Courttia Newland is the au~~thor~~ ~~of~~ ~~the~~
novels *The Scholar* and *Socie~~ty~~* ... ~~and~~
the anthologies *Disco 2000*, *~~...~~*
is Editor of an anthology o~~f~~ ...
IC3. He lives in West Londo~~n~~ ...
www.myvillage.co.uk/urban ...

Praise for *Society Within*:

'Pulls no punches in its description of estate life as a mixture of
community and ghetto . . . his strength lies in the depiction of
violence and menace'
Independent

'It is the ambition and scale of Newland's book that really
impresses. Every one of the stories has some kind of engross-
ing and subtle moral point to make; almost all the characters
are alive with tenderness and hope . . . an impressive achievement'
Guardian

'Newland writes with a compelling lightness, utterly lacking
in hyperbole or machismo . . . it is quite easy to imagine
Newland becoming one of this country's most important
social commentators in years to come'
Glasgow Herald

'Newland has a sharp curiosity that gives him both a maturity
beyond his years and an energy that reinforces his youth'
Independent on Sunday

'As a literary culture, we are chronically short of this sort of
fiction. Voices like Newland's provide a vital counterpoint to
the likes of Bridget Jones'
Financial Times

Snakeskin

Courttia Newland

An *Abacus* Book

First published in Great Britain by Abacus in 2002

Copyright © Courttia Newland 2002

The moral right of the author has been asserted.

A CIP catalogue record for this book
is available from the British Library.

ISBN 0 349 11509 5

Typeset in Palatino by M Rules
Printed and bound in Great Britain by
Clays Ltd, St Ives plc

Abacus
An imprint of
Time Warner Books UK
Brettenham House
Lancaster Place
London WC2E 7EN

www.TimeWarnerBooks.co.uk

Acknowledgements

Give thanks to the higher spirits for guiding me through this novel. Once again, a shout goes out to all my road peeps for their efforts to keep me mentally, physically and spiritually alive, and all my publishing peeps for believing in my art. On a more specific note, One Love to Gilda O'Neil, Uchenna Izundu, Suhky Dhaliwal, Riannon Williams, Yin Tsoi, Stephen Thompson, Tashee Meadows, my Thailand buddy Oz, Riggs O'Hara, Carl and Sandie, Jade McCubbin, as well as Nabil for the much-needed breaks. Not forgetting everyone at Portobello Houseshare for your much-appreciated patience! Big up Rajeev (I was convincing myself as much as you, I reckon!), Ray Shell, Alex Wheatle, Barney Platts-Mills and Ghanim Shubber for your remaining interest; also Carol Moses and Bobby Joseph for allowing me to be inspired by Akira's memory. Thanks to Will, Duncan, the staff @ Uncle's and Maggie @ Nectar for keeping me well fed, Jonathan

Barnett for the musical advice, and all the people that helped me gather the ammunition needed to fire off my first draft. Apologies to everyone I've forgotten and everyone I ducked in order to get this book finished – I hope the read is worth the inconvenience! RIP to Kendo, whose spirit is still felt. On a last note, this book is also in memory of Dora Boatemah OBE, whose community work was an inspiration to many, including myself.

'And each stroke of his tongue ripped off skin after successive skin,
All the skins of a life in the world . . .'

—Anon

Snakeskin

1

It seemed as though London was in flames.

I followed the Saab across Vauxhall Bridge, my own Audi a two-car distance behind, the sky awash with rays from the lowering sun. Deep orange faded into fiery red, setting the city ablaze as though Hell had come visit for the day. The colours spread like some all-consuming conflagration. The illusion of fire reflected from slow moving traffic, road signs and surrounding buildings until the brightness of dusk almost blinded me. I retrieved my sunglasses from the glove compartment. Hell became murky, tinged a rusty shade of brown.

I took a peek in my rear-view mirror, knowing what I'd see. Darkness – though from my viewpoint, I couldn't see the fade from fire into night. After that, I had to pay attention to my quarry again, as he passed a set of lights on the south side of the bridge. He angled right, heading west. A black cab tried to overtake me, beeping with indignation as we almost collided. Shrugging uncaringly at the driver, I let him through, knowing my prey's destination. When the cabbie passed, I slid in lane, taking the right turn behind him.

Another set of red lights, sitting neatly on the edge of a gentle bend. I sighed and stopped, watching the Saab edge away, then lit up a cigarette.

The radio was tuned to Jazz FM's drive time show. R&B was making my speakers throb, but I wasn't really listening. My mind was going over the same old thing; the same thing that had been bothering me for the past six months. It was torture, yet I couldn't stop it. There was no escaping the truth. It was apparent in every impatient tap of my fingers on the steering wheel; the lethargic yawn as I waited for the lights to change. Apparent in my every emotion.

Green light penetrated my thoughts. I eased the car forwards and resumed my former alertness, overtaking the cab, driving dirty to recover lost time. I caught my prey at the Rockwell Park Estate, but he didn't enter, instead keeping to the main road as I knew he would. He went through the lights, where he joined the Brixton Road and headed north, accelerating smoothly along traffic-clear streets.

When he reached the Angelldown Estate, he took a right, then another, easing his vehicle tentatively over the speed bumps. I parked my car outside the entrance and got out, then opened the boot; retrieving my camera, three rolls of film and a quarter of weed wrapped in cling film. I left behind the Nike gym bag, which contained two books and my licensed Taurus. I'd long decided I'd be too occupied to read. As for the gun, it wasn't necessary on a job like this.

Walking slowly, I stuffed the tools into my pocket and followed a through road, head moving right to left, surveying the dusk. The blocks were quiet, despite the handful of school kids making their way home in scattered groups. His shark-grey Saab 9000 was parked in the centre of squat, yellow-brick buildings, just past a brand-new basketball court-cum-football pitch. I approached the vehicle, running my hand over the boot, roof and bonnet admiringly. When I'd had my fill, I headed for Mr Bruce's flat, whistling between my teeth.

Preparation consisted of removing my sunglasses, adjusting my clothes, then taking a gulp of breath before ringing the bell. Mr Bruce opened the door almost at once – he certainly moved quickly for an eighty-two-year-old. He stared at me distrustfully. Since this was close to his usual expression, I decided to see if he might've remembered. Producing my stinkiest shit-eating grin, I took a step towards the door, just in case it abruptly shut in my face.

'Hello Mr Bruce, how are you on this fine evening?'

'Who de hell ah you?'

My vague annoyance only stalled me for a moment.

'It's me, Mr Bruce. Ervine James. I called around two weeks ago . . .'

'Me nuh know nuh *Er*vine James . . .' He paused and slapped his toothless gums together, making a sound like a foot stuck in deep mud. 'Me know a *Dan*yel James. Use ah live on de lickle hill in Sain' George. Wha' dem name it? Uh . . .'

'. . . The private investigator?' I continued, forcing my sentence like a battering ram against his. 'I used your back bedroom last time I was here. I *paid* you to use the back room . . .'

Mr Bruce was looking confused.

'Investigatah?' he repeated haltingly. 'Me nuh waan talk to nuh investigatah!' The door was closing but I'd anticipated this, so I put my right foot in the way. It closed on my Reebok loafer. Hard. I swallowed my pain as well as the urge to swear.

'No Mr Bruce, it's not you I'm investigating . . .'

'Fuck arf before me call de police!'

The door slammed against my foot again, then once more. This time the pain travelled from my instep up the inside of my thigh ending just below my groin. I groaned.

'*Ow*! Mr Bruce . . . *Mr Bruce*!' I really didn't want to say the next thing, but I had no choice; it wasn't looking good. 'Mr Bruce, I've got the quarter of weed, remember? I'm not investigating you, I swear it! You can have the weed if I can use your back bedroom for a few hours. Honest – I'll even show you if you want!'

Miraculously (or maybe not so miraculously when I thought about it), the door paused mid-slam. Mr Bruce's face slowly re-emerged, looking wily and sly. His gnarled hand, brittle from age and arthritis, made beckoning movements. Using the door handle as a crutch, he took jerky steps until he could see enough of my face to talk.

'If you is a pri-vate investigatah, show me yuh ID nuh!'

Which I should have done in the first place seeing as I'd wasted so much time being clever. There's really no such thing as an ID for private investigators in this country. That shit only exists in American movies and shoot-'em-up shows. Still, I'd had one made up by a printer to appease the odd doubting Thomas, and never once regretted the pittance I'd spent.

Mr Bruce grabbed the wallet from my hand, letting it fall open so he could scan the words and picture. He glared at the leather in concentration before handing it back.

'Me nevah know dem 'ave black investigatah! Heh, heh, *hey* . . .' He giggled long and loud, almost like a child. 'All right. Mek me see de 'erb.'

I showed him the quarter. When he made a grab for it, I pulled back.

'Uh-uh. Let me use the room and I'll give you the herb afterwards.'

'Nah man, it nah go suh! Me waan de 'erb firs'!' he screamed.

Fuck! This was taking longer than it should. Admitting defeat to save time, I handed the cling-wrapped bundle over, reflecting that an *old man* had talked me down. My earlier thoughts in the car came back like a boomerang – sudden, swift and deadly.

'All right, there you go,' I told him, watching him inspect and sniff at the weed professionally. He looked up and winked.

'*Yes* man! Yuh all right still Mista Pri-vate Investigatah! Heh, heh, *hey* . . . Come nuh . . .'

I stepped over the threshold, pushing the door shut before following the pensioner inside. The flat was both musty and untidy, its grime-marked walls bearing crooked pictures of relatives and islands on the other side of the globe. It was like a time capsule in there and the Sixties wallpaper certainly didn't help. The atmosphere was cold and still; an atmosphere in accordance with a man who was waiting to die.

Mr Bruce led me to the back room. It was a bare place, the one bed minus any duvet or blankets. I nodded in acceptance. He smiled, my friend again, then stepped into the passage leaving me to work alone. I got busy assembling my tripod. With the camera locked in place, I moved it towards the window, pushing the zoom lens through a hole I'd cut in the net curtain on my last visit. Looking through the viewfinder, I slowly turned the lens with my right hand until the focus was correct.

The game they'd played last time was only just beginning, though I was sure it would remain unchanged. I'd been told the man was almost religious in his attention to routine, and to date he'd done nothing to disprove this. Inside the flat directly opposite me, in a place I presumed to be *their* back room, a naked woman came into view. She danced to music I couldn't hear, winding her body low, moving closer towards the curtainless window. That was the bit I couldn't understand; it was almost as though they wanted someone to see them.

The man was sitting on the edge of a bed, watching with great delight. He was small, with no muscles to speak of, even when I zoomed in close. He looked at least forty-five or fifty, with glossy black skin and the slightly nerdy look of someone who'd lived better than most. He was naked. I snapped off a few close ups to get the roll going, wincing slightly at the sight of his tiny, limp penis.

The woman was also middle-aged, but she was fat and hefty everywhere the man wasn't. Her body rolled as she moved and danced, her flesh firm despite her bulk. She was in good nick for her age, performing for the man with a vigour that I had to respect. When she stood in front of him, grabbed her right leg and lifted high enough to make him gasp, I snapped off a few more shots, then lightly applauded her efforts while simultaneously shaking my head in disbelief.

I returned my eye to the viewfinder as the action got more heated, the click and roll of the camera becoming methodical background music. The woman gyrated and postured, running her hands up and down her unyielding offering of flesh, playing with herself for her partner's pleasure. She rubbed jiggling breasts in slow motion. She squeezed thick nipples and rolled them between her fingers. The man looked impressed, yet her little show didn't excite me. Even when she licked her index finger to the knuckle, trailing it along the round stomach, between her legs and inside with a gasp I could only see, my mind was detached. Unlike my camera I was focused on the job, not the sexual encounter before me.

The man had obviously waited as long as he could. He got to his feet, turning the woman roughly so that her face was up against the window. Grabbing her shoulders hard, he entered from behind and began thrusting his hips in a jerky, rhythmless fashion. The woman's large breasts bounced and moved as if dancing by themselves, even though her legs had long stopped going. The sight repelled me. I pulled focus to take a wide shot of the *back* shot, and before the thought had time to fully arrive, I'd collapsed onto the bare mattress in a fit of laughter, which said a lot for my state of mind.

Eventually I managed to stop laughing. I'd had enough voyeurism for the day. Flicking the camera to timer, I waited for the click and whirr, feeling a sting of discontent even as my pager began to vibrate. I regretted not bringing a good book with me after all.

Even though the message had hinted at prompt action, I remained in Mr Bruce's flat until the fading light made any more work impossible. After that, I packed up my things, said my goodbyes, then left the block and looked around for the nearest payphone. It wasn't hard to find. I fed the box with coins and dialled Maya's mobile number from memory. There was a hiss of empty space before the phone rang, loud and clear. Before it even finished that first dial, Maya picked up.

'Wha' blow?'

I huffed disappointed breath into the receiver, realising that somewhere inside I'd been hoping she'd changed, wised up, come round. Her opening sentence was enough to remind me how far we'd drifted apart, and how close to the shores of that other world Maya remained.

'D'you have to talk like that?' I complained sourly. 'I'm not one of your mates on street, you know. You could at least say hello, especially since we haven't spoken for so long.'

She groaned in return, the rhythmic snap and pop of her gum echoing faintly as she waited for me to finish.

'*Hi* Vinnie. Satisfied?' she drawled in return, a lot less defensively than I would have anticipated. It was a reflex action that came with the job I suppose, but as soon as I began wondering why she wasn't angry, the answer came to me in a flash. She wanted something. Probably something small and insignificant, yet a favour nonetheless. Until she got what she wanted, Maya was more than prepared to tolerate any grief I doled her way. Which meant that for a while at least, she might be prepared to listen.

'What can I do for you?'

She giggled, sounding embarrassed.

'I need you to help me out, I'm in a bit a bovva,' Maya chuckled, confirming my suspicions. 'I'm in Streat'am Common, but I got no money to get home or nothing, Vin! I called Reggie an' his phone's off, so I'll be stuck here all night if you don't come an' get me, man! You're the only person I know wid a ride, you gotta help me . . .'

'An' what are you doing in Streatham Common?' I seethed accusingly. Maya fell silent for a tenth of a second before bouncing back.

'Come on Vinnie man, do I ask where yuh at all the while? No. 'Cos I respect dat you do yuh own ting, innit?'

"Cos I'm not fifteen years old, Maya,' I countered, glancing at my credits. 'Look, my money's nearly finished, but wait by Streatham Common Station an' I'll be there in fifteen minutes. You're lucky I had a job in Brixton.'

Maya squealed loudly in delight. 'Oh, thanks bruv, you're a dappa! See yuh—'

The phone cut off and I heard my money tumble into the BT collection box. Still faintly annoyed, I replaced the receiver and headed back to my Audi, threw my camera in the boot, then exited Angelldown, turning left onto the main road.

On the short journey I kept my mind busy musing over Maya's antics. To be perfectly honest, I hadn't formed more than a passing thought of her or the others for a very long time. It was this job, see. This job becomes an obsession, in for a penny in for a pound, and before you know it you feel better in the shadows, never quite seen, as much a mystery as the cases you'd been hired to solve. That was a PI's life. You could easily forget that it had been almost a year since you'd seen your baby sister, and even when you did it was no more than a fleeting exchange of greetings. You forgot about your mother and younger brother, telling yourself you had no family so the solitude was an easier meal to digest. Then, when the reminder finally comes, as it inevitably does, you pretend not to be hurt by the distance between you and them. Everyone attempts to go on behaving as if everything's normal, but they can't because everything isn't. Lives have changed, feelings have changed and people have changed. Acceptance is the first step in moving on.

I realised just how hard acceptance could be as I pulled my car up next to the railway station and saw her walking my way. It was hard not to react, dressed as she was in a leather mini-skirt, knee-high boots and a top that gave an unobstructed view of her stomach and cleavage, though God knows I tried. When she'd been growing up I'd been a barely recognisable face in the family home, never sticking around for long, always busy living my own life. I was in my mid-twenties when Maya had been in Pampers, which meant she'd grown up much closer to Douglas, who was now twenty. Whether it was just an unaccountable aspect of her nature, or because she was the only girl, or had grown up on a notoriously bad estate, was hard to tell; the fact remained that Maya had grown up wild.

She slid into the passenger seat, while I tried not to dwell on the change in her features, her manner. The once baby-pretty cutie still lurked somewhere, although a struggling teenage vixen seemed desperate to take over. Maya had grown, both outwards and upwards. She wore make-up – only the faintest of eyeshadow and lipstick, yet enough to transform my sister into a new breed of woman. She looked older, wilder almost, her eyes telling stories I had no wish to hear. It was hard to hold my tongue when faced with the sight of her. She made it even harder when she opened her mouth.

'Wha' gwaan, bruv?' She leaned across the gear stick and placed a smoochy kiss on my cheek. I sat stiff as plasterboard, giving her only the tiniest of glances.

'I'm OK, Maya. How are you?'

'I'm cool, man, serious. Well, I was until I got stuck in dis shit hole. Can we go now?'

'Where shall I drop you then?'

She screwed up her face and thought.

'Uhh . . . Reggie's, if you could.'

I stared. Maya threw her head back onto the car seat, exasperated.

'Harlesden! He lives in Harlesden, Vinnie! Gosh, I bin goin' out wid the brer for a year and a half now, I woulda thought you'd know what area he lives!'

I pursed my lips and turned the car around, directing it back towards Brixton, outrage building with every turn of the steering wheel. When I eventually finished the manoeuvre, I spat my reply from the side of my mouth. 'So you were thirteen when you started seeing this guy?'

Maya crossed her arms and looked out the passenger window, ignoring me. I knew that my attitude had set the tone for the entire ride, and felt a little guilty for how I'd treated her, though I couldn't alter my feelings. She was my baby sister, the youngest in the family. I saw my own failure every time I looked at her, remembering how my mother had named her after Maya Angelou. I hadn't read any of her books, but my sister's behaviour seemed to be a far cry from that of the great woman. Even now, I couldn't understand what had happened. Maya had been the smartest of us all; she was reading at three, could write by five, and had the highest eleven plus grades in her whole primary school. By rich people's standards, that may have been ordinary, but on the estate she'd beaten the loop and was on a clear and admirable path. Then she hit secondary school. Something happened during that time. Maya began growing up much faster than anyone had anticipated.

'So what were you doing all the way in Streatham?' I asked, trying to take on the tone of an enquiring friend, rather than a demanding parent. She shrugged.

'Jus' at some garage dance, innit. My friend said she was gonna pay fuh me to get in, but when we get dere she didn't 'ave no money, her man was supportin' her, y'get me. Suh dat was it.'

'So she left you outside?'

Maya snatched a look at me, as if to gauge how much of the truth I needed to hear.

'*Yeah . . .*'

I snorted loudly. 'Great friends you got, Maya. Leaving you in a place you don't know, where anything can happen, dressed like you are—'

'Like *what*? How am I dressed?'

She instantly looked livid. I'd done the exact opposite of what I'd intended, which had been to patch up the tear that had occurred between us, not wrench it apart. Biting back my answer, I was left with nothing else to say, instead turning my attention back to the road. We drove through Brixton, Oval, Victoria, Park Lane, then Notting Hill and Shepherd's Bush in complete silence. However, as we finally moved up Wood Lane, Maya turned around in her seat. The anger in her eyes was evident. All at once, she looked even more stunning than she had as a child.

'Listen, Vinnie, I gotta tell you dis before we get where we're goin; after all, I dunno when I'm gonna see you again, do I? 'Cos you're never around are yuh? I can't see why you're tryin' it all the time, goin' on like I'm some foolish girl who dunno nuttin' more about life dan workin' in McDonald's an' gettin' pregnant, but lemme tell you now, if you think dat's me, you got anovva ting comin'. OK? Jus' 'cos I don't talk like *some* people an' dress like dem, don't mean I'm stoopid, right? Ask Mum if yuh don't believe me! Ask who passed all her mocks, den come back an' start tryin' to tell me about myself. You don't even know me, man! My own brudda don't even know me!'

Shame was burning my face. Somehow, I knew that Maya was right. More than that, I knew we had to go through with this now, while the opportunity to find some common ground still existed. If not, there was a good chance I could lose her for good. Humility seemed the best course of action.

'I know I don't,' I admitted sadly. 'And I don't intend to have a go at you, honestly. I just see you're in Streatham on your own at night and it worries me, Maya, of course it worries me. Supposing I hadn't been where I was . . .'

It was the right move. Generously enough, Maya was smiling now, a hand on my shoulder as if attempting to absorb my woes.

'Dat's anovva ting,' she chided gently. 'Don't you think I'm worried about *you*? Look at yuh man. You got a beat up ol' ride, mash-up clothes, half the time nobody even sees you . . . If yuh makin' money, yuh hidin' it real good. So why d'you do dis, Vinnie? What for? It don't seem to make you happy, fuh real.'

As she said this last, I found myself pondering her words while she waited for my reply, giving me time. Why *did* I do this job? In all of the thinking I'd been buried underneath for the previous few months, I was pretty sure I'd never asked that question. Yes, money was tight. My cases had pretty much all dried up, apart from the routine 'affair jobs', which were still few and far between. Yes, there was little satisfaction. Solving the limited cases of cheating lovers wasn't exactly difficult, and my boredom had been growing like a hardy weed. So why had I resorted to such a tiresome form of employment?

'It's the only thing I've got left that I'm good at, Maya.' I spoke before my conscious mind could stop me damning myself. 'I've tried everything else. This is it.'

She turned that over in her mind, then grinned again, letting go of my shoulder, settling back in her seat. At that moment – and only that moment – my worries for her were gone, and I felt confident in her ability to take care of herself. When she spoke again, I had time to wonder if the talent I'd long believed I possessed was in the blood, a hereditary part of our make-up that we shared.

'Well do it den,' she told me sassily. 'Do it as good as you c'n fuckin' manage.'

We snatched a glance at each other, stone-faced, hardly daring to smile.

I dropped her outside a cluster of council houses not far from Jubilee Clock, then watched her ring the bell, greet her boyfriend, wave and go inside. A niggling feeling told me I was wrong for letting her stay here, but what could I do? As she said, I was hardly around. I could lay no claims to her life unless I intended to take responsibility for it, and we both knew that was not on the cards. At least I could console myself with the thought that we'd built some bridges in the last forty-five minutes. Finally managing to smile at that thought, I turned the ignition and moved my car towards the High Street, heading home.

2

The following afternoon I spent time developing pictures in my dark room, really no more than cupboard space in the office I rent. Watching the couple's sordid actions materialise once more had a negative effect; they sapped my strength each time I pinned the wet prints on my makeshift clothes-line to dry, the red light casting a cheap glow. Checking my watch, I worked as fast as I could possibly manage. Pinning up the last with five minutes to spare, I went into my office to wait for Mrs Donaldson.

My business – James' Private Investigations – was based just over the river in Farringdon, North London. My office was one of over 400 identical rooms in the large building, once the administrative end of a moderately successful stationery firm. The company had moved premises in the early Seventies and the building stood empty for ten years, before it was sold off in the spending spree Thatcher created. With ingenious thinking and foresight, the purchasers split the building into separate offices, renting and creating what existed today: a steady, profitable business that weathered the violent storms of the Eighties, stood firm in the rebirth of the Nineties, and was now marching proudly across the Millennium.

I sat in my black leather chair, relaxing as I leaned back and closed my eyes. Even blind, I could map every item in the room down to the pencils, pens and erasers on my broad wooden desk. The two wooden office chairs opposite me, a resting-place for prospective and hard-earned clients; the coat and hat stand in the far corner of the room, looking like a refugee from a Philip Marlowe show (the programme had always been my favourite); the selection of family photos, hung just above a row of filing cabinets that contained records representing almost three years of work. All these things and more made up my office space. My kingdom. I was fiendishly proud of everything I owned.

The intercom buzzed. Sadie, my receptionist, calling from the little cubby-hole outside my domain. I thumbed the 'answer' switch.

'Hey Sadie.'

'Mrs Donaldson to see you, Ervine.'

I closed my eyes again, only replying after a long pause.

'All right, send her in. An' when you've finished those accounts you can go.'

'Thanks, Ervine.' There was a definite note of sympathy in Sadie's voice. 'Take care . . .'

'OK, see you tomorrow.'

Taking my finger from the answer switch, I leaned over and dug inside my desk drawer, retrieving an A4 envelope containing the last set of photos I'd taken. I regularly censored the worst; there was no way Mrs Donaldson was seeing the ones hung up in my DIY dark room, no matter how good her money was. An inner vibe told me she wasn't the type of woman to take that kind of news well.

My office door rattled.

'Come in!' I yelled in my most commanding tone.

Mrs Donaldson floated into the room as gracefully as a black swan, head held aloft. She was a tall, regal-looking beauty, bearing the haughty, middle-aged demeanour of a woman who knew men had once laid themselves at her feet and drooled. Sometimes they still did. She wore a caramel-coloured fur, dotted with black around the collar, while on her feet she wore knee-high burgundy boots that I knew cost over £500. Her make-up was carefully applied. As she moved into the room, staring at me with those wide, cat-like eyes, I could smell her favourite scent – *Joy* – filling the air with sweetness, lust and money. She reached out a black gloved hand. I got to my feet as casually as I could, taking her fingers firmly and matching her stare; gazing deep into her grey eyes, which she took as a sign of respect.

'Mrs Donaldson,' I muttered, nodding my head.

'Ervine . . .' She took her seat and eyeballed me directly. 'Is the news good or bad?'

As usual, Mrs Donaldson got straight to the root of her dilemma.

'Mrs Donaldson' – I paused, partly for dramatic effect and partly because I wasn't sure how to broach this delicate subject while doing the job I'd been paid for – 'Mrs Donaldson, I know this can't be easy for you—'

'So make it easier and get to the point,' she told me with a wave of her hand. 'And I do wish you'd call me Katrina like everyone else. My God, you make me sound ancient.'

I smiled in acceptance and held her gaze once more.

'OK then, Katr*ina*,' I conceded, putting emphasis on the fact that it was the first time I'd used her given name. 'Although Mrs Donaldson *sounds* ancient, people only have to look at you to know that it's a bare-faced lie.'

Katrina Donaldson chuckled a low and throaty laugh at that, relaxing in her seat and crossing long legs, still watching my eyes. As much as I didn't want them to, they couldn't help their quick flick downwards. I saw her long fur jacket fall open at the knee, exposing bare flesh all the way to the upper thigh. When my eyes returned to her face, Katrina Donaldson wore the hint of a smile.

'Continue,' she said, with that smug look women sport when they know they've got exactly what you want. I cleared my throat.

'Well, you see, Mrs – Katrina. It seems to me that your husband *has* been engaged in the activities that we suspected him of, and he's been visiting this woman for quite some time. Over my sixteen plus hours of surveillance—'

Katrina groaned loudly, cutting me off once more. '*God*, this is all so *for*mal,' she insisted. 'I thought you were going to get to the point.'

I held my hands up, defeated once more, then reached onto the desk and handed over the envelope. She took it, frown lines creasing her face where there had once been none.

'You better look at these before I go any further. I think they cover what I'm trying to say.'

She opened the envelope, looking at the black and whites one by one. Mr Donaldson in various compromising situations made a haphazard pile on my desk. Holding on to his companion, looking lovingly into her eyes; a walk through the park arm-in-arm, serene expressions on both faces; the naked companion sitting astride Donaldson, feeding him fruit, with laughter all over her face. Photo after photo appeared in front of me and with each I expected some kind of reaction. But nothing. When her hands were empty and the pile complete, I touched the tips of my fingers together, appraising her remarkable control.

'I'm sorry, Katrina. I can't imagine the hurt you feel—'

'Oh, I'm not hurt,' the woman contradicted, shocking and

cutting me off for the third time. 'He's a stupid fool of a man who hasn't a thing going for him besides the size of his bank balance. Nothing more, nothing less.'

In dangerous waters now, I desperately tried to play agony uncle to Mrs Donaldson's denial of pain.

'I don't mean to be presumptuous, Katrina, but surely you feel *something* for the man,' I persisted, unable to believe she could be so blasé. 'After all, you paid a lot of money to have him tailed and photographed.'

I flicked the pictures with an idle finger, then formed a tent with my fingers once more, waiting for her to burst into tears.

Instead, Katrina Donaldson looked me in the eyes, then threw back her head and laughed as though she'd got all six on the lottery. My mouth dropped open. The bad feelings came back, rendering me speechless, incapable of further argument.

'Do you really think a woman like me would fall in love with a man like *that*?'

She pointed at the photos. My mouth flapped open and shut like a dying fish.

'But Katrina, you—'

She did her trick again.

'I only married the man for his *money*, Ervine; I thought you would have realised that. With the evidence you've efficiently supplied, I have more than reasonable grounds for divorce, and more than reasonable grounds to take at least half of everything he owns, wouldn't you say? I mean, come on, you took the photos Ervine, the man's worse than pitiful in bed. I haven't let him come near me for the last year. *That's* the reason he's sleeping with that Brixton whore.'

Well, well, well, I thought to myself, shocked more by her willingness to share this information itself. In my three years' work experiencing various dramas and problems in this city of millions, I very quickly found myself becoming immune to surprise. I'd long ago accepted that some people have strange motives and behave in ways I would never dream of. Over the years my immunity has become a necessary tool of the trade. I carry it at all times and it has certainly saved me from more sticky situations than my Taurus.

'What do you think of that?' Katrina smiled.

At least I could dig into my trusty bag labelled 'Standard Client Statements' for an answer.

'I'm not really paid to think, Katrina. You can use the pictures however you see fit. It makes no difference to me.'

The feline gleam in Katrina's eyes was back again and I didn't like it. I didn't like it one bit.

'I can use the photos however I please?'

'Of course you can. You paid for them. They're yours.'

She continued smiling and eyeballing me. Ever seen a cat focused on a plate of food at a dinner table, licking its lips as if entranced? That's the way Katrina looked at me. I'd never played out a scene like this when I'd daydreamed about being a PI, years before I started the business. I hadn't any 'Standard Client Statements' for the shit brewing in the air, I was sure of that.

'So,' she began, sitting upright, 'if I decide to use this evidence – the evidence you've given me – as a right to kill my husband in the name of justice, you'd have to let me do it. Agreed?'

I had to give my brain a moment to process exactly what she'd said.

'No, I strongly disagree,' I barked when I found my voice. My finger inched beneath the desk, probed, then found the emergency button that let Sadie know I was in trouble. I pushed hard. 'If you were to commit murder I'd be forced to take you to the police and turn you in. There's no ifs, buts or maybes about that, Katrina.'

She rolled her eyes as if to chide me for being so dramatic.

'But what of client confidentiality? Doesn't that mean anything? After all, I have paid you.'

I was looking at her seriously. The fun and games were over now. Katrina Donaldson was talking some dangerous shit.

'You paid me to tail your husband and take photos. That's *all* you paid me for. I will not turn a blind eye if you decide to make your husband pay for cheating on you, I can assure that.'

Jesus, I wish she'd stop smiling. The grin on her lips was distinctly predatory, like the flat, frozen grin of a Great White. I pressed the emergency button again, wondering why the hell Sadie didn't answer. Then I remembered: I'd sent her home.

Jesus Christ.

Katrina Donaldson got to her feet, placing her hands on my desk, leaning forwards so she was looking down on me. The expression of amusement on her face did nothing to quell my misgivings.

'You know what, Ervine? I think I'd have to seduce you to get you on my side, what d'you think? I've seen those old films. I know how it works. I mean, I couldn't possibly have you running to the police, so I'd have to ply you with the offer of immeasurable wealth. And give you my body in the meantime, while we wait for his will to come through.'

'It would be illegal for me to take any form of a bribe, Mrs Donaldson,' I trotted out this old and frequently used statement breathlessly. The reversion to her surname wasn't an accident either. Before I could say any more she stepped back from the desk, fingers moving along the buttons of her caramel fur like a concert pianist approaching a crescendo. When that was done, she threw the coat open and dropped it to the floor.

'Turn *this* down – if you dare,' she told me confidently,

running her hands along beige skin touched with a hint of red.

She was completely naked. I'm not joking; she wasn't wearing a stitch apart from those knee-high boots, along with extravagant-looking rings on her fingers and in her pierced ears. It was true that her skin looked smooth and baby soft. It was also true that where Mr Donaldson's companion was tubby, Katrina's body was pert and toned. She obviously worked out. She'd done well to look so good.

Nevertheless, before my current vocation as a PI, I'd spent five years' hard time in the Second Battalion Parachute Regiment of the British Army. Even fought for my country during the Falklands conflict back in '82, seeing things that forever changed my life. Although I made no friends, had a lukewarm career, and hated ninety per cent of my time there, one of the things I'd always loved was the deep sense of discipline I received. Without some sense of discipline in a man's life, he becomes weak, unable to function, left to the whim of emotions and desires with no control over either. It was this sense of discipline that made me instantly write a new 'Standard Client Statement' for future situations.

I moved around my desk and to her side. She held her arms aloft as if to embrace me, wrap me in expensively perfumed charms and sex the pride back into her unfulfilled body. I dodged her premature hug, instead ducking and roughly picking her coat from the floor, shoving it into her outstretched hands, pushing her towards the office door.

'I don't *fuck* my clients, Mrs Donaldson. Especially not the more mature women, if you know what I mean.'

She shook herself out of my grip, her features contorted and vex.

'You *bastard*!'

The slap came from nowhere, stinging my face. I put a hand to my cheek and glared. Time to switch tactics.

'That one was for free. Next time I hit back. Got it?'

She glared at me, spitting fire, all pretence at civility vanished.

'Ignorant street bastard . . . You're not on my level, you know. No matter how well you speak.'

'Got it?' I repeated, ignoring the bait and grabbing her wrists.

'Let me *go*! I'll scream rape,' she warned dangerously, as I tried not to look at her body.

'I'd rather you just left, Mrs Donaldson—'

'*RAAAPPPE!!! RAAAAAAAAAPPE!!!*'

I couldn't believe what was happening. If anyone saw this I would be the one fucked, I knew it as sure as I knew my name. According to the TV documentary programme *Dispatches*, rape is what my people do best. If the police were called I'd be guilty before proven innocent; no matter how strong my ties were down at the station.

The door rattled open once more.

'Thank *God* you've come.' Mrs Donaldson wasted no time, completely ignoring me and turning towards the newcomer. 'I thought he was going to—'

Sadie came into the office. At precisely that moment she looked as heavenly as an angel – I wanted to kiss and hug her to thank her for being there. Sadie was forty-plus years, built like a very large man, and a former night-club bouncer who took no shit. Standing in the doorway like a judge, she destroyed whatever morale Katrina Donaldson had.

'You better leave this office before I throw you out myself. Ervine tries to help you out an' you come with *this*? I swear to God, you leave from this place right this minute – an' if I hear the R word come out yuh mouth one more time, *I'll* be the one doing the rapin'! Yuh get me?'

Oh yeah. One other nugget of information about Sadie. She swings both ways. Which I suppose Katrina Donaldson already knew. If she didn't, she certainly got the message.

With an I'm-above-all-of-you sniff, she struggled into her fur coat and stomped out of the office. I followed, feeling determined and grim, wishing the day would end.

'Where yuh goin'?' Sadie called, spinning around to face me.

'Just making sure she leaves, Sade!'

Katrina stormed her way to the main corridor, then paused and turned on her heel.

'Fuck *you*, Mr James!' she spat, before slamming the door shut and disappearing from view.

Delayed shock flowed through me in waves. I stood motionless, replaying the incident to see if it could've been handled with more skill. A metallic sound of laughter wafted into my ears. First I took no notice; then I realised where it came from – Sadie's neat and tidy desk. The intercom was set to 'listen'. And Sadie was still laughing, her hoarse chuckles loud enough to make the tinny speakers crackle harshly.

I marched back into the office. She was holding onto the desk with one hand, while the other was clutching at her stomach. Her massive shoulders shuddered up and down, and a look of pure mirth was on her face. When she saw my expression she laughed even louder.

'Oh God . . . If you could've seen how you looked . . . I've never seen you go on so nervous . . .'

She was off and laughing once again. I stood prone and annoyed, watching her glee, far from amused.

'You were listening to the whole thing?'

'I had to,' she gasped between breaths. 'She told me she had a present for all your hard work – a present you wouldn't be able to refuse. The chance was too good to miss, luv. Don't get vex, I wouldn't let anything happen to yuh!'

I shook my head in dismay.

'She was talking about murder, Sadie!'

'Only to get you into bed, you fool. Honestly Ervine, you've got to liven up a little. "*It would be illegal to take any form of a bribe*",' she mocked, winking at me, then coming closer and taking my hands. 'Your mother would be proud she's raised such a responsible young man.'

'Don't be sarky,' I sulked, feeling like a little kid.

'I'm not, I'm bein' really serious, darlin'. You're doin' all right, you know. You should stop punishin' yuhself, beatin' yuhself over the head when you don't even know the reason. *Live* a little, Ervine. Take chances. You are allowed to actually *enjoy* your life.'

I was nodding with her, allowing her fingers on mine, thinking about what she said.

'I *do* know the reason why I'm punishing myself, Sadie.' I paused, unable to go any further. She was prompting me with her eyes, until she realised I needed more persuasion.

'Go on,' she nodded.

'Well . . . You see . . .'

There was no way I could possibly tell her. Sadie had three kids, two of whom were under ten. She worked another job in the evenings. Her hours in my office were nine to five, though whenever she ran over, like tonight, I tried to pay extra. She often told me how much she relied on the work I gave her. My mother always praised me for what I'd done. There was no way I could possibly let her know what I was thinking.

'Never mind,' I muttered. 'It doesn't matter. I just had a hard one today.'

'Are you sure?'

'Yeah . . . Yeah, I'm OK . . .'

Sadie was peering into my eyes with deep intent. I forced a smile. She pulled a face as if to say '*Enough*', then rubbed my hands and let the subject drop.

'You should get some rest,' she ordered. 'Tek a bath and watch a flim or someting.'

I let go of her hands. 'Will do, Sade. I'll do exactly that. I'll lock up and go right now.'

She smiled my way. 'You go on. I'll tidy tings in here and lock up.'

'Thanks, Sadie.'

'S'all right, luv. Just make sure you rest, OK?'

I got my coat and left as fast as I could.

3

The Claybridge Estate NW10 was the home of my saintly mother Tazanne, along with my two younger siblings. Notorious as a 'black' spot in London, many stories were told and secrets hidden between those dusky grey blocks and narrow alleyways. My clients among the estate were numerous – varied in race, sex and age. I worked my way through the traffic, occasionally tooting the horn and waving my hand before pulling to a halt in the car park of my mother's block.

Dougie answered the front door. Though my younger brother, he was six foot three, which made him easily as tall as me. As usual, he was chewing. Dougie never seemed to go more than sixty seconds without some item of food in his mouth. He chewed and grinned; an ugly sight, though I was glad that he looked pleased to see me.

'Wha' you sayin', bro?' he champed loudly.

'I know Mum taught you not to speak with your mouth full. I was there,' I joked, straining for a hearty voice, though there was a tiny ball of hardness inside me.

Dougie shrugged and grinned some more, stepping back to let me inside without a word of reply. The flat was as small and confined as I remembered, overpoweringly dark. Long ago, my mother had tried to give our home some grand touches, but then found maintaining them – and her growing family – too hard. Since then, the house had become stuck halfway between decent and overwhelmed. Assorted clothes were everywhere, pushed under stairs, boxed and hanging out of cupboards, or draped over banisters like animal hides. Familiar cooking smells and the sight of family pictures along with the same old ornaments were small comfort to my inherent unease. I had to restrain myself from bolting out of the door in fear of becoming the teenage youth who had grown too big for the nest once again.

Dougie navigated us through the flat with relative ease and comfort, something I'd never quite managed at his age. I followed him into the kitchen just like the old days.

'How dat greenery stay?' he asked, ambling towards the fridge.

I shrugged. 'Ain' got a clue. You know that thing ain' really my scene. I don't think I'll need any more off you, though. Not the way today's job went.'

'Yeah, *yeah* – I know yuh all smokin' big bongs on the sly blood, you should jus' come clean. Or would bunnin' weed fuck wid yuh positive image?'

I pulled a huge false smile, declining an answer, then noticed a girl sitting at the kitchen table smoking a strong-smelling spliff. She was light-skinned or mixed-race, I couldn't tell which. Her long hair was so straight and black it gleamed like freshly laid Tarmac. She gave a little wave hello. I waved back, then leaned against the counter.

'Wanna drink?' Dougie offered.

'Yeah, is there any juice?'

He nodded. 'Won't be a sec . . .'

No one said anything while my brother poured the drinks into three plastic tumblers. When he handed me mine, I gulped it down in one.

'Thirsty,' the butter-coloured girl noted. I smiled in agreement.

'So what's goin' on? You seen Maya?' I asked.

Dougie barely contained a spluttering chuckle of laughter.

'Lissen, bro, my girl's gone mad up now, trus' me. Mum went diggy on her the other day. True she's goin' out wid one out dere Harlesden yout', an' my man's got her ravin', drinkin', smokin', all dat shit. You gotta talk to her man, straighten her out or suttin'. My girl's goin' on too raggo fuh her own good.'

Frustration provoked by the day's toils and the strong possibility that my sister had lied to me pushed my temper over the edge. Dougie caught my mood swing straight away. I appraised him, *really* studied him hard instead of being blinded by the façade of sibling relations. He'd always been the most sensible member of the family. But my visits here were so infrequent that I was long used to us playing the same old brother/sister/mother/son roles; three years of looking *through* my family, rather than at them. Now I'd noticed the dark, charcoal-like smudges beneath Dougie's eyes, they were impossible for me to *un*-see; like the after-image of the sun when you turn your head. I looked at the girl's mannerisms, clothes and eyes. Reluctantly, I saw she had dark smudges, too.

Dougie was matching my gaze, still chewing hard, unable to understand my frosty demeanour.

'Whassup wid you?' he huffed, shuffling around on the spot uncomfortably.

'*Whassup*?' I echoed angrily. 'I'm just wondering why *you* don't take the time to straighten her out, Dougie? She's your sister too. Or don't you care?'

Both youths froze, caught out by my severity. The girl wore a cautious expression, shoulders hunched as though watching a storm-blackened cloud and expecting rain. Dougie's mouth dropped open. He looked at the girl, silently begging for assistance.

'Wha' you goin' on like dat for, Vinnie?' he whined, sounding alarmed. 'You know I care about Maya, man. I try talk to her but she don't hear, her ears too hard—'

I borrowed Mrs Donaldson's trick. 'Maybe you'd be a better role model if you stopped smoking that crack,' I sneered witheringly. 'How the hell's she supposed to respect a brother that's such an obvious junkie?'

Nothing. Only harsh breathing while he fumed. I thought he might try to attack me; had a moment of fear, even though I was older and stronger. I had to stare him out, make him back down. After realising the face-off was useless, he threw his tumbler among its unwashed companions in the sink, rushing past me and out of the room. Doors slammed, informing the household of his rage. The girl remained sitting at the table, occasionally dragging at her spliff the way an asthma sufferer would suck on their inhaler. We avoided each other's eyes, embarrassed by the ugliness of the scene. I looked at my feet. Time passed.

'My name's Tanya, by the way.'

I looked up, feeling awkward at letting her break the silence now it was over.

'Ervine.'

More silence, apart from Tanya inhaling and exhaling smoke.

'Oh, sorry . . .' She offered me the spliff. I shook my head. She smiled to herself and spoke to the wall in front of her.

'You shouldn't have said dat. About the crack, I mean. He really feels bad about it. He wants to stop.'

Fatigue made my reply seem strained and weak.

'It's not enough just to want, you have to turn it into some kind of action. I know my brother. He *likes* what he does.'

Tanya pulled a face. 'How well d'you *really* know 'im? Ay? We bin goin' out fuh ages, an' I hardly ever seen you around.'

I shrugged and turned towards her, stepping closer to the table.

'I've been working very long hours,' I explained quickly. 'But never mind me, I'm not the one with the drug problem. What about you? Do *you* ever want to stop?'

Smiling faintly, Tanya took a deep drag of the spliff, then leaned back and blew out slowly, lazily, puffing little circles in the midst of all the smoke. Her eyes were half-closed; she looked wistful. For the first time since setting eyes on her, I realised how young and pretty she was. After the realisation came a rush of fear for her – then more for my brother and sister. I'd faced the harsh realities of the world they inhabited. I'd seen it wreck the lives of men and women with twice their strength.

'Yuh good,' she chuckled in a low tone. 'But not dat good. Yuh bruvva already told me what you do. I'm not gonna let yuh play mind games wid *me*.'

I held up my hands, knowing that my words and efforts were futile.

'Fine. In that case, I'm gonna go see my mother. Tell Dougie I'll see him around, OK?'

'Safe,' she exhaled, before I left the room. But something told me I hadn't heard the last of that issue. I couldn't ignore it forever.

Mum. No matter how long we spent apart (sometimes years), I always felt the same when I saw her. She was eternal, time-less and constant, never shifting, never changing, always there. If I look back, she always had a hand in the new direc-tions of my life, encouraging me, urging me on, *believing* in me. That was the most important. If I was honest, I saw her more when I was feeling down than when things were going well. She recharged my batteries and had never once com-plained.

I sat on the edge of her queen-sized bed, surrounded by photos of my extended family and deceased father. One particular picture kept catching my eye: the one of me and my army mates in full combat gear, just before we'd gone over to the Falklands. I remember posting my mother that picture. I can also remember how shit scared we'd all been. When I'd eventually got back from the war and spent decades knocking around doing dead-end jobs, Mum had made me realise I could run a business. She even lent me the money to set up an office.

Mum was lazing on her bed, propped up by pillows, an open tin of assorted biscuits on her night table. *London Tonight* was on TV, the volume turned down. She chewed on Bonbons and Custard Creams, listening to me with that vacant expression I'd come to recognise as deep thought. When I finished, she said nothing for a long time. Then she wiped crumbs from her Reggae Boyz T-shirt and sat up.

'Suh yuh serious den? Yuh waan give up all yuh hard wuk?'

'I wouldn't call it giving up. It's just admitting this work isn't all it's cracked up to be. It's boring, mundane, tedious and slow.'

Mum's thick eyebrows were raised in disbelief.

'Yuh call watchin' some bloke gettin' his leg over *tedious*? You should try servin' custard to over four hundred school kids, then you'd know the meanin' ah the word.'

Like Sadie, and indeed like many West Indian immigrants, my mother mixed Jamaican patwa with London slang to form a colourful cocktail of rhythm, sound and words. I often found it strange when Sadie talked to a client using one voice, then to me using another, with little or no effort.

'Watching ugly people having sex isn't my idea of fun,' I told Mum. 'An' to tell you the truth – I know this is gonna sound ridiculous, right – but to tell the truth, I just thought . . . you know . . . I thought being a PI would be a bit more . . . *exciting*.'

'Exciting,' my mother repeated, though she said the word very matter-of-factly. If she was surprised, she didn't let on. She offered me a biscuit. I took a chocolate digestive and ate; it was her turn now.

'I remember when you was ten years old an' me did buy yuh dat lickle detective set,' she began jovially. 'The one where yuh had a magnify glass, invisible ink an' a fingerprint set among udda tings, right? I had a box ah biscuit in de house, jus' like these.' She pointed at the tin. 'But they was in me bedroom, hidden away, jus' fe meself. Now me ave a lickle drink up one night, OK? Invite a whole 'eap ah people dem. When de drink up done, I come fe me biscuits an' the whole lot ah dem nyam! Whoever nyam dem left de empty box, nuttin' else! Me was vex, yuh see! But me son – me son tell me he cyan work out who teef dem!'

I was nodding now. I knew this tale and had heard it told before, many times over. But like a child's bedtime story, the plot didn't matter. It was the telling of the story; the time and care taken to say it.

'Suh yuh come in me room. Get out yuh fingerprint kit. Dus' de tin, de walls, de door handle. Yuh find suttin' yuh did call matchin' point. Den yuh tell me Mrs Johnson teef me biscuits. But me nevah did believe yuh. Me tink it was Douglas, or more to de point, yuh cousin Sasha – she was a lickle rascal in dem days, always inna yuh business. But you tell me, "No Mama, it had to be Mrs Johnson". An' yuh show me de prints yuh tek from everybody at de drink up. When me see dem, sure enough, dere was no way on dis eart' me could deny it!'

We laughed in remembrance of old Mrs Johnson down the hall – dead now, but shamed into buying a new box of biscuits by little old me, long before she eventually passed away. After that, understandably, she'd never quite trusted me, always giving me terrible looks when I passed her on the street. Part of me had been hurt by her sour reaction, which is why I'd never used the detective skills I'd learnt on my family.

Until today.

Mum grasped my hand, startling me from my thoughts. She eyed me critically, her gaze penetrating my skin and looking into my soul.

'Yuh *good* at what you do, Ervine. Dere's nuttin' wrong wi' dat. Use it to help de people dem dat need it.'

I cast my eyes down at her wrinkled hands, brown skin rough as elephant hide from hard work. I couldn't tell her I didn't think I was as good as everybody made out.

Mum kissed her teeth and shuffled about on the bed.

'Yuh 'ear 'bout what happen to dat MP?' she asked suddenly, decisively, her words slow and carefully chosen. 'De one whose daughter die a few mont' ago? Dem nevah find de killer, yuh know?'

I knew the girl she meant. Every black person in London knew.

My mother smiled. 'Go home an' get some res', do. I've bin tinkin' about dis fe awhile, an' it seem like de right time to mek some call. Jus' mek sure yuh go to work tommora like normal. Yuh promise?'

'Yes, Mum,' I said, unable to argue, even now. I got up, then kissed and hugged her tightly.

'Wait fe de call,' she told me as she squeezed my sides. 'Tommora, you jus' wait fe de call . . .'

The drive to my Finsbury Park home was mercifully traffic-free. I picked up an Indian takeaway and a bottle of Hennessy, my thoughts unconcerned with other late-night drivers. I should really have had an accident for all the attention I paid to the road, but someone must have been watching over me and I arrived safely. My thoughts were on those crazy, hard-to-work-out things called options, and the decisions that they eventually led to. I'd paid my mother's advice close attention. There was no doubt she believed in what she'd promised, but I couldn't get excited about intangible things. When I received the call she'd forecast, my enthusiasm would be secure, and I'd be able to think and deal with the results accordingly. Until then, I was still riding a downward slide of few jobs and little money. Unless that changed, I couldn't think of any reason for good cheer.

I parked my Audi directly outside my block. My council flat was amongst a small cluster of others on a road of older, privately owned houses – inspiration towards a higher standard of living. God alone knew the times I'd looked longingly from behind net curtains, dreaming of the things I'd do to a home like that when I could afford it.

Fumbling for my keys, I opened up, heading straight into the kitchen with my food. The flat was fairly new and I was only the second occupant of the one bedroom, bathroom, standard-sized living room and tiny kitchen. Every room was a challenge in the art of space management, yet the flat was great to come home to; like my office, it gave me a proud feeling of possession.

The bathroom and living room were painted (turquoise and jade green respectively), and I'd purchased more paint for the bedroom; I just needed free time to apply it. The living room had a natural, organic feel going on, with wooden tables, bookshelves and chairs, carvings and chess sets of stone. I'd treated myself to cable TV and bought a DVD player off the back of a lorry so I could watch all my favourite films in style. The bedroom was less of a show, geared towards basic creature comforts – a large king-sized bed, mini CD stereo and built-in wardrobe with a healthy selection of clothes. Friends remarked on such an obvious bachelor's pad, but I made no apologies for that. I had lived there five years and would buy at the first opportunity.

Spooning the food into a large wooden bowl, I poured the brandy into a short glass with some ice and Coke, then settled down in front of the TV. On cue, the cat flap in the kitchen rattled loudly. Renk, a feline version of B.A. Baracus, strolled

into the living room and saw me sitting with my dinner, then
yowled at the top of her lungs. She was jet-black, a tartan
collar and tiny bell around her neck, huge grey eyes blinking
in silent demand. I was pissed. Renk's eyes reminded me of
Mrs Donaldson. After the day I'd had with that particular
client, the similarity didn't help her entreaties.

I frowned, tried to ignore her, ate on. She continued to yowl
even louder, moving closer and staring into my face.

'Shit, Renk, you pick your moments!'

It wasn't her fault she had the eyes of a bitch. Swearing
some more, I jumped up and went back into the kitchen, the
cat padding at my heels, then winding through my legs as I
dug into a cupboard for a tin. Two minutes later, the meaty
smell of chicken and rabbit Whiskas filled the air. I smiled
down at Renk, feeling pleased with myself: joy brought to the
animal world by strong, benevolent owner. I watched the cat
eating before remembering my own food, and returned to the
steaming wooden bowl.

Picking up the remote control, I switched to a movie channel. They were showing *Raging Bull*, the Martin Scorsese
Oscar-winner and a favourite of mine. I'd missed the first fifteen minutes, though the rest of the film was definitely worth
watching. Resting the bowl of food on my lap, I sightlessly
spooned huge mouthfuls, while Jake La Motta fought the
world on my TV screen.

4

Sometimes, mostly at night, I couldn't stop thinking. My mind worked overtime, assaulted either by worries or happy moments, depending on the balance of the day. I'd be up the whole night watching TV and drinking brandy, in an attempt to get back to sleep. If that didn't work, I'd write in my diary, read, drink Camomile tea . . . anything to persuade my mind to switch off.

Loneliness also kept me awake. My bed had long been empty, so I ploughed myself through days filled with work, usually falling unconscious as soon as my head touched the pillow. Hours later, I'd wake up filled with unappeased longing, the ghosts of old lovers floating above my headboard, going through detailed replays of places, times and positions.

That night, my thoughts were filled with murder and politics. The feeling was chilling, though laced with an excitement I hadn't felt for years.

Next day, I quickly fed Renk, then took an early trip to my local library. In a small room, I looked over the newspapers of three months before. It didn't surprise me that only black publications treated the story as headline news. I checked the entire list of broadsheets and tabloids to find that there was little mention of the information I sought. What I did find was no more than an obituary column.

BLACK MP LOSES DAUGHTER
IN SHOCKING SOUTH BANK MURDER

In a bizarre occurrence, Viali Walker, daughter of Labour MP Robert Walker, was found brutally stabbed to death in an alleyway, yards from Central London's Globe Theatre. Twenty-one-year-old Viali, a Law student in her final year, told a friend of the family she was meeting her father at the Purcell Rooms that evening. Robert Walker denies any knowledge of this claim.

I closed the paper, returning my attention to the handful of black publications. The largest printed a colour picture of the victim and father together in a photo studio. Viali Walker had been a bright, fresh-looking girl with a cute, dimpled smile and large brown eyes. Her father was a portly, greying West Indian with the fixed expression of a bulldog hungry for a bone. Nevertheless, the resemblance between the two was unmistakable. It was in the eyes, lips and shape of the brow.

According to the paper, Viali had told her flatmate she was meeting her father for seven, travelling to the South Bank via an underground train from Ladbroke Grove. Apparently, the young woman hadn't spoken to her father personally.

Someone had phoned on his behalf, someone she'd assumed worked for or with him. She was wrong. At eight-thirty a number of screams were heard from an alleyway not far from the Globe Theatre. They were ignored. At nine, a number of homeless people found Viali's naked and mutilated body. She'd been sexually abused and beaten.

Robert Walker claimed he knew the killers. A far-right political party called The Foundation had been sending hate mail to his office and home for many years. I knew very little about them, but vague reports described the party as a hate group prone to violent attacks on immigrants of all kinds, though no such accusation had ever been proven in court. There were also rumours that they came into multicultural towns, stirred up the locals, then left in a wake of mayhem, even causing a few small-scale riots on occasion. While many people disputed their involvement in these events, there was no question that this hate group existed.

As time passed, Robert Walker had told the reporter, the party grew more vocal about their racist intentions. They sent a letter bomb to the office, stuck abusive posters up at his family home, and even told him they'd attack his family if he didn't quit as MP. Despite this, and despite the fact that Walker had kept all the letters as evidence, police refused to question Foundation party members. So far, the total number of arrests was zero.

None.

I read the other papers and the story remained unchanged. They all spoke of Viali in glowing terms: her loving personality, her intelligence; her ability to have fun no matter how gloomy the occasion. I looked at her photo once more, staring into the eyes, seeing if they gave away anything that hinted at the life she'd led.

She'd been good-looking, with the strong kind of brown complexion I liked, the colour of demerara sugar. She was wearing a tight-fitting dress. I wasn't surprised to find myself feeling attracted to her, a lot of men must've felt that way when she was alive.

After photocopying the information, I left the library and strolled into the office at half past ten. Sadie was already typing away, God bless her. I kissed her forehead, gave her the flowers and thank you card I'd bought earlier that morning, then retired to my sanctuary and put my feet up. Closing my eyes, I felt myself reeling from lack of sleep. I checked my diary. Nothing. I twiddled my thumbs. Switched on the TV.

Teletubbies. Crap film. Crap film. Science programme. *Style Challenge*.

Jesus Christ.

After half an hour's torture, I buzzed Sadie.

'Any calls, Sade?'

'Nah, luv; it's bin real quiet so far. I thought Mrs Donaldson would be steamin' up the lines cussin' an' makin' up noise, but even she ain' bovvered. Who yuh pissed off?'

'Everybody,' I returned with a chuckle, sitting back and closing my eyes once more.

Remembering I had a novel in my desk, I dug amongst the shit I'd stored until I found it. *The Insult* by Rupert Thompson. Whenever I had free time, I lost myself in his darkened world.

Typically, just as I kicked back and found my page, the intercom buzzed. I answered immediately. Nerves made my stomach feel light.

'Sadie?'

'A Mr Walker for you on line one, Ervine.'

'Thanks, yeah.'

I took a deep breath. It was show time. Picking up the phone, I pressed it to my ear. 'Hello?'

'Ervine James, what a pleasure to talk to you.'

His voice was baritone and full of melody. Although the West Indian accent was evident, it came with a middle-class lilt my mother and Sadie could never capture, no matter how versatile their linguistics. There's something about an educated Jamaican accent that makes me feel proud of my heritage, never mind the fact that most white people can't tell the difference. It always underlined the truth: we, as black people, are not all the same. Some of us can't understand one another. Shit, some of us don't even *like* one another.

'Mr Walker,' I measured my greeting with what I hoped was just the right amount of respect, 'thanks for taking time to call . . .'

'Oh, that's no trouble, no trouble at all. Now, Ervine, you do know that I've met you before don't you?'

'Really?' I was intrigued.

'Yes, yes, when you were no more than a little boy. You see, I met your mother way back in Nineteen . . . Nineteen . . . Well, let's just say I met her a long time ago!'

Amazing. Three months ago the man had lost his only child; now, here he was, cracking bad jokes on the other end of my line. I mentally applauded his strength of character. Robert Walker seemed an interesting type of guy.

'How did you meet?'

'We lived on the same road in Windrush days,' Walker told me. 'Shepherd's Bush, when everything was cheap. I bought a house just by the Green for four t'ousand pounds in Sixty-two. Nowadays, those houses go for up to two hundred t'ousand!'

'The good old days, huh?' I said nostalgically, lighting a cigarette and imagining the world I was too young to remember.

'Well, they weren't *all* good, I have to admit,' Walker admonished smoothly. 'But some of those days were great, yes they were. Your mother's a good woman. She was very close to my wife back then, and she's been a tremendous help through our trauma. I wish Viali had known her a little better. There were so many people I wanted her to meet.'

A crackle on the line as silence fell. I noted the pronunciation of her name. *Vee-ar-lee.*

'I understand the police are no closer to solving things, Mr Walker. I looked through the press cuttings. I really don't think they give a damn.'

'Please, Ervine, call me Robert. And you're right on both counts,' he sighed, while I shook the ghost of Mrs Donaldson's voice from my ear. 'I truly believe I know who killed my daughter,' Walker continued. 'I've been receiving death threats from a certain right-wing movement for some time. I gave the police all the letters, but they say there isn't enough evidence to link them to this case.'

'I know,' I told him steadily. 'I read that, too. You understand that I don't work in quite the same way as the police. I have a fee, of which half is paid before I begin—'

'I'll give you five t'ousand pounds cash if you can start right away.'

My mouth hung open. From somewhere far away, Walker was calling my name. I retrieved my senses.

'Ervine?'

'Yes, Robert, I'm here. Uhh . . .' My brain still felt numb. 'Don't you want to meet up first?'

'Of course, I'll need to check your credentials, that goes without saying. But I want my daughter's killers found. Where are you now?'

I told him. He gave me the address of The Tabernacle, a community centre based in Ladbroke Grove. He would be there all day as part of a Role Models' programme. We could go for a cup of coffee and discuss the job.

When I put the receiver down, I immediately decided I had to thank my mother. Her phone rang twice before I remembered she'd be at work. Nervous energy enveloped me. When I could contain it no longer, I threw my arms in the air and roared as loud as I dared.

The recently refurbished former church gleamed and sparkled in the sun, as I walked the long path that led to the entrance.

Face-painted infants and their proud parents passed me along
the way. Once inside, I looked around to see Robert Walker sitting in a café area with a scattering of men and women. I
paced around until he saw me, then waved and pointed at an
empty table a little way from the suited group. Five minutes
later he slid into the seat opposite me, clutching two steaming
mugs of coffee.

'Hope you like cappuccino,' he winked.

'Love it,' I thanked him in return, though I would've drunk
turps for a chance at that money.

Looking at him through my own eyes, I realised the photos
hadn't been far wrong. He was bigger in the flesh, but also
greyer. His demeanour was cheery, but his features sagged.
The man in front of me looked twenty years older than the one
I'd seen on TV months ago. He puffed a heavy breath, as if
he'd guessed my inner thoughts, wiping his eyes tiredly with
a silk hankie.

We immediately got down to business. Walker offered me
the five thousand pounds cash, which would secure my dedication to the case. A further ten thousand would follow if I
found the murderer. He'd pay all my expenses, including
food, travel and any nights spent in a hotel, providing I could
prove the stay necessary. Regardless of his promise to check
me out, he asked very little about my work or personal life,
and didn't seem to question whether I'd take the job. That
seemed a bit strange, but who was I to argue with a reasonably rich client? When Walker was finished, he casually asked
for some form of contract.

'Just a guarantee of the terms and conditions,' he
explained.

'No problem,' I replied agreeably. I already had a standard
contract that covered that type of thing, so I handed it over. 'If
you could take a look and sign as soon as you're happy, I can
get started right away.'

He looked up. 'Really? So soon?'

'Well, look over the contract, then I want you to tell me everything you know about Viali. Her favourite food, favourite hang outs, favourite friends . . .'

'I'll take you to her flat,' he enthused helpfully. 'She only lived a couple of streets away.'

'That would be a great start. You can bring me up to speed as we go.'

He signed the contract and we left the building, walking around a corner to Ledbury Road, just off Westbourne Park Road. Walker limped up some concrete steps opposite a small estate, then rang a ground-floor bell and waited with his arms behind his back. A woman's voice answered the intercom. After an exchange of words, there was a buzz and a click. We went in.

'How long did Viali live here?'

'Around eighteen months. I own it, but she paid the mortgage in the form of rent. Viali insisted it was that way. She was very independent.'

We pushed our way through the door as a woman appeared to greet us. She was tall, willowy almost, thick locks streaming from her lime-green hairwrap like jungle vines. She wore an African print dress and her feet were bare. Walker smiled at the sight of her. They embraced.

'How are you?'

'Fine, fine . . .'

The woman looked my way.

'Afternoon,' I greeted.

'Hello.'

Walker introduced the woman as Dominique. Close up, her angular ebony face was intelligent, proud and strong rather than pretty or demure. Her eyebrows raised when she heard my occupation, but there was no further reaction. I asked to be shown to Viali's room. We walked through the flat, which was stylishly decorated with a strong Afrocentric theme.

The bedroom was much the same. African literature lined the walls, while Malcolm X and Che Guevara posters stared sightlessly down on us. Her bed was made. Teddy Bears and other cuddly toys lolled on the duvet as if they owned the place.

'I haven't touched a thing,' Dominique explained from somewhere near the door. 'I wanted another flatmate at first, to help out with bills, but we couldn't stand to move her stuff. This is the way it looked when she left.'

'The room will stay exactly as it is,' Walker broke in firmly, and for the first time I saw his calm exterior crumble. Ignoring them, I stepped deeper inside.

'Have the police looked over this room?'

Dominique nodded her head.

'They took a token look, but said there was no evidence of any importance to be found.'

I opened a desk and found a small grey diary nestled within. Picking it up, I turned it over in my hands.

'What about this?'

She shrugged thin shoulders.

'Yeah, they *took* it, but they didn't *do* anything with it.'

I held the diary out in Robert's direction. 'All right to look?'

He nodded once. 'Take it.'

I flicked through. It was an engagement form of diary rather than the kind you write memoirs in. I studied some of the dates.

'When did your daughter pass away?'

'November the tenth.'

I looked up the date. There was only one appointment: Dad, Purcell Rooms, at seven. I turned to the back of the book and saw a list of names and numbers. Pocketing the diary, I faced the MP.

'Could you both draw me up a list of Viali's best friends?'

They nodded in unison.

'And the address where she worked if you know it.'

I wanted a sense of this girl: what she ate, the music she liked, her taste in men . . . Any of those things could lead me to the truth. And that's all any detective is: a man who seeks the truth; a man obsessed with knowing why events occur.

5

After getting the names and addresses of Viali's best friends from Walker and Dominique, I bagged a recent picture of her from her room. It was a holiday snap. She was wearing a sky-blue bathing suit, skinning her teeth against the background of a hotel pool. Behind her, a bather was caught mid-dive, half in and half out of the water. I wondered where the pool was and what she'd been thinking. She looked happy. She also looked good.

Someone cleared his throat behind me. Walker.

'I thought you might want to get paid at last.' He smiled and handed me a padded manila envelope. 'My contact numbers and all my details are in there. Please feel free to call. And to check the money,' he added as an aside.

I followed the latter advice to find it was all there. Five thousand pounds in crisp fifties looking fresh from the Royal Mint. I tucked the envelope under my arm, feeling reborn.

'Thank you. You don't know how much this helps,' I told him honestly.

'Well help *me*. Please find my daughter's killers.'

I nodded 'yes', unable to stop myself looking into Walker's eyes. Tears had sprung into them, making them glisten as he faltered on those last words, while his lips trembled and he clutched tightly at his chest. I crossed the room, taking one hand and placing the other on his shoulder.

'I swear to God I'll find them, Robert.'

I rarely say that to a client, but today was different. I'd decided if I couldn't solve this case then I wasn't really a PI. I'd sell up, buy a shop, or go abroad and start another less strenuous business with the money I had saved. This job was the test that would make or break my dreams.

Walker gulped back his sorrows, then squeezed my hand in return and said nothing. He didn't have to. His eyes expressed his hopes and fears, the lines encircling them putting an age to his grief like tree stump rings. We shook once more and he said something about letting me get on with my job. I called goodbye to Dominique before leaving the flat.

Entering the first telephone box I came to, I dug for change. A twenty pence piece gave me the opportunity to inform Sadie I'd taken the job, then I asked her to phone my police contact for some inside information.

Next stop was the nearest mobile phone store. Up until now I'd made so little money, I made do with a pager for communication. Half an hour later, I was connected and heading towards the address that Walker had given me as Viali's place of work, somewhere in Soho. On the way I phoned Walker and Sadie, passing on my new number.

Parking is a hard thing to do in Central London, yet I secured a vacant meter and fed it like a loving mother would a fat child. The workplace address led me to a coffee shop on Wardour Street called Freedom Café, full of twenty-something university students and tourists. Entering, I relished the smell of espresso mixed with cigarette smoke, and the confined bustle of the West End. Taking a seat near the counter, I decided I was still high from my cappuccino. I ordered an orange juice and took stock of the place.

It was a large, brightly lit space split into two sections. The bar area was at the back of the building, while a seating area made up of sofas on one side, tables and chairs on the other, took up the front. Garage played in the background. The staff were young and trendy, the young lady who took my order plain yet cute – a white girl with a half-friendly, half cautious smile; a London smile. The rest of the staff hung around the counter by the bar. There were two guys and another girl who talked to each other in some European language I couldn't quite catch.

At close to four PM the bar was around a third full. Due to its location, I knew it'd be heaving on a Friday or Saturday. The waitress brought my orange juice. I paid and pocketed the receipt, glad I wouldn't be shelling out on the West End rip-off prices myself, thanks to Mr Walker. Sipping on my drink, I watched the afternoon clientele come and go. When my juice was done I stepped to the bar, looking keenly at the staff gathered there. They watched me for a second, then one of the guys stepped forwards.

On closer inspection, he definitely wasn't English. His dark hair and sun-ripened skin indicated time spent in a climate much warmer than the UK. He was short and stocky, wearing one of those muscle T-shirts most bartenders have these days.

'Can I help you?'

The accent was European, as I'd suspected, though hard to place.

'I dunno, maybe you can,' I replied, placing my ID on the bar. 'My name's James, Ervine James, and I'm a private investigator.'

The young man frowned.

'You know, I'm hired to look for people as well as performing other good deeds. Kinda like a bastard police force . . .'

My thin humour was lost on the bartender, who simply stared at the picture in my wallet. People often did that. I always wondered what they hoped to find in my face that had them gazing so intently.

'Anyhow, I'm looking for anyone that might've known a girl who worked here. Viali Walker . . .'

I replaced my ID card with the picture of Viali in her swimsuit. The bartender scrutinised her form for a long time. Soon, it became too long.

'Do you recognise her?'

He shook his head.

'No – I only work here one week.'

I nodded slowly. 'What about them?' I said, pointing at the three remaining bar staff. They were watching me closely, talking with their heads together and eyebrows furrowed. My bartender shrugged.

'Christophe may know. He's been here longer than all of us. Everybody is here longer than I. I'll ask.'

I nodded, then stood back while he walked over to the youngsters. While they talked, I looked around and waited. In front of me, two women, one black and the other white, were sitting close together, speaking in circumspect tones. They were middle-aged, both sporting identically shaved heads, and were a little dumpy, as though they'd been fashioned out of Play-dough and moulded to their seats. I noted them as lesbians, feeling a little bad for branding them by such obvious attributes, until they kissed on the lips as the white woman went to the ladies'. The black woman, left on her own, saw me looking and turned her gaze to the floor, embarrassed. I wondered how come she seemed shamed, when her partner clearly didn't give a damn who saw them.

'Excuse me?' I turned to see the other two bar staff standing in front of me. 'You're looking for Viali?'

The speaker was a thin girl with short black hair, a hoop earring in her eyebrow and a Red Hot Chilli Peppers T-Shirt.

Her companion was a tall, thin-faced guy with bleached blond hair and an easy smile that showed train-track braces on his upper and lower teeth.

'Did you know her?'

'We worked with her for around six months,' Train Tracks told me with another faint accent I couldn't place. His eyes were filled with sympathy I couldn't understand until he spoke further. 'Uhh . . . Um, you *do* know what happened to her, yes?'

I nodded rapidly.

'Yeah, sorry, I do. I'm a private investigator, hired to investigate the murder. I'd like to know some things about her time here.'

I gave them the ID and they passed it between them, then handed it back gravely.

'We'll tell you all we can,' the girl said, a determined look on her face. I sat on a barstool and got out the pad that I carried for these occasions.

'OK – first, gimme your names.'

'I'm Juliet, this is Christophe.'

'Hi, I'm Ervine James . . .'

I set about asking them routine questions: how long she'd worked there, how she was received, did she make any enemies . . . After five minutes, it was clear everybody had loved her. Juliet showed me a stack of thank you notes she'd received from customers, and even a handful of anonymous Valentine's cards, sent by lonely businessmen, no doubt. It didn't take much longer to see that Christophe had been one of her admirers. A little probing in the right place easily revealed the depth of his esteem.

'. . . What I thought of her? Personally? I thought she was beautiful,' he said candidly, looking me dead in the eye. 'She wasn't just attractive, either. It was like . . . She didn't know the effect she had on people. She was kind, very kind to everybody she met. Once a *Big Issue* vendor came in here to sell those crappy papers. No offence to them, but really, the paper is rubbish. Anyway, it was raining outside, and I'm sure he was just looking for shelter. Our manager screamed at the man, telling him to get out, he was stinking up the place . . . Then Viali heard all this from downstairs. She came running up to our manager and, how did she say it? She hexed him?'

'You mean cursed him?' I helped, hiding my smile.

'Yes, that's right!' Christophe beamed, his braces reflecting the bright lights of the bar. 'When she finished, the manager was so ashamed, he gave the man free coffee and let him stay as long as he liked. Any of us would have been sacked if we'd shouted like that.'

'That's right,' Juliet agreed. Her eyes filled with tears. 'Viali always was good to me. I'm from Serbia. Not many people are good to us here. Viali always said she had an . . . obligation to understand what we'd been through. I never knew what she meant until she died.'

Juliet broke off. Her face turned lobster red and a tear escaped her eye. Guilt chided me for having provoked this kind of response.

'You know, you don't have to do this if—'

'I will finish. I *must* finish,' she said resolutely. Christophe found her some tissues in a drawer beneath the bar. She dabbed at her eyes and blew her nose while customers watched.

'Where's your manager today?'

'Day off,' Christophe replied. 'He usually takes a week day off, leaves me in charge.'

I leaned closer to the bar. The easy questions were over. I needed both of these youngsters to think.

'Now, I want you to concentrate very carefully on what I'm gonna ask you next. Did you ever see any suspicious people lurking around Viali? Maybe one of her admirers turned nasty?'

I flicked one of the Valentine's cards with a finger as both
youths swapped stern expressions. Juliet shook her head at
once. Christophe thought a little longer, but then sighed and
shrugged.

'No, there was no one. I was watching her all the time. I'm
sure I would have noticed someone behaving like that.'

I'm sure too, I thought to myself, noting the serious look on
the bartender's face and marking him mentally as a suspect. I
didn't really think he'd be so open about his affection if he was
the killer, but the old adage in this business clearly states: You
Never Know. I closed my pad and put my pen away. I was
done here. For the time being.

'So I can find the manager here any day except Wednesday?'

'Yes,' Juliet whispered, her throat still affected by her tears.
'Uhh . . . How close are you to finding the murderer?'

I offered a limited twitch of the lips in their direction.

'Well, I've only just started on the case, but I'm pretty sure
I'll wrap it up quickly.'

They nodded gravely, neither knowing that my words were
simply candy to a bawling child. I gave them what they
needed because it suited me. I had no idea what twists and
turns this case would lead me through, and nothing they had
said got me closer to the truth of Viali's death. All I was building in those preliminary questions was the truth of her life.
Pondering that thought, I shook Christophe's hand and kissed
Juliet on the cheek, before leaving Freedom Café for the murky
London streets.

Driving through the beginnings of rush hour traffic, I crossed
Westminster Bridge and headed south, just to the other side of
the Thames. The building that Viali had named in her diary
and the spot where she'd been found were no more than a
mile apart, according to newspapers. I thought a stroll around
the South Bank could rustle up some answers to the questions
dancing like hyperactive children in my brain.

After paying an extortionate rate to place my vehicle in a car park beneath the Hayward Gallery, I walked up some nearby stairs to the Purcell Rooms where Viali had believed she would meet her father that night. The wind whistled through me, causing me to zip up my jacket. The wide expanse of the River Thames gave a sharp bite to the chill, while South Bank Centre flags fluttered forlornly. The Millennium Wheel loomed above the overground train line to Charing Cross like a giant hamster's toy. The sparse gathering of tourists took pictures and pointed at the varied sights with glee, presumably impervious to the cold.

I tried to imagine the area as Viali had seen it. It was a lonely kind of place. Apart from myself, there were no black people or any people of colour. I wondered if she would've noticed that, whether it would've made any impact in her pro-black mind. Burying my head in my jacket, I turned and walked away from Bankside jetty, in the direction of the Purcell Rooms.

Digging into my pocket, I checked that I still had Viali's photograph, grateful for the warm blast of air that greeted me as I pushed through heavy doors. A black security guard in a suit and tie watched me curiously. I nodded his way; he nodded back without a smile, yet without malice. The box office, intended as my first port of call, was closed and devoid of humanity. I decided to try the lobby area to see if I could find anyone behind the bar, then question the security guard as I left the building.

The lobby was a ragged symphony of commotion and activity. An extravagantly dressed middle-aged woman stood by a grand piano, singing war songs to an audience of disabled kids and OAPs. 'We'll Meet Again' resounded around the huge area, while more able-bodied pensioners danced with painful-looking steps. The wheelchair-bound children watched in delight. It all seemed quite sad, and I felt that familiar fear return, the fear of growing old, growing weak, growing incapable. I told myself I'd stay and watch, then began walking away when I saw the closed bar area. Nobody in here would have seen Viali that night, I reasoned. Even if they did, I bet none of them would remember.

Turning back, I walked towards the doors that led outside. The black security guy was leaning on the box office counter, looking bored. I approached him.

'Excuse me . . .' I began.

'Whassup bro?' he replied easily.

This threw me. Most black people in the UK are self-conscious of their colour in a working environment, scared they may be seen as 'too black'. 'Too black' is often equated with 'too strong', which usually ended up becoming 'too much trouble for us'. As a result, most of us played the loyal Negro role in a setting such as this, believing that made our colour invisible. This was new to me. It was also great.

'I'm cool,' I responded in kind, after taking a beat to recover. The guard noticed my surprise, and although he didn't say a word, I could see the amused smile in his eyes. 'I was just wondering if you'd been working here long? I was looking for a friend of mine, but I'm not sure if she still works here . . .'

There was no need to tell him why I was here if he knew nothing. A sixth sense told me that the fewer people who knew what kind of job I was doing, the safer I would be. From what I knew of The Foundation, if they had killed Viali they were well connected enough to get rid of me too, no hassle, no fuss. After all, I was nobody in their world.

'Well, I've bin 'ere just under a month,' the security guard told me. 'What's your friend's name?'

I waved a hand.

'I wouldn't worry, it doesn't matter then.'

The guard shrugged.

'Oh . . . Well, sorry bro . . .'

'No worries, blood. Later.'

We nodded at each other once more. In the lobby behind me, the middle-aged singer was striking up an enthusiastic rendition of 'Daisy', cheerfully backed up by her pianist and willing, if incapacitated, audience. I stepped outside without a backward glance.

Standing on the street where Viali's body had been found, it was hard for me to stifle my disquiet. It just didn't make any sense.

True, the confines were dark, silent, and far enough from the main walkway of the South Bank to conduct any secret, sordid business. But it was also yards away from the Globe. Had nobody heard her cries and attempted an answer? The papers said the closest thing to witnesses were some late-night commuters who heard screams at eight thirty. Yet no one had called the police. No one even mentioned what had been heard until the murder investigation was in full swing. Even then, passers-by claimed they had seen nothing.

Why? My mind screamed, anger coursing through me fast and hot, like the passage of my life-blood.

The street was called Bear Gardens. It was deathly quiet, the noisy London bustle becoming a muted murmur the deeper I walked into its depths. I looked back, glancing at my watch and counting the space between the scattered groups of passers-by. The first was around a minute and a half. The next was five. And this was early evening, close to six PM, nowhere near the time when Viali had been murdered.

Here was a concentrated testimony to the ultimate act of racism, though my thoughts at that moment were not on death at the hands of right-wing extremists, or a father's harassment by those same animals, walking upright in the guise of men. I couldn't fail to notice the towering height of St Paul's Cathedral, which loomed on the other side of the Thames. This, along with the other numerous symbols of English society, had stared impassively over the scene of

Viali's death. The cathedral glow illuminated the night sky, though its bright eye hadn't managed to fall here, on this alleyway, where it was needed. As I gazed at the dome, blue police lights flashed and wailed noisily on that side of the Thames, the very sound insulting to my ears.

This travesty was a weight too heavy for me to bear. I stepped back towards the South Bank, letting the bitter wind wipe hot tears from my eyes.

6

It was the following afternoon. The sun was bright and high in the cloudless sky, the air refreshingly cold. I turned my car heater up full blast. I was heading west, my driving aggressive, grim determination filling my mind. Once again I'd been through a night of whirlwind thoughts and no sleep. The combination didn't help my demeanour.

Today's destination was King's College University, situated deep within the West End. I parked my car in a square surrounded by ancient-looking buildings, then began my stroll around the massive site. The students I saw were mostly young, gathered in groups reflecting their varied racial backgrounds, rarely transcending barriers the outside world had erected. The clustered groups of ethnicity worried me somewhat. I wondered if they found things easier that way.

Stopping a group of Asian students, I asked for directions to the reception and effortlessly followed them to the front of

the building. Earlier that day, I managed to get details of
Viali's Dean from her father, who had known the man as a
personal friend. The call I made to book an appointment
revealed a deep-voiced, well-spoken man, with a penchant
for long, thoughtful silences. After some hesitation, he agreed
to meet. I hadn't managed to check up on him yet, though
David Wren seemed to have gleaned some interesting work
from Viali, judging by an essay Walker had given to me and
which I'd scanned through. Wren had given a good grade and
scribbled his endorsement of her views in neat, well-scripted
handwriting.

As I waited at the modern-looking reception desk, all wood
panelling and bright lights, I could feel the eggs I'd eaten for
breakfast churning. A well-lit sign informed me that I was currently standing inside the Strand Entrance. Posters advertising
study groups and the student magazine, *Kings Bench*, could be
seen everywhere. Youngsters milled around, enjoying their
lunch break. An elderly white woman behind the reception
desk came forwards, a full yet questioning smile on her face.

It was the age, I told myself. *Had to be my age.*

'Good morning,' I beamed politely. 'I was looking for David
Wren. I'm told he teaches Law here.'

'Do you have an appointment?' she enquired, an eyebrow
raised.

'Yes I do, for two o' clock.'

'One moment . . .'

As she turned to the phone, a sudden thought grabbed me,
so obvious I had to follow through. I reached into my pocket
for Viali's photo.

'Excuse me . . .'

The receptionist stopped mid-reach and returned her attention to me slowly, wearing a somewhat exasperated expression.
I took no notice.

'Have you worked here a long time?'

She thought about that. I could see her sifting through

hundreds of reasons why I might ask the question. Finding none that stuck, she nodded.

'Ten years next September. May I ask why?'

'Of course you may. My name's Ervine James . . .' I laid my ID alongside Viali's photo. 'I'm a private investigator looking for the killers of this young lady. Do you recognise her, or know her at all?'

I tapped the celluloid with my index finger and waited. She peered at both items on the desk then stared at me, her mouth a lipstick-coated O of astonishment.

'*Ooooh* . . . You mean a PI? Like the ones on TV?'

I grinned. If I had a pound for each time I heard that . . .

'No, not quite like that, but the general idea is the same. Now did you know this student? Her name was Viali Walker, she was the daughter of a Labour MP—'

Her face lit up like a firecracker, bright colour and all. It was compelling, yet disturbing to watch. I almost feared for her life.

'Oh *yes*! Yes of course, I remember. Not that I knew the poor child, but it caused such a commotion on site. Students crying . . . classes cut . . . Oh, her poor family. You're such a good man taking this on . . .'

I'd made a new friend but needed progress more than allegiance. Scooping up the photo and ID, I indicated the queue that had formed while the aged receptionist lamented.

'I'm sorry, but I really should speak to the person I came here to see if you didn't know her personally . . .'

'Of course!' The woman gushed. 'I'll get him at once.'

She picked up the phone and dialled like the spirit of youth had taken over her knobbly fingers. That was the great thing about these types. If they were against you, you were up shit creek, yet if they *liked* you . . . I smiled apologetically at the students waiting behind me. They shrugged, looked away, or smiled back.

When I turned to face the desk, someone tapped me on my

shoulder. I twisted my head around, to see a broad-shouldered Asian guy. He was good-looking, possessing piercing green eyes and sideburns that joined his beard, everything trimmed to perfection. Like many of the Asian students, he was dressed in smart casual garments, brand new shoes and a smattering of gold. His arm was outstretched and his hand open.

'Can I get a look at that photo?'

'Sure.'

I handed him the picture then paid him no mind. Another tap on my shoulder. I faced the Asian guy yet again. He gave back the picture.

'Know her?'

He nodded forlornly.

'Yeah, yeah I did as it goes. I knew her quite well. We kind of went out together.'

Behind me, the old receptionist had returned.

'Mr James? He said he'll be down to get you in a second.'

Now I was torn. I'd wanted to talk to some students while I was here, and this guy seemed like the perfect start. Experience had taught me that most people hated to talk to PIs. Even when they relented, the interview was undertaken as reluctantly as an HIV test. Any stalling on my part could lose me either, or both of my volunteers. I had to tread carefully.

I made a split-second decision. 'Could you tell him I'll be five minutes? I've found someone I'd really like to talk to.'

She nodded fast.

'Don't worry, I'll explain,' my new friend replied vigorously, making me breathe a sigh of relief. Leaving the matter in her capable hands, I followed the Asian student past some lifts and on through swing doors into the college.

'We'll go to the student bar. We can talk there,' he told me. I nodded mutely. My anticipation had returned.

We walked down a long corridor and into a stairwell, then up two flights of stairs until we reached the Student Union. The bar was a welcoming expanse of couches and round wooden tables, much like the furniture of any local pub. Windows looked out onto the Embankment side of the River Thames. Top Ten hits were playing somewhere above us. Pretty female students with free time on their hands tended the bar, which was cheap and amply stocked. I offered my volunteer an alcoholic beverage; he declined and went for an orange juice. I ordered a half-pint, inwardly admonishing myself for drinking on the job, conscious that Walker was paying.

We settled down and I began the interview, taking things slow, my questions even, simple and unthreatening. Experience had also taught me that if I slipped up and caused any alarm, my witness would only clam up. The student responded casually, with little or no sign of nervousness, though he hardly glanced in my direction for the whole interview. He spent the majority of our conversation looking at his hands or the wall behind me with the deadened gaze of the blind. He spoke as if he was reciting the words to himself, committing them to memory.

His full name was Ravinder Singh Kapoor. He lived somewhere in West Hanwell and had known Viali from the beginning of the previous term. As I guessed upon entering the university, mixing across the racial divide was not the norm, particularly if you were brought up a Sikh. Despite this restriction, Ravinder claimed he'd taken one look at the attractive student and knew the expanse was a gulf he had to cross. He sipped at his orange juice as he told how he'd fearfully made small talk, ever on the lookout for so-called friends that would expose his intentions to his parents. Encouraged by Viali's openness, the small talk grew into longer chats between classes, drinks in the bar (devoid of alcohol on his part, he quickly assured), lunch in coffee shops outside university grounds.

'And you initiated all this?' I asked.

'Yes, at first,' Ravinder admitted. 'But she never refused.

Pretty soon she offered to take me to lunch. I could see we were getting to be friends.'

'Go on,' I motioned eagerly.

The blossoming friendship between them began to attract the attention of other students. Most did not like what they saw. Ravinder told me that black students, particularly males, would bad-mouth him and act aggressively when they saw him around the building. Females wouldn't say much (when they did it was under their breath), though sour looks definitely made their feelings plain. On his side of the fence, Asian students of all kinds would simply act as if Viali didn't exist, when before they had been best of friends with the girl. Their male counterparts would hound him about the friendship, stressing how bad it looked for him to be seen out in the open with a girl who wasn't his kind. Funnily enough, Ravinder was quick to tell me, close friends didn't give a damn what either of them did. They saw it as none of their business and rightly so. It was the people that knew them least that thought they knew best. They began meeting secretly in an attempt to make things easier.

This badly backfired. When they were eventually seen together, it was assumed they had to be a couple. After all, why would they hide if they had nothing to be ashamed of? At this point in their friendship, there had been no sexual activity, though in Ravinder's own words, they 'both knew it was on the cards.' The tension between them had been building for some time. If either of them *had* made a move, things may have been different.

Then Ravinder received the e-mail that tore him apart.

```
Ravinder, I'm sorry but my life is too
complicated for us to continue seeing each
other the way we have been. It's not anything
you've done - it's all down to my stupid
mistakes and me. I hope you can understand
what I'm saying.
```

Viali disappeared, failing to reply to Ravinder's following e-mails. Two weeks later, news of her death was all over the university.

Looking at the youth from across the wooden table, I found sympathy rising within me, but with an effort I pushed it away. There was no room for emotion here. If the truth were known, I felt a little of what his fellow students probably had back then. Ravinder had managed a touch of something none of us could hold.

I hated myself for thinking like that, but there it was. The chipped tooth in the winning smile of a supermodel. My brother would have been pleased if he'd known what was running through my mind at that moment. Or would he?

'You know that your confession makes you a suspect,' I informed him coldly, half-expecting him to squirm with unease. I was irrationally relieved when he stared back easily, even though I told myself it meant nothing. Maybe he *had* aroused some sympathy.

'Fine,' he mumbled. 'I've nothing to hide. Do you want my address?'

'Yes please.'

I took out my pad. He scribbled down his details, finally watching his fellow students as he wrote. They were congregating solidly. Some leaned at the bar, turning away as we looked up. Others simply stared boldly in sets of three or four at their tables, letting us know they'd seen us noticing them. When they were sure they had our attention, they whispered to each other and laughed.

'Friendly lot,' I commented. Ravinder dismissed them with a shrug of his shoulders.

'I try not to think about them most of the time. Since Viali died I can't stand to see them.'

'Figures,' I agreed. He gulped back the rest of his orange juice and stood up to leave.

'Hey, just one question before you go, won't take a minute.'

Ravinder sat back down, sighing and finally looking straight at me with those wide, green eyes. I realised how impossible it was for Viali not to have been attracted to him. If his story were the truth.

'Why did Viali call the whole thing off if she was so adamant about seeing you before? I mean, she'd had to deal with all the stick from other Asian students, and probably from black ones, too. Why go through all that just to call it off when you'd got so close?'

Ravinder was silent for a long time. I was even more aware of the whispered voices from students, the ticklish feel of malicious eyes, the giggles, loud even over the sound of Brit Pop. He closed his eyes. When he opened them, I saw the strength of his sorrow.

'I heard . . . I mean, they reckon—' He stopped, flicking his eyes to the right, letting me know exactly who *they* were. '— she'd been having a fling with a lecturer of hers. Mr Wren. He took her for Law.'

Ravinder stared while I tried to keep my face neutral.

'D'you know him?' he continued.

'No . . . No, I don't. I just didn't think Viali was like that,' I stammered, momentarily confused.

'Neither did I,' the student replied brusquely. 'Can I go?'

'Yeah, sure.'

He got up once more and left while I sat there composing myself. That was the first indication that this case was going to be more complex than I could've imagined.

Ravinder's accusation weighed heavily on my mind as I went back to the reception area and informed my aged friend that I was ready to see Mr Wren. While he had been convincing enough to make me almost sure his story was true, part of me warned myself not to be too eager, to see what happened before revealing what I'd been told. If the student were right, Wren would earn the place of number one suspect, even though the motive seemed a little weak. Although relationships between students and lecturers were frowned upon, the troubles they caused were never severe enough to provoke murder. Viali was a grown woman; I honestly doubted that the lecturer's job had been threatened. But there might be something deeper that had occurred between them. If this was so, Wren might just expose what it was without any prompting.

The receptionist put a call through to the lecturer. Within minutes, I was climbing another narrow set of concrete stairs, which led to a corridor on the third floor. I followed door numbers until I came to an office at the far end. David Wren's name was proudly inscribed into a chunk of knotted wood along with the accolade *Head of Law*. The words had been etched or burnt into the log, then placed on the office door.

Very *nice*, I thought, reaching out an involuntary hand to touch the varnished finish.

'Ah, ah, ah . . .' a voice warned to my left.

My fingers froze. I turned my head towards the voice without lowering my hand. A young girl with short brown hair and distinctly Mediterranean features sat before me, her eyes the lightest hazel, crested with dark eyebrows that framed the curious expression she wore. There was a bag of books by the side of her chair, though I couldn't see the titles. A further three empty chairs were lined up beside her, outside another office door. I'd been so wrapped up in my thoughts over Mr Wren and Viali Walker that I'd passed without even noticing her.

'I wouldn't do that,' she said helpfully. 'David don't like people fiddlin' with his bit of wood. He makes stupid jokes about tarnishing his name to hide it but he gets really pissed off if he catches anyone touching the thing.'

I masked my surprise, turning to face her. She was watching me with a smile, seemingly pleased at spotting me when I'd so obviously thought I was alone.

'Is that so?'

'*Yeah* . . . It's silly, I know, but everyone's got their thing, int they? I think he got it made in Jamaica or suttin, he's always goin' on about Jamaica anyway. I ain't bin meself, but I see his pictures an I thought I wouldn't mind it you know. Take a six-week break, laze on the beach and go diving, that type of thing? Me auntie went last year and I was gonna go with her but I couldn't afford it and she went wiv me cousin, lucky bitch. Are your parents Jamaican?'

'Yeah,' I replied, amused and a little stunned by her non-stop flow of words.

'Thought so. It's not like you can tell but I thought so. Something told me. You must give out a vibe or suttin.'

'Must do,' I grinned. 'Look, I gotta go, but what's your name?'

'Christy.'

There was a hint of suspicion in her reply.

'All right, Christy, I gotta see Mr Wren, but I'd like to talk to you afterwards. Don't look like that, strictly business, honest.'

She made to ask *what business*, but before she could I put a finger to my lips.

'Tell you later. When I come out. Wha' d'you reckon, up for it?'

Christy shrugged her petite shoulders, leaning back in her seat. 'Dunno. Depends if I manage to get in that room before midnight.' She inclined her head towards the other office door. That nameplate was metal and said: *Gloria Harris*, *Head of English*.

'All right, fingers crossed.'

'OK,' she replied. 'See you later maybe.'

'Sure . . .'

I knocked beneath Wren's nameplate, pressing my ear flat against the thick wood of the door. There was a faint, 'Come in', beneath the mahogany, I was sure. I gave the young woman another quick nod and pushed my way inside the room.

Wren's office was much smaller than I might have imagined from outside, had I paid my imagination any mind before I entered. It was long and thin, a double-glazed window opposite me; on the right side of the room, shelves crammed with box files and encyclopaedias loomed threateningly over the paper-laden desk. Wren was sitting before his iMac computer, which was precariously placed on a table, just another brick in the wall of mess invading the tiny space. If it weren't for the existence of box files and five-tier filing cabinets, I would have seriously doubted Wren's ability to manage his department. As it was, those things alone provided order, while everything else in the room screamed the opposite. Including David Wren.

He was a head taller than myself and wide-shouldered, with a large chest and arms much broader than my own lean frame. A round face was topped by tousled black hair that hung limply above his eyes, which were the faded blue of an icy winter sky. His nose and lips were thin. Baggy slacks and a crumpled red shirt with the arms rolled up to his elbows were the nearest Wren got to a suit and tie.

He raised himself from the computer and crossed the tiny room to greet me with a slightly defensive smile, while I scrutinised him from behind the veil of my eyes. David Wren had the rugged good looks of your typical youngish lecturer, and was already betraying a manner that seemed a little nervous. We shook hands. I waited as he busied himself extracting another chair from somewhere amongst the chaos.

'So, Mr James, you managed to find me at last! I was worried you'd got lost, or maybe our students had frightened you away!'

'Not at all. I just met a student who knew Viali actually, and I wanted a quick interview in case I never saw him again. People are funny about detectives. I'm sorry for the delay.'

'Not a problem. I was just finishing off some marking,' the lecturer said amiably.

He handed me a stool he'd found under a pile of unopened post. I sat. It would probably become pretty uncomfortable after a while, but I could bear it for now and its hardness would probably make this interview go quicker. I continued watching Wren, waiting to see if anything that I said caused panic, or the slightest reaction of any kind. He sat back down at the table and moved the computer mouse as he spoke. Drives whirred and spun. I assumed he was saving his work.

'Which student did you interview?' he asked absently.

'Uhh . . . Ravinder . . .' I consulted my pad. 'Ravinder Kapoor.'

I studied Wren's eyes as I said the name. He was looking at the wall behind me, the icy blue gaze blank, even though his large head nodded in recognition. No reaction. *Good*, I thought to myself, *but not that good*. My suspicions were aroused by his lack of direct response. If Ravinder and Viali had been close, then Wren, as her lecturer, would have seen them together. He would have known Ravinder if only to say hello. But here he was, nodding with a closed mouth in what I saw as an ineffective attempt to distance himself from the name.

'Sound familiar?' I probed. Wren frowned lightly.

'Vaguely . . . Stocky Asian student? First year Law or something? He and Viali were quite good friends?'

'That's right . . .' I paused as I wrote in my pad that *yes*, they all knew each other. Wren's admission had done him no favours. 'So tell me, how well did you know Viali Walker? It might be best if you start from when you first met and go from there.'

'Sure,' Wren muttered, chuckling a little and looking at his hands. 'Though I have to warn you, I'll be going back a bit.'

'Take your time,' I urged softly, my pen poised. After some nervous shuffling the lecturer began.

David Wren first met Viali Walker thirteen years ago. Her father had been running as Labour Candidate for Hammersmith and Fulham, giving speeches in libraries and community centres. Wren lived in Fulham with his wife and three children, finding himself increasingly concerned with the politics of his borough. He decided to attend one of Walker's vote-rousing campaign speeches, the venue an old church near Shepherd's Bush Green. He took along his oldest child, Libby, aged twelve; but left his wife Sara and his two other children at home.

'I was curious about Robert,' Wren smiled faintly. 'It was interesting to see a black MP with such obvious passion and understanding for his community, who could then be seen at, say, a luncheon for senior bankers, and feel completely at home in both environments. Walker intrigued me back then. He still does, I have to admit.'

I wrote about that, then looked up at the department head when I realised he was watching me scribble.

'So you went to see Walker speak, and . . .'

'He blew me away,' Wren enthused eagerly, picking up my cue. 'It'd been a long time since I'd heard someone who excited me that much. Robert was an eloquent and intelligent speaker, just as I'd been told. I had to talk with him afterwards, but I'd been to so many of those things I knew exactly how it would go. You know, the speaker steps away from the lectern, down from the stage and into the arms of his adoring – or sometimes *un*adoring – public. I was right. As soon as he came down, Labour supporters and journalists mobbed him. He couldn't move for all the people. So I told Libby to sit back down and we waited. When they'd finally finished with him, I had my turn.'

Wren had expected Robert Walker to be tired from all the questions, but was received as eagerly as the MP had previously attacked the microphone. They talked for at least fifteen minutes ('though not *strictly* about Labour policies,' Wren admitted keenly). Mostly the lecturer queried the MP on a more personal level: his own wishes for the future, his thoughts on the handful of black MPs in the city, his views on

UK life. Pretty soon they found they had a lot more in common than their young daughters, who played amongst the pews while their fathers broke bread. They vowed to stay in close contact and debate more in the future. That meeting saw the beginning of a long-standing friendship.

As Viali grew older, David Wren remained close to the Walkers. There were garden soirées in spring, barbecues in summer and Christmas dinner parties in winter. Through her teenage years, Viali, always a keen and able student, redoubled her efforts, with Wren as a major source of assistance. He saw her through GCSEs at fifteen, then guided her through A levels in a series of long-running tutorials. Of course, during this time they grew to know each other well enough to become friends in their own right, adult to adult. Wren was forty at the time. Viali was eighteen. She'd had precious few boyfriends and was finally beginning to notice men.

'I suppose I knew Viali had developed a crush on me,' Wren admitted, head down, body language screaming his shame. 'She'd come to my house for tutorials, and while my children played and my wife made Sunday dinner we'd sit in the study so we could work. She . . . She was very touchy, you see. She'd look into my eyes, giggle, hang on to my every word. My wife couldn't ignore how she was acting.'

'Didn't she get upset?'

'Of course. But over the years she'd seen it happen with other students. Crushes are a regular teenage thing, as you know. Sara trusted me. So help me God, I'd never faltered before.'

'Before?'

There was at least a minute of silence after I spoke, which I left intact, allowing the lecturer time to say what he meant. Wren was deeply upset about his actions, responding by tiptoeing around the truth rather than tackling the subject head on. He wrung his hands together, fidgeted nervously in his seat, refused to look me in the eye as though fearful of my reaction. Ravinder had indeed spoken the truth. While I watched, Wren did an amazing job of reading my mind.

'You must've heard some of this already. From the students, yes?'

His eyes finally lifted to face me head on. I held the gaze.

'I'd like to hear what you have to say, David.'

Wren shrugged, returned his gaze to his lap.

'I was flattered, of course. I mean, who wouldn't be? Viali was a stunning girl, easily as smart and articulate as her father. She was bright, witty – her family nickname was "Sunshine". All of her fellow students thought the world of her.' He looked up again. 'What I'm trying to say is, it wasn't just a physical thing. I'd grown to love her.'

'What about your wife?'

'I loved her too,' Wren whispered simply. 'My feelings towards Sara hadn't changed. I didn't even sleep with Viali until her twentieth birthday; subsequently, it only happened four or five times. We knew it wasn't right, but we couldn't stop ourselves.'

I kept my mouth shut. My opinion meant nothing, even though my more cynical mind wanted to ask how he could do such a thing. Walker had treated this man like one of his own; Wren had repaid him by sleeping with his daughter. I began to grow angry, only holding my temper with the thought that, despite his confession, Wren hadn't tried to justify his actions.

'So what about Robert?' I asked bluntly.

Wren sighed, fidgeted, shrugged. Said nothing. I waited some more. Finally, there was a huge puff of breath.

'We never told him. To this day, he doesn't know.'

I scratched my temple with the end of my pen while I thought about Wren's words, then wrote those down as well, aware of the following silence. When I glanced up, the lecturer was stifling a sob, huge tears rolling down his cheeks. When he saw I'd noticed he grunted and venomously swiped at his eyes. I saw a tear arc its way across the room as though shot from the tips of Wren's fingers. Mentally steeling myself, I proceeded.

'I have to ask this question, David, please forgive me. Where were you on the night Viali died?'

The atmosphere in Wren's office abruptly changed. His expression told me he seemed insulted I'd even asked.

'At home with my wife and children,' he growled sternly. 'I'd seen Viali that day, in this building and this room. We talked over some work.'

'Only work?' I cut in quickly. Wren glared, then self-consciously wiped his eyes again and cleared his throat, his face red.

He'd been reading a novel during his lunch period when Viali knocked on his office door. At first, they had indeed talked over her studies, as well as general college gossip. Then, he claimed, Viali turned frisky. She sat on his lap, kissing his neck and distracting him from his reading.

'How did she seem? Angry? Did she act at all disturbed?'

'Not at all. She seemed happy as larry, full of chat and jokes as always. Until someone knocked at the door. We had to pretend no one was here. I wasn't happy about her timing, so we agreed to meet up the following night. I went home that evening and watched the nine o' clock news with my wife, my children, my eldest daughter's boyfriend and his best friend. The next morning we heard about Viali on the radio.'

'Can I have the names of your daughter's boyfriend and his friend, please?'

Wren's voice trembled as I scribbled down the details. My mind was flying, the next sentence I said detached from that room, David Wren and all his problems, big or small.

'Good thing you two never had sex that last day. You'd be a prime suspect now.'

When I got no reply, I glanced up from my pad to see David Wren scowling at me coldly. I apologised, of course, and Wren accepted somewhat dully. Yet I knew that the damage was done. The lecturer clammed up, answering further questions in an unco-operative tone that clearly displayed his dislike. Somehow, he didn't seem to care that he was incriminating himself by looking pointedly at his watch, or giving me hard glares. His behaviour brought the interview to a close, forcing me to put away my pad and pen. By then, I was pretty sure the man was hiding something.

We stood close in the tiny office, shaking hands before I was gently nudged towards the door and eventually out of the room. I stood in the quiet corridor and took in the familiar smell of bleach, the hum of industrial vacuums and the chatter of cleaners. School and all its many memories came back to me, quickly pushed out by thoughts of Wren. Did I like him? I wasn't sure. Was he lying? I thought so. Something about that interview bothered me; something about *him* I couldn't put a finger on. His nervous manner had only grown the deeper I'd dug, and those tears could well have been an outpouring of guilt. I sighed and relaxed, letting my shoulders fall, letting the questions go, finally remembering Christy and our conversation.

She was gone from the chair where I'd found her. I took a business card from my inside pocket and placed it there, noticing the seat was still warm. That thought made me smile as I walked with my hands in my pockets, along the corridor and out of the university.

7

As much as I would have liked to, I simply couldn't ignore the presence of the police in my line of work. Before my army career I'd been just like every other growing London youth who loathed the Met, even fearing the thought of dealing with them when I became a PI. At first, my working contact was purely negative. After having been mistakenly arrested for stalking in the same area for the fourth time running (I'd been tailing a suspect), I got talking to a friendly detective down at the station. We stayed in touch after I was released from the cells. Every now and then the detective would throw some work my way, or help me out by running a name and some prints through the computer. DS Alain Birkett was my cherished secret weapon, an exception that proved the rule amongst the police force.

I walked into the station and gave the desk sergeant a nod, then sat on a row of chairs while he went into a side room and put the call through to Birkett. The atmosphere in the reception area was thick with tension, though the desk sergeant's whispers were the only words said. A large white woman dressed in a T-shirt and tracksuit bottoms was sitting next to me, breathing like a marathon runner who'd just crossed the line. A girl I took to be her teenage daughter was seated beside the woman. She was thin as a stick of fudge, pale and worried-looking, casting a frown at her mother and wincing at her every breath. I tried to block them from my attention, but couldn't escape their words. They continued the conversation interrupted by my arrival.

'Dis is fuckin' stoopid,' the daughter said in a matter-of-fact tone.

The mother's head snapped around. She jabbed a thick finger at her daughter.

'Don't you fackin' start! Don't you start, d'you 'ere me?'

'Well it's true,' the daughter whined. 'I didn't *do* nuthin' wiv Daryl, I dunno why you're carryin' on like dis. Get on my nerves, man . . .'

This last was said to herself, wrapping thin arms around a similar torso, while throwing the torso back in her seat. The mother ignored her outcry, focused only on her own litany, which served as a response.

'You let dem rape you. My little girl's been raped. You let dem gits rape you . . .'

Amazingly, the daughter kissed her teeth at that, the long, drawn out sound cutting the air like a scimitar.

'You're so *stoopid* . . .'

All of this was followed by another testy silence in which I felt very uncomfortable. I sat perfectly still, as though the slightest movement meant my joining into the argument, giving my opinion. The mother sniffled and took more deep breaths. The daughter mumbled but didn't act that bothered, even though her mother seemed to think she'd suffered a serious assault. Despite my reluctance to get involved, my mind couldn't help wondering how someone 'let' themselves get raped. Wouldn't that constitute sexual consent? Unless she was underage. *Leave it alone*, I told myself. Sometimes I couldn't stop. The desk sergeant returned, looking my way.

'DS Birkett will be out to see you in a minute,' he informed me crisply. After an almost imperceptible hesitation he turned towards mother and daughter, addressing them soberly. 'Have you calmed down now, Mrs Jenkins?'

'I was calm in the fackin' first place! Never mind calm – I wanna see a proper policeman, right this minute—'

My shoulders twitched ever so slightly. When I sneaked a glance at the desk sergeant, he'd raised a huge hand, palm up. The meaning was clear.

'Mrs Jenkins, I insist you stop using that language in the station—'

'*Well let me* see *someone. Then I'll leave an' fackin' well swear outside!*'

The desk sergeant glared at her, bad temper bubbling beneath the surface of his skin, causing veins to pop like corn in his temples and forehead. Mother, daughter and desk sergeant played an intense game of eyeball, where the stakes – pride, self-belief, power – were mountain high. I felt trapped between their criss-crossed sight lines, like a man wandering onstage in the middle of an opera.

The side door that led to the cells and offices deeper inside the station rattled open. Alain Birkett, tall, fresh-faced and cheerful, smiled my way in greeting. 'All right, mate?'

'Yeah, not so bad.' I stood and willed Mrs Jenkins to use her head before it was too late. It took longer than I imagined, but she eventually piped up.

'When can I see someone about my daughter? I wanna make a statement—'

'Someone will be out to see you if you're patient, Mrs Jenkins,' the desk sergeant crooned, smooth as salve on a wound. I raised an eyebrow at Birkett as he walked towards me. His flat eyes were locked on the scene before us.

'Everything OK out here, Woods?' Birkett spoke crisply, his tone as compressed as his gaze. The desk sergeant's words left his mouth before the detective closed his lips.

'Everything's fine, sir, all under control.'

Birkett swept his eyes over mother and daughter in one quick motion, then nodded and inclined his head towards the station entrance. He was outside before the woman had time to gather the heart for another go. I followed in silence.

Outside the air was fresh, the sky a confident blue. I erased the mother's dilemma from my mind as I joined Birkett on the concrete steps, unable to hold back my satisfied grin. He smiled, the skin on his thin face stretching to form laughter lines around his eyes and mouth.

'Good to see ya, Jamesy, good to see ya! So ya finally lined up a big one!'

'Finally.'

I couldn't stifle my pleasure. Birkett cuffed me on the arm.

'Congratulations Ervine, well done. You deserve it.'

'Thanks, mate.'

We stood grinning at each other until it got awkward. Birkett gestured towards a pub across the street.

'Fancy a quick bevvy, yeah? I shouldn't, but . . .' He shrugged.

I smiled a little warily. It wasn't the suggestion that he may drink on duty that heightened my concern. I'd been worried about being seen with Birkett, and the pub he was pointing at was a police haunt, mainly due to its proximity to the station rather than any drinker's loyalty. Police and private investigators aren't supposed to mix, an unspoken rule I'd always adhered to by being discreet. I managed to justify my forthcoming deviation by telling myself that not only was this a special occasion, but I was also a man who came and went as I pleased. After all, there were a lot of things Birkett and myself shouldn't have done. We always ended up doing them anyway.

Crossing the road, I entered the pub nervously. It was full, mainly with off-duty police and elderly regulars languishing in Snug bars. I sat at the nearest table while Birkett went to the bar, nodding at men and women I'd come to recognise over the years, including a plain clothes officer, who didn't look pleased. Although I'd been dealing with my Met friend for close to three years, I still managed to feel uneasy when faced with his colleagues, many of whom despised what I did. As of yet, nothing had been said directly, but the studied looks I got made it plain they had a good idea why I was there. Their organisation had been branded a failure. Robert Walker had openly chastised them as a whole. Now here I was, taking on the case they'd been publicly informed they couldn't solve. I had to move carefully, as their dislike and gossip could land me in trouble of all kinds.

Birkett came back with my orange juice and a half-pint for himself, skirting the tables and canteen-style banter with an old hand's ease. Once seated, we clinked our glasses together, bearing conspiratorial grins, even while I noticed many pairs of eyes on us.

'To your continued good fortune,' Birkett toasted.

'I'll drink to that.'

He swigged long and deep, then gasped as his glass thumped on the wooden table.

'This is a tricky case, Ervine. You solve this and you'll never be out of work again, I promise you.'

I sighed, brought down to earth. I'd already seen the more negative truth in his words.

'Have you brought the files with you?'

He frowned in distaste.

'With all this attention? You must be mad. No, I sent them to your office in the post; they should arrive today, tomorrow at the latest. It's all on floppy disc.'

I smiled to myself. Sometimes I forgot what a technological age we lived in.

'So tell me about her, Alain. Tell me what *you* know.'

Birkett swirled lager around in his glass, looking at me head on. His eyes were green and flecked with speckles of brown like the eggshell of some rare, exotic bird. He pursed his lips.

'What *I* know? That'll take two seconds. I know that all the evidence connecting The Foundation is purely circumstantial. I know there are as many suspects as there were people that knew her. She was a lovely girl, Ervine, stunning to look at, loved by everyone, which meant they all wanted a piece of her. Trouble was, no one seemed to have much of a real motive for murder. Even those racists.'

'What about her college lecturer, David Wren? They had some kind of a fling, didn't they?'

Birkett was nodding. 'Yeah, that's all in her file.'

'Any criminal tendencies? He seemed jumpy when I interviewed him. Like he was worried about something I couldn't put my finger on.'

The detective gave me a sharp look. Any hint of a smile had disappeared.

'Didn't he tell you?'

'Tell me what? All we talked about was the affair.'

Birkett cleared his throat. The noise of glasses, chit-chat and the digital cash register faded to a low-level hum, on the periphery of my hearing.

'David Wren was arrested months before Viali was killed, sometime late last year,' the DS told me evenly. 'Apparently his wife called her local police station, claiming he was acting violently towards her. When he was taken in she dropped all charges and we never heard any more about it. It's all in the file.'

I sat back, then took another gulp of my orange juice, drawing faint consolation from the fact that I'd known something wasn't right.

'Was she badly beaten?'

'Nah. A few cuts and bruises, a black eye. That's all.'

'Isn't that enough?'

'I've seen worse. A hell of a lot worse,' Birkett confided.

'Wasn't the wife questioned about Viali?'

'Just like everyone else that knew her, but there's a house full of witnesses claiming Wren was with them. Including her.'

'Yeah, that's what she says, but . . .'

Birkett frowned deeply. 'You think they'd lie? There's nothing to suggest they did. Besides, they all knew the girl as well as he did.'

I shook my head, gazing deep into my glass.

'They could say what they like, Alain, and no one would believe otherwise. They're middle-class, white and English. How could they possibly lie?'

Birkett shot me a strange glance, studied my expression, then dismissed my words and glanced around the pub, embarrassed. Our conversation ceased. We fell into another awkward silence, this one longer and more intense than the last. It seemed I'd struck a nerve.

Finishing our drinks quickly, we walked out of the pub and back into bright sunshine, still silent and full of thought. I felt slight regret for voicing my opinion so loudly, though not for any of the views I held and expressed. Assumption was often used as another form of English prejudice – assumption woven by stereotype into a garment of deceit; a clothing that all society seemed to be wearing. I had no qualms pointing out the frayed seams, yet was wary of Birkett harping on about some imaginary 'chip' balanced precariously on my shoulder.

I looked over at the DS. He was yawning and stretching beside me while I mulled curiously over his new information. There was no doubt about it: Birkett had sobered my excitement. I cursed myself for not saving time, pushing David Wren further when I had the chance. Lost in thought, I was brought back to earth by the feel of his consoling hand on my shoulder.

'Don't worry. It's not exactly something Wren would share with you. You'd have to get that kind of evidence from someone else.'

I frowned in distaste. 'I knew something was odd; he was defensive from the start. I should have pushed harder.'

The fingers squeezed tight and let go.

'Don't worry about it, Ervine. You're right, you know. I mean about what you said back in there. I reckon you might have a chance at this one. Maybe you're what this case needs.' Birkett grinned again. 'You know what you have to do. Just don't forget to call me if you need anything else, OK? No hesitation.'

Surprise almost made me speechless. Birkett had a way of doing that, no matter how vocal I was concerning my dislike of the world he was so much a part of.

'Will do.'

I watched him step from the pavement and raise a hand in farewell, crossing the street, then striding up concrete steps into the station. I stood smiling at nothing until a police car rolled past, the occupants staring my way, faces blank. I stared back until they drove out of sight, then headed for my car, unease seeping into my bones.

It was lesson time back at the university, a silent hum of working brains steady beneath the low sound of traffic and chattering of birds. Striding along the corridor towards Wren's office, I stifled a bad feeling as I rapped three times on the door. The wait for a reply was as painful as any I'd had to endure as a school-going teenager, forcibly sent to the head for a crime I wouldn't admit. When there was no answer, I compelled myself to accept the obvious. The dean was busy teaching a class I hadn't been told of. I knocked once again, groaning in frustration at the silence, turning to make my leave.

Then I saw him.

He was poised just past an open swing door at the opposite end of the corridor, as if he'd headed for his office and stopped in his tracks when he'd seen me. A handful of files were clutched tightly against his stomach, his eyes on mine in the steely-eyed focus of the hunted. Annoyance flashed across his face. I stood waiting, hands in my pockets and heart thumping hard, wondering how the lecturer would react now he'd been sighted.

Realising there was no other way to behave, Wren continued stepping hesitantly towards me. I forced myself to smile and act calm.

'Hey David, how's it all going?'

I stuck out my hand as the lecturer approached. He shook and released it as though it belonged to a leper.

'It's going fine, Mr James. What can I do for you?'

He was hurriedly unlocking his office door, waves of nerves spilling from his bulky frame. The jangling of keys and tremble in his voice bolstered my confidence, which in turn fuelled my casual tone.

'I was wondering if you had time for a few more questions, David. Things have come to light which I'm sure you'd like to discuss.'

'Well, I'm very busy . . .' He opened the door, stepped halfway through, then faced me. 'Can't it wait until tomorrow?'

'If you could take five minutes it would save a lot of hassle later on.'

I left the ball in his court, retaining my nonchalant, non-aggressive stance. Wren scrutinised me some more, then his eyes fell. He pushed the door aside and headed into his office. I followed, closing the door behind me as he threw his collection of files onto the messy desk, skirting the room like a cornered mouse.

'I'd appreciate it if you could make this quick, I've a lot to get on with—'

'You never told me about what happened with your wife, David. The beating, the arrest. Why was that?'

I'd let the question fall, wanting to see how he caught it. There was silence as the wind left his sails, then he sagged visibly and grasped for his wheeled chair. He fell rather than sat down, rolling the chair backwards, a hand rubbing at his huge head, his skin pale.

'Why was that, David?' I repeated.

When he looked at me, I finally saw how dark-rimmed and red his eyes were. All focus in them was lost.

'You asked me about Viali, not my wife. Besides, I assumed you already knew. You're the detective for God's sake – you're supposed to *know* these things . . .'

I pounced on his chair, spinning it around so he was looking directly into my eyes. Even then he couldn't hold my gaze.

'That's *bullshit*, David, and you know it! The police might not think the two are connected, but it makes you a suspect in my mind and you knew it would! Is your wife sure you were where she claims, can you tell me that, David? If I told her you'd been sleeping with Viali, how sure would she be then?'

The lecturer's mouth hung open. I'd scared him, perhaps too much. I had to tone things down, ease my aggression.

'Did the police ever come back to check your wife's statement? Or anyone else in your family?'

A mute shaking of the head. I forcibly bit back the anger in my words and followed my hunch.

'What time did you leave for home that day, David?'

'Uhhh . . .' He was looking at the ceiling, brow furrowed with strain. 'Seven, eight o' clock, I really can't say.'

'That would put you home by nine at the latest, right, to get back to Fulham? Nine thirty if there was traffic?'

'I suppose you're right.'

'And you went straight home?'

'Yes, of course.'

'Which means you couldn't have got to the South Bank in time to meet Viali?'

'Well, the report said she was there by seven, and—'

'What would you think if I said that you were lying about leaving here between seven and eight that night?'

I let that hang a moment. Wren was looking pitiful, his mouth working nervously.

'What d'you mean?'

I perched myself amongst the papers and files strewn across his desk, letting him stew. He tracked my every move.

'What would you say if I told you someone had seen you, in this building, on that night, leaving at four instead of seven?'

It seemed as though Wren would say nothing. While he gaped, I produced my notebook, holding it high for him to see.

'I bumped into Mrs Andrews downstairs before I came to see you, David.'

He was frowning in confusion, lost in the twists and turns of my questioning.

'Mrs Andrews?' I prompted. 'The receptionist who works by the main entrance of the building? Dark hair, short, quite old . . .'

'*Andrews* . . .' Wren breathed, slowly and surely, remembering. His head dropped into his hands once more.

'For an old lady she's got an amazing memory,' I continued casually. 'Really amazing. She knows everyone's timetable to the minute, whether you're taking tutorials, giving a lecture or taking a field trip, you know, stuff like that. She told me that you had a free period this afternoon actually, and a free one that day. So you left here way before seven or eight. You left at four and she saw you.'

He slumped in his seat as equal measures of fact and

unspoken accusation washed over him. Sweat made his pale face glisten. His voice was a pained whisper.

'What do you want?'

I shrugged. 'There's no evidence to tie you to Viali's death yet, but if it exists, I'll find it, I think you know that. I want you to tell me everything you know about her, including all the stuff you missed out last time. If I find you've been lying again, I'll hand Mrs Andrews' statement over to the police, let them deal with you. So talk now and talk straight, all right?'

He gave a vigorous nod in reply.

'So where did you go when you left here?'

Wren attempted to stall, but one look at the unforgiving set of my face was enough to erase any thought of non-co-operation.

'I –Viali had to pick up some things from her father's office in Ladbroke Grove, so I offered to drop her there. She left before me and waited a couple of streets away. I followed ten minutes later and picked her up. That's all I did, took her to work, had a drink with her, then I went home!'

There was a pleading tone to Wren's words and his eyes implored me to believe what he said. I still wasn't sure if he was telling the truth, though time and a look at the files would put the pieces back into this puzzle. My hunch that he and his family were lying had paid off. I was happy my instincts had been proven right, but that still didn't make this man a killer. He had an affair to hide, which may have motivated his own untruths. Yet why had his family lied about what time he came home?

'So how long did you drink with her, David?'

'An hour. She said she had to meet her dad at seven, so we stayed in a bar—' I frowned his way. '—The Ion Bar it was called. She left around six.'

'What did you do after that?'

'Stayed in the bar, then went home.'

'For how long?'

'I don't know – two hours at the most.'

Which would put Wren home at the time he'd said in his first interview. His wife and family *had* told the truth. My hunch had only been half-right, though half-right was better than a whole wrong.

'It's OK, David, I'm not gonna tell the police. Yet. But in return, I want the address of Robert Walker's office. And that might just be for starters.'

I got out my notebook and took down the address, marvelling at the cowardly display before me. Wren had been remarkably easy to break and the sight wasn't pleasant enough to warrant me hanging around.

'All right, I think that's enough fun for today.'

Wren ignored my words, eyes on the wall directly in front of him, a fist in his mouth as if to block any further confessions. I lowered my head, tipping an imaginary hat and heading for the door. I managed two steps before Wren spoke.

'Mr James?'

Halting, I closed my eyes before turning back, wishing the two steps had in fact been the four that would've removed me from the room.

'I know that this sounds suspicious in light of what I've told you today, but it's the truth . . .' I raised my eyebrows expectantly. '. . . Viali did say that there was a man at that office whose attentions bordered on harassment. She constantly complained she was going to tell her father and I never heard what came of it.'

I said nothing in reply, simply staring at this now child-like man before me. Wren thumped the armrest of his chair angrily, the blood flooding back into his face.

'You don't believe me?' he growled dangerously.

My reply was toneless.

'Would *you* believe you?'

Wren could only reply with more of his silence. Leaving it at that, I walked from the room.

❋

Paying little mind to David Wren's wild accusations, I headed towards the Labour Party office, a half-hour drive away. He was right: I did find his sense of timing suspicious. Still, at this point in the game everything was viable, everyone was under suspicion, which meant many people would soon hate me. This was just another thing I'd grown accustomed to in my job: the loneliness, the alienation. Even murderers had the possibility of finding like-minded friends who provided solidarity. A PI unintentionally makes an enemy of everyone.

The office was on Ladbroke Grove Road, a main street that became alive with music, food and floats come Carnival time. For now, there were only rattling buses lumbering through afternoon traffic, bearing paint as red as a supermodel's lipstick. The office itself was a converted basement flat which stood out from the others on that block, red also the most prominent colour on the Labour Party logos and posters across the front of the flat. Even pots bearing expensive and beautiful plants lined up beneath the flat window were that vivid blood red.

I rang the buzzer and was let in via an intercom system. Inside, the conversion took on the appearance of a doctor's waiting room, with a trademark reception area not far from the main door. Labour propaganda was everywhere. I approached the receptionist, a plain black woman who seemed eager to please, stating my business. She told me Walker was out of the office, but none of the staff had any qualms about being interviewed, though she stressed the police had questioned them all.

It didn't take me long to go through everyone there. I found her father had given Viali a job during her summer holidays in order to earn extra pocket money and gain work experience. She'd enjoyed it so much, she came back for several years afterwards, even doing the odd day when she became a student and worked at Freedom Café. Carrying out the most menial jobs, Viali made tea, took dictation, and wrote letters, as well as performing other basic secretarial tasks. Her boss found her pleasant, polite and clever, claiming she never complained, no matter how mundane her duties.

Everyone was quizzed over Wren's claim that a male staff member had harassed Viali. No one had a clue what I was talking about. There was only one male member of staff, a spotty bespectacled youth who took Viali's place when she began her university studies. Two minutes was long enough to ascertain his innocence.

I took everybody's details and left the Labour Party office, drove to my own to collect Birkett's floppy disc file, then headed home.

My phone rang sometime in the early hours of the morning, waking me from a death-like slumber. Prising the crusts of sleep away, I wrenched my eyes open only to see Viali's face on my laptop screen, watching me twist, groan and yawn. Her files had been an interesting read, until fatigue got the better of me, wrestling me into bed within an hour. I struggled to a sitting position feeling waves of dizziness crash through me. Beside my bed, the phone continued to ring. I decided to count to ten then pick it up, while Renk looked sleepily annoyed from her bed on the floor. By fifteen I still wasn't ready, although the phone still rang. Throwing caution to the wind, I snatched up the receiver.

'Hello . . .'

My voice sounded weak even to my own ears. The voice that came back, however, blazed with a fury I was completely unprepared for, stunning me into confusion.

'How *dare* you interrogate my staff members for no good reason? I didn't pay you to come and disrupt my place of work!'

I recognised Robert Walker's voice, bellowing into my ear. My heart began thumping in my chest. I couldn't quite get my brain to work at its normal speed.

'Mr Walker—'

'I don't like the accusations you're making either, Ervine. What's this about Viali being harassed? Do you think I'd allow my daughter to be harassed while she worked in my own office? I'll admit I didn't like certain lifestyle choices she made, but do you seriously believe I'd allow that to go on?'

'Mr Walker, I was merely following—'

'I don't want to hear your excuses, I want action, Ervine. I want you to do your job! You should be following up what I told you about The Foundation, not wasting time questioning innocent people! Do you hear me?'

There was nothing else to do besides agree and argue my case later, when I had all of my marbles in one hand. I felt myself nodding.

'I hear you, Mr Walker. I'll get on it from—'

'*Good*,' Walker rasped.

The phone clicked, leaving me with the dial tone whining in my ear. Putting the receiver down, I fumbled for my watch, giving the face the most cursory of glances. I never marked that time physically or mentally, merely turned over and went back to sleep without a second thought. Months later, when everything was over and done with, I realised bad luck dogged this case from that point onwards.

8

The studied calm of Viali's face greeted me once again when I awoke later that morning. It was nine thirty, and the anger of Walker's phone call still reverberated in my brain, pleasant as a hangover. While I could see why he'd got upset at my line of questioning, the fact that he'd seemed quite amiable until the orbit of my investigation grew big enough to encircle his world was worrying. A little further thinking on the subject had me fumbling on my night table for a pack of cigarettes, lighting one and frowning at the ceiling as his sentences paraded through my mind.

'. . . I'll admit I didn't like certain lifestyle choices she made, but do you seriously believe I'd allow that . . .'

Even in the context of this case, his words were somewhat strange. What lifestyle choices had Viali made that her father hadn't liked? How important had his respect been to her anyway?

The urgent questions refused to let me go. I couldn't resist rolling over in my bed and looking at the files on my computer screen once more, needing to reacquaint myself with the ins and outs of Viali's life before I went out on my rounds. Besides, it made very interesting reading. Much of the information I'd looked over yesterday had been uncovered during the last week's work, so I concentrated on Viali's exact movements on the day she died. The file detailed her flatmate Dominique seeing her at home around eight thirty in the morning, then witnesses from her local corner shop saying she'd popped in a little after nine. Various college students saw her attend class for ten on the dot, in a lecture that went on until twelve; after that, she went to the library for two hours' study. The report didn't know what happened between the library and Viali's trip to her father's place of work, though I'd covered that ground. In defiance of her angelic image, she'd been locked with Wren inside his office.

Smoking the last of my cigarette, I crushed it in an ashtray, wondering how the police could have failed to question Mrs Andrews. She'd told me they hadn't asked her anything, though I quickly reminded myself that their loss had become my gain. There were so many university witnesses that they could be forgiven for missing the odd one or two; and of course, they didn't have the vested interest I had. As Birkett had implied, my altered perceptions of suspects had already created some headway. That led me to the thought that maybe, contrary to Wren's belief, Walker might indeed have known what was going on between his old friend and daughter. Maybe that was the 'lifestyle choice' he'd been so strongly against. What lengths could that knowledge drive a father to?

From my own investigations the previous day, I knew Viali hadn't stayed at the Labour Party office for long. Her former boss told me she'd used the phone, sent a few e-mails, then made small talk about her father before leaving to rendezvous with David Wren, I presumed. The entire visit took no longer than twenty minutes. When Viali's boss mentioned the calls and e-mails, I'd immediately wondered who she'd been talking to, though when questioned further the woman claimed ignorance. I badly needed that evidence. There was a chance the real person Viali met had contacted her, or The Foundation had sent threatening e-mails.

After writing a few words in my notebook about finding someone who could crack her QuickMail password, I spent the next ten minutes wrestling with my PhotoShop programme. It was fairly easy pasting Viali's police photo onto a poster outlining minimal facts of her death, together with an appeal for witnesses, above my new mobile number. When it was done, I printed a copy and got out of bed.

The police had questioned a worker at the South Bank, so I took down his name, got washed and dressed, then climbed into my Audi and drove south of the river once again. On my way, I stopped off at Rymans for a packet of Blu Tack and 200 photocopies of the poster I'd printed.

The scene around Southwark Bridge and Bankside hadn't changed. I got to work putting posters on walls, fences and doors every twenty feet or so, starting from the alley beside the Globe Theatre, then working a westward trail until the Millennium Wheel turned slowly on London's skyline. I hadn't asked permission, assuming the severity of the crime would keep the posters where I'd put them, at least for a while. My gloves made the job much harder, yet were more than necessary in the cold of the day. When I reached as far as the Royal Festival Hall, I consulted my notebook. The police witness had been found inside this building. I put away my Blu Tack and posters, then pushed through glass doors.

The lofty airiness of the Hall never failed to impress me as a kid and still packed a solid punch. A bustle of middle-class arts enthusiasts and foreign fellow devotees moved about assuredly, which made me feel I should do likewise. Internally prompted, I approached a glass booth that bore signs announcing TICKET AND SALES POINT, thumbing my trusty note-book. Michael Josiah, head chef at The People's Palace restaurant, was the witness I was looking for. I entered the booth, which sold poetry books and postcards, asking a girl behind the counter where I could find the restaurant. Taking the directions I was given, I headed for a pair of elevators snuggled haphazardly between the men's toilets and a cloak-room. The restaurant was on the third floor. The lift arrived quickly, with no more than the slightest bump. I noted how far removed this was from the lifts in all the council estates I knew, before exiting into a large lobby area.

I could already see the restaurant on the landing opposite me. Stopping by the main entrance, I took a look at what they had on offer. Who knew, I might even end up having lunch there and charging it to Walker, just to make me feel better about taking his shit. One look at the set lunch menu speedily changed my mind. As I didn't have a clue what most of the dishes were, I didn't fancy their chances of making me a believer. Nevertheless, The People's Palace looked like the type of restaurant you'd bring your wife to – high class and very impressive, a casual show of good taste.

Stepping through more glass doors, I found myself immersed in the sounds of idle chatter, hearty laughter and clinking cutlery. Dark-suited waiters moved gracefully from table to table like worker bees collecting pollen, never still for a second. The main reception was a small wooden booth not far from the doors. Another dark-suited man saw me coming and approached. I automatically tensed, more than prepared for a scene.

'Table for one?' the thin-faced, earnest-looking man enquired.

I was slightly ashamed, fully expecting a classy place like this to throw me out on my pointy little ear just as soon as look my way. It had happened before and would do so again, no doubt. In my loafers, jeans and plain black jacket, I wasn't

exactly the best-dressed man in town, and to top it off, I was
black. I peered at the gold-coloured nametag on the man's
lapel – *Jason Brindley, Assistant Manager*. My smile was impossible to contain. I could grow to enjoy this kind of treatment.

'Actually, I was hoping you could help me track down your
head chef. Michael Josiah? He does work here, right?'

Jason was frowning slightly, though I soon learned this was
due to curiosity.

'May I ask what it concerns?' he questioned.

I dug out my dodgy ID and handed it to him. 'I'm investigating a murder case, Mr Brindley. Viali Walker, daughter of
Labour MP Robert Walker? Your chef gave evidence to the
police when it happened; I'd just like to hear what he saw in
his own words.'

Jason took a random glance at the ID, quickly handing it
back. He had a sincere manner, something about him giving
the impression that he did everything in a hurry; that even
when he was still, he exuded pent-up, nervous energy.

'If you'd like to wait by the bar, I'll see if Michael can spare
a moment,' he told me helpfully, walking away when I smiled
in thanks. I followed him to the long marble-countered bar,
seating myself on a stool and waiting while he disappeared
behind a partition-like wall.

The bar was minimally decorated, a red lamp and a bowl of
limes at one end of the counter, a huge bouquet of multicoloured flowers at the other. The restaurant itself was much
like everywhere else in the Festival Hall, mostly glass and
steel, with huge examples of modern art hung high. Opposite
me, a window stretched the length of the room, overlooking
the Thames. You could see the old Shell building and the busy
rear of the Savoy hotel amongst a wide panorama that glit-
tered like an open jewellery box.

A man in his mid-thirties who I assumed to be Michael
Josiah came out dressed in chef's whites, with Jason in tow.
While the assistant manager inclined his head Josiah's way

and left, the chef dried his hands on a dishcloth, then held one out for me to shake. He was a tall, stocky black man, with coffee-dark skin and a look of abject curiosity firmly attached to his face. I looked down and saw that what I'd taken for a dishcloth was really a wispy, cartoon-looking chef's hat.

'So you're the private investigator?' he smiled inquiringly. 'I didn't think you'd be black!'

I grinned in return and gave a tiny shrug of the shoulders. Black people never expected it. If white people noticed they never mentioned a thing. As for me, I was just as surprised to see a black head chef.

'Yeah, I get that a lot, I'm used to it,' I admitted casually. 'Listen, Michael, is there anywhere quiet we could have a quick word? It's about Viali Walker.'

'I've got an office at the back of the kitchen,' he said soberly, turning and pointing behind the bar. 'Come right through.'

The walk into Josiah's domain was like stepping into another world. The large, clinical-looking kitchen area was filled with more chefs, bustling and talking over the hiss of frying food. Five cooks were lined up on the other side of the room, chopping various meats, eyes never straying from their tasks. Steam rose along with the smell of seasoned fish, making my stomach rumble even though I'd eaten on the way. We passed a washing-up area and what looked like two miniature metal lifts, before taking a left turn that led into a modestly furnished office. Josiah motioned me inside, shutting the door and grabbing for a chair, shoving it my way with absent consideration.

'Take a seat, Mr James. Would you like anything to drink?'

I declined and settled in my seat while Josiah sat by his wooden desk.

'Busy out there,' I began cheerfully. 'You'll probably be rushed off your feet by lunchtime.'

'You're not kidding,' he complained wryly. 'It's great business, but hard, hard work. Good thing I like to cook!'

He gave a big hearty laugh at his own weak joke. I gave thanks that this wouldn't turn into a repeat of yesterday's interview. I needed today to go well for the sake of my self-esteem.

'Smells like great food,' I chuckled, wasting no time. 'Now in case you're wondering why I'm here, it's nothing big OK? I just heard you'd seen Viali the night she was murdered. I wondered if you could tell me what you witnessed.'

'So you've taken over the investigation?'

'Yeah. That's right.'

Josiah's beam got wider. 'Congratulations! It's about time they got a brother seeing things through. I'll tell you everything I remember.'

He reached out and shook my hand once more, though he used a great deal more force this time, looking into my eyes with unmistakable pride. My emotions stirred again. I reminded myself of the promise I'd made, to solve this case or quit. No matter what grief Robert Walker threw at me, what suspicions I had, I would put my all into this. I could promise no less.

Josiah had witnessed very little that day, though enough to become the last person on record to see Viali alive. The chef first sighted the student going to meet her father outside the Purcell Rooms; he'd been working a long shift and decided to have a break and cigarette outside, to hell with the cold. He escaped on the pretext of buying his wife an anniversary gift, then left the building and saw Viali walking by. Josiah knew who she was because he'd seen her pictured with her father in *The New Nation*. He lit his cigarette and caught her up.

'Because I liked her father,' he cautioned seriously. 'Nothing more.'

'OK,' I conceded. 'Would you say you'd seen her around seven PM?'

'More like ten to,' he corrected.

He walked Viali to the Purcell entrance, asking after her father, saying how proud he must be that she was growing so well. Leaving her at the doors, he walked back to some concrete benches lined up outside The Royal Festival Hall. He didn't know why he lit another cigarette, yet did it anyway, then watched seagulls glide across the river and trains rumble through Charing Cross Station. He supposed that somewhere deep inside, he'd been waiting to catch a sight of Robert Walker. Of course, that meeting never took place.

During his wait, he'd occasionally sneak quick peeks Viali's way. At first she remained much as he'd left her, reading a book held in one hand, stamping restlessly from foot to foot to keep warm. At twenty past seven he saw her walking away towards the National Film Theatre, shadowed by four skinheads. Josiah remembered feeling a little concerned, until he saw Viali talking quite chattily, even laughing with the men before disappearing around the edge of the building.

'I still can't believe what I let happen,' he told me in dismay. 'So many white kids wear their hair short, you can't jump to conclusions like when we were young. So I let her go.'

'Michael, you know there was nothing you could have done. It wasn't as though they were dragging her away,' I consoled soothingly.

'Yes, but she'd told me she was meeting her *father*. By the time I remembered I had to get back up here, and . . .'

He sighed, pushing for a smile, finding his cheeks and heart too weak. Reaching over, I patted his shoulder awkwardly while getting to my feet. He had already told me more than the police report. I wasn't prepared to push for more. Viali had laughed with the men as she'd walked away. That didn't fit with what I'd presumed so far, suggesting that she'd known them vaguely, or even quite well.

Sincerely thanking Josiah for his help, I left the restaurant with a cold and heavy heart. I knew what the hell I was doing – a blind man could see what was going on – yet dumb old me was fooling myself again. Walker had been right to scream at me, I decided right there and then, only he didn't know why I was skirting the issue. To me, it was as painfully clear as the bright blue sky of the frosty afternoon.

To cut a long story short, I was scared. From the beginning I'd been running away from people I'd known I had to question, people that played a major part in this case. The four men Viali had left with were suspected Foundation members, mystery figures I'd been in no hurry to put names to. That would mean paying a visit to a bookstore in the heart of racist London, an alleged front for their right-wing organisation.

My office had a quiet, expectant air, even though the waiting area was devoid of people. Sadie was typing on her PC. As usual, she'd been great at holding the fort while I was on the road. I couldn't help thinking how lucky I was to have her on the payroll.

'Still quiet?' I enquired as I entered.

'Yeah, 'fraid so,' she moaned casually. 'We 'ad a couple calls askin' fuh estimates, a couple from Robert Walker askin' for you, that's it. Robert said he couldn't get through on yuh mobile.'

'I had an interview so I switched it off. What did he say?'

In reality the phone had never been on, as I'd been in no mood to talk to anyone from the outside world. My feelings hadn't changed.

'Nothing much, jus' that he needed to talk to you. Oh, an' Ervine?'

I stopped by my office door. There was no need for any hunch to tell me what was on Sadie's mind.

'Uhh . . . You haven't paid me last month's wages yet. I'm kinda behind on my rent an'—'

I raised a hand, stalling her request. She was right, of course. She hadn't been paid for almost two months due to the lack of any decent jobs. Taking the money out of what Walker had given me wouldn't leave me with much after I paid off my other debts, though I did have my credit card. There was no question guilt would eventually force me to do the right thing. Trouble was, that would leave me broke again.

'All right, Sade, I'll put two months wages in your account for you as soon as, OK?'

She responded with a perplexed scowl.

'Are yuh sure yuh can? Don't forget, I'm the one who jus' did yuh accounts. You're skint, unless you got any regular income you ain' tellin' me about?'

I managed to give her a reassuring grin, even though I didn't really mean it.

'I wish I did, though that isn't your worry. I'll sort something out for myself, just don't let it go this long again without reminding me.'

'OK, whatever you say . . .'

Cursing my poor financial situation, I left the reception area and went into my office. After all the traipsing around of the past few days, it was good to be back in the space that I knew as my home, despite Sadie's justified complaints. Producing the disc with Birkett's information, I forced my worries away and loaded the Viali files onto my office computer then went on-line. Hopefully I could find an Internet site that provided the exact address of The Foundation's London base.

I typed the organisation name into my favourite search engine. In moments, a long list of companies with a matching name appeared on-screen. These included *The Nobel Foundation*, *The European Science Foundation* and the *American Foundation for the Blind*. I found what I was looking for beside a description that read: *Political Party, dedicated to the cultivation of Anglo-Saxon heritage – click here for registration and membership.*

Following instructions, I was instantly bombarded with images I'd long avoided, a visualisation of people and

ideologies in direct conflict with my own. The Foundation
seemed to be an amalgamation of hate groups the world over,
with various images and logos bordering the home page as if
paying homage to brothers in racism. The Nazis, Ku Klux
Klan and the National Front were just some of the many
groups represented. The headline logo, an outline of a house
surrounding the word Foundation held up by an armless pair
of white hands, was the backdrop for their introductory spiel:
a brief paragraph outlining some type of mission statement.
Reading those words didn't help the feeling that I had wandered into the lion's den without a clue as to whether I was
Daniel.

```
We, the collected citizens of Great Britain
registered below, solemnly vow to uphold the
beliefs and ideals that made this country a
world leader, bringing health and prosperity
to true British citizens. We are opposed to
the disease called multiculturalism, The
Black Death spreading through our land,
believing Britain for the British, Africa for
Africans, Asia for Asians, Israel for
Jews . . . Our personal lives come secondary
to our life's work, which is to restore the
British Empire to its full, unblemished
glory. We, the undersigned, vow to take
necessary steps to win back our country and
restore hope to our people, whatever the
cost.
```

Below those words was another *Click here for registration*
button, next to one that proclaimed casually: *More.* My curiosity aroused, I moved the mouse until the arrow rested on the
former, then did as I was told. A name and address box
appeared on-screen. I noticed that registering would also

provide free e-mail – @foundation.co.uk. I filled the box with bogus information and pressed *Register*. Another page appeared.

```
Congratulations new member, welcome to the
fastest growing political party this century!
Please feel free to surf our site, which
details events, fundraisers, and our Internet
radio show! You're in good company, as you
can see from our members' list, which
contains over 8,925 members!
```

There followed a never-ending list of names, far too many to read, even though I attempted to scan them all. This was no band of unemployed school leavers, all shaven heads and bovva boots. This was a financially strong, well-organised collection of right-wing sympathisers whose danger had been seemingly downplayed by the media.

The scariest part of the site by far was that number: 8,924 people who agreed with the party's racist agenda; every new member that signed up instantly added to the total. As I sat taking this in, dumbfounded, the number rose by five. Another dizzy spell made my head spin. The number went up by a further two members as I watched, deeply disturbed. They weren't strong enough to vote The Foundation into power yet, but who knew what horrors the future could bring?

I went back to the home page and continued my search for the fraternity's HQ address. When I clicked *More*, I found yet another hidden world; just as confusing, though way more sinister than the hustle and bustle of Josiah's kitchen. Even though I'd known it existed in some form or other, I'd been largely unaware of how deep the horror went. Events such as marches, meetings and raves showed just how well organised the party was. You could download hate bands with names like 'The White Devils' onto MP3 at no charge. There were pages advocating the forcible removal of 'non-European' citizens from these shores. I had to laugh at that. They couldn't possibly ask for the removal of 'non-British' people; there'd be nobody left on the island.

It took a great deal of searching before I finally found what I wanted: a mailing address tucked away at the bottom of the letters page. Jotting it down in my notebook, I left the website with a bad taste in my mouth.

As soon as I drove into Eltham, South-east London, I felt the vibe: a stifling, pensive kind of watchfulness. I could feel my heart beating, sweat under my armpits, hairs rising on my neck and prickling my skin like pins and needles. At the edge of my hearing came the haunting voices of eight black and Asian youths slain by racists in this one little town, and the lone voice of an innocent white youth killed in return. Areas like Brixton, Shepherd's Bush and Ladbroke Grove were exceptions that proved the English rule. In those places, racism disguised itself beneath a cloak of regeneration, skulking about like Jack the Ripper in ye olde London. This was the true face of the country. Those multicultural towns were simply pockets of safety, in which the immigrant population of the Fifties had settled; the poorest, most run-down areas. Somehow we'd let that fool us into thinking those areas were the status quo; that a place like Eltham was relegated to times gone by.

I parked my car in a side street and walked the short distance to the bookstore, wary of my surroundings. My gun was in its holster, the latter tucked beneath my scruffy black jacket. I was taking no chances. The store, a tatty blue-painted shop front with no sign or any other form of advertising, looked closed. Shutters were up, so there wasn't even a chance of peering through any dusty windows. Various posters advertised an Aiya Napa Garage compilation, amongst other things. The whole scene looked quite ordinary. Still, I couldn't leave without checking things out.

Approaching the front door tentatively, I knocked the letterbox three times, then waited until I found a bell just above my head, pressing hard. It was working all right; I could hear the ring, yet there wasn't a sound from inside the shop. After waiting a little while longer, I turned and saw an old white man watching me through narrowed eyes. He held a snow-white Yorkshire Terrier by the lead with one hand, a wooden plastic-tipped walking stick in the other. The dog bared its teeth, growling until its owner jerked the lead. Then it quieted and sat on his foot, breathing hard. I smiled their way, silently appealing for calm.

'Hey there. How you doing?'

The old man said nothing in response.

'Do you have any idea what time the bookstore might be open?'

Still nothing. The dog remained on the old man's foot, staring at me with its mouth open, as if dying to communicate but unable to spit the words. At that point, the old man opened his mouth and spoke in one of the broadest South London accents I'd heard. His dog looked upwards, cocking an ear as if taking the point his master was making into careful consideration.

'You stay away from dat shop if yuh know what's good fuh you, mate. Stay well away. You'll only get 'urt if yuh don't.'

This was like one of those stalk n' slash movies. *Return of the Racist Dead*. I stepped forwards, a hand to my heart as if he'd caused deep offence.

'Wha' d'you mean? Who'd wanna hurt me?' I asked, pretty sure this was the only contact I'd be making.

The old man paid no mind and began shuffling down the street, dragging his dog detachedly behind him. I followed, repeating my question, until quickly remembering that, in this area, a six-foot-three black man tailing an old scrawny white man was not acceptable. I stopped, chiding myself for being stupid, letting the old man potter away, his walking stick keeping slow time on the pavement. While I looked around, taking careful note of the still closed bookstore behind me, I realised that yes, I had been noticed.

A tall, skinny white youth was eyeing me hatefully from a bus stop across the street, a deadened expression on his face as he slouched against the metal rain shelter. He never moved when he saw me, never flinched, made a face, or even ran. He simply lounged and looked. Even as I caught his eye, the youth rubbed his nose and returned my stare, casual as the day was cold. In that brief period, time seemed to halt. We could have been the only human beings in the world, judging by the attention we paid each other. My street pride kicked in. I refused to back down, eyeballing the youth with no fear, daring him to take the next step.

He responded by pushing himself up with a shoulder, spitting at the base of the bus stop and walking away, hands in his pockets, a primordial gait to his step. I had half a mind to follow, but the youth's provocative behaviour was way too suspicious for me to take such obvious bait.

Casting a look at the closed bookstore, I decided to continue this fight another day, when I didn't feel so alone.

9

My night's sleep had been fitful; my dreams filled with dog-walking white men who pointed fingers and issued silent warnings as their rotting flesh fell to their feet like over-ripe fruit. Not surprisingly, this didn't fill me with joy as I opened my eyes to light streaming through my bedroom window. I yawned loudly, rubbing sleep from my eyes, struggling from beneath my covers then stumbling into the bathroom. Fifteen minutes later I emerged, clean, if not awake. Today I planned to see if I could find a way to glean Viali's e-mail password and read her correspondence, before I went back to Eltham and that closed bookstore. I was resolute in my decision to do this. Neither the old men of my dreams, nor the young thugs of reality would prevent me from performing that necessary task.

Feeding Renk, then myself, I proceeded to leave the house, still a little unsettled by vivid reminders of the previous night.

Although I was putting a brave face on things, my dreams often had a foreboding quality that, at the very least, warned I had a problem my mind was attempting to digest. Now I'd faced my fears by knocking on the bookshop door, I knew I was in for more dreams, a prospect I didn't exactly welcome with open arms.

Preoccupied as I was, I couldn't fail to see what was attached to my front door as I turned the key in the lock. Staring mutely, I pushed my hands inside my pockets, hypnotised by the words and logo before my eyes. When I'd seen enough I tore the poster from the door, looking up and down the road, wondering if the bearers of this gift were lying in wait somewhere, watching to see how their present had been received. I even took to the street, marching as far as the nearest corner. No suspicious characters were in sight. Going back into my flat, I raged at the audacity of such a move, then got on the phone to DS Birkett, dialling his work number from memory.

'DS Alain Birkett?'

My friend sounded brisk and awake. I took a deep breath.

'Yeah, Alain, it's Ervine.'

'Ay, what's goin' on? How'd the disc work out?'

'Fine, mate, I got all the info on my computer now.' As I spoke I realised how short of breath my anger had made me. I consciously forced myself to calm down. 'Actually, that wasn't what I was calling about. I gotta bit of bother on my hands.'

'Oh yeah?'

I could almost see him settling into his seat and putting his feet up, preparing himself for what I might have to say.

'Yeah, mate. See, yesterday I took a trip to that bookstore in Eltham, you know, the one where they reckon The Foundation's based? This morning I wake up an' leave my house to find they left one of their propaganda posters on my door.'

There was a harsh intake of breath that made the phone line crackle. Other than that the policeman said nothing. I continued.

'Now, I dunno how they got my address, and I don't really care, but you know I'm licensed to carry a gun, right? An' I'm not jokin', if I catch any one of them near my property—'

Birkett jumped in before I could incriminate myself further.

'Ervine, Ervine, stop right there, mate . . .' he soothed, his voice as relaxed as it had been a minute before. 'Now, first off, you don't wanna be talking like that, especially not to me. Secondly, I want you to tell me a few things. Did they enter your house?'

It was immediately obvious where this was leading. Even though I knew I would have taken the same approach in his shoes, the thought didn't make me feel any less isolated.

'No, not that I know of.'

'So you couldn't legally shoot them for being on your property as they never even crossed your threshold. If they did and you used that gun, you'd more than likely go to jail for a very long time, never mind where they were. Do you understand that, Ervine?'

'Yeah I do,' I muttered, disgusted by his words, even though I knew they were true. 'But what about the poster? Doesn't something like that constitute a threat?'

'Were there any threatening messages on it?'

I gave a deep groan of disgust, providing Birkett with enough of an answer.

'Listen, Ervine, I feel what you're going through, believe me I do. I'd be livid if they put that shit anywhere near my house. The fact of the matter is, they haven't done anything wrong in the eyes of the law. Even if we caught them red-handed putting up another poster, there'd be nothing we could do legally, besides telling them to stop, or maybe getting a court order against the individual that did it. And d'you know how many members they've got?'

'I do now,' I grumbled, wondering if Birkett might take that the wrong way. I still needed him in my corner, even if we didn't see eye to eye.

'All I can say is keep doing what you're doing,' he encouraged, ignoring my words. 'You're obviously onto something, or they wouldn't have come to you.'

I couldn't help getting annoyed at his casual response. Between Walker's chastisement of two nights ago, and Birkett's lack of any real commitment, I was beginning to feel a tiny bit used and abused. The trappings of law meant I would be unprotected until it was too late for help, or until I took things into my own hands.

'Why can't *you guys* be onto something?' I seethed brutally. 'Isn't that what you're paid for?'

'Not anymore,' the detective shot back. 'Now it's what you're paid for.' He stopped for a minute, perhaps realising how harsh his own words sounded. 'Listen, Erv, bring me some real evidence an' I'll be down on these guys like a Streatham slut, no word of a lie.'

The conversation was at a clear end.

'All right, mate. Lemme go and get on wiv my job then.'

'No probs. Sorry I couldn't help more, and be careful with that shooter, yeah?'

I grunted a reply and put down the phone, feeling patronised, hard done by, plain misunderstood. The Foundation poster stared up at me, its logo, mission statement and most of all, headline – BRITAIN FOR THE BRITS, SUPPORT OUR CAUSE – jarring me to the pit of my stomach. Anger took hold. Before I knew it I was tearing the thing to pieces and depositing those pieces in the bin.

Panicked, though keen to deny the emotion, I went around my flat making sure every window was locked. When that was done, I remembered Walker's call to Sadie the day before, and decided to let him know what his late-night message had got me into. Leaving and locking the house, I switched on my mobile and walked the short distance to my car, still fuming at the morning's morbid revelations. In no time there was a strident beep from the handset. I looked down to see I'd received an answer phone message.

After some fumbling, I retrieved the message to find that it was from Viali's flatmate Dominique, saying she had some urgent information to pass on. Frowning, I started up the Audi and pulled away with the phone tucked under my chin, following the voice options and dialling the call return facility. Dominique answered after three rings, saying there were details about her flatmate she hadn't told me, things that she knew I needed to hear. Would I mind meeting at her home and maybe going for coffee?

Against my better judgement I said yes, angling my car westwards, wondering what new surprises the already eventful day had in store.

Dominique was sitting on the steps that led to her main front door when I arrived, a tartan record bag by her side. She was dressed in tight-fitting jeans that emphasised long and supple legs, topped with a knitted purple jumper and matching scarf for protection against the cold. Her locks were tied in a bun around her head, giving her strong features a subtler, more girlish look. She sighted me at once, stepping nimbly onto the pavement before opening the passenger door and climbing in.

'Hey!' she smiled as she slammed the door, facing me with a grin. 'How's you?'

'Good,' I replied, a little thrown by her change of appearance and demeanour. 'Where d'you want to go for coffee then?'

'D'you know the Portuguese Café on Golborne Road?'

I shook my head. 'I know Golborne, though.'

'I'll direct you,' she told me decisively, pulling the seatbelt around her shoulders.

Five minutes later we entered the coffee shop, a favoured haunt of Moroccan, black, and Trustafarian patrons alike. We joined a queue that never died, shouted our orders over the noise of percolation and mid-morning chatter, then walked to the back of the shop where a row of barstools and a hi-table provided just enough space for comfort. All the way, I tried to keep my eyes from Dominique's lithe body, which had a few more curves than her previous toga-style attire had suggested. Although thick, her jumper was tight, clinging to firm breasts like an embrace, ending high enough to expose a behind as round as a prize watermelon. Even as she sauntered through the café, I could see the attention she was getting and the cool way that she handled it.

'So!' she beamed, when we were eventually settled in our seats, dark cherry lip-gloss making her smile even more enticing. 'How's everything going? Got any leads yet?'

I sipped at my café latte before answering, almost as if that would break the spell she was unconsciously weaving. I smiled at her use of the word 'leads'.

'No, none yet. I'm really in the early stages of the case, you know, seeing what evidence matches with the police report. Hopefully I can build a clear picture of Viali's movements. Any holes I find will expose where I need investigate further.'

Steam from the coffee veiled our faces. Dominique was nodding in studied concentration.

'Been doing this long?'

'Well, I've had PI business for about three years. Other than that, I've wanted to do this my whole life.'

'Married?' she smiled, leaning forwards in her seat. I laughed and she joined me, only pausing to take a bite of her toasted croissant. 'Well, there's not many good-looking black men in London that own their own business, are polite enough to pay for breakfast, and are also single. I gotta know which side my croissant's buttered, fast!'

'I hear you,' I admitted, still chuckling. 'I gotta tell you, though, if it's a rich man you're looking for, you're better off grabbing someone who can pay for breakfast on King's Road!'

Dominique snorted.

'Yeah, right. The odds of finding a conscious black man who can do that are about the same as finding a conscious black prime minister!'

'How d'you know I'm conscious?' I smiled, baiting her. As open as she was, she refused to bite.

'You're on this case, aren't you? Lord knows no one else would bother with it.'

I took her point and sipped more coffee, reminding myself that I had very little time if I was to get everything done.

'So, Dominique, what was your call about? Why the urgency? I thought you'd told me everything the other day?'

'Oh, I haven't told you the half,' she mused, noting my raised eyebrows. 'An' I couldn't really. Not with Robert listening.'

I waited for more, my stomach doing a slow flip-flop inside my belly. It looked like this was the interview I'd been praying for. I reached for my notebook and pen.

'Go ahead.'

Dominique gave a theatrical sigh, playing with the silver rings on her long, nimble fingers.

'All right, lemme get this over with,' she complained with a wry face. 'This is so bad! Even though she's dead, I still feel like I'm betraying her.'

I gave no reply. Seeing I wasn't going to give reassurance, she had no choice but to continue.

'OK. Viali might not have been as . . . straight-laced as police reports and Robert Walker would have the world believe,' she began stiltedly. 'In fact, she wasn't straight by any means. She took drugs.'

Despite her warning-filled introduction, I looked up in surprise. No one else had mentioned this.

'What kind?'

'Purely recreational. Weed, the occasional E . . . The pills weren't that often, I know that much. She couldn't tell her father, though. He would've hit the roof if he knew she'd done it even once. And she was paranoid bad about her dad finding out she smoked puff. Everything's about image to Robert, it's his primary concern.'

Dominique looked sad and wistful, her mind's eye focused on something far away from the coffee shop.

'Anything else?'

'She had a boyfriend. I mean, you already know about David, right?' She waited pensively for my agreement, then dropped another bomb. 'Well, it wasn't him. David fancied himself as this older man she was head over heels about. It wasn't the case, believe me. Viali knew that particular relationship was going nowhere. She was in for the kicks, plain and simple.'

My expression made her laugh aloud, grabbing the attention of the friendly staff, who smiled back good-naturedly.

'Yeah, the real Viali was not created in her father's image, trus' me,' Dominique persisted, still laughing, seeming to relax now the worst was over. 'She was a smart girl, but a human being just like the rest of us. Anyway, this boyfriend of hers was a Nation of Islam minister, which is why she couldn't come clean about him either. Would've ruined her dad's all-loving media persona to have any relation, political or otherwise, to any non-passive organisation. Talk about out of the frying pan and into the fire.'

'She certainly picked 'em,' I agreed casually. 'What's his name?'

'Charles Muhammad. They call him Slamma on street. He works at their West London branch.'

'OK, I know where that is . . .' I took her words down haltingly, inwardly cursing my hard-to-read shorthand. 'Anything else?'

'Too much . . .' Dominique rolled her eyes and puffed once

more. 'You know Viali worked at that coffee shop in Soho. Freedom Café?'

'Yeah?'

'Well that was her first job. Her second was at a strip club down the road from there. The Lipstick Parade or something like that. She said she only worked the door, you know, wear a low-cut top and short skirt, get the punters in . . . But who knows what else she got up to. She did it for at least six months, and it's not like she couldn't keep a secret. If I know anything about her, I know that much.'

'The Lipstick Parade you say?'

'I think so.'

I took the name down, my tone and expression clinical.

'And you're sure Robert Walker didn't know what Viali did for money? Sure enough to stake your life?'

She opened her mouth, thought about what she was saying, then frowned and shook her head.

'No . . . No, I'm not that sure at all. Does it matter?'

'It doesn't matter one bit, Dominique, not one bit. I was just wondering.'

All this information added to the black marks I was mentally placing beside the image of Robert Walker MP. From what I could make out, the possibility of Walker knowing what his daughter had been up to was rapidly increased by Dominique's evidence. Hadn't he said himself that he might not agree with the way she'd lived? What father would abide the fact that his child was a stripper?

Finishing my scribbling, I noticed Dominique staring at me, a tiny smile pushing the corners of her lips. We were sitting close enough for our thighs to rest tightly together, the warmth of her leg sending lurid signals to places best left well alone. An urge to touch her was building by the second.

'Is there anything more?'

She shook her head, the half-smile still playing across her face.

'Then I gotta ask something about you,' I continued, putting down my pen. 'Kinda predictable, but I'm curious anyway . . . Why are you telling me all this? Why not the police?'

Dominique leaned over our coffee mugs until she faced me head on, looking directly into my eyes. She was so close I could see my breath lightly ruffling the strands of wool on her purple knitted jumper, and with each person that passed her seat, the strands undulated like seaweed on an ocean floor. I concentrated harder on that minute detail. It helped take my attention away from the rest of her.

'Well, I couldn't tell the police for obvious reasons,' she murmured softly. 'Mostly to do with Robert's reputation. As for why I've chosen to tell you,' she lowered her eyes. 'Haven't I made that plain enough, Ervine? Or shall I make it plainer?'

She rested a warm, nimble-looking hand on my upper thigh, fingernails lightly brushing my balls, heat from her palm causing me to harden instantly. We were eye to eye, oblivious to the other customers, who were equally oblivious to us – after all, couples regularly frequented this coffee shop. Dominique softly rubbed where her hand had previously been content to lie still. I looked around at the varied faces, sure that someone would notice. No one did.

'Didn't you see the way I was looking at you when you came to the flat?' she breathed.

I shrugged a reply. 'No, not really. I was workin'.'

She grinned abruptly, the confident beam of a woman who knew that my eyes amplified the thoughts I couldn't quite vocalise. Knew what was next, as precisely as the knowledge that two came after one.

'So do you notice now? Or are you still too busy for a break?'

Sadie's voice prompted me forcefully from somewhere deep inside my head. I took Dominique's nimble fingers, entwining them with mine.

'Let's go to your flat. Is that OK?' I murmured.

She grabbed her record bag and marched out of the café without another word, or even a glance to see whether I'd follow.

Everything after that moment was lost in a blur of urgency, including our heat-filled journey towards Dominique's home, charged with the fervent energy of lust. Once inside the flat she led me to her bedroom by the hand. There, we kissed with the hunger of the physically starved, filling ourselves with a taste of the other. I couldn't keep my hands from roaming, unbuttoning jeans, pushing them past her hips, pausing to let her remove them fully while gazing at firm mahogany thighs. I caught myself watching as Dominique smiled, secure in my arousal. We speedily undressed and embraced as soon as we could.

'Wait.'

She prised herself from my clutching arms, then walked towards a writing desk in the corner of her room. I was content to follow her one-word demand and see what she had in store. Her body betrayed a strength that her features had only hinted at. The lightly sculpted muscles of her shoulder blades and arms rippled as she moved; the deliberate border of her waistline flowed into the curve of her hips, gentle as the crest of a wave; her buttocks broad and plentiful; her legs strong and shapely.

Dominique raised herself until she was sitting on top of the desk, which was bare apart from some books and writing pads. When she was sure it could take her weight she looked me in the eye, then leaned back and opened her legs as far as her position would allow.

Her sex was shaved low. She rotated her hips, her flesh rippling as she played with her heavy breasts, pinching the nipples until they were dark like cherries. One finger strayed below her waist. She exhaled thin breath from between her teeth, throwing her head back in pleasure.

Watching wasn't enough. I walked her way slowly, thinking that if I didn't go steady, this would be a quick and very disappointing encounter. Heedless of these thoughts, my bare feet brought me closer. I bent and kissed her thighs, the skin as hot as pepper sauce, nibbling and gently tugging at flesh until she groaned. She became moist in seconds. I stood, selfishly unable to wait, looking down on inner thighs that shone with perspiration. Placing her arms on my shoulders, she traced the outline of my lips with a sharpened nail. I licked her fingertips before entering.

Ease of penetration brought back everything I had missed during the long, dry spell of my bachelor's life. Dominique's inner muscles enclosed me as tightly as my own fist on many a lonely night; but the heat – the heat made all the difference. That and my smooth slide deeper inside, aided by Dominique's wetness, her wide-eyed, open-mouthed gaze, and sharp fingernails digging into my back. Her heels rested on the cheeks of my behind. She used them to pull me deep until our hips met. Gasping as I withdrew, coated with her juices, I pulled back further, rubbing against her, then penetrated again, our cries in harmony as the odour of sex rose from between us.

What little foreplay there had been was over. Our unspoken agreement was that that would come later. This time was ours. We fucked in natural rhythm, a steady movement that caused me to pant and sweat lightly, while Dominique murmured for more, hips moving to meet my thrusts. At first I thought I couldn't control my inevitable orgasm, but when I came close to the edge, I slowed until the moment passed. Eventually, it faded altogether. From then on, I moved harder, keeping a pace that eventually made Dominique shout aloud, our thighs slapping together as though applauding a job well done. The sound became more fluid the longer we continued, until she was biting my shoulder, bawling my name as I moaned into her ear, the books on her desk falling to the floor, the desk itself thumping against the wall.

Over our passion we realised we were making a lot of noise. I backed away while Dominique slid from her sitting position, turning her back on me and bending over the desktop. Holding her hips, I entered once more, pushing deep, keeping our contact close so I was never less than halfway inside. Her ample behind was wobbling, dark like guava jelly, my eagerness urged by the warm feeling of inner muscles contracting around me with every thrust. When I slowed, Dominique slid herself along the length of my hardness; when I moved faster, she let our bodies meet with fluent ease. I found myself grabbing at her breasts, forcing her flat on the desktop, going harder the louder she yelped in delight.

My lower belly tensed. Remembering I wore no condom, I withdrew, watching months of pent-up frustration splash her buttocks and the back of her thigh. Dominique turned to face me, wiping the semen from her body with one hand, then studying the stark contrast between the dark of her fingers and the white of my seed.

'Been a while?' she panted breathlessly.

I could only nod in reply, caught as I was within the ravenous clutches of orgasm. She wrapped long arms around my shoulders and nuzzled against my neck, sending shivers down the right side of my body.

'Let's try and make up that lost time,' she whispered.

I took her hand and led her towards the bed.

10

I didn't know what time it was when I eventually woke, though I was sure it wasn't morning any more. The playful shouts and yells from kids walking home after school told me it was some time past three PM. Almost a whole day wasted. I cursed myself for allowing such a distraction to last so long. Putting a hand to my forehead, I blinked at the featureless white ceiling. Dominique lay beside me. The duvet covers were strewn around her naked body, a pulse in her neck beating as though begging for freedom. She cupped her crotch tenderly, her mouth wide open and her snores light, yet deep enough to denote an advanced state of sleep. I decided to let her be, looking around in a belated attempt at pulling myself together, taking note of the possessions that made up her room for the first time.

It was a little smaller than Viali's own private space had been, though large enough to be quite comfortable. A chest of drawers lined the wall at the foot of her bed. The desk, a useful participant in our actions, was on the right-hand side, close to where I lay. Amongst the scattered books and pads we'd knocked over was a blue button attached to a plain greeting card that read: *If you don't stand for something, you'll fall for anything!* That made me smile at Dominique's sleeping form, before I scanned the posters of Sojourner Truth, Marcus Garvey, and the infamous image of Malcolm X, *By Any Means Necessary*, which also graced Viali's wall. A built-in wardrobe was on Dominique's side of the bed, its panels painted to resemble a field of grass in sunset. The red, orange, pink and green colours were soothing enough to make me want to close my eyes once more, but there was work to do.

I forced myself out of the bed and over to my scattered clothes. When I eventually stumbled into them, I sat on the bed, gently shaking Dominique's shoulder. She twitched, then turned over and frowned at me, her face screwed up tightly, embedded with sleep.

'Whassup?'

'I gotta push on. I'm well behind time.'

She fumbled for my hand, rubbing tiredly then resting my palm against her waist.

'That's OK. Do what you gotta do. I'll be in touch.'

'All right.' I rubbed her hip softly. 'I'll see you soon.'

'OK.'

Depositing a dry kiss on one cheek, I got up and left her to roll back into sleep. Leaving the flat, I switched my phone on. It beeped to say I'd received some messages, then rang before I could even check them. Sadie's warm voice greeted me.

'Ay what'm, yuh get a phone an' yuh cyaan answer it? Who yuh hidin' from?'

I smiled as I reached my car, opened the door then got inside, the phone to one ear, making a mental note to buy a hands-free kit.

'Nah, I just been taking your advice Sade. Living a little, you know?'

Her reaction almost blew out my eardrum. I had to pull the phone away so as not to become deafened.

'*Wah!* You mean you bin shack up wid some 'ooman den?'

'Kinda. I just took a little break, that's all.'

There was a tiny pause.

'Ervine, me hope yuh nuh spen' dat good man's money on Soho prostitute, yuh hear?'

I had to laugh at that.

'*No*, Sadie man, what d'you think I am?'

'Is check me ah check,' she laughed in return, sounding pleased with herself. 'Anyway babes, I'm only calling cos Robert's been on the phone every hour on the hour, askin' for a progress report or suttin'. He wants to know why you ain' callin' back . . .'

There was an easy answer. Not only had I earmarked Walker as a potential suspect, but the man had also soured my mind with all his ranting and raving during our last conversation. I didn't like him dictating how I should do my job, even though I knew there was a kernel of truth in his accusations. Allowing a man like him to make demands of me wasn't good. It would be all too easy to find myself running around at his every whim, without any clue as to what had really happened to his daughter.

'Tell him that while I'm out in the field, I'll keep the phone switched off. It'll be on this evening, so he can call me then.'

'All right me dear. Yuh waan me phone 'im for you?'

'If you could.'

'OK, an' you can tell me wha' you bin up to when you get back!'

I could hear the smile in her voice, and pictured her leaning over her desk, the phone receiver tight against her ear, brow furrowed. Promising to relay all details, I shut off the phone and put it in my pocket. Dominique's unexpected new 'lead' deserved my immediate attention.

Driving the short distance to Goldhawk Road, Shepherd's Bush, I found myself mulling over my new evidence. Did I believe Dominique's claims? The answer had to be yes. She had no reason to shit on her deceased friend. Still, I intended to look for a motive, even though gut feeling warned I'd come up empty-handed. The missing links that kept appearing as I dug ever deeper into Viali Walker's life made me wary of making any assumptions, which was a very good way for a PI to feel. My excitement and interest in the young woman was growing, though my suspicion that I was overlooking some vital piece of evidence loomed, the prospect as disturbing as the promise of nightfall within cemetery walls.

Reaching Shepherd's Bush, I parked beneath some elevated London Underground tracks. On the opposite side of a main street, Goldhawk Road, was the entrance to an infamous local market, a long-standing feature of the town. Varied races, mostly represented by their women, scuttled in and out of shops, faces intent with the prospect of bargain hunting. Fruit stalls, video stalls and clothes stalls were pushed together, each fighting for rightful breathing space. Weaving my way through the prams, wandering children and dour-faced pensioners, I came to a blue door wedged between a local supermarket and battered-looking TV repair shop. A push on the intercom system was rewarded by a pleasant voice of greeting. I asked for Charles Muhammad and was buzzed in.

Taking the stairs and bypassing other offices housed inside the building, I found the Nation of Islam entrance on the second floor. The woman behind the intercom voice was sitting at a desk just past the doorway, dressed in what I recognised as standard Nation attire – a long dress-like garment coloured a simple white, topped by matching headgear. I smiled as respectfully as I could manage, declaring my business. The receptionist asked me to wait and buzzed through, informing Muhammad he had a visitor.

A young, bald-headed man with glasses passed the desk while nodding in greeting, then headed towards a door further along the landing. I returned the gesture, sitting and gazing at pictures of Honourable Elijah Muhammad, Louis Farrakhan, and other lesser-known Nation soldiers I didn't recognise. From what I could recall on the strength of my limited knowledge, the Hon. Elijah Muhammad formed The Nation of Islam sometime in the early Thirties. After generations of being downtrodden by segregation, race riots and regular lynchings, African Americans were more than ready to embrace a religion that denounced white America and proclaimed the black man a superior being. By the 1950s, with Malcolm X as national spokesman, the Nation of Islam had gathered an overwhelming amount of support from the black community. It continued to grow even after X's assassination, under the guidance of his prudent replacement, Minister Louis Farrakhan. Over the years, Farrakhan had been maligned for alleged anti-Semitism. Both Conservative and Labour governments banned him from the UK, despite the fact that he was no mass murderer, or General Pinochet-style dictator. Though his fight against the ban had made his name on these shores, Farrakhan was best known for organising the Million Man March. Many supporters agreed that this was his biggest achievement to date.

I couldn't help thinking that I wasn't entirely convinced by the Nation as yet; indeed, if I'd agreed with everything they said, I would've joined up a long time ago. I knew that what they were fighting against was a stone-cold reality, and that the media vilified them more out of irrational fear than any definitive cases of actual harm. I liked the idea of their Sunday Schools, which taught English, Maths and other fundamental subjects from a black perspective. However, I found their separatist ideology very hard to swallow; after all, what worked in the United States, a home for segregation, would be difficult to import. Moreover, I would love to see a Million *People's* March.

After five minutes of these random thoughts, I was approached by a tall, clean-cut black man whose demeanour was serious, yet full of polite charm. He was fully dressed in Nation of Islam attire, which comprised of a dark suit, a white shirt and red bow tie with a white moon and stars logo. For headwear, he had a Naval-style cap, for footwear he wore black shoes shiny enough to reflect the ceiling lights. The man stopped in front of me, introducing himself as Charles Muhammad. I took close stock of him while standing and exchanging a firm, reverent handshake.

Muhammad possessed what I liked to call 'S-Curl good looks', his carefully cultivated style closely resembling that of a male model. He was aged mid- to late twenties and was dark-skinned, yet his eyes were the misty grey of a gloomy Monday morning, topped by eyebrows thin enough to be manicured. A narrow nose rested inconspicuously above butterfly lips. There was only a hint of facial hair around his jaw. I couldn't help but note the glance of admiration the receptionist shot his way; his handsome looks obviously attracted attention.

Ignoring the receptionist's gaze, Muhammad wasted no time in asking my business. When I mentioned Viali, a shadow passed his face and he responded gravely. Instructing his receptionist to hold all calls, he led me to his office and I followed, already deeply perplexed by his nature.

The room was spacious and neat, filled with thickly bound books, along with a gathering of more than adequate leather chairs. Much of the furniture emitted an odour of age. A bright, new-looking PC sat upon a wide, lengthy desk. A window at the far side of the office looked out onto Shepherd's Bush bus garage. I watched a number 94 inch its way towards a bus wash, then turned my attention back to Muhammad, taking the nearest seat I could find.

'How can I help, Mr James?'

The man's voice was deep and melodic, laced with a sub-dued boom that I guessed came from lots of public speaking. There was certainly a pattern when it came to Viali's choice of partners. She seemed to have liked robust, striking men, the kind that turned heads, though race didn't seem to matter. I waved away his formality as I busied myself getting out of my coat.

'Ervine. Just Ervine will do,' I replied easily, wanting Muhammad to feel as relaxed as possible. 'I really just wanted to go over some minor details concerning your relationship with Viali Walker. To get things straight in my mind, so to speak.'

'You want to work out whether you think I killed her,' he returned evenly, looking directly into my eyes. As his words contained no malice, I shrugged feebly; he'd hit the nail first go, yet I didn't mind admitting it.

'Well, yes, you could say that. After all, it's what I'm paid for,' I replied, feeling relaxed and comforted by his direct approach.

'Any ID?'

I opened my wallet and tossed the card to him. Muhammad looked it over before passing it back respectfully, as though he was holding an ancient talisman. He rolled his chair back a little, bending at the waist.

'Who paid you?'

I smiled thinly. 'I can't reveal my client, it's unethical. Now, is it OK to talk, Mr Muhammad?'

'Charles,' Muhammad grunted, his head buried inside a drawer he'd pulled from his massive desk. I could hear the movement and shuffling of many objects, and frowned until he sat up, placing a small metallic object next to the computer. A Dictaphone. 'I'm more than happy to talk with you, Ervine – as long as I can tape the conversation so we're both clear on exactly what was said.'

'Fine. As long as I can take notes.'

We grinned at each other conspiratorially. Muhammad tested the tape with that old familiar *one, two* refrain. When he was sure it was working, we began.

'So how long did you know Viali? When did you meet?'

'Maybe six, seven years ago. We knew each other through school friends, though we went separate places. I'd not long left Greenside High. Viali went Avery Park, which meant we had some of the same friends.' He lent back in his seat idly. 'Avery was filled with doctors' and diplomats' children, mixed with regular estate kids. She hung around with my friend's sister, so we knew each other from around the way, only to say hello.'

'*Friend's sister* . . .' I scribbled quickly. 'So when did you two first start dating?'

Muhammad screwed up his face. 'Lemme see . . . It must've bin when I was around twenty-four or something like that, so Viali must've bin around nineteen. We saw each other on an' off until she died, though when it happened we'd bin goin' through an off patch for quite some time. I always thought we'd get back together at some point; I'd bring her round, we'd get married, that would be the end of that. Allah obviously had other plans.'

My hunch came suddenly. It was more like a sting of static electricity than a jolt of white lightning, but still an interesting way to angle the conversation.

'Bring her round to what? The Nation? Didn't Viali share your beliefs?'

From what Dominique had told me, a belief in the traditions of Islam was furthest from the young woman's mind. As I expected, Muhammad was shaking his head, while staring at me with a great deal more respect. I noted that was another thing Viali's men all had in common: remarkable eyes.

'Yuh good at yuh job, Ervine!' Muhammad was grinning. 'Maybe we could find some work for you here sometime!'

'Maybe,' I agreed. 'But I'd have to finish this job first.'

He took my point, sobering and swallowing hard.

'Yuh right, of course. Viali couldn't deal with the unlearning it took to be a member of this family. The release from the shackles of a society that enslaves our minds like it once enslaved our bodies was too great a disruption. Even though we were in love, she still clung to Western ideals. Instead of assimilating into the culture of Islam, she tried to link the two ideologies. They had to clash.'

'And you wanted her to join Islam?'

Muhammad was nodding eagerly. 'Very much. Not only would it have benefited her spirit, she would have bin an asset to this organisation, I swear. I reckon she could have turned it into something resembling what they got in America, an army strong enough to call a million men to one place at one time. An' yuh know what? Although I couldn't get her involved with the Nation of Islam, I never doubted her dedication to the race. In that respect, her father taught her well.'

I let him have his say, deciding to follow a lead the conversation and Muhammad had unwittingly given me.

'You and Robert Walker never saw eye to eye, did you?'

The minister shot me a contemplative look, then attempted to take it back when he saw I'd been waiting for that very thing. He laughed once more, but said nothing. I pushed a little further.

'Did you ever argue with him or Viali? Did he know how close you two really were?'

Now the respect Muhammad appraised me with was akin to the gaze of a hunter looking straight into the eyes of the beast he was stalking. It was much more than a simple, measured stare. He was finally taking me seriously.

'You *are* good,' he breathed carefully.

Pride gave my reply. I kind of hated myself even as it came out of my mouth.

'Thank you. Now please be aware that I'm not trying

to trap you. The truth will simply save us all some time, and I intend to find the truth now rather than hear a rehash later.'

The minister gave me a blank glance, which gave me time to think over what I'd just said. *The ego has landed*, my inner mind chided. I focused on Muhammad and made sure that none of what I was thinking showed on my face. It was quite a struggle. He proved my success by shrugging and relaxing even more in his seat.

'I don't think yuh tryin' to trap me; you're a man doin' yuh job, that's all. I was jus' noticing how good you was at it. *Now*,' he gave me that stern, level-eyed stare again. I got the feeling this guy was a lot smarter than he liked to admit. 'You were askin' whether me an' Robert Walker got on. The answer would have to be no, though I'd say we got on like blood brothers if I didn't know at least four people who'd tell you different. An' you asked did he know about me an' Viali? That's easy. No way.'

'Why not? I mean, I know why Viali didn't want him to know. What were your reasons?'

He smiled the bright and breezy grin of a man on sure ground.

'Simple. I'm a peaceful guy that don't like complications. On top of that, I very much wanted Viali to be mine. In the beginning at least, that meant keepin' the relationship a secret. If we planned to marry, we knew her parents and brother would have to be told.'

I jerked to attention, my seat rolling backwards a good few centimetres. Muhammad was watching my reaction with a teeny smile tickling the corner of his lips.

'Sorry, Charles, you kinda caught me with that one,' I breathed swiftly. 'What do you mean by *brother*?'

He stared at me.

'No one told you?'

'Does it look like they did?'

His smile was beginning to get very annoying, though I knew I was pissed about missing something important rather than any genuine dislike for the man.

'Yeah, Robert Walker had an affair with some woman way back when, which resulted in a son two years younger than Viali. His wife knows about it an' they patched up the holes a long time ago, so Viali an' the son used to see each other quite regular. After all, they were brother and sister.'

My mind was on fire. Why had nobody mentioned this? It was all I could do to think straight with all the possibilities.

'Did you ever meet him?'

'Years ago, when we were all still in school. I used to see her with him when he came down to visit. I haven't seen him since then. I don't think he comes down so much now they're older, you know.'

'Comes down from where?'

'Dunno. Up north somewhere.'

Muhammad was straining hard and coming up with lots of nothing. I truly believed he didn't have any more answers, so I decided to let him off the hook and take my questions about this 'son' elsewhere. Dominique would be my first port of call.

'All right, don't worry about that. So what happened next? Viali refused to convert?'

He nodded slowly, once, twice, then four, five times, finally letting out a huge exhalation and sadly shaking his head.

'Yeah. That was it for our relationship. What was I supposed to do, give all this up? I'm one of the youngest ministers on record. Marry a non-Muslim, to hell with the consequences? Destroy her father's career when the papers found out what I was a part of?'

Muhammad spat choices as though asking me to pick, when we both already knew it was an impossible task. Of course, I couldn't tell him the relationship had been doomed, even when you discounted the grisly fact of Viali's untimely death. Both factions would have forever regarded a union between a Nation minister and Labour MP's daughter with suspicion. I raised my hands in acquiescence, putting my notebook and pad away before struggling back into my coat. The young minister looked up at me, his own surprise affixed to his face.

'What, is that it?' he gasped.

I smiled. 'Yeah, it is for now, Charles. I might get back to you at a later date.'

He was watching me with a hint of unmistakable suspicion in his eyes.

'Leave yuh number with the sister at the front desk, jus' in case I need to contact *you*,' he semi-demanded. In that instant I caught a glimpse of the confidence that gave him this cherished position at such a young age.

'Sure,' I replied, making my way to his office door. He got to his feet, moving around his desk in order to see me out. I waited until we were face to face.

'Where were you on the night Viali died?'

One more moment. There was one more moment of surprise on his part, briefer than the first, yet somewhat stronger and more real. When it passed, Muhammad was speaking again, steady and without hesitation.

'I was at a Nation rally in Manchester, with eight other Nation members and close to one hundred spectators. I gave a talk on media and the modern black youth. It went down really well.'

He was standing almost to attention as he said this last, but it was OK. I believed him, more or less.

'I'm sure it did,' I told him warmly. '*Assalamu Alaikum*, my brother.'

'*Wa'Alaikum as-Salam*,' he replied, handing over a small business card. 'Stay in touch, Ervine.'

I couldn't help smiling at this young man, whose fresh and seemingly honest manner was very likable. Taking the card and putting it in my coat pocket, I found myself sincerely hoping that he, more than any of my other interviewees, wasn't Viali's rapist and killer. I touched his fist, then approached the front desk to give the receptionist my mobile and office number, before leaving the building with my mind whirring with fresh information. As I approached my car and slipped the key into its lock, sixth sense told me to look across the road. My stomach was Slush Puppy within seconds.

Two white guys sat inside a battered blue Mini Metro, obviously waiting for something. The driver was unashamedly looking my way, dark eyes blank and full of malice. He was so huge and the car was so small, his knees were practically pushed beneath his chin. His medicine-ball face was unshaven and coarse. His passenger was a string bean of a youth, as tall as his mate, but with next to no surplus meat on him. He was busy reading a tabloid newspaper and chewing on something unconsciously.

It was the kid I'd seen at the bus stop in Eltham.

Pretending to scan the general vicinity, rather than recognising them for who they were, I got into my car. Gunning the engine, I set off praying that I'd made a serious mistake. The men I'd seen were probably West London labourers on a long lunch break. I was being paranoid. Taking deep breaths, I drove on towards Soho, pondering what the hell I was going to do about chasing up this half-brother.

When I dared, I looked into my rear-view mirror and saw the battered blue Metro cruising a steady two-car distance behind.

11

Dread invaded my mind and body. My hands instantly tightened on the steering wheel. Sickening images of my own grisly death at the hands of those two men, obvious Foundation affiliates, flashed into my head.

Cursing myself for playing hero back in South-east London, I got with the program, turning over my few options. First was to make use of my gun, which was locked inside the boot of my car; but my career, not to mention my life, would be over if I dared. Second would be to try and lose them in the afternoon traffic. The streets on the way to Soho were probably the busiest in London. Third option was to pull over and ask them what the hell they wanted, though that would undoubtedly lead to a fight, and odds were clearly not in my favour. To swing things further in favour of option two, I was approaching one of the best spots to lose a tail: the Shepherd's Bush roundabout. Deciding this was the best course of action, I immediately began making my move.

For starters, I widened the gap between my Foundation friends and myself, so there was a four-car distance separating us. This was done slowly and casually, weaving into space and ignoring the horns, before pulling up at a red light. Thanks to my nifty driving, I was now at the head of the queue. To my right was the Shepherd's Bush shopping centre, a tired collection of chain stores that had finally combined into a mall. To my left was the Underground station, which spewed a constant flow of diverse commuters onto the West London streets. I glanced in the rear-view mirror. My pursuers sat tensely inside the Metro, their faces serious. Even so, they seemed to lack any suspicion, which was more than I could've hoped at that minute.

The lights turned yellow. I lifted my foot from the clutch and the Audi leapt forwards. There were more traffic lights placed just before the roundabout entrance; those were the ones I was really trying to beat. Many a journey had seen me caught by the first and second set in turn, so I'd been forced to become adept at rolling through in one go. The only people caught in the trap were those unaware that the lights worked in unison, stemming the flow of vehicles on that busy intersection. I powered past set two as they rested at amber a moment, then got caught by a third set on the actual roundabout, just beside the Thames Water Tower. Set three had been red for a while.

A look in my rear-view informed me that my plan had worked. I could just about see the Metro at the second set of lights, hemmed in by many other cars. While I was chuckling to myself, my lights turned green and everyone moved. I took the third exit onto Holland Road.

This was a long and drawn out route to Soho, but more than necessary if I wanted to lose those thugs; plus it gave me time to think. From Holland Road I drove to Kensington High

Street, then all the way to Hyde Park Corner and onto Piccadilly Circus. From there I took back roads until I was amongst neon lights and the tiny streets of Soho. I parked in Soho Square and fed a meter, then grabbed my gun out of the boot before beginning my search for Lipstick Parade.

I knew that I was scared – too scared to lie to myself, though not enough to drop the whole thing along with Robert Walker's money. The Foundation knew where I lived, what car I drove and where I'd be at any given time, yet I had no protection. Add the fact that this case was getting more bizarre with each new suspect, and doubts began to flow as cold and fast as a mountain stream. If I was honest, I was no nearer a solution than I'd been when I started my investigation. Admittedly, it was still early days, but none of the people I'd seen so far had aroused that hunch, or given me even the slightest indication that they may have committed murder. Which meant I had them all under suspicion. Which in turn meant that my head was filled with so much information it could easily come apart at the seams.

The truth was I had begun to feel uneasy. In my whole career I'd never handled a case as big as this. The misgivings I'd long been feeling about my ability to do the job were tugging at my coat-tails, begging me to pay them mind. Each turn I made revealed a new facet of Viali's life – her background grew more complicated the further I dug. Almost everyone I'd met seemed to have something to hide or some vague reason for animosity, however irrational or obscure. Anyone's reason could have been justification enough for murder, provided they had the inclination.

I usually found that my client's personal life was of no concern to the case; here, it seemed of utmost importance. The fact that Walker's career had been in danger due to Viali's work ethics, forbidden relationships and his own affair, was another dark area I feared to tread, yet knew that I must. For the first time as a PI, I was forced into questioning the motives of my employer almost as much as I questioned the suspects. Did I have any semblance of truth within my grasp, or was my overeager mind clutching at straws? Or worse still, was I running further from the real killers – The Foundation? Was I constantly fooling myself?

The answers refused to make themselves known as I stepped warily southwards into Soho. There was a strange air, almost as if some furtive form of cultural exchange was being performed, fluid like the shift between day and night. Traders in the local market stripped their stalls down to metal skeletons. Shops ejected last customers, then turned their lights out and locked the doors. Businesspeople moved swiftly through dirty streets, bearing sightless expressions, ignoring the scattering of red lights. As the sunlight began to fade, scantily clad women appeared in selected doorways, smoking cigarettes and beckoning at passing men.

Deciding that these 'doorwomen' would undoubtedly know the place I was looking for, I asked the next one I came across, a heavily made-up Thai with a diverse selection of piercings.

'Lipstick Parade no good. You come here, pretty girls,' she ordered, trying her best to sound demure. I pulled a face.

'No thanks, I'm lookin' for a friend of mine. Do you know where it is or not?'

Thai looked disappointed, as if I'd failed some test of my manhood, though she gave me the directions anyway. I ambled along the busy streets, taking tentative rights and lefts until I found the place halfway down a grass-thin side alley. The name of the Lipstick Parade was scribbled above a pursed pair of lips on a signpost outside. The neon in both lit up repeatedly, one after the other. A plain black girl in a PVC outfit highlighting her obvious assets watched me humourlessly. The Lipstick Parade would win no awards for originality, but if answers were as easy to find as the place itself, I could quite possibly leave a happy man.

'Hey baby,' the PVC-clad doorwoman mumbled with next to no enthusiasm. 'Wanna come inside an' see what we got?'

I stopped and hesitated, unsure of how to tackle this.

'I wanted to ask you some questions if that's OK . . .'

The girl frowned, creasing her heavily made-up face and making her look severe, somewhat unattractive.

'What kinda questions?'

I showed her my ID and the photo of Viali, one after the other.

'Did you know this girl?'

PVC gave both items a quick glance, then handed back the ID. When she studied Viali's photo the second time, her frown disappeared and was replaced by open-mouthed concern.

'That's Viali, right?'

'So you knew her . . .'

PVC looked up at me.

'What happened?'

It was strange how easily the fear beneath the been-there-done-that façade took over, claiming her as its own. I realised at once that it had always been there, waiting for bad news of this nature.

'Viali was murdered. I'm heading the investigation into her death.'

'*Oh my God*,' PVC breathed, a hand to her mouth. She stumbled back into the doorway. Before her shoulder touched the wall, tears were flowing down powdered cheeks. Motionless, I watched her mournfully attempt to pull herself together.

'When . . . When did that happen?'

'Three or four months ago. I'm sorry, Ms—?'

She took a huge gulp of air.

'Francis. Erica Francis.'

I dug into my coat pocket for a tissue, then found an old packet of five and passed one over. She mumbled her thanks while blowing long and hard, eyeliner streaked across her face like war paint.

'*God*, I'm sorry . . . It's just shock. I can't believe that could happen to *her*.'

I hoped I was nodding in a manner that conveyed my utmost sympathy.

'This might be hard, but I'd like to ask you and your colleagues some questions, you know, try and piece together the details of her life? Would it be possible to talk?'

Erica was nodding.

'Yeah, course . . . Come downstairs and meet the other girls.'

We walked inside, then down a steep set of stairs that bore a threadbare carpet that had seen much better days. The faint smell of damp came from all around. Walls were cracked in many places; they were also plain and unpainted. At the bottom of the stairs was a tiny box-like room where two women sat on a sofa opposite the doorway I'd just come through. A large desk was placed on the right, guarded by another scantily clad female. On the left was a curtained doorway that led to a second room. As I glanced around, Erica prodded me back to the moment, ushering me impatiently towards the lounging women.

'Good afternoon, sir, and how are you?' the older of the two purred in welcome, a slight Caribbean lilt to her accent. She was a heavyset woman aged around forty, wearing ordinary black leggings and a matching croquet top with a T-shirt beneath; a pierced nose was the only indication she may have been influenced by her surroundings. The girl next to her was a blonde and blue-eyed cutie, dressed in figure-hugging jeans and a boob tube, no older than twenty. Both were looking expectantly my way, until Erica informed the women of the real reason for my presence.

The young girl behind the reception desk, who reminded me of Sporty Spice, instantly broke down in tears. The older black woman expressed her grief though a glassy-eyed stare at the crumbling walls, one hand rubbing fitfully at her breast.

The blonde girl looked uncomfortable. Erica told me she was new and had started the job long after Viali left.

I asked the women if they minded answering my questions. At once, they all agreed to participate. The blonde girl was told to make a 'back in 10 minutes' sign and put it on the street door so we'd be able to talk in peace. While she left to carry out the task, I was given her space on the sofa. The sniffling reception girl brought me a glass of Red Bull and ice, then the women gathered their chairs around me, looking grave. I'd just met my most eager interviewees yet.

Sporty Spice's real name was Alexis. The black woman was called Charlotte. The blonde, who stood nervously at the foot of the stairs attempting to look inconspicuous, was Nina. I introduced myself and told them of the job that I'd been given.

What followed was the toughest interview I'd ever undertaken. None of them had heard about the fate that had befallen their former workmate. Up until then, the grief I'd seen had been intense, yet dulled by time, whittled into practical baggage that was easy to carry. The remorse of these women, however, was as fresh, real and tender as an open wound. There were a great deal more tears, though for the most part their sorrow was displayed in silence. My questions were answered eagerly and with unbridled sincerity, though I became ever more disturbed as the interview progressed.

The Viali that had become a 'hostess' in the Lipstick Parade was a far cry from the young woman known to her friends and family. Charlotte told me how she had got talking to Viali while she worked at the Freedom Café, and struck up a passing friendship spurred on by regular visits to the coffee shop. Tired of hearing the young woman's complaints about her lack of money, Charlotte had said she had the perfect job for a pretty girl like her. Within a week Viali was moonlighting, standing in the Lipstick Parade's doorway, enticing punters to spend.

I was quickly assured there was no sex involved in her work. Viali would bring the customers down into the curtained room, where they were pampered and shown a drink menu. The Red Bull I was sipping would cost me two pounds as a paying customer, though Coca-Cola was priced the same. The punter was then informed that for £250 they would be given 'a full and complete night's service' and the company of the hostess for as long as they liked. If they refused, they were politely asked to leave. If they agreed, some calls were made and the customer was escorted to a tiny room where there was another girl ready for a night of passion, which, unknown to him, would last approximately ten minutes. Viali would go back to the door and start all over. She earned ten per cent commission on every customer, growing adept at her work in a very short space of time.

Erica and Alexis took over the story, explaining how Viali became drunk on the money she was bringing in and the varied opportunities to make more. Working in Soho put her in direct contact with men long used to dangling the golden carrot on a stick. After refusing many offers to make money on her back, Viali was offered a job as a stripper. With only the smallest of qualms, she took the work, performing three nights a week alongside Erica for a number of months. It was easy money, the young women told me, yet the student soon wanted more. When asked if she'd prefer a nearby lap dance club, she readily accepted.

As time passed, her former work colleagues began to see less of Viali. She stopped working at the Lipstick Parade, stopped dropping in to see Alexis, Charlotte and Erica, then even stopped working in the Freedom Café. While Erica continued performing at the strip club, Viali left for the higher paid lap dance venues, breaking all contact with her friends. Now, months later, Erica and Charlotte still blamed themselves for Viali's decline, insisting they'd 'never imagined such a decent girl would go so far'.

'Tell me about those lap dance clubs,' I prompted Erica. 'Were you allowed to take men home if they were willing to pay?'

Erica threw Charlotte a worried look. She was given a stern nod, the older woman casting her eyes at the CCTV camera fixed into a corner of the room and putting a finger to her lips.

'Officially it's not allowed,' Erica finally whispered. 'But unofficially . . . Yeah, it happened all the time. The punters was always after a bit more, especially when me an' Viali finished wiv 'em.'

'So what about Viali? Did she ever leave with anyone?'

'Yeah, loads ah times.'

'Any frequent customers?'

Erica gave me a direct stare, then shook her head.

'A few guys tried to handle her like dat. She weren't 'avin' it an' she called security if they got pissed. Viali got greedy, she didn't get stoopid.'

While I appreciated the fact that Viali had used good business sense, I remained crushed by these new revelations. A doorwoman was one thing, but I didn't relish the prospect of telling Robert Walker his daughter had resorted to prostitution; or worse, the possibility that he may have known all along. If he had, that would change his status from tentative to definite suspect. What further intrigued me was the thought that, broke as Viali was, she didn't exactly suffer from a lack of opportunity, so she must have performed at the clubs for personal enjoyment. That said something about her character that was disappointing in a very real sense, as well as introducing hundreds of suspects that I was unable to trace or put names to. This case was rapidly becoming a maze, and I was already lost in its confines.

'Are you sure she slept with these men?' I asked, unwilling to believe it was true.

Erica was nodding sadly.

'I started first, then when she saw nothin' bad happened, she didn't see why she shouldn't try it. Viali was like that about sex; she was open and didn't really 'ave no hang-ups. Her love life was pretty active, she always had a new bloke on the scene, so her way of thinkin' was, "why not make money?"'

'So she was promiscuous?'

Even though Charlotte looked unhappy at my incredulous line of questioning, she didn't say anything. Erica thought my question over for a long time before answering.

'Well, yeah . . . I mean, she was kinda wild, you know. She liked to have a good time, and she didn't mind doing whatever for that to happen. That was all. She loved life, an' . . . an' people . . .'

Erica's bottom lip trembled. She apologised to the room as a whole, getting up from her seat in a jumble of arms and legs and disappearing behind the curtained partition. Moments later, a loud sobbing could be heard. Nina followed her through while I numbly put away my pad and pen. Charlotte stood with me, her eyes damp.

'I think that's all you'll get from her. Sorry we couldn't be more helpful . . .'

I shook my head. It would be hard to overstate how helpful this visit had been.

'That's fine, you've been great, all of you, though there's one last thing I think you could help with. Could I possibly have the names of the clubs where Viali worked?'

Alexis nodded and told me she knew the places, going behind her desk and scribbling on a scrap of paper, which I placed into my pocket without looking. I was tired and drained by the day's proceedings, reminding myself that it'd been all go since this morning. Mentally, an enticing picture developed, involving good food, a hot bath and my feet up in front of the TV with the company of my cat. Prompted by this vision, I left the sorrowful atmosphere with a head bowed from the weight of surplus knowledge.

On the street, peep shows and other doorways bearing signs advertising 'models' of varied persuasions surrounded me. I stood on the threshold of this outside world for a moment, lighting a cigarette and taking a deeper look at Viali's photo. The smiling, carefree picture had me shaking my head in disbelief; it was next to impossible to imagine her in this environment, selling her body. So why would she do it? Just for kicks? Or had she been forced into the sex trade?

Taking another puff on the cigarette, I put the photo away and walked from the door, my mind busy turning over what I'd learned. I'd gone no further than two steps when huge hands grabbed at my shoulders, spinning me around and forcing my face into the nearest wall. I heard a doorwoman gasp and shout at my assailant to stop; his profanity-filled reply was enough to silence any heroism. I struggled until a solid punch to the kidneys made my legs weak and the air rocket from my mouth like a pea from a shooter. Warm breath caressed my ear and cheek.

'Lissen Mr fackin detective, leave it alone, all right? Ya little investigation's pissed my friends off, an' yuh don't need to be Sherlock to know who they are, you followin'? I catch you at it again an' you'll be in pain fuh a long time. *Stop tryin' ta stitch us up*. All right?'

There was another punch in my kidneys. This time, I couldn't help groaning. I tried to muster more defiance, only to find any rebellious ideals had left along with the wind in my body.

'*All right?*' the voice repeated.

He needed a reply, especially as I could hear people gathering around us, muttering their disapproval. Realising that there was dignity in silence, I pinned my mouth shut, as if it were possible for my agreement to dive from my lips of its own accord. As I might have guessed, my attacker was only left with violence. I felt another blow, this time to my ribs, then I was left sagging on the pavement while onlookers eagerly rushed me. My view of the mystery assailant was blocked. I wanted to beg them to move, but found myself so short of breath I couldn't produce the words. The only glimpse I managed was of my attacker's broad back, that medicine-ball head and a black bomber jacket that bore the words THE FOUNDATION in thick yellow thread.

Knowing none of my aches and pains were fatal, I waved away the worried expressions from good samaritans and headed for my car. Inside the Audi, I put my key in the ignition, sitting still for a minute without starting the engine, desperately trying to stop despair washing me from head to foot. Things were not looking good. Progress was minimal and the sneaky feeling that I might be in over my head was rising by the minute. The more I discovered, the more I saw, the more I knew I was swimming way out of my depth. It was only a matter of time before I sank to the bottom of this ocean without trace, having failed in my most important case to date.

Pride alone made me turn on my mobile to check for messages, jumping slightly when the handset beeped loudly. Just as I was about to check who'd called, the phone began to ring. The number was instantly recognisable.

'Shit!'

I had to answer. I'd been dodging the call for days. Taking a deep breath, I pressed a button and spoke as lightly as I could.

'Hello, Ervine James—'

'Ervine! Where the hell have you been? You're a hard man to track down, even with a mobile phone!'

I closed my eyes and leant back in my seat.

'Sorry about that, Robert, I can't receive calls when I'm in the field. I could be on surveillance, or carrying out an important interview. Please accept my apologies.'

Walker gave one of his characteristic exhalations, the sound rumbling like a thunderstorm in the tiny loudspeaker.

'Of course, of course . . . I just wanted to see how things were going really, or if you'd found any leads . . .'

The use of the word 'leads' reminded me that I'd spent the majority of my day holed up in Dominique's bed. From there I'd seen Charles Muhammad, and ended up right here, parked in the middle of Soho Square. There wasn't one positive thing that I could tell Robert Walker. I honestly didn't have a clue what to say to the man.

'Everything I have so far points squarely at The Foundation, Robert, but I'd prefer not to speak about it on the phone—'

'I understand,' Walker broke in. 'When shall we meet?'

There was no way I was meeting him tonight. I was shattered, plus I needed time to think about how I'd reveal what I'd discovered without the MP having a heart attack right in front of me, or wanting to murder me himself.

'Tomorrow morning,' I suggested tiredly. 'I need some time to collate the information.'

He hummed and hawed a bit, even though he had no choice. We set the time and place – midday in my office.

'That's settled then,' Walker said cheerily. 'Twelve o' clock tomorrow. See you then.'

'See you then, Robert.'

'And Ervine – thank you.'

'You're—'

Before I could reply, Walker had hung up. I looked at the phone with my mouth still open until I realised what I was doing and pressed 'end', pushing my lips into a thin line, starting the car.

12

When I arrived at my office somewhere near eleven the next morning, I was in reasonably better spirits. I'd followed my inner urges the previous night, running a bath hot and deep, wallowing like a hippo in mud until my skin wrinkled disgustingly. Later, when I'd fixed myself a modest vegetarian meal of noodles, carrots, mushrooms and courgettes, I settled down to a night of watching bottom-rung cable TV. The endless offering of American sitcoms and chat shows allowed me something to focus on other than Viali Walker and her sordid life. If the truth were known, I could see the young woman was fast becoming an obsession. My every waking moment was taken up by thoughts of her. When I closed my eyes I could see her smile, glinting with an innocence that I now knew was a lie.

On the way to Farringdon I worked out what I'd say to Robert about his daughter's varied forms of occupation, going on the assumption that he hadn't already known, despite my suspicions to the contrary. I decided that, much like the photos I'd regularly delivered on my last case, some serious editing was required. So, I'd tell Walker about Muhammad and her 'hostess' job, but would leave out the stripping and all that that entailed. Gossip being what it was, her secret would come out one day. When that happened, the shit would truly hit the fan. Even though Viali's spirit was in another place, part of me felt guilty about what I'd unintentionally started. Instead of performing the task I was being paid for, I'd only managed to churn up hidden secrets that to date had managed to stay buried with her.

By the time I walked in on Sadie at her desk, I'd stifled my guilt successfully, even giving her a smile and friendly peck on the cheek. She responded with the kind of look usually saved for drunks and madmen, recoiling from my lips and narrowing her eyes.

'Hello, Ervine. How come you're so cheerful?'

I was flicking through the morning's junk mail, knowing there was nothing of interest by the plain and simple brown of the envelopes.

'I dunno, but there's no use in being down about things you can't change. Life has to go on,' I crooned, in a sickly-sweet voice I would never have used ordinarily. Sadie was still peering with a face as hard as granite.

'So you haven't heard?'

I sighed inwardly, fearing the worst. This 'haven't you heard' shit was getting to be a regular occurrence.

'Oh, for bloody hell's sake! Haven't I heard *what*?'

My rudeness was ignored as Sadie laboured in a struggle to express her news. Her mouth was working and her fingers clutched at her desk. All at once, a tear escaped her eye. The hollow feeling in my stomach returned, my insides telling me that I'd fucked up somehow, maybe irreparably so . . .

'Robert Walker's dead, Ervine. His wife found him in their house this mornin'. He's bin stabbed to death.'

There was a moment where I didn't believe her. Where everything went a hazy grey and my soul felt as if it had left my body, unable to take more punishment. For a few precious seconds I was soaring over her head, over my own head, looking down on a tableau that was frighteningly painful to watch. There was Sadie, tears running stealthily down her cheeks. And there was me, frozen before her in surprise, wide-eyed, rooted to the spot in disbelief. When I blinked, I was back where I started and Sadie was on her feet, leaning over the desk, calling my name in a bellow that brought back my army days. Telling her I was fine, I turned on my heel and left the office. My guilt had returned, completely and undeniably.

I could vaguely picture where Robert had lived from the address on his business card, and from what I'd been told by various clients over the years. Gossip in the black Community spread as fast as it did in any other, and the MP made no secret of his desire to live amongst the common public. In fact, his working-class leanings had stood him in good stead over the years and his popularity in the polls was always rock solid. After Viali's death, support and sympathy for Walker and his policies had grown. This was reinforced by the solid mass of people filling his street when I arrived.

The police were already there, a section of the road cordoned off by yellow tape surrounding the house. Parking a little way from the scattered onlookers, I wandered past curious people until I reached the police line, trying to get somebody's attention. A group of vans was stationed on the opposite side of the cordon. Police officers of varied ranks were milling about, though none took any notice of me. I raised my voice until a burly looking sergeant walked my way, a deep ridge of mistrust firmly fixed across his brow.

'If you'd like to leave the area, sir . . .' he began authoritatively.

I responded by telling him of my relation to Robert Walker, asking if I could speak with his wife to ascertain whether I could be of any help. The answer was a quick and forceful 'No'. I stressed my point, saying that as I'd been involved in the investigation of one murder case, I could have information that shed light on what had happened here. It was a downright fabrication, of course, but what else could I do other than lie? The sergeant responded by asking to see some identification.

Shit.

Without a pause I was reaching for my wallet, handing it over. The sergeant opened it up, studying the information long enough to cause me to sweat, even though the weather was cold and breezy. A suited man came out of the house, walking down the garden path towards us. My gatekeeper caught sight of him. I could see the chain of logic all over his face.

'One moment, sir . . .'

He left me to approach the man, whom I assumed was a plain-clothes detective, my wallet still in his possession, much to my dismay. Moving his colleague to one side, they spoke in low tones with their heads bowed, occasionally pausing to shoot furtive glances at me. The sergeant showed his superior my ID. I winced as he took it out of the wallet, looking at the laminated card from front to back, staring my way once more. He finished by handing it over to the sergeant, who nodded briskly and returned.

'Hey, how'd it go?' I muttered weakly. There was a vague possibility that I was about to be arrested as prime suspect in this murder case, putting the lid on an already terrible week. The sergeant remained expressionless, giving no clue as to what to expect.

'See that man over there?'

He pointed at the suited detective, who was watching us with an eagle-eyed stare.

'Yeah . . .'

It was all over, bar the cuffing.

'That's Detective Inspector Ryder. Go over an' see him, he'll take you through to see Mrs Walker.'

At first I was sure that he was joking. It was only when his unsmiling face remained unchanged that I realised I was in. The sergeant gave back my wallet with another curt nod, then, trying not to smile at my success, I returned the gesture and ducked the yellow tape, walking nervously over to where Ryder stood.

The detective's face was thin and wretched-looking with pockmarked cheeks. His eyebrows and hair were thick and dark, and he wore his suit with as much style as a clothes hanger, not that he seemed to care. Ryder stuck out his hand as I approached; I shook it sternly and quickly before letting go. His fingers were sandpaper dry, his handshake cold.

'Detective Inspector Carl Ryder,' he introduced himself formally.

'Ervine James, private investigator.'

Try as I might, I couldn't match that zeal.

'I know who you are,' Ryder said crisply. 'You're Birkett's detective friend, aren't you?'

I smiled wanly. *Now* this little scene made sense. Birkett had managed to come through for me yet again.

'Yeah, that's right. D'you know him?'

Ryder gave a limp shrug.

'Only through Sunday football. Birkett plays midfield like a girl, you can tell him I said so. Wanna follow me through?'

Nodding, I trailed in his wake as we entered the house, which was filled with more police officers, though the air was busier and charged with more light-hearted banter than outside. From the interior, the Walkers' house was modestly extravagant. We walked through a games room where a full-sized snooker table took centre stage, and another large room containing hundreds of shelved books, a modest stack system, and a long dining table surrounded by at least twelve seats. Apart from those items, everything else in the house was fairly low key, until we came to the foot of a winding set of stairs. To the right of the stairs was another door. Ryder warned me to watch my step. Forensics were everywhere, dusting and collecting unseen evidence from available surfaces, paying us no mind.

'What's through there?' I asked the Detective Inspector.

'The kitchen. That's where Robert Walker was killed. Mrs Walker's upstairs in the bedroom.'

I nodded in understanding, climbing the stairs behind Ryder, which were large and wide with examples of African art hung all the way to the landing. He guided me towards a spare room that only contained a neatly made bed and wooden chest of drawers. I followed willingly, frowning as I entered. Ryder gently closed the door behind us.

'What's going on? I thought I was being taken to see Mrs Walker?'

Ryder gave me a stare as blank as a sheet of white paper.

'You still are. I just wanted to ask some questions of my own, Mr James. Like where the hell did you get that corny ID?'

I looked up sharply, only to be heartened by the fact that he was smiling, though the grin seemed far too wide for his thin, sallow face.

'I had it made up. That obvious was it?'

'Not to an ordinary civ. But I wouldn't advise you show it to any more police officers.'

I laughed along with him and easily agreed, willing to play the ignorant if it got me what I wanted.

'So what can I do for you then? I'd like to help out if I could,' I told him amiably, though the strain at being neutral and polite was growing difficult.

Ryder leant against a wall and produced a pack of cigarettes, offering the pack, then pushing forwards an ashtray that sat on top of the chest-of-drawers. No doubt this had become the designated smoker's room. I took one and lit up casually, glad that I was being treated like an equal. Across the room, Ryder did the same.

'I already know from Birkett that you took this case. He called through as soon as he heard about Walker, saying you might turn up and advising me I'd do well to look after you. You're lucky I came outside when I did, Ervine.'

I made grateful noises and repeated my question, still mystified by his decision to help. Ryder puffed on his cigarette contentedly.

'I want you to tell me everything you've learned so far. About Viali Walker, her father, this family . . . Everything.'

Now I understood. Ryder wanted me to cover his background information, but that was OK. It was worth it just to have the police on side, especially in light of my recent tussle with The Foundation. Starting from the day I'd received the initial call from Robert Walker, I went though everything from my Freedom Café jaunt, to my troubles with David Wren. Contrary to Ryder's request, I omitted everything pertaining to the Lipstick Parade and what I'd learned about Minister Charles Muhammad. After all, I didn't want the police muscling in on everything I did. And somehow, exposing those things felt too much like speaking ill of the dead.

Ryder listened carefully, sometimes asking minor questions, mostly remaining silent and thoughtful, all attention focused on my words. When I was finished, he puffed a tired breath of air, then caught himself and winked.

'Thanks for that, Ervine, much appreciated.'

'No problem, whatever I can do.'

He was appraising me with the expression of a proud parent. I almost expected him to lovingly tousle my head.

'So what happened?' I asked, finally voicing the question

that had plagued my mind all the way here. Ryder casually
ticked the points from his fingertips.

'Emilia Walker comes home around eight PM, after attend-
ing some literature workshop over in Tottenham. She heats up
some food, comes up to her bedroom around quarter to nine,
eats, watches telly, reckons she's asleep no later than ten thirty.
A little past eleven PM, she hears Robert come home. He's
talking to someone, but she doesn't know who. Emilia says
she's sure about the time because she checked the clock in
their room. She tries to wait up for him, though you know the
score – she's tired, she's just got to sleep and all that, she can't
do it. When she wakes up at around five this morning, he still
isn't there. She goes downstairs and finds him in the kitchen.
Dead.'

Ryder had run out of fingers and resorted to studying me to
see what I made of all that. If he was hoping I'd hazard a
guess at the culprit from that information alone, he'd reached
a state of desperation easily matching my own.

'How did he die?'

'Stab wounds to the chest and stomach incapacitated him,
though he could've lived through that, even after all that time.
They weren't that deep. The fatal wound was one in his upper
thigh. It hit the femoral artery, and you know the rest, I'm
sure . . .'

I blew out a long and lengthy breath, giving no reply. It'd
been a long time since somebody I knew had died in such terrible circumstances. I'd stayed well clear of situations that
involved any killing after my Falklands stint, which was probably why I spent my career tailing cheating husbands instead
of taking cases like this.

'Might as well have stabbed him in the jugular,' Ryder elab-
orated, just in case I didn't get the picture. I quickly changed
subject.

'How'd our man get in?'

'Well, there's no forced entry, so he must've either had a key, or Walker let him in. We're going through a file of all the people Robert knew right now. Believe me, it'll take a long time.'

'I can imagine,' I responded, thinking of everybody that could have had something on Walker, liked though he was. 'Find the weapon?'

Ryder snorted disgustedly.

'We should be so lucky. They're still looking.'

We stood in silence, the air filled with our criss-crossing thoughts. Why had Walker been killed at this stage, when he was no harm to anyone? Since Viali died his profile was so low key he was practically unseen. Surely he wasn't that much of a threat to The Foundation's well-being; so why would they, the prime suspects, do it? If they'd already killed Viali, wasn't that enough of a warning?

Ryder cleared his throat.

'All right, Ervine, ready to see Mrs Walker?'

I took a deep breath. The answer was no, but I wasn't telling him that.

'Yeah, let's go.'

We moved into the large bedroom, where a huge walk-in wardrobe with central mirror and Hollywood style make-up section loomed above us. The carpet was thick and plush, my loafers sinking into its warmth. The walls were painted a deep burgundy red, the solid colour laid as thick as dried blood. Sculptures and the odd vase, African or otherwise, dotted the room and gave a cosy atmosphere of good spirit. There was more artwork, though the pictures were larger and had a more personal feel than the ones on the stairs and landing. In a far corner there was a small writing desk, easily dwarfed by a regal leather chair, its colour closely matching that of the walls. A concerned-looking WPC and a large black woman I took to be either a close friend or family member were both guarding the chair. There sat a black woman, staring away into a space that no one else could see, ignoring the minor invasion overtaking her house.

Emilia was a small, photogenic woman, every part of her tiny and compact in a doll-like way. Though her face was lined and thin, even in grief she still bore the beauty that had drawn Robert many years ago. Her hair was braided and tied back, the streaks of grey that ran through it easily visible from where I stood. Back in the late 1950s, when Walker had first come to prominence as a political leader, justly protesting the unfair treatment of West Indian and African immigrants, Emilia Scott had stood firmly by his side. They were married sometime in the early 1960s. A look at black London's limited history books pictured Emilia and Robert at each pivotal moment of the struggle for equality. She was the strong, p-assionate firebrand for whom diplomacy was just another tool in her box. When that failed, she used harsh words and strenuous campaigning to win the justice she rightfully demanded. Mostly, Emilia Walker was known simply for her unbeatable will to survive.

Ryder approached the widow cautiously, as though her plush carpet was embedded with hidden traps. If she noticed his presence, she gave no indication. The WPC got to her feet in a quick movement, while the second black woman eyed him casually.

'That's OK, Hepburne, you can relax,' Ryder told his subordinate, who looked relieved. 'I just wanted a quick word with Mrs Walker, if that's all right with you.'

Ryder angled his last words at the leather chair, as well as Emilia's companion. At the mention of her name, Emilia Walker slowly raised her head, squinting as though she was gazing directly into bright light. Her eyes were slits, the lids swollen with the weight of her tears. She was nodding unconsciously.

'Yes, of course, you must do what needs to be done,' she croaked hoarsely. Sorrow slipped through me like ice water.

'Give us a moment alone,' Ryder told the WPC.

The unknown black woman looked quizzically at Emilia, who nodded in reply. Without another word, the women left. Before I was even ready, it was my time. Ryder turned to include me in the conversation, while Emilia looked me up and down, a perplexed set to her delicate expression.

'Mrs Walker, this is the man your husband hired to find who's responsible for your daughter's death – Ervine James.'

Her eyes widened and I felt that cold fear once again. Stifling my misgivings, I respectfully bowed my head.

'So sorry to hear about Robert, Mrs Walker. I had a lot of respect for him.'

Emilia lowered her eyes somewhat, as though the thought of what had happened to her loved one was too much to dwell on.

'Thank you, Ervine. Now tell me something. Is it really true that Tazanne James is your mother?'

Her soft accent was reminiscent of West Indian seas and sands, a balm to my disturbed state of mind, even though tears had scuffed her throat. I managed a half-hearted smile while Ryder looked a little confused as to where this was leading. To his credit, he never said a word. I nodded my head in response.

'Then you must know that I met you as a child,' she continued. 'You couldn't have been any older than three, four at the time. Your mother was – still is, in fact – a good, kind woman.'

'Your husband said that he thought he knew me,' I told her, then kicked myself when I saw her close her eyes tightly. When she opened them again, Emilia was looking straight at me.

'Come sit on the bed. Both of you.'

We did as we were told, then awaited further instruction like errant schoolboys. I was pleased by the respect that my new-found colleague afforded Emilia Walker; my estimation of him had risen markedly over the last five minutes. Emilia took each of our hands in her own, though unlike Ryder's her fingers were warm, soft, comforting. If she noticed the coldness of the detective's hands, she refused to mention it. We waited pensively for her to speak.

'Each of you has a job to do; equally important, yet as separate as the colour of your skins. Carl, you must do your level best to find my husband's killer. Don't let it become a repeat of my daughter's investigation; do that, and the black community will distrust the police even more. People are disillusioned, fed up with the beatings, the unsolved cases, the acquittals. I know it's a hard burden to carry, but you're a good man, I feel that. If anyone can make it right, it's you.

'Ervine, I know you must be feeling bad about what happened to Robert. Remember that it's not your fault. I also know you had your disagreements with my husband. Robert could be bullish at times, but we both need you. Honour his memory by completing the task he gave. Give our people the hope that somewhere along the line, justice *can* be awarded us.'

I heard myself speak from somewhere far away, in a voice that didn't belong to me, though I was powerless to stop it. It was the voice of all my insecurities, all my fears.

'I don't think I'm living up to your husband's expectations,' I told her ashamedly, unable to look at her. 'I've questioned loads of people and I'm no closer to knowing who did it than I was at the beginning. I'm sorry to say that, but I don't want to lead you on and tell you everything's going great when it's not.'

I could feel Ryder's eyes burning my cheek, yet I took no notice, concentrating on this important confession. Emilia deserved the truth. The thoughts I'd just expressed had never been told, though they'd been rattling around my brain like a pea in a whistle for days. Emilia looked sympathetic, but unconcerned by my revelation. I couldn't help feeling a little bit uneasy.

'Don't worry, Ervine, we knew this would be hard,' she told me in what was meant to be a comforting voice. 'The police had a whole team of men investigating and couldn't find anything, isn't that right, Carl?'

It was obvious that admitting this was like swallowing cyanide for the Detective Inspector. He braced himself and took a deep swig.

'Yes. Yes, you're right, Mrs Walker.'

'All you can do is your best,' Emilia whispered. It was clear that she was addressing us both. 'Can you promise you'll do your best, at least? That's all I ask. I need to know who took my family before I'm called to join them.'

We muttered *yes* in unison, our sombre voices mingling in a monotone that would've brought no joy had I been Emilia Walker. Nevertheless, it seemed enough to satisfy the lady. She sat back in her chair and closed her eyes.

'Now go, both of you, and continue with your work. I need some time by myself. I've been molly-coddled all day and I hate it. I might even sleep if I'm permitted.'

We got to our feet, bowing our heads like knights before a queen.

'Of course,' Ryder told her. 'I'll make sure WPC Hepburne is right outside your door if you need her.'

'Thank you, Carl, you've been a great help.'

She was already sitting on the bed and slipping her shoes off, then swinging her skinny legs up onto the duvet. I bowed my head once more.

'Take care of yourself, Mrs Walker.'

'You too, Ervine. You've got the number here so call anytime you like. It'd be good to catch up with you and your mother.'

'I'm sure you'll be hearing from her soon, for the nine nights, at least.'

Her eyes were closed and she was nodding softly in reply,

breathing as though she'd instantly drifted away. Ryder gently tugged at my arm, inclining his head towards the door. I shut my mouth and left Emilia to the solitude of sleep.

13

Ryder offered to take me over the crime scene, even though he knew I had no desire for blood and guts, or to see Robert Walker as a chalk outline on linoleum. After sticking around for a few more hours out of vague camaraderie, I thanked the policeman for his hospitality, promised to update him if necessary, then hastily vacated the house and went back to my car. There, I sat breathing harshly, images from the last few days circling my thoughts like flies. I stayed that way until I noticed people on the outskirts of the crowd elbowing their friends and watching me curiously. Starting my car, I left the street and drove without any true destination.

Back at the house, I'd attempted to tell Ryder what had happened outside the Lipstick Parade, when I'd found myself manhandled by the unknown thug. He'd responded much like Birkett, saying that there was nothing he could do; I remained as unprotected and vulnerable as before. If I wanted to drop the case, he'd continued, that was up to me. But in light of Emilia Walker's pleas, could I possibly bring myself to do that?

Somewhere in the pit of my being, I knew Emilia's confidence should have buoyed me up and held me aloft so I could fly mountain high until I brought her daughter's killer to light. Instead, my soul responded by withering like a raisin. All I could think about was the fact that yesterday I'd been accosted, and the next morning a man lay dead. If that wasn't a clear indication that I was in over my head, nothing else would suffice.

So here I found myself, caught between a rock and hard place in every sense of the phrase, only the rock was a woman I'd respected from afar most of my adult life. The hard place was death, plain and simple, I had no doubts about that. Deep inside, I also had no doubts who was behind this double killing, this destruction of a family. It was as Robert Walker had told me from the start, and I'd disbelieved him. Not only had I distrusted him, I'd also believed that he may have murdered his own daughter.

That's why I knew that it was over. No more. Because there was no way that I was returning to Eltham without back-up. And even if I risked inciting the biggest racial conflict London had ever seen by involving Charles Muhammad, there was no guarantee that would bring the murderers to me. I'd thrown in the towel, even though nobody knew it yet.

As the thought sunk in, I was brought back to reality by the fact that my throat was bone dry. The idea that I should drink to my new decision was a spark that soon roared, and where better to drown your sorrows than Soho?

Knowing no answer, I drove into the West End.

Once there, the question of where I should go arose. Remembering what the girl at Lipstick Parade had told me, I fished in my coat pocket for the names of bars Viali had danced in all those months ago. Finding the crumpled piece of paper, it only took a few directions from a shop owner to stumble across the first club on the list, Blue, situated in another squashed alleyway at the centre of the red light district.

This was more Viali's style, I noted, as I walked along the rain-dampened pavement, though I realised this knowledge was a recent acquisition. There were lights and erotic glamour, gay bars and stores selling bondage gear, all crammed so tight you could OD on visual candy – if you liked that sort of thing. Viali clearly had. I pictured her wandering these streets on lunch breaks from the Freedom Café, day in and day out, scared she'd be seen but unable to stop herself. I saw her entering shops tentatively for the first time; the next with more abandon, then the next without a care.

Strip clubs had never held any appeal for me. My army days had seen me use the services of the odd prostitute, but I'd never got used to paying good money just to see a woman take her clothes off. More than anything, it was a wind up I couldn't afford. I'd always felt disgruntled on the rare occasions when I'd been face to flesh with strippers, so to speak. But now I was thinking that maybe there was something I'd missed, both in the nature of the work and in the context of this case.

Stepping to the ticket booth, I was faced with a huge man impeccably dressed in a black suit and tie. Handing over my money, I was charged fifteen pounds entrance fee, and given what looked like an old cinema ticket in return. The man told me the club was two doors down. The ticket entitled me to one free drink. Also, as long as I kept the stub on my person I could come and go from the venue as I pleased until three AM. I doubted I would stay that long, but smiled my thanks and walked a little further along the alleyway.

Here, I came to a large awning, with so many light bulbs surrounding the entrance it was painful to look. Colourful pictures of women wrapped around poles were everywhere, looking more like movie stars than any strippers I ever saw. In the centre of all the posters, red carpeted stairs led up until you could see no more. I studied the differing poses to see if Viali had made the Hall of Fame. A voice broke into my concentration.

'Evening, sir.'

Another heavyweight in a matching suit and tie. I gave him my ticket and he ripped it in half, then repeated the warning to keep my torn stub in a safe place. Pushing it deep inside my coat pocket, I climbed the red carpeted stairs. When I reached a set of swing doors, I eased through to find myself in a small bar area. A skinny white girl in a loose-hanging glittery dress was serving drinks, her smile slightly forced, almost non-committal. She wasn't the prettiest of sights and was wearing way too much make-up, but I ignored all that and sat on a barstool, returning her thin grimace. Ordering my free drink, a brandy and Coke, I looked around at the other customers: a group of guys sitting in a comfy corner of the room. They looked like tourists, talking and laughing amongst themselves, surrounded by their drinks, mostly bottles of beer. Directly behind me was another set of swing doors, the top window deliberately covered so punters couldn't see what lay beyond. Music from behind the doors pumped through speakers placed above the bar. The pasty-faced girl jigged half-heartedly as she placed my drink before me. I grabbed the glass and slid off my barstool.

'No alcohol allowed in the main room. You'll have to drink that here,' the woman ordered, eyeing me distrustfully.

I returned to my seat without a word of argument.

That night marked the beginning of my swift demise into the darkened world of depression. I'd known it was coming, yet the finality of its arrival bowled me over, leaving me sprawling and dazed in its wake. Running away from what I'd known to be the truth had been a wrong move, I saw that clearly; it was now obvious to me that I should never have taken this case on. I'd been feeling I wasn't up to the task of detective work for a long time, that I'd shied from serious cases to protect myself. Now my quest for survival meant a man had been killed by my negligence. There wasn't a damn thing I could do to change that.

Sorrow and alcohol is a powerful mix, guaranteed to intoxicate a man's body and spirit to the point of pollution. It was hard to think when I felt so guilty at what I'd contributed to, and my guilt spanned so many people my head began to pound. My mother, who I hadn't called since taking on the job she'd lovingly secured me, was one of the people I'd let down most: Christophe from the Freedom Café; Michael Josiah; Erica and the girls from Lipstick Parade; Robert Walker himself, and his wife, who even now trusted me when I couldn't trust myself. Worst of all, I felt that I'd failed the spirit of Viali, a beautiful girl who deserved more than a shabby would-be detective fighting for the peace of her eternal soul.

I took out her photo and laid it on the counter before me. The wide smile and demerara complexion caught me for a moment. I bent my head closer. If only I'd seen her in the flesh. If only I'd had a chance to witness that smile, then my whole life would be different and I'd be another man, not the one scarred by inner-city living and a war where I'd seen my friends lose eyes and arms. A man who moved in the circles she'd inhabited would've been free of those things. His wealth would be of his own making. He would have been attractive to her, blessed with a gift that not only drew her to him, but also claimed the rest of the world: *success*.

I believed success came to those who were given an intangible something at birth. And if that something wasn't concentrated enough, or another being had more of the stuff, or if you weren't given any at all, then you were doomed to failure, forever and ever, amen. I'd spent a lot of my life believing that I was one of those unlucky people, destined to live without a bite of the Golden Apple, no matter how hard I fought or worked. So regardless how I tried, it would always be this way, whether on this case or in my life, and I'd better get used to it.

After reaching my sombre conclusion, I put Viali's photo away. I remained at the bar and continued to drink more brandy, diluting the first three with Coke, downing the rest straight along with a little ice. I was trying my best to get drunk, though I couldn't say why it wasn't happening; yes, I was tipsy and slurring by my sixth, but I wasn't gone yet. I needed more. Striking up a friendship with the pasty-faced barwoman, I bought her a requested vodka and Red Bull for her troubles. The group of tourists moved between the main room and bar three times, finally blowing kisses in my drinking buddy's direction before leaving. Other men came and went through the swing doors. Pasty-face finally asked a very sensible question. If I'd just come to drink, why didn't I go to a normal bar? I shrugged my shoulders loosely. Why not indeed? When I told Pasty this, she gave me a double brandy on the house and said that since I'd paid the fifteen pounds, I might as well see what was on offer. Part of me saw the sense in what she was saying. I decided to give it a try.

Sliding from the barstool wasn't that difficult, though as soon as my feet touched the floor, the reality of my situation became apparent. I grabbed at the bar to keep myself steady while Pasty smiled and told me to watch myself, before I got thrown out for disorderly behaviour. Taking her warning very seriously, I thanked her, stumbling my way into the main room.

Disappointment was the first thing that struck me. There were at least forty or so cinema seats, all in a circle around a raised stage where the stripper, a leggy half-naked Asian girl, performed with lacklustre attention to her audience. Her sequinned bra and knickers already lay on the floor beside her. The scattering of men sat with blank expressions that only became animated when she danced in front of them, swinging around the pole in slow time to the lightweight R&B being pumped at high volume. Most of the men were middle-aged or older, apart from a group that looked to be in their late twenties. They puzzled me by their excited pointing and grunting, until I realised they were deaf mutes. I took stock of the scene. There was a moment where I wanted to go back to the safety of the bar and drink more brandy, though something inside me rebelled at the thought of where that might lead. I sat at the back of the room and steeled myself.

When her song ended, the Asian girl picked up a couple of ten-pound notes thrown beside her underwear, then left the stage via a back door. An unseen woman's voice told us that we'd just seen Bunny. The next girl up was called Diamond. A tall, European-looking brunette in a leather thong came from backstage, caressing herself while another song blasted from the speakers. The group of deaf mutes clapped and stamped their feet, obviously pleased by what they saw. The brunette smiled at them, wrapping her legs around the pole nearest their seats.

I lost track of time while I brooded in that noisy room, my mind far away from the girls, who changed places every four or five minutes. What had Viali's stage name been? Had she enjoyed being on show like this? Was it an ego boost of any kind to be leered at by such men? For all of the protests I'd heard against this trade on the basis of feminism, from the immediate picture it seemed these groups of sad, tired, unattractive men were the ones being exploited for financial gain. I lost count of the number of times old codgers, who could barely lift their arms without trembling, stuffed crumpled notes into G-strings in return for a quick feel of young flesh. Instead of finding it erotic, I saw the whole thing as melancholy in the extreme, unable to imagine Viali onstage with those girls. Some time later, Bunny the leggy Asian was back. I got up to leave and she smiled my way, perhaps hoping to win a quick ten pounds, but I ducked my head and went back to the bar. Ordering three straight brandies from Pasty, I proceeded to knock them back one after another while she watched them disappear incredulously. High in ten seconds flat, I mumbled a goodbye and stumbled down the stairs, while the suited doorman watched my exit, amused.

Night in all its splendour caressed the Soho streets. I looked at my watch and was amazed to find that it was nearing six PM, which meant I'd been inside the club for near enough three hours. I knew that I should go home before I ran into trouble of some kind, but had no inclination with Robert Walker's death and the Foundation poster fiasco fresh in my thoughts. Trying not to trip over my own feet, I dug into my coat once more and retrieved the crumpled scrap of paper, memorising the name of the second club where Viali had worked. Recognising the street name, knowing it was a short walk from where I stood, I decided to pay another visit under the subdued pretence that I was still on the job.

Half an hour later, I was queuing up outside Whispers, a huge establishment that strove for a classier image than the club I'd previously attended. Huge concrete steps led to heavy black doors. A model-like blonde was on the ticket desk, wearing a simple black dress that seemed expensive and revealed very little. All the signs and photos announced that this was a lap dance club, which promised a more stimulating experience than the mundane display I'd only just managed to struggle through. Feigning a flimsy degree of sobriety, I paid with more cash, left my coat in the cloakroom, then headed towards another set of heavy black doors at the end of a grey and white tiled landing. Beyond them, according to the signs, was where it all happened.

It happened in a space the size of a small concert hall, with a huge stage and seven glistening poles placed in varied spots. Each had a dancer attached, sensuously winding themselves to disco music while the audience, made up mostly of expensively suited men, sat in alert groups and watched with eager eyes. There were younger men too, even some couples scattered around the hall, while barmaids dressed in little more than bathing costumes roamed from table to table, taking drink orders. The place was packed and buzzing with the sound of chatter. I found a vacant table and sat down, taken aback by my new surroundings.

A passing barmaid approached me. She was another bottle blonde with ink-black roots and a body as curved as it was lean. Smiling politely, she offered a drink menu, directing my attention to a gathering of women seated in a far corner of the hall. The prices for differing forms of table dance were rattled off one after the other in a stilted monotone. I declined the women, instead asking for another brandy, this time with a Coke mixer. My barmaid nodded politely and left.

Somewhere between the last club and this, the alcohol's effect had faded, allowing me to realise where I'd ended up. Disgust at myself ran thick as I took in my surroundings, though there was one way I could maintain some dignity. Producing Viali's photo once more, which had taken on all the significance of a lucky talisman, I placed it firmly on the table. She looked at me with that same familiar smile. The barmaid appeared above my shoulder with a drink on her little black tray. I paid, leaving her a hefty tip. She was moving away from my table until I called her back.

'Hey, how you doing?'

My voice sounded hoarse and thick, mostly due to the strain of pitching it over the music. The woman looked at me questioningly.

'My name's Ervine James, I'm a private investigator dealing with a murder case. This girl, Viali Walker, was killed around four months ago. She used to work here. I'm trying to piece together the people that knew her.'

Looking up at the woman to see how much of this was making an impression, I noticed she looked dubious. I passed her my open wallet. After reading, she sat next to me and

picked up the photo, holding it beneath one of the lights surrounding the tables, screwing up her face.

'She used to work 'ere?'

Her normal speaking voice was as cockney as Sid James. I
nodded.

'I don't recognise 'er, but maybe one of the other girls will.
Can I lend this a minute?'

She held up the photo and I nodded once more. She got up,
grabbed her tray and headed for some girls in the corner.
Sipping at my drink, which was quite strong, I promised
myself I'd take it easier on the brandy this time. I watched the
barmaid do the rounds with Viali's photo. She went through
all the girls, who shook their heads one after another, then
went to the bar, passing it to a white guy serving drinks. I
narrowed my eyes as he held the photo up to the light. Next
thing I knew, he was picking up a cordless phone hung on the
back wall.

Deciding to leave them to it, I looked around the club,
immediately catching the eye of a woman seated at another
table not far from mine. She was white, yet curiously tanned,
with dark black hair that fell all the way to her hips. She wore
a one-piece lavender-coloured dress with a plunging neck-
line, and a hem that ended dangerously close to her upper
thigh. Her body had the busty yet supple grace of one of the
table dancers; still, she sat alone drinking what looked like
red wine. My eyes couldn't help lingering on such an attractive sight. She continued to stare, eventually smiling. Timidly,
I allowed myself to smile back.

The barmaid returned, breaking my concentration.

'Hi . . .' she murmured.

'Hi.'

I forced myself back into the moment, while she returned
Viali's photo with the most human smile she'd managed.

'None ah the girls knew her, but the barman said he'd
seen her perform here. He called the manager, who said he

remembers her vaguely or suttin'. He'd like a word if you don't mind. I'll take you up.'

'I don't mind at all,' I fumbled, feeling a little nervous. The 'manager' was probably just some gangster placed to keep things in order, but I had to finish what I'd started, even though I was gutted that I'd left my gun in the car.

Downing my drink, I got to my feet. Attempting to ignore the gaze of the woman in the lavender dress, I followed the barmaid through the club and customers, heading backstage.

I was walking along a dank corridor as glamorous as an empty warehouse, while girls in various states of undress ran here and there. It was hard to ignore all the nubile bodies, so I gave up trying, feasting my eyes on well-toned dancers' breasts, thighs, butts. If my barmaid noticed, she never said a thing, instead leading me up narrow stairs and into a quieter corridor that was a little better looked after. Though there were still cracks in the plaster, paintings and mirrors hung on veined walls. The threadbare carpet was marginally more becoming than the chipped wood I'd walked over moments ago. My barmaid led me to an unmarked door at the end of the corridor, where she knocked as loudly as she could. I only just heard the subdued call to enter, and followed, pondering on the number of offices I'd visited since taking this job.

This one was nothing special. Bare to the point of poverty, it boasted one desk, one hardback chair, one leather chair (occupied), one leather sofa, some blinds, and that was about it. No music, no computer, no books. The only form of entertainment was a series of TV screens that surveyed the action in and outside the club. The manager seated behind the desk looked Eastern European at a glance, his hair somewhere between brown and blonde, his shoulders wide. He wore a purple suit with a sky-blue shirt and tie that screamed money. This man and lavender dress downstairs would've made a lovely colour co-ordinated couple.

The barmaid introduced us; I learned her boss was called Ivanhoe. That was all, no surname. If I'd had any inclination to laugh, the manager's stern gaze swiftly quashed it, as he grasped my hand and shook. Ivanhoe had the rounded-yet-hardened face of an Army veteran, his eyes black circles in his face. There was an angry line of long and fleshy scar tissue just above his right eyebrow. His fingers were a series of thick sausages, the knuckles protruding as though the flesh covering them was stretched at the seams.

Ivanhoe asked the barmaid to leave us alone. For a long while after that he said nothing, simply watching me over the broad black desk that looked as heavy as stone. I left the silence intact. This man made my former thoughts of sobriety laughable and I felt every drop of alcohol I'd consumed.

'So,' Ivanhoe began, his accent faint, though still apparent to the discerning ear, 'I'll make this quick as I have lots to do. You're looking for the man who murdered . . . Viali, that was her name?'

'Yes.'

'If it was a man, isn't that right?'

'Yes.'

'Nothing to say it couldn't have been a woman who killed her, no?'

I pulled an ugly expression of disbelief.

'Well, she was raped. So there must've been a man involved somewhere along the line, even if you're right.'

Ivanhoe grimly rubbed at his chin.

'A terrible thing. I knew her well, saw it in the papers when she was killed. I didn't tell the girls, though. You must understand that kind of news is bad for business. I don't think her father would have been pleased to know she worked here either.'

'You heard he was killed this morning, right?'

He left his chin alone and placed his hands on the desk.

'Yes. It's a terrible tragedy.'

Leaning forwards, I was very aware of the increased pounding in my head as a reaction to any movement.

'I'll make this brief and spare your time, Ivanhoe. You look like a man who relies on instinct, has a knack for feeling things out. I need you to tell me if there was anything out of the ordinary about Viali, anything out of place or slightly off-centre about her on any of the nights she worked here. Was there anything that struck you as strange—'

'Yes, yes, I understand the question,' Ivanhoe said moodily, speaking in the tone of a spoilt child. I sat back in my seat, not wanting my eagerness to come across as ineptitude or the unskilled approach of an amateur. The manager closed his eyes. Although I'd been playing my speech by ear, it seemed as though I'd guessed right. Ivanhoe was an instinctive man, judging by the time that he gave my query. Eventually, he was forced to shake his head.

'No. No, there is nothing.'

My faint hope plummeted like a meteor. There'd been a moment when I'd felt like I was on the case again, in both senses of the word. I sighed in defeat. Ivanhoe was still frowning furiously at his desk.

'Then I suppose . . .' he continued softly.

Despite myself, despite everything, I found myself desperate to hear what he had to say. The words emerged so slowly I wanted to prise them from his mouth with my bare hands.

'I suppose there was . . . something . . . Though I'm not sure . . . whether . . . it would help . . .'

My mouth was hanging open, my eyes silently urging him on.

'There was a man . . . He regularly came to look for Sunshine—'

'Sunshine? What's that, her stage name?'

And her family name, according to David Wren. Ivanhoe, thank God, seemed to catch my enthusiasm.

'Correct. He only came on weekends, mostly Saturdays . . .

He'd sit drinking at the bar until she finished her shift, then he'd escort her home, week after week. All the other girls assumed he was her boyfriend, but she never said a word to any of them, never told them who he was . . . Sunshine was a good table dancer, but a private girl. She kept herself to herself. No one was surprised when she left and didn't come back.'

'What did the guy look like?'

He mused with a distant look in those indigo eyes.

'Very tall, thin guy. Good looking – not that I like men, but the girls would always comment. Well-dressed, the smart casual type. Shoes and jeans.'

This was all very interesting. The image of Charles Muhammad immediately came to mind.

'What kind of complexion did he have?' I continued. Ivanhoe was frowning once more. 'Would you say he was black?'

The manager peered my way in an intense manner that sent involuntary shivers through my body. He wasn't the kind of guy I'd like to get on the wrong side of, I was very aware of that. The fact that he was capable of violent action emanated from his pores like body odour, though he seemed unaware that he gave off such a strong vibe. Nevertheless, I held my head portrait-still.

'He was pale,' the manager said casually. 'His skin was more . . . I don't know . . . More yellow than yours.'

Damn. I'd thought I had this character firmly pegged, but that didn't sound like Charles or David Wren. Even Ravinder didn't fit that description. I was lost, confused again, slumping into the hardback chair, rubbing my head tiredly. Ivanhoe was silent, allowing me time to think.

'He came by every weekend?' I finally puffed in exasperation.

'Most weekends. Sometimes he wouldn't come back for a while, then he'd turn up again.'

'There were no arguments or fights?'

Ivanhoe shook his head from right to left, as though his ears were waterlogged.

'Never. Sunshine always acted very friendly towards him. He was the same. They seemed very comfortable together.'

I was clutching at straws and we both knew it. It was quite possible that Viali had picked up yet another admirer on her travels – someone that I, and probably everyone that had known her, had no clue about. It was generally agreed that she'd been a secretive young woman. Trying to find all the people she'd ever met was a task that could easily last my whole lifetime; a thought that sobered me quicker than any other.

'Mr James, I know you mean well, but I really have a lot of things to get on with,' Ivanhoe was saying, his face set into the nearest approximation of concern he could manage. I got to my feet.

'Of course, thank you for your time. It was a pleasure to meet you, Ivanhoe.'

'And you sir, good luck! If I can help in any way, don't hesitate to return!'

I replied in the positive, even though I stepped into the corridor secure in the knowledge that I'd never come back. The taste of my own inadequacy was as bitter as bile. Tomorrow morning, I would get on the phone to Emilia Walker and let her know I was off the case, no matter what she said. After that, who knew where my life would lead? Even though I felt as though I'd let everyone down, including myself, the relief that my decision gave was surprisingly good. It felt like the right thing to do. I even managed a faint smile as I walked along the empty corridor and down the dank, narrow stairs. My instincts told me I'd finally reached the beginning of a new life. What that meant was a question only time could answer.

Ignoring the writhing girls onstage and others dimly lit by

tableside lamps, I moved quickly across the hall, leaning hard into heavy doors. Collecting my coat from the cloakroom, I was depositing some gold coins in the tip jar when the heavy smell of Gucci *Rush* crept beside me. I swivelled to find the woman in the lavender dress standing at the counter in all her glory; and believe me, there's no better sight to a troubled man than a beautiful woman. Face to face, she was more attractive than I'd previously judged. Her lips were bursting with plump ripeness, her eyes a sparkling nut brown, her tight dress barely containing the strength of the woman it held. She inclined her head towards the main doors while the cloakroom attendant looked on, a smile on her pale face.

'You're leaving?'

The accent was hard to place and could've come from anywhere within London.

'I think I've seen enough beauty for tonight.'

She smiled to herself and looked at her feet, clearly pleased by my words. I regained a teaspoon of pride.

'Would you like some company?' the woman asked.

This was getting weirder by the minute. Either Ivanhoe had sent her to spy on me, or luck was letting me know that it still existed; it just picked its time and places very carefully. The question was, could I afford to turn away the chance that the latter might be true on a paranoid whim probably fuelled by nothing more than brandy fumes?

The woman took one look into my eyes and knew my call. She collected her leather jacket. We left the club.

My beautiful companion called herself Elaine. Yes, she had formerly worked at the club we'd both attended, but not for a few years. She'd been drinking with friends nearby and when they'd caught their Underground train home she'd stayed around, walking familiar streets before passing her former place of work, deciding to see who was still there. Most of the girls were new, but the guy on the door remembered her. She

also knew Ivanhoe, though she hadn't seen him that night.
Yes, she'd heard many violent tales involving his name. No,
she'd never heard of Viali Walker.

'Why all the questions?' she asked when I eventually fell
silent. The coffee shop we'd found was busy enough to make
you feel like everybody had something exciting to say, or was
engaged in some most important conversation. Steam rose
from behind the stacked plates, reminding me of my last visit
to a place like this. If I got lucky with this woman tonight, I'd
never wrinkle my nose at the café latte lifestyle again.

'I'm just curious about you,' I told her sincerely, thinking
that if I was really going to pack the job in, it meant a radical
change of personality. My curious nature had been with me all
my life. It would be hard to let it go when it had driven my
being for so many years.

'So what about you? Why were you there?'

I considered telling her the truth, then buried the thought
and smiled over my mug.

'I just like women. I'd never been somewhere like that
before and I thought, "why not try?"'

Those plump lips parted slowly, revealing a smile as enticing as the telltale swell of her bosom, which had long caught
my eye. Elaine moved closer, allowing a clearer view.

'That's very honest,' she murmured. I was grinning now.

'Why lie?'

When we stared at each other brazenly, I knew there was
nothing more to be said. Over her shoulder, I could hear a
couple of guys talking in Italian, faces sick with jealousy. We
drank up and left while they tried not to watch Elaine's spell-
binding exit from the coffee shop, her warm fingers grasping
mine.

14

Over the course of our night I'd promised to take Elaine home. I drove my Audi southwards through Westminster, and on past Elephant and Castle as the ancient grandeur of the West End gradually gave way to the modern dilapidation of North Peckham Estate, an army of spiritless tower blocks that marched as far as the eye could see. It gave me no joy to wind the car through the centre of those buildings. The few scattered residents that I saw watched us drive past like townspeople in those old Western flicks: expressionless faces that showed no emotion, heads following our journey. Heeding Elaine's directions, I parked in a small area at the rear of one of the blocks. Apart from the tinny sound of music from above, all was quiet.

'Is that all ri—'

I turned in my seat, shocked to find that Elaine had a foot up on the dash and a hand between her legs, which moved as though it had gained its own life. I'd seen a lot of things in my time, yet the image of this woman sprawled in the front of my Audi had me speechless. Her fur-lined leather jacket was wide open on either side of her torso, as if mimicking the actions of her limbs. She threw her head against the car seat, opened her mouth and emitted a low moan, almost as if I wasn't there. Her hips rocked and jerked in slow motion movements, her lavender dress a bunched ripple of material around her waist.

There was nothing more I could do, other than what I'd already fantasised. I reached over the gear stick and kissed her, testily at first, then with more passion as she responded. My hand clawed at her dress, pulling it from her left shoulder, taking a firm pink nipple between my thumb and forefinger. I squeezed tight. Elaine writhed, panting and kissing me harder, fingers working at my fly until I was hard in her hand. As she drew her nails gently across that hardness, her fist moved in a motion as liquid as the hips of the lap dancers I'd just seen. Occasionally, she bent her head as I leaned back to accommodate her, licking from my balls to the tip and back again. She looked up with a tiny smile, pushed me back into the driver's seat, then leaned over and took me in her mouth to the hilt. Even in the dark of the car, I could see my shaft glistening like an unsheathed sword as her lips travelled along its length.

Urged on by the scents of sex, I lifted her head and tugged at her hips. Elaine got the message, climbing onto my lap, my hardness still firm in the palm of her hand. We had to open my door to give her enough space to sit astride me, then she moved her knickers to one side and lowered herself. It was a tight fit. She backed off, rotating her hips against my tip in slow revolutions. The tightness turned soft and moist as body lotion. She tried again. This time I slid inside, feeling her part almost unwillingly, until her arse cheeks bumped softly against my thighs.

Her hands were all over my body, pinching my nipples beneath my shirt, gripping my shoulders as she bucked harder and panted into my ear. I was insane with lust and didn't care who saw, or how much noise we made, pushing my hands past her coat and onto her abundant breasts. Elaine started to move faster, her rocking more abandoned, her cries higher pitched. She was so wet that the one time I came out of her, there was a noise a little like soapy hands rubbing together. Once back inside, we continued until she screamed and shuddered, grabbing me tight, pushing her hips solidly into mine.

In the resulting calm, we heard voices from the front of the block. We laughed and kissed more gently, ourselves again.

'*Well*, that was naughty . . .' She kissed the tip of my nose and smiled brightly.

'You OK?'

I didn't know why she wouldn't be, it just seemed like the best thing I could ask at the time.

'I *am* . . .' Elaine wrapped her arms around my neck, my softness wriggling out of her of its own accord. She hummed contentedly. 'You didn't come, did you?'

I shook my head, unworried. It'd still been a great bout of sex.

'Listen,' she continued in the same breath, 'I gotta little one upstairs and I need to check on her—'

'You got a kid?'

Normally that wouldn't bother me, but since it'd never been mentioned in all of our talk I felt I had a right to be a bit peeved.

'Yeah.' She was looking serious now. 'Is that a problem or somethin', cos I know some blokes—'

'Nah, nah . . . It's . . . Yeah, it's cool. I don't mind kids . . .'

That wasn't exactly a lie, but it wasn't the whole truth either.

'You sure?'

'Sure I'm sure.'

'OK!' Elaine's pretty beam was casting light once more. I was struck by its intensity as she spilled out of her dress in front of me. 'I gotta check on my little man, then you could come up in around . . . say, fifteen minutes. If he does wake up, I'll have him back to sleep by then, and *you* . . .' She kissed me once more. '. . . are gonna come like a fuckin' volcano. Does that sound good?'

'Sure bloody.'

My mind had resorted to schoolboy terms of speech, such was my limited vocabulary at that point. Elaine massaged my temples, causing me to close my eyes in pleasure, finally running her hands down my chest and climbing out onto the street. When I opened my eyes she was looking down on me, her lips graceful crescents, her eyes small sparks of bright light.

'You're a good guy. Thank you,' she breathed as she shrugged her leather jacket into a more comfortable fit. 'It's flat forty-two on the fifth floor. Come up in fifteen, OK?'

'OK . . .'

Elaine waved and walked into the block via the fire exit, a little shaky on her feet, otherwise fine. I watched those firm thighs disappear, then relaxed onto the headrest when I heard the metal door bang shut. *What a night*, I thought contentedly. Nothing like this had ever happened to me. I had a feeling that I'd be recommending lap dance clubs from now until I was old and grey. To help with the fifteen-minute wait, I switched on my radio. Jazz FM was still on the dial. I relaxed to the sounds of Ronald Isley singing that she was all he needed, the perfect end to an extraordinary night. My muscles unwound, my ears tuning out the external sounds of music, whistles of greeting and the occasional rhythmic beat of passing footsteps. Content, I smoked a cigarette that tasted better than ever.

Not long afterwards, I flicked the smouldering butt out of my window. I was dozing, if not fully asleep; anticipation would never let me miss a second round. My mind was just

going through an elaborate rewind of the entire night with
Elaine, when realisation sat me up like a sudden scream. My
mouth hung open, my gut wrenching at my own stupidity.

'I gotta little one upstairs and I gotta check on her . . .'

And two minutes later . . .

'I gotta check on my little man, then you could come up . . .'

Male pride obscured the fact that Elaine had lied. About her
kid, probably about her name, definitely about the flat number
that she lived at. I felt in my coat pockets.

'Fuck, no!'

My wallet. I'd had my wallet on me all night and it was
gone. The sneaky little bitch had robbed me while we were
fucking. I couldn't believe I'd fallen for that ancient one, surely
the oldest in the book. The ID was expendable I supposed, but
the cash . . . I had to get that money back, there was close to
£300 in that wallet.

I got out of the car in an explosion of movement. Looking
around for estate dwellers, I went into my boot, checked the
safety on my 9mm Taurus and stuck it firmly into the small of
my back. Locking up, I went for the fire exit, only to find there
was no handle on my side of the rusted door. Cursing her
ingenuity, I walked around the front of the block to a main
entrance, only to be faced with intercom buzzers for over 200
flats. I finally saw how well I'd been deceived.

Peering through the small panes of glass on the main door,
I saw a man at a reception booth asleep in front of a portable
TV. Bingo. Ringing the reception buzzer hard, I kept my finger
there until he jumped up in confusion. He responded by
swearing, although I couldn't hear him do it. More buzzing
got him up and over to the door like a grizzly bear woken out
of hibernation.

'Why you buzz like that, huh?'

The man was stocky and dressed in a thick jumper and
jeans, his accent decidedly West African. He wore his displeasure like a warm overcoat in the chill of the morning.

'Listen, you gotta help me man, I've just been robbed. Some woman had sex with me and nicked my wallet and I . . . *What?*'

Although he'd been quite serious at the beginning of my speech, when I reached the part about my wallet, the man began to giggle. I felt my anger rise, wondering if I'd have to use my gun to prove my point, especially if he kept laughing.

'*What?*' I repeated, growing angrier still.

The African's head was bowed as he chuckled some more. My hand was already sneaking towards the Taurus. Before I could make that final move, he was up again.

'*Oh* . . . Oh, I'm sorry my friend, it's just . . .'

Narrow-eyed and tight-jawed, I waited for his explanation.

'. . . It's just . . . This has happened many times before. I see many men like you taken for a ride . . .'

'So you know who this woman is?'

The man looked at me, a smile still attached to his face, while his red-rimmed eyes were hard and grim. He opened the door as far as it would go.

'Come my friend.'

There was the usual blast of hot air from the above-door heater as I entered, following the African back to his desk where he resumed his former place, feet swung up on the imitation wood. When he was firmly settled, he returned his attention to me.

'Listen, my friend. As you are a brudda I help you. I know you struggle like me, it's not nice to struggle and be robbed. Am I right?'

'Yes,' I muttered impatiently, ignoring his sermon. 'What d'you know?'

He pulled down the corners of his mouth. 'There's squatter on da twelfth floor, always holding party and creating lots of noise. Some people who live next door say it's the women who rob men like you.'

I was nodding in understanding. There was no guarantee

that block gossip was right, or even that this man was telling the truth. Still, I had no option other than to check.

'What about you? What d'you say?'

He lifted his hands to the heavens, exposing cream-coloured palms. 'Hey, what do I know, huh? I sit here an' know nothin', you wid me?'

'Yeah, all right,' I scowled. 'What number?'

'One one eight. Twelfth floor.'

'OK, thanks, yeah?'

I stepped swiftly down the long hallway towards the lifts. When the metal doors shut and I started to rise, I took out my gun and flipped the safety off, preparing myself. The lift doors jerked open.

I stepped onto a ravaged landing where the black soot of an old fire had scorched the walls and front door of the first flat I came across. Loud music came from another flat at the end of the hall. I recognised the tinny sound I'd heard from inside my car. Gun in hand, I crept carefully along the passage. The music was coming from one eighteen all right, the other numbers on the landing told me so. Fully alert, I spotted something on the floor beside the rubbish chute. Proof, as if I needed more at that stage.

My open wallet lay where Elaine had presumably thrown it. I picked it up and flicked through briskly. The ID was there, though my credit card and all the cash I'd had was gone, probably for good if I wasn't fast. I looked up at one eighteen, then flipped my gun safety and put it away. There was a subtler way to handle this, armed with my ID and some good luck.

Walking up to the door, which was a plain pink colour that shouted neglect, I gave a robust knock on the letterbox and waited. The music coming from the flat was making the wood tremble, but it never went down, not even a decibel. I knocked again, much harder. A long while later, I heard locks turn and click. The door opened to reveal a short, skinny white man. He

looked unclean and had a weasel-like face with marble grey
eyes, along with a plume of hair that ran in a straight line
from his forehead to shoulder blades. Earrings that looked
like chicken feathers adorned his ears. He sneered cruelly at
me.

'Yeah, whadda you want?'

I flipped open the wallet, letting my ID show and imitating
DI Carl Ryder's formal tone.

'DI Earl Johnson. I have reason to believe that a woman
who lives at this address witnessed a serious car accident
tonight. I'd like to have a word with her please.'

'A car accident . . .'

Weasel was thinking that over, a finger to his stubble-
roughened chin. His voice was nasal and could grow quite
irritating if I heard it much longer.

'Yes. She was wearing a leather jacket, lavender dress?'

He thought some more, those eyes never leaving mine.

'Wait there . . .'

Weasel disappeared inside the flat and the door banged
shut. I wandered to the opposite wall, leaning against it. Five
minutes passed. I could hear voices from the flat, but couldn't
make out what they were saying. Once or twice I swore I
heard loud women's voices, yet when I strained my ears, they
disappeared like smoke on an updraft. I shut my eyes,
inevitable fatigue descending on me. The front door of the flat
jerked open with a whine of indignation.

When I opened my eyes, there was another white guy looking around the door like a sentry on first watch. He was thin
and mangy as an old hound, limp hair spilling down his forehead, arms tattooed from shoulder to fingertips. Faded jeans
and an army-green athletic vest was all the man wore. He
looked dangerous enough to arouse a tingle of disquiet, so I
pushed myself upright as he walked from the flat and down
the landing.

'Y'all right mate?' I began jovially.

'Fuck off.'

Even though I'd expected some animosity, I was still put out by the speed of his false start.

'What's your problem?' I asked, arms outstretched in a peaceful gesture. The man continued to bear down as if I hadn't spoken.

'Jus' fuck off, you black bastard . . .'

His insult was the straw that broke my weary back. All the pent-up frustration of the last few weeks came to an overflowing head that I just couldn't contain. If I'd seen the other two guys behind him, I probably wouldn't have done what I did next; but I didn't, so I did. The punch surprised even me, and tattooed guy certainly never saw it coming – a flowing uppercut that landed squarely on his jaw, knocking his head back so far I could see his Adam's apple jutting like a plum stone. His legs wobbled like stilts, then collapsed. When he fell, there was nothing to stop his head from cracking against the landing wall, the sound very audible in that small space, even over the music coming from the flat. Then he was down, sprawled on the thin brown carpet, eyes fluttering rapidly and a trickle of blood running from his mouth. The three of us standing looked at one another, each a little surprised by what had just taken place.

Then they erupted.

These two were clearly lager louts, boasting matching beer bellies and stocky frames, almost like a drunken Tweedle Dum and Tweedle Dee. They surrounded me in seconds, shouting and swearing as loud as they could manage, the odd racial obscenity thrown in for good measure. Tweedle Dum began with an open-handed slap; I caught his meaty hand and twisted until he yelped and turned red. I felt a crashing blow to my temple from Tweedle Dee, and while I saw stars he used his massive belly to bounce me along the landing step by stumbling step. When my head cleared, Dee was still in front of me, though Dum was gone. There was an abrupt tug on the collar of my coat before I hit the floor on my arse and was dragged backwards towards the lifts, fighting all the way.

Reaching for my gun was now impossible, yet I still had the presence of mind to remember Birkett's words and feel quite wary about using it. This was Peckham, after all. If the police were called and I was caught with the Taurus I'd be in trouble that could get me killed in custody, I didn't doubt that. Besides, even though I wasn't doing too well, I could tell these men were street brawlers who'd been lucky enough to fight their own ilk up until now. I doubted if they'd ever fought an ex-soldier. What made a battle with us so difficult was that even if we were down, we never gave up.

Spurred on by that thought, I responded by hooking my legs into Dee's and twisting, hard as I could. He resisted, but the drink I could smell on both of my adversaries affected his balance. Eventually, he went down like a shot elephant. I turned myself over until my hands were flat on the floor, causing my coat to dig into Dum's fingers and his grip to loosen. He stopped dragging and let go of my collar with one hand in order to get a tighter hold. Instead of pulling away, I got on all fours, then put my head down and butted, aiming for his groin. The howl of agony I heard confirmed a direct hit. Although Dum never fell, he let go of my coat, which was good enough for me.

I got to my feet, surveying the scene. Tattooed guy was on his feet again, holding his jaw with one hand and the wall with another. Dee was standing too, giving me a sneer that told me he was ready to continue, although he was breathing in a manner that proved his exertions had already worn him out. Dum had his forehead against the wall and a hand cupping his seed bag, eyes closed, his attention diverted by his deep-seated pain. It seemed I'd won that round.

'You know why I'm here,' I said to Dee, the only one who seemed capable of any conversation. 'All I want is my money, then I'm gone. OK?'

'You'll 'ave ta go through me ta get it, cunt!' the fat man panted. I rubbed at my head casually.

'OK. If that's what you want . . .'

I shot a quick glance over my shoulder to make sure Dum was still incapacitated, then walked towards Dee, each of us sizing up the best way to start. What happened next was a relief for us both in some small way; neither of us wanted to be seriously hurt over this.

'Oi! Oi, you lot, you can stop dat shit right now! I've called the police and they'll be 'ere in five minutes, so unless you wanna wake up in a cell, yuh best fuck off! All ah yuh! Wakin' up my fuckin' daughter wiv yuh crap . . .'

The four of us had been so caught up in the heat of battle that no one heard the front door open, or the arrival of the woman spectator. This neighbour's mention of the police made me freeze in my tracks. The possibility that I'd feared had arrived. Dum, Dee and Tattoo guy took the cue they'd been offered, scuttling painfully into their squat like crabs on a lonely beach. I, with nowhere to run, stood mannequin-still. I knew the woman hadn't seen what I looked like yet; of course, I wanted things to stay that way, but I had to leave this council block fast. I hoped my speedy exit would win me some points with this unknown lady, so I could come back to the squat sometime and resume my search for what was right-fully mine.

Convincing myself that revealing my face was all for the best, I turned around – to find myself so stunned, all thoughts of the police flew away and left me with a joy I'd rarely ex-perienced. We mirrored each other's open-mouth gaze for what seemed a millennium, staring from head to toe and back.

'Ervine?' Carmen Sinclair muttered as the squat door slammed shut, clutching her dressing gown tighter and peering down the landing. 'Nah . . . Dat ain' Ervine James, it can't be!'

'Shit,' was all I could reply at that time, such was the improbability of who I was faced with.

The woman in front of me was an old school friend. Moreover, she'd been near enough my closest confidant back in the days of run-outs and Children's BBC. Both my Claybridge Estate neighbour and my only platonic female relationship at the time, we'd baffled everybody with the amount of time we spent together. Before school, after school, over weekends and holidays, we remained side by side from first year to fifth. Secretly, as they'd learned to keep their comments about our friendship between themselves, both our parents thought we'd eventually marry. But it wasn't to be. Against the odds, we stayed friends for years after we left school, which further confounded everyone that knew us.

Then I joined the Army.

That was the beginning of my slow, yet unavoidable slip from the world that I'd grown up in, the people that I'd known and loved, the estate that had been my only home. When I returned, London had changed too much for me to rekindle anything other than a distant spark of affinity. Most of my friends were hustling, driven mad, in jail, or worst of all stone dead. Carmen had got pregnant and set up house with some South London guy as far as anyone knew. Eventually her parents had left Claybridge and immigrated to Barbados. The last time I'd seen my friend, the day before I left for an Army life I'd thought was forever, we promised we'd stay in touch. As sincere as that pledge had been, those words remained as they stood: a promise, not fact or resolution by either of our standards. If it had been more, I wouldn't be staring in shock at this person, with the look of a grown woman but the face of a girl previously just another sad image in my memory.

Carmen was stepping along the landing, a half-smile on her face, while her eyebrows twitched like an old woman attempting to focus. I did the same, part of me thinking that this was like one of those romance movies, where the couple race across the beach and into each other's arms, only at a fraction of the speed.

'I'm seein' things, right? You're not my friend are you?' she was saying softly, her lips hardly allowing the sentence to be formed. I reached for her hands. She must have recognised me at that point, because she let me. We stared at each other in disbelief.

'It's me, Carmen,' I reassured her steadily. 'I know this is crazy, but it's me.'

Carmen looked from head to foot once again.

'Wha' you doin' 'ere? Furthermore, wha' you doin' fightin' on my landin'?'

Her face creased as she said this, finally remembering the reason she'd come out of her flat. Thanking the voice of Birkett for urging me not to use the Taurus, I looked around at the dirty collection of doors, wondering how long we could remain here before my three attackers returned.

'Listen, Carmen, you won't believe the shit I'm gonna tell you, but you gotta lemme in. Quick, before them idiots come back.'

She could manage no vocal answer, giving only the sternest glare she could muster. Eventually, she couldn't hold back her emotion. Next thing I knew, Carmen Sinclair was hugging me hard enough to make breath wheeze from my chest. I wrapped my arms around that tiny, familiar body and began to squeeze tightly in return.

15

I know what the song says, but *waking* up is hard to do when you're hungover, and you've spent the previous night brawling with unknown louts. My head was thumping as though embedded with Djembe drums; I could hear them with the greatest clarity, even though the tiny flat was silent and still. When I opened my eyes, the light of the day was sharp enough to make me wince in pain. I grabbed at the blanket wrapping me like a mummy and drew it over my head, hoping sleep would return with little effort.

Last night, from its miserable beginning to its amazing end, had to be one of the craziest I'd ever experienced. To lose, then to gain, only to lose and gain at the end was a rollercoaster ride I never wanted to repeat. If there was one thing I could say about my life at this point, I knew that it certainly wasn't boring, not at all. The trouble was, excitement wasn't quite the buzz I'd previously imagined. Excitement seemed to *hurt*.

I'd spent the residue of the early hours talking with Carmen, telling her everything that had happened since we'd last met (which took a matter of seconds), then everything that brought me to her flat. She sat on the edge of the sofa not saying a word, generous lips half-open as she listened to my tales of Robert Walker, Charles Muhammad, Ivanhoe and Dominique. Without hesitation I told it all, unconsciously remembering times past when Carmen and I shared every secret we had. Back then, I even knew that she'd started her period before she told her mother, we had been that close. When I finished my story, I was faced with the realisation that this was a woman I hadn't seen in over fifteen years. Things might have changed between us. Disquiet wormed its way into my stomach, even though it was too late; the words had already left my lips.

'So what d'you think?' I'd asked when I was done.

The years seemed to roll away from me in the briefest of moments. Suddenly, I was four years old and Carmen's family had moved into the flat three doors away from ours. My mother took me along when she'd welcomed them to our estate, and while they talked we'd stared at each other from behind our parents' legs, smiling haltingly though refusing to speak. It was strange how clearly I remembered that first meeting, though even stranger that the recollection had never left. When we were teenagers, Carmen and I realised this was a shared memory. Over our years apart, I'd found myself pondering whether it was one she still harboured.

'Wow,' she'd replied to my tale, breaking me free of the recurring memory. 'Dat's what I think. You've had a mad life, Vinnie.'

'So what about you?' I asked, ignoring her use of my family and old estate name, though it was good to slip back into that familiar groove. 'What've you been doing all these years?'

In response, Carmen had only managed a slightly sad-dened look. She spread her arms wide and sighed.

'Jus' here innit,' she'd grumbled sombrely. 'Same old ting, really. Tryin' to make ends meet.'

Briefly, Carmen told me the South London guy I'd heard about all those years ago left soon after the miscarriage of her first child. I reacted sadly, but she waved my words away with a casual hand, saying it was a long time ago and the wounds had long healed. She met someone else a few years afterwards, ending up having a daughter with him; they'd split too, though this guy managed to stay around. Since then, she'd been living in this flat and working part-time in a bagel bar while signing on. She also collected the pittance of housing and child benefit the government offered, finding it hardly enough to clothe and feed two. Carmen saved the best until last, following that with a photo of her daughter, Akira.

'My little star,' she'd said proudly, unable to stop her face lighting up with pride as I returned the photo. I smiled, shaking my head at the thought that this woman I'd grown up with was now a mother, like millions of others. Carmen said we could save any further revelations for the morning, unfolding a makeshift bed from her sofa, with seat cushions for pillows and a thick woollen blanket for a duvet. When she'd left for her own bed, I'd managed to stay awake for all of about two minutes before falling into a slumber that almost resembled death.

Now I was awake, I could feel faint pangs of hunger that accompanied the pounding of my head. That alone made me pull the blanket back, looking around the tiny living room. It was the usual council affair: cramped with possessions that included a wide-screen TV and Kenwood stack system courtesy of the local crack-heads, Carmen had told me. Pictures of Akira and her parents were everywhere, most of the latter taken in and around their Barbados home. Her father still wore that same, easygoing smile. Her mother's formerly long auburn hair was now cut to shoulder length, bearing streaks of grey that made her look very distinguished. Beneath these photos, a fake wood cabinet took up most of one wall, its shelves stacked with every Disney film that had been produced. Scribbled drawings that resembled Mr Messy of the Mr Men, entitled *Mum, Dad and Me*, were pinned on the back of the living room door, penned by Carmen's daughter no doubt.

I had just taken note of this multicoloured artistry, when the living room door swung open. Before I could collect myself, Akira stumbled sleepily into the room, wiping her eyes as she walked, heading straight for the TV. Carmen's features had been melded into hers; they had the same wide brown eyes and rounded face, though Akira's complexion was the milky brown of a Galaxy bar rather than the tanned beige that came from mixed heritage. It was almost as if the little girl was a scaled down version of my old friend, or an exact duplicate of Carmen at the same age.

Akira only realised she wasn't alone when she reached my spot on the sofa. There, she stopped dead, staring without shame.

'Hello,' I whispered nervously. 'How are you?'

She said nothing, casting her eyes down at the carpeted floor, tiny fingers winding in and out of each other. I sat up on the sofa and checked that my gun was safely put away, then inched a little closer, moving slow.

'It's OK to watch TV if you want. You can put a cartoon on.'

The little girl looked up when I said this. She was smiling and had been all along. It was the most beautiful thing I'd seen in a long time, causing dimples to appear at the corners of her mouth, her tiny face a picture of angelic charm. In fact, I was a little thrown at the sight of such perfect innocence in such awful surroundings. At once, I felt myself wanting to be this little girl's protector, her mentor, the person that guided her through life until she was old enough to protect herself. Although it was slightly scary, it was also as pleasing as the moment I'd looked down on baby Maya for the first time, knowing she was a life that I could nurture and shape. The years had passed and I'd failed since then concerning Maya, but here . . . Here was innocence once more.

I reached out a hand, offering peace. Akira looked down at the floor again, then back up, still smiling. Ignoring the hand, she carefully stepped towards the sofa, sitting as close to the edge of the seat as her tiny backside would allow. I found the TV remote, passing it over. She clicked a few buttons and on it came. Carmen's crack-head friends must've fitted cable too, for Akira went straight for the Cartoon Channel. *The PowerPuff Girls* exploded onto the screen. We sat in silence, Akira watching the trio of young superheroes' wondrous adventures with an awe that was hard to feign.

By the time Carmen limped tiredly into the living room, our silence was long gone, the two of us talking back and forth like old pals. Her mother's wispy curls stuck up like Einstein's, her thin body swamped by a large woman's nightgown. I'd forgotten Carmen sometimes wore glasses, her hazel eyes peering out from behind black frames that made her look much like a secretary. My old friend was a little astonished to see me conscious, even more surprised to find me comfortable and willing to get up early with her daughter after this morning's drama. She listened, amazed, as Akira steadfastly gave me a first-hand education in all things Toon, from *Dexter's Laboratory* to *Ed, Edd and Eddie*. Quickly hugging and kissing her mother, the little girl went back to her running commentary, telling me who the bad guys were, which characters she liked best. At one point in *Dexter's Laboratory*, a villain was punched by a superhuman mother so hard, he slammed high speed into the wall of a bank he was attempting to rob. Akira threw back her head, roaring with manic laughter so loud it had to be false, then turning my way.

'That was funny,' she grinned.

'Not so loud, Akira,' her mother returned sternly. 'One more cartoon den you get ready fuh school, d'you hear?'

Carmen busied herself making a quick breakfast of soft

boiled eggs, fishfingers, baked beans and toast cut into soldiers, then disappeared into the bedroom to dress her
daughter while I flicked the TV to a news channel. I caught
the newscaster in the middle of a report on the death of
Robert Walker, unable to stop myself frowning when he told
viewers there were no leads. A sombre DI Ryder appeared,
pictured outside the Walkers' home with a mike shoved in his
face, saying lots of nothing. Carmen and Akira came back
into the room. The child was dressed in a simple primary
school uniform of a blue skirt, a little blouse and a blue sweat-
shirt with the name PECKHAM WOOD emblazoned on the
front. They sat down, Carmen on the sofa, Akira on the floor
between her legs. The little girl looked half-frightened to
death. Her mother leaned down and dipped her finger into a
pot of grease, then began kneading her hair with half an eye
on the TV.

'So wha' yuh gonna do about all dat?' Carmen asked when
the newscaster finally signed off and went on to the Middle
East.

I didn't really want to say. My decision to pack in the case
hadn't changed, though I couldn't stop feeling a little
ashamed, especially after seeing Emilia on-screen appealing
for someone to give the murderer up, or come forward and
confess. I scratched my head while mother and daughter gave
me identical inquisitive looks, the little girl's head jerking like
an epileptic as Carmen tugged and pulled. Their likeness was
amazing.

'Still gonna give the whole thing up?' Carmen continued
matter-of-factly, before she saw the surprised look on my face.
She laughed a hearty donkey's bray. I immediately heard
what her daughter had been trying to imitate, while Akira
smiled tightly at the sound, despite her pain. 'You forgot yuh
tol' me innit? Vinnie man, you ain' changed at all, still got a
story for all seasons! I thought yuh done know yuh can't lie to
me!'

All I could do was join in with my friend's loud laughter. She was right as usual. I'd always been one to compartmentalise what I said and whom I said it to. Except with her. To top things off, the strangest thing was that we really *hadn't* had any sexual leanings towards each other. That was just another unfathomable aspect of our old relationship.

'I know how yuh feel, but they need yuh. Look at dat woman, what's her name . . . The wife, she needs you man! You know the police ain' gonna be able to catch whoever did it—'

'Yeah, that doesn't mean I will,' I broke in seriously. 'Honestly, Carmen, I ain't got a clue, I don't know where to begin. I'm all messed up, and it might just be best if I leave it, that's all I'm saying. I'm doing more harm than good if I carry on this way.'

My friend was shaking her head. 'I don't believe dat. One of those guys you questioned is the killer. It's jus' a case of findin' out who.'

I winced slightly at the ease of her statement.

'Yeah, but *how*? They're not gonna come to me an' admit everything—'

'Pressure dem. Dat's the way they always do it on TV innit?'

Inwardly, I was groaning in agony. It was hard to bite back my disdain at those words, though I just about managed, remembering who I was speaking to. What had I been thinking, talking shop with someone like her? What the hell did Carmen Sinclair know about detective work? I didn't mean to disrespect my old friend, but I knew she was wandering dangerous territory with her particular train of thought. *TV indeed*, my inner mind sneered in reply. The worst thing was she thought she was doing me a favour.

'Carmen,' I spoke in a voice of finality. 'It's over, man. I'm not doing this any more. I've made my decision.'

My friend had a look in her eye that I didn't much care for.

She shrugged all the same, patting her daughter's back and leaning away from her. Akira's hair was intricately patterned with lines, twists and bunches all wrapped up with pink and blue ribbons as bright as spring flowers. She looked beautiful. I told her so and she responded with a shy smile.

'Go,' her pleased mother ordered, pushing her towards the living room door. 'Get yuh books and bags den Little Miss Durben is gone!'

When she had left, Carmen turned on the sofa gravely.

'If yuh drop dis now, you're always gonna be wondering if yuh could've done a bit more, Vinnie. I think you should allow yuhself da privilege. Other than dat, I'm jus' glad yuh alive an' well an' functionin' wid all yuh faculties. Nowadays, dat kinna shit is a blessin' from high.'

'Yeah,' I muttered soberly. Part of me knew that everything she'd just said was the truth, yet I still fought against it as uselessly as a middle-aged man fighting the idea of growing old.

'You gonna walk Akira to school wid me? I think she'd like dat,' she finished on a brighter note.

I took her hand and smiled, telling her yes, I'd like that too.

The grey of the morning matched the grey in my head as we followed the trail of parents and children gravitating towards a small red building. Akira skipped, sang and played around us, sometimes finding school buddies amongst the procession, always running back to tell us what new gossip she'd found, or jokes she'd heard. Seen this way, mother and child were an impressive team. Carmen was hailed many times. Almost every parent seemed to know Akira by name. It continued this way until we reached the school gates, where, after a quick peck on the cheek for each of us, she was spirited away by the sound of the bell, the laughter of her friends, the greetings of her teachers. Maybe I was just a little emotional of late, but I felt a lump in my throat as she ran into the doors, turned and gave one last wave, then disappeared. I felt a little stupid; after all, I hardly knew her. However, when I looked at Carmen a mirror of my feelings was cast over her features, the corners of her mouth turned down. We pulled wry faces. *C'est la vie*.

'She's amazing,' I complimented sincerely. 'I've never met a kid like her. I've never met *anyone* like her.'

I'd already noted that my friend was always careful to speak very casually about her daughter. Despite that, there remained a note of barely withheld love whenever her name was mentioned.

'Yeah, dat's my Akira. Quiet, but deadly. Takes after my mum in dat respect innit?'

'Oh yeah, definitely.'

We thought over the truth in that.

'Well, uh . . . About yuh money an' card,' Carmen stammered all of a sudden, looking a little embarrassed. 'Um . . . I think I know some people who might be able to get dem back.'

My quizzical look produced that braying donkey-like hee-haw of a laugh again. It was kind of hard to resist.

'Cee, I don't wanna know,' I chuckled with her. 'If you can that's good, but I don't want to know. Promise you won't tell me.'

'Girl Scout's Honour!' She stood to attention and saluted right there on the pavement, amongst all the buggies and parents and little dogs as cute as the children they'd been purchased for. 'Gimme your number and I'll call you in a coupla days whatever happens. OK?'

We swapped our details, then hugged tight again. There was no doubt that it felt good after the loneliness I'd been fighting for months. Although my physical needs had now been fed, my spiritual loneliness had endured. Previously, there had been no one to confide in, no one I could talk to and expose my weaknesses. The release of speaking my mind to someone I could trust was a joyful feeling of weightlessness, a loosening of my chest. I relished the newfound emotion as we walked back to Carmen's block, swearing once again to stay in each other's lives.

'Ay Vinnie, I hope you bin sensible wiv all dem girlies,' she stated roughly, as we reached the car park. I gave a thin smile and shrugged. Looked at the pavement, said nothing.

'You used protection, right?' Carmen demanded, eyes wide.

'Well . . . No, but it was kind of difficult at the time—'

The creamy palm of her hands flashed in front of my face before I'd even started explaining myself.

'OK, don't say nuttin'! You're a big man an' dere's nuttin' I can say that you don't already know, so I won't even bovva. Jus' don't do it no more will you? Can you promise me dat?'

The seriousness of her request took me by surprise. I watched her stern face to make sure I hadn't misjudged her manner, then nodded when I realised that, no, she wasn't making a joke.

'I promise, Cee. I know it was stupid.'

'Well as long as yuh do,' she responded, her tone dismissive in the extreme, similar to the voice she'd used with Akira when ordering her to get ready for school. 'I'll call you.'

'Sure . . .'

Watching Carmen go inside the block, I turned over her words. She was right, of course. Although my sexual conquests of late had been the stuff of fantasies, I stood to lose a lot more than my wallet could hold if I didn't begin taking precautions. Part of me was chuffed that someone was concerned about my well-being in that way. In fact, it made a more than welcome change. Inside my car, I remembered scenes from the morning's adventure and was forced into manic laughter. How close had I come to ruining my life? With

that thought in mind, I phoned Sadie and told her I was sick
with a stomach bug, then went home to think over my next
move in the cold light of day.

It took until the morning after next for me to remember
Dominique.

16

Through all of the flattery, all of the information, all of the sex, Dominique had never mentioned the fact that Viali had a brother. She had to have known of his existence; she'd lived with the girl and knew Robert Walker too, so their secret must have come out at some point. We hadn't spoken since Robert Walker died, another task that had been swept under the carpet as I dealt with every new element of the case. As I was technically finished, there was no need to rectify the matter, but I was still annoyed that Dominique had ... Well, not exactly lied to me, but not told the whole truth, either. Looking through my notepad I saw her work address scribbled on the inside cover: a video drama project back in Ladbroke Grove. After ladling Whiskas for the MIA Renk, I left my house, on full alert for any unwanted visitors.

The previous day and night hadn't managed to change my mind where quitting was concerned, yet I needed to know the truth as Dominique saw it. My inquisitive mind would never let me go through the agony of wondering why she hadn't passed the information on; moreover, I felt that I was owed some kind of explanation. Deep within, I told myself that going to see Dominique changed nothing. I was investigating for myself, nobody else. Even then, I could feel Carmen's magic words working on me, though I was taking great pains to pretend it wasn't so.

The project was located in the back of what looked like an old primary school, though time had eroded its magnificence until the beauty of the building could only be imagined. Inside, I was directed up stairs to a plain, unvarnished wooden door. Knocking twice, I was commanded to enter. Doing so, I stepped into the midst of unchecked chaos.

Video cameras, the guts of video cameras, tapes, monitors, computers and people were all crammed into a space that would have looked large if it were empty. A wooden partitioned area at the far end of the room was set up as two separate digital-editing suits placed side by side. One of the doors was wide open. I saw a Macintosh G4 wired up to smaller, more compact-looking cameras than the ones under repair in front of me. Heading towards the first person I saw, I asked for Dominique, only to be pointed in the direction of the closed editing suite.

A knock and push revealed her dressed in Africanwear once more, sitting with some young white kids while carefully going over the fundamentals of a computerised editing system. Until I made my appearance, the youths were hanging onto her every word. The expression on each face was slightly annoyed at the interruption.

'Hey, Ervine.'

Dominique's tone was neutral, her smile faint and subdued. My entrance had sobered the room in less than five seconds.

'I just wanted a quick word about some news I found concerning Robert Walker. You *do* know what happened to Robert, don't you?'

'Yes,' she mumbled quickly, shooting a glance at the young men. 'Give me a moment you guys. Tell you what, see if you can drop that scene in, the one we transferred with Billy in the park. If it doesn't work, we don't have to save it. I'll be back in a moment.'

The boys nodded and leant forwards, their concentration gratefully directed at the computer screen. I stood to one side to let Dominique pass, following her out of the room and down some stairs into an even smaller film-maker's stock room. There, I was surrounded by rows of videotape boxes, each one numbered and filed in alphabetical order, stacked on shelves rigged as high as the flaky ceiling allowed. Dominique pushed the door shut, locking it with a key she produced from her pocket. When she turned my way, her eyes were downcast and wary.

'What's wrong?' she asked wearily.

I got straight to the point, telling her everything Charles Muhammad had passed on about Viali's half-brother, passion and anger fuelling my words. Part of me expected her to react with outrage or shock. Instead, she threw up her hands and laughed.

'It's no official secrecy act, Ervine, the whole family just thought it'd be better if he was kept out of the spotlight! Mason's nothing special, they only keep quiet about him 'cos Robert didn't want the media prying into his private life. No one was hiding anything! If Charles made out we were, he's havin' you on. It's common knowledge Robert had a son, believe me!'

I hated being played for a fool, then have the person make out like it was all in my mind, a hallucination. Dominique wasn't going to get away with it this time. I wanted to throw a spanner into her works, and though I knew that following my instincts was a risk, deep down I relished the thought, even after all my previous misgivings about the validity of my talents.

'You had an affair with Robert, didn't you Dominique? That's how close you had to be to find out that secret of his, wasn't it?'

She gave me a harsh look, then couldn't hold my enquiring gaze and dropped her eyes, coughed once, put a shaky-yet-clenched fist to her mouth and began to cry, all in rapid-fire succession. For once, I was not drawn into sympathy by a display of grief. Digging for tissues, I ended up passing her the whole packet, disappointment a hard and sizeable ball in my chest. She blew her nose loudly, cursing in a bunged-up manner. Someone brutally knocked the stock room door. When there was no answer, they turned the handle insistently. Dominique jumped to attention, rounding on our unseen intruder.

'Jus' give us five minutes!' she screeched loudly, her voice roaming several octaves in one sentence.

'Am I right?'

I had to be persistent if I wanted an answer, though I couldn't help feeling that it was cruel to behave this way. Dominique was blowing and nodding all at the same time.

'Yeah, we had an affair. How did you know?' she whispered in disbelief. I shrugged, refusing to let my pride get the better of me like back in Muhammad's office.

'That's what I do. It makes perfect sense that if you knew something that secret, your relationship with Robert had to be closer than just being Viali's flatmate. That was it. Now can you tell me how long you were seeing him?'

It turned out it hadn't been long, a matter of them sleeping together four or five times over the course of the three years Viali lived with Dominique. The first time was completely unexpected, she told me. Robert had come to see Viali and, finding she wasn't in, he'd stayed around, which eventually led to a sexual encounter. Dominique said all this as if it were a chemical equation, x plus y equals sex. When I asked if they were scared Viali might have caught them, she told me yes. Of course, that only added to the excitement.

From then on, they met up twice as a planned escapade, when he came to the flat while Viali was at work, and once as an attempt to curb their desires which led to more sex. The last two encounters were due to the fact that they were supposed to have parted, but Walker had 'talked her round'. Strengthening Dominique's guilt was the knowledge that, to this very day, his wife didn't have a clue what they'd done. As I listened, I had to wonder who else Walker might have slept with. Had Emilia guessed what her husband was really like? I reckoned that if she knew about this half-brother, she must have had an inkling of his desires, which in turn would make the widow another tentative suspect in his murder. That didn't exactly fill me with joy.

Unable to listen to Dominique's confession anymore, I changed subject, asking if she knew more of the brother: his full name and exact address, for example. This was a long shot bound to miss. Dominique only knew that his name was Mason Nathaniel Booth, and he lived somewhere in Leicester, only don't ask the exact place. By then, annoyance at what I'd heard about her antics with Walker had seeped into my bones. Though I'd believed I was immune on an emotional level, I could barely hide my displeasure. Snapping my notebook shut, I decided to leave before my feelings made me say something that I later wished I'd kept an afterthought.

'Why don't you look in Viali's diary? The one that you took from her room?' Dominique offered enthusiastically.

'I'll do that,' I told her truthfully, moving towards the locked door. 'Now I better get on with things. I'll see you about.'

I could see Dominique was trying to get me on-side again, and unwilling as I was for this to happen, deep down I knew she *had* given me good advice. I'd forgotten about the diary since taking it from Viali's bedroom and depositing it inside my office drawer. Maybe it could help me crack a few more secrets.

She lightly touched my right arm. Within my mind, a voice screamed at her to stop. This was translated into body language that also begged her to reconsider her actions. There was no chance of that, judging by the keen look in her eyes.

'You gonna call me?' she breathed, unable to turn the question into a statement, as I imagine she might've meant it.

I stopped in my tracks and ran through a thousand diplomatic answers, even though they all came to the same conclusion. In the end, I thought it best that I speak the truth.

'No. No, I don't think so, Dominique.'

She took it bravely enough, swallowing hard and looking me face on, though her eyes sparkled unnaturally as she unlocked the stock room door.

'OK. Like you said, I'll see you around.'

'Yeah, see you around,' I shot over my shoulder.

I walked past her and into the corridor, only to step into the midst of stares emanating from curious students. Concern for Dominique and distrust of me fought a strange-looking battle on the gathered faces. Ignoring their dirty looks, I kept moving, making sure I walked out that building with my head held high and without a backward glance.

Paranoid, I checked every parked car around me before I got into my own and drove an intricate route back to my office. As much as I was enjoying the idea of being out in the field, it wasn't fair leaving Sadie to fend for herself. Though I knew she could cope, the last thing I wanted was for her to feel rejected or ignored; right about now, I needed her in good spirits. A vague plan was beginning to hatch. When I reached my office I'd phone Emilia and give her the bad news, then see if I could take on a few smaller projects, ones where I felt that I knew what I was doing. Today's victory proved that I had some detective skills at least. It was important to remind myself of the fact.

The curveballs came thick and fast from the moment I walked into Sadie's neat and tidy domain, leaving me little time to contemplate the plan I'd only recently constructed. The first came with the sight of Carmen Sinclair sitting on one of my waiting room chairs, talking eagerly with Sadie as if they'd known each other their whole lives. Akira was with her mother, sitting on the reception desk exposing scuffed knees, so busy drawing with coloured pencils that she didn't even notice me. The two women turned my way with embarrassment, as if they'd been caught in the midst of some terrible gossip.

'Hi Vinnie!'

Even though Carmen clearly sensed the vibe, she tried her best to pretend nothing was amiss by wearing a broad banana-shaped smile across her open face. She was conservatively dressed today, in a simple beige skirt and jacket with a thin, elegant black blouse to match. Her curly hair was tied severely against her head, leaving a modest ponytail dangling, giving her a streamlined, no nonsense look.

'Hey Carmen. How you doin' Akira, Sadie?'

I did the rounds by kissing each female on the cheek, then stood up and looked around questioningly, waiting for an explanation. Akira drew and spoke to herself beneath her breath. The women boldly returned my stare, leaving a moment of pensive quiet hanging in the room.

'Some letters came,' Sadie informed distantly, passing them over. I frowned at her unusual manner, taking the envelopes and scanning through while turning my attention towards Carmen.

'So what brings you here so soon?'

She gave me that fruity smile again.

'I jus' come to check on yuh Vin, make sure tings was OK since the other day. I tol' you, I ain' lettin' you go easy dis time round!'

Sadie laughed a little self-consciously. I suddenly realised she might think Carmen was the mystery woman I'd promised to tell her about when she'd caught me on the mobile leaving Dominique's house. That would account for some of her strange behaviour at least.

'D'you wanna come into my office a minute?' I asked my old friend, finally deciding this weird situation called for some privacy. Carmen agreed. After telling Akira to stay outside with Sadie, she followed me through, all modest perfume and clip-cloppy heels. By this time, I was frowning to myself. Something was going on. Even though I was eager enough to prise information from Carmen, I maintained a calm manner as I drew out a seat for her and went around the desk for my own. Once the office door snicked shut behind us, Carmen wasted little time.

'You know I'm yuh bes' friend, right?' she grinned, making her dimples appear at double their usual depth. I rubbed my temple blindly, feeling the pulse.

'You're funny, man . . . Yeah, of course you are. Why, what's up?'

Without a beat, she pushed a hand into her pocket and brought it out holding another envelope. She handed it over.

'It's not all there, but I got the credit card and most of the cash back,' she told me brightly.

It was true. I opened the envelope to find £180 in crumpled and dirty notes; over half of the £300 lavender-dress had stolen. The card had already been stopped, as I'd given up hope of retrieving it, though I could now rest assured that my hard-earned money wasn't being spent by someone else. I looked up at my friend, who was wearing a what-the-hell-did-you-expect type of expression. It suited her.

'You said you didn't wanna know, so don't ask me about the crack dealers on the landin' below dat scare living daylights out ah dem squatters. Don't ask me about anythin'. Please.'

Laughing, I peeled off fifty pounds and passed it over the desk with great flourish. Carmen smiled in thanks, taking the money and pocketing it without any hesitation. I had to smile at that, secretly glad she hadn't given me the old, 'oh no, I shouldn't' routine. When she was done, she relaxed and looked around the office, taking stock of my gathered possessions as if she'd only just noticed them.

'So, yuh thought about what I said the other day, Vinnie?' she finally exploded, as if the words had been beating for freedom against her lips. I covered my eyes with my fingers, only to hear that hysterical laugh once again. So that was what this scene was *really* about.

'Come on, man, wha' you goin' on like dat for, you must ah thought about it a moment! Sadie says you ain' even bin in fuh the last two days, so you had time.'

'I hope you haven't been tellin' her what I told *you*,' I rasped in reply. 'I thought you two looked a bit overfriendly.'

Carmen waved a tiny hand in dismissal.

'*Nah* man, not at all. But she's worried about you, Vinnie, it's obvious. We're *all* worried about you, even Akira. You know how perceptive kids are. Yesterday she says to me, "How come Uncle Ervine's so sad—"'

'*Uncle Ervine?*'

Though you couldn't tell by my tone, I was pleased with my new moniker.

Carmen smiled and continued.

'Yeah, uncle! I tol' yuh she loves you off but yuh don't wanna believe me. Anyway, I was talkin' to Sadie an' we come to the agreement yuh takin' on too much, Vin. It's not right you got all dis responsibility on yuh shoulders. No one can take dat kinna weight without bucklin'.'

I didn't like where this was leading. Carmen was talking too much like a runaway train, almost impossible to slow down or stop. Nevertheless, I was still curious.

'So?' I challenged.

'So, I think it's time you considered a division of duties.'

She seemed very proud of that sentence, sitting before me looking smug, even though I didn't get it.

'A *what*?'

'A division of duties. Meanin', I think it's time you get yuh-self a partner. Meanin' me.'

So there it was. I slumped in my seat. The thought of a partner was a theory that had long been banished, and the thought that it could be Carmen was in a realm all by itself, an undiscovered country. I honestly didn't know what to say. Although it wasn't exactly the most repellent idea in the world, it wasn't the best either and I knew that my musing was showing all over my face. I'd never liked the idea of a partner, a sidekick; it always seemed as though that person would become an extra burden, someone that would slow me down, get in my way, argue with my methods. Worst of all, I was such a loner there was bound to be some clash of person-ality somewhere along the way. I couldn't even imagine being out in the field with Sadie.

The positive thing about Carmen's offer was that I knew the personality clash was never going to happen, unless she'd changed in some drastic way. I'd seen no evidence of that yet. The negative was she had no clue about detective work, she'd already showed as much. Without meaning to, my friend had put me right back where I was the day I'd left Robert Walker's house with Emilia's plea ringing in my ears. Should I or shouldn't I?

'Carmen, man—'

In response to my lame words, my almost rejection, she leaned forwards and seized what she seemed to think was her moment.

'*What* Vinnie? What? You're blatantly strugglin' wiv dis job an' I can help, yuh know I can help. To tell you the truth I do need some work, or I wouldn't be askin' . . . Still, the way dis could run, both of us would get what we want don't yuh reckon? I got some ideas fuh you too, cos I've bin thinkin' about the case an' . . .'

She broke off when she saw I was sighing heavily. This was not the kind of thing that I wanted to deal with. My good feelings were dissipating as fast as sugar in cappuccino. Fragile as I'd become these days, I really didn't need this scene.

'All right, Cee, can I jus' open my letters an' think about it?'

'Sure,' she agreed cordially. 'D'yuh want me to wait outside?'

'Nah, it's cool, you can stay. I'll only be a minute.'

Feeling the weight of her eyes, I picked up the first of the envelopes and ripped it open, guessing rightly that it was a bill. My electricity bill to be exact – sixty-three pounds. Despite myself, I cursed for giving the fifty away so readily. Mentally discarding both the letter and that thought, I turned my attentions to the next. It was a plain white envelope, with next to no markings. Tearing it open, I revealed the back of a cheque. Carmen sniffed elegantly.

'The Lord giveth an' the Lord taketh away,' she commented in a hushed voice, referring to the bill, something she readily recognised. I gave her a funny look, which she returned in kind, then focused my attention back on the cheque in my hands, flipping it right side up.

The amount was made out for ten thousand pounds, signed by Mrs Emilia Walker.

I could hear Carmen asking what was up as I read the note that came with the payment, saying she was impressed with how I'd grown up, how Ryder had expressed his confidence in my abilities, and how in her heart of hearts she knew that I'd do what was required. That was all it took. Though to be perfectly honest, it wasn't Carmen or even the words on the page that tipped the balance. It was the sight of all those noughts behind that perfectly formed ten. Ten grand. Call me mercenary, but I'd have to be crazy to turn that down, no matter what I thought of my abilities, and I wasn't going to.

Which meant I may need some help after all.

Over my euphoria, I remembered Carmen was in the office with me. She craned her head to see what had affected me so, half-leaning over the desk in eagerness. When I raised my head, she had the presence of mind to back off and regain some poise.

'What's dat all about?' she quizzed. Ignoring her, I focused on my own immediate needs; like any man, most women would probably say.

'Carmen, listen carefully, this is very important. I want you to tell me your ideas on how we should move on with this case. Better still, tell me what you think the next step is.'

'What, now?'

'Yes, right now. This very minute.'

I waited with a feeling of excitement. This seemed right and I wanted her in, needed her in if I was going to take that money, yet the bottom line was, she had to be good. Carmen fulfilled every criterion I could think of, and what she didn't have could be taught, but she had to be very good.

'OK . . . I would . . . Umm . . .'

Come on, my mind prompted impatiently. She was blushing from chin to forehead, her jaw moving like the mouths of the deaf mutes I'd seen back at the strip club.

'I would . . . Try look at all the suspects . . .'

Damn. That was bullshit talk.

'. . . An' I would see which one ah dem I hadn't spoken to . . . See, I was thinkin' the only person you ain' seen dat figured in her life is the brudda. So you might as well tick him off yuh list seein' as he's the unknown factor an dat . . .'

Carmen stopped when she glanced at me to see if I was following, then noticed my smile. Her dimples naturally reappeared.

'Is dat OK?'

I couldn't help chuckling. My old friend was charming and smart without even trying. I couldn't believe I hadn't noticed that two days ago. Now the blinkers were fully removed, I was never putting them back on, I promised myself that much.

'You were perfect, Carmen. *Fucking* perfect. Now I just got one more question. D'you ever have trouble finding a babysitter?'

She was grinning with me now, allowing herself time to realise what that meant.

'Nah, no trouble, Vinnie. No trouble at all,' she beamed.

17

I had to bring Carmen up to speed on all of the evidence I'd gathered: the files Birkett had given me, the information Viali wrote in her diary, even my hasty shorthand notes were all taken to her Peckham flat and laid out on the living room floor. While Akira was told to go and play, we pored over everything, a task that lasted well into the night. It was good to have someone else's opinion, and very good that the questions Carmen asked made me think deeper about our suspects and their motivations. Much later, Akira tottered out of her room way past her normal bedtime of seven, looking sleepy and frustrated at her confinement. As soon as she'd been night-dressed, told a story and tucked in, Carmen came back bearing two mugs of tea. We continued until she complained she'd go mad with all she'd learned. By then, it was almost one in the morning.

I spent the night in Carmen's flat, sleeping on her sofa.

After surfacing only to behold another seamlessly cloudy London sky, I got straight on the phone to call Emilia and thank her for her money, but more importantly, to get the low down on Viali's half-brother. This was a difficult subject to broach. It's not easy to talk to a widow about the illegitimate son of her recently deceased husband. True to form, she responded willingly enough, giving me all the details she possessed, including his full name and address, along with a mobile number. By that time, Carmen and Akira were going through their daily hair ritual. I quickly and politely got off the phone.

'Mason Nathaniel Booth is twenty-one, mixed-race, and lives five minutes' drive away from Leicester centre,' I told them self-importantly.

'Dat's up north, right?' Carmen frowned into the back of her daughter's head.

'Yeah – well, the Midlands anyway.'

'S'up north to *me*,' she grumbled moodily. I'd forgotten how gloomy Carmen could be in the mornings. Still she'd partly talked me into this shit; there was no way I was going easy on her.

'So d'you think we should go up to Leicester? Could your sitter look after Akira?'

Carmen pulled a face that was clearly negative.

'I gotta ask her first ain' I? Tell you what, though, I don't even think we should rush to go up dere yet. Not before we've checked out a few more tings down dis way. An' you *know* what I'm talkin' about . . .'

It was my turn for a morose expression. Last night, Carmen clearly and precisely pointed out that unless I engaged my prime suspects, I was unable to either wipe them from my list or attach the murder to them. Without their interview I was stuck in a rut of my own making, which might have contributed to the fact that I'd been running around chasing my own tail for so long. She made me promise to go back to

Eltham to face the men who were behind my attack in Soho, though she agreed the smart move was to join forces with Charles Muhammad and the Nation before I went 'bowling down there', as she put it.

We cleared up our mess, locking up and dropping Akira with a curiosity-drunk neighbour who looked me up and down appreciatively, then winked Carmen's way before ushering her little girl inside the flat. Amused at the neighbour's antics, I noticed myself watching Carmen as we rode the lift to the ground floor, and slipped through a fire exit into the car park where my Audi was waiting. Today, she'd left the corporate look alone, going for jeans and a simple tracksuit top, along with trainers and a casual light jacket. Earlier, when I'd asked her about her choice of clothes, she'd said she needed something to run in, which didn't help my worries. Pushing the thought into a corner of my mind, I found myself unable to keep from staring as I unlocked my car doors.

Carmen had always been cute and fresh-faced in school. These days, her younger self hid deep beneath the surface of her skin, emerging only in a stray smile or sassy glance, both of which remained as they'd always been. Her eyes were still intelligent, large and brown, but where there had once been true innocence, time had cast a shadow that darkened her features no matter how brightly they attempted to shine. Where her skin had once been smooth, it now bore marks that hinted at her age. Where her smile had been full and unchecked, it was now weighted with hesitance. Only her freckled nose betrayed a faint trace of the former tomboy that had so frustrated our male friends. When we were kids, young men from my estate would have loved to get with Carmen, even though they knew she'd never been particularly interested in guys. Not that she was into women; Carmen was just one of those teenagers who turned their back on the whole girlie thing. Somewhere along the line she'd decided that guys, especially the ones around our way, looked like they were having more fun.

Though her innocence had faded, something just as strong had grown to replace it. There was an assured confidence in my old friend, something unshakable within her psyche. Her serene air made her all the more whole in my eyes. Finally, I saw what my friends had noticed all those years ago.

Carmen realised that I hadn't turned the ignition, giving me another of her belittling looks, even as she smiled faintly.

'Wha' you doin', Vinnie man? I thought we had to get on.'

Turning to face her, I started the car just to show that I was aware of her concerns.

'How come you haven't got a man around you, Carmen? I know you've got Akira, but she's a lovely kid an' you still look great. You're not old enough to be a grass widow.'

She gave an ironic little laugh, looking out of her window and watching the school kids racing past kicking tennis balls. Their screams faded into nothing while she stared pensively. I heard her sigh long before the answer.

'How'd you know I ain' got a man?'

I shrugged, even though I knew that she couldn't quite see me.

'I don't know that at all. So, have you?'

Carmen turned back to me. Despite our surroundings and everything else I guessed she'd experienced and hadn't told me yet, those brown eyes still twinkled like the North Star.

'I think you should drive, Vinnie. A woman's gotta have some secrets, even from a detective innit?'

I grunted an agreement and left it at that. My query was gone, though definitely not forgotten.

Back at South Bank, Carmen suggested that we take down the Viali posters and try making one-to-one contact with people who might live or work in the numerous buildings lining the Thames. As my phone had never rung with a call from any witness, I was decidedly sceptical, yet Carmen was so eager and enthusiastic I was convinced into giving it a go. We reached the riverside to find a light drizzle falling, the odour from rain-blackened concrete permeating the air. People ran from shelter to shelter with coats over heads, while the sky above them resembled a dirty woollen blanket. Carmen grumbled and flipped up her hood as we set about visiting pillars and walls where I'd placed Viali posters. We split up to save time, each working yards from the other.

As I did my rounds, I was disheartened and sickened by the evidence which proved why I hadn't been inundated with calls. Some pillars that I knew I'd covered were bare. Others still bearing posters now wore funny faces, big tits, or had the letters NF scribbled over them. Other pillars had only half a poster left. The more I saw, the further my desperation grew. Up ahead, I could see Carmen marching from spot to spot without a pause, occasionally stopping to waylay the odd passer-by and ask if they'd seen anything that night. Forcing my despair to the back of my mind, I continued until we reached the entrance to a small subway, where Carmen returned to my side. I had to laugh at the sight of her stomping animatedly back to me, the green hood along with her diminutive size making her look like a rogue character from a Tolkien novel.

'Shut up you,' she blasted in response to my laughter. There was a scrunched up collection of posters in her hand, and a thick wad of Blu Tack. The exertion of the walk had sent blood rushing to her face, though I could swear she was enjoying herself.

'How far d'yuh put dese things anyway?' she continued unchecked.

'A little way past the Globe Theatre.'

'Where the hell's dat?' she squealed indignantly.

'Just before the next bridge along,' I pointed, knowing the gesture meant nothing. 'Come on, we've done most of them anyway.'

We entered the subway, ignoring a resident homeless couple holding court with a sign, a scrawny dog and tattered old blanket. I was surprised to see most of the posters here were up and relatively unharmed. Stripping them from this surface was no problem, so I rapidly moved along the wall while Carmen did the same on the opposite side. The mechanical nature of the work ensured that I eventually became lost in deep thought. When I finished and looked back the way I'd come, I noticed the homeless couple solemnly watching us work. Taking a look at the shape of their blanket, I could see their hands tightly linked beneath the material. Another hunch tickled my brain.

'*Hey!*' I called loudly, almost startling the wits out of Carmen. '*Hey!*'

My voice echoed spookily in the subway confines. The homeless couple stiffened and held their heads straight, facing the green tiled wall in front of them as if they hadn't heard a thing. I made a big deal out of pretending to curse myself, then tried again at much the same volume.

'*See anything suspicious the night when that young woman was killed? Her name's Viali Walker. She—*'

'What the fuck are you doin'?' Carmen hissed suddenly from my side. She'd appeared out of nowhere, pulling her hood down viciously and glaring up at me with a look of disgust.

'They might've seen something, Cee,' I began feebly. She was smart enough to pull me up immediately.

'So? Wha' yuh gonna do, shout it out of 'em? Damn, Vinnie, yuh gotta learn how to deal wiv people!'

Then she was off, marching her resolute way towards the homeless couple, each of them watching her approach gingerly. So far so good. When she finally reached the duo, I could tell she was introducing herself as the good girl and me as the bonehead, which was all great now passion of truth was flavouring her words. I saw the homeless couple nodding along with Carmen, then begin to reply in stilted bits and bobs, which lengthened the further their conversation progressed. My good cop–bad cop introduction had borne fruit. Finally, Carmen squatted beside the couple talking ten to the dozen, and they let her. Perfect. She'd proved herself yet again. There'd be no more tests for Carmen, save the situations I couldn't possibly manufacture. And I was sure there would be plenty of those.

Moving slowly, so as not to further corrupt my bad impression, I headed for the homeless couple's spot. Their grimy faces were thin and malnourished, their eyes dead, as if they'd already taken in far too much for any normal human being. Like a TV with just one little light to let you know that they still functioned, these kids were forever on standby. And they *were* children really. No more than twenty, either of them. While most of their generation raved, worked or studied, here they were camped out in a damp and dreary subway as a living symptom of London's diseased streets. Who knew whether they'd be rescued, or if they'd plunge into an abyss so deep I could find them thirty years from now, drinking Kestrel to numb the pain of rejection and wearing faces the wrong side of eighty.

By the time I reached the youths, Carmen had both flowing in steady discussion. If there was one thing she was an expert at, it was the art of communication. The young man was a tortured white kid, sporting bleached blond hair Eminem-style. The girl beside him was an Asian whose baleful stare reminded me of a mournful Cocker Spaniel. Their mongrel lounged between them, a head between its paws as though the idle chatter of humans drove it to boredom. Carmen heard me coming and stood up excitedly, the dog's head rising with her. Her murderous expression had disappeared like a boiled sweet on the tongue.

'Dis is Hadiah and David. Guys, dis is my partner, Ervine James. Vinnie, these guys think they saw something. They're more than prepared to tell us what they know.'

The couple was still busy looking blankly at the green tiles before them, but my heart went out to both of them all the same. They looked so pitiful and defeated with their blanket around their knees.

'Only if you promise to call me Davey,' the bleached blond guy quipped, as heartily as his situation allowed. His girlfriend smiled faintly, though her face was coloured with slight distrust. Based on my earlier behaviour, I couldn't blame her.

'I promise,' I grinned, the hope of their assent behind my attempt to win points and confidence in one go. 'Let's find somewhere we can talk with a little more privacy . . .'

The Globe Theatre had a small restaurant area on the second floor. Our witnesses tied up their dog (who was introduced as Mister), then we took them upstairs and gave them the run of the lunch menu. Before we knew what had happened our table was laden with soups, home-made burgers and drinks, yet they finished the lot and left their plates virtually spotless. I quickly realised Hadiah's quiet nature couldn't be ascribed to simple mistrust. She was shy, the type my elders liked to call 'inner'. Davey, on the other hand, was a South London wide boy whose mouth, once revved up, could run like an Olympic medallist. Despite these and their more obvious differences, it was easy to see the two were both deeply in love. By the time the meal was over, Carmen and I swapped amused looks of agreement. It was clear we liked them both. When Davey had burped and farted his appreciation (not giving a damn who heard him), we settled down to hear a twin account of Viali's last night on earth.

In a quiet whisper of a voice, Hadiah said she'd spotted Viali walking through the subway with the four skinheads in tow. She couldn't see their faces clearly, though she did notice they were fairly nondescript, dressed not in stereotypical skinhead gear, but Nike trainers, plain shirts and puffer jackets. In fact, the only resemblance they had to the racists of my parents' era was the butchered number one cut that had become a world-wide symbol of abuse. Hadiah asked the men for change as they passed the couple's spot, and was rewarded with a sullen look from the largest of the four. Viali turned and dropped some money in their hat, then rolled her eyes and chastised the men, while walking on. When they left the subway, Hadiah commented about the glance she'd received. Davey urged her to forget it, which before long proved impossible.

'Would you remember their faces if you saw them again?' I asked seriously. Carmen was quiet beside me, focused on every word said.

'Probably,' Davey confirmed. Hadiah nodded.

'How were they acting towards each other?'

'Like best friends,' Hadiah muttered, almost inaudibly.

This suspicious aspect of Viali's final night was still very strange. It was clear they'd befriended her in some way before her death. But why had she trusted them so easily?

Hadiah continued by saying they sat in that spot for a further forty-five minutes before cold moved them on. Wrapping up their blanket, they put a ragged lead on Mister, heading for Southwark Bridge. Just before they reached the concrete steps, Davey thought he heard raised voices coming from a nearby alleyway; Bear Gardens, no doubt. They stopped and listened until the cries were so loud even passing pedestrians took notice. Mister began to growl aggressively in that direction.

Davey readily admitted his initial reaction was a desperate urge to leave the area. He would have followed the inclination if his girlfriend hadn't clearly heard a woman scream. She urged him to investigate.

'So we walked down the alleyway . . .' Davey narrated in a cold, toneless voice. 'The closer we got, the more we could tell summit weren't right. Mister was barking, which they must've 'eard 'cos this massive bloke comes out from round a corner an' tells us to turn around an' go back. Real polite about it, no trouble, even though you could tell he was hard as fuck. Anyone could see that.'

'The same guy from the subway?' Carmen broke in.

'Yeah.'

You could almost see the memory dancing across Davey's forehead as he winced. Beside him, Hadiah's face was similarly set.

'Describe him,' my voice demanded gently. I took out my notepad, almost unwilling to break the confession-like calm that had overtaken both boy and girl. They spoke in polite turns, reaching unconsciously for each other as the words spilled like the trickle of water from a faulty tap.

'He was *huge*, fuckin' huge . . .' Hadiah remembered.

'. . . Had a head like a basketball, little piggy eyes an' no neck . . .'

'. . . Had a scar on his cheek, really big it was . . .'

'. . . An 'ee was like . . . kinda bald, like Phil Mitchell, yuh know, an' as big as one ah dem WWF geezers. Not as much muscle, though, he looked fat t'me . . .'

The couple stared at each other questioningly, before nodding once.

'Is that all right?' Hadiah finished, as she invited Carmen and myself back into their orbit. I smiled as I wrote.

'That's brilliant, really,' I agreed truthfully. The couple looked relieved.

'So what happened after dat?' Carmen persisted. The Asian girl cleared her throat, turning her head towards the window and the tugboats floating on a murky Thames.

Hadiah, unlike the wilting flower persona my mind had created for her, had refused to back down, asking Mystery Man why they couldn't pass. As he attempted to concoct some story, Mister began to bark with more frenzy. Just as Mystery Man's violence began to bubble to the surface, Davey decided to let the dog go. A dumb thing to do, but kind of brave nonetheless. While the man turned, distracted, the couple took the opportunity presented and raced past him on the pretext of chasing their wilful mutt. Davey's plan proved successful – to a degree.

It was clear that when the youths rounded that corner, they reached a turning point in their lives, never to be retraced. This was made evident by Hadiah's muffled sniffling, the way Davey's jokes dried up, the way they both began to shiver as though the temperature had dropped ten degrees. Carmen wrapped an arm around the Asian girl while I rubbed consolingly on Davey's back, although we were painfully aware we could do no more. What they had seen would remain with them until they reached their graves. There was nothing they could do to change that. All they were able to affect was the way they dealt with such an experience.

Hadiah, who had turned the corner first, saw the backs of many men along with quick glimpses of Viali. The student was being pushed by a man in the centre of the group, a tall, thin man who was shouting in the girl's face. In turn, Viali looked distraught to the point of hysteria. She was shouting something about murder until Mister's overzealous barking diverted the men towards the homeless youths. The assailants looked at each other, confused for a moment. One turned and walked their way just as Mystery Man came from the other direction.

Davey had been so busy calling Mister, he didn't see the fist descend on his temple, or hear Hadiah's scream. Next thing he knew, he was face down on the concrete with fireworks flashing before his eyes and Mister licking his face with a rough tongue, listening to the arguments above his head. He was dragged at least ten yards, then deposited on the cobblestones with a final warning from Mystery Man to stay away. Davey needed no more instruction. Though he sympathised with the black girl and agreed with his girlfriend's pleas that something should be done, he saw no reason for anything more to be done by them. Others had heard what was going on. On a busy stretch like this, *someone* would get involved. Wouldn't they?

The answer was written on their faces as they described how they'd run away, spending the next few weeks in hiding after they read of the murder in a discarded *Evening Standard*. Months later, they emerged and returned to the stretch of concrete they knew best. They were sitting at the top of some steps that led to the Charing Cross overhead walkway, when they were approached by a livid-looking Mystery Man. He threatened them at once, warning that they keep their mouths shut, or one of them would lose a companion. As he left, he reminded the couple of how laughably easy they'd been to find.

'Did you ever see him again?' Carmen asked, filling the silence with her thoughts.

'Yeah, after you stuck dem posters up,' Davey returned stoically. I gave a weak smile of guilt, though even that didn't last long when faced with their stone grey faces.

'So you saw them?'

'Uh huh,' Hadiah agreed with little enthusiasm. 'Wasn't long after the mystery guy came back, sayin' the same shit about us not talkin'. We said we hadn't talked by now, so why would we start?' Here, she began to smile hesitantly. 'I dunno ... I suppose we got pissed off, but that wasn't the reason we—'

'*I* got pissed *fuckin'* off,' Davey flamed, scowling at his empty plate, while I looked around at the other customers, scared they could hear. 'Who the *fuck* d'they think they are pushin' us around jus' cos we're homeless? Think they can take the piss. I'll grass on dem racist cunts, I don't give a fuck. What have I got to lose? *Fuck* 'em ...'

I stole a fearful look at Hadiah. It seemed as if she was angry too, although her steamy expression was aimed in her boyfriend's direction. Her arms were crossed and her eyebrows knitted tightly.

'Davey was gettin' *nightmares*,' she growled stiffly, looking at him, daring he say otherwise. He opened his mouth to try, took another glance at his girl, then checked himself and returned his eyes to the plate. I swapped another amused look with Carmen. Contrary to the size of his mouth, it was clear who wore the boxers in this relationship.

I noticed Carmen twitch her eyes twice in Davey's direction, instantly catching myself thinking, *Damn she's good.* Because she was. She was also correct when she claimed she knew how to deal with people, probably more right than she would ever know. Carmen realised that if we allowed Davey to continue feeling bad about himself, his neurosis would grow until we might be on the receiving end of his screamed profanities. If Carmen had noticed Davey's character traits so quickly, she must've also seen that as strong as Hadiah could be, she wouldn't act without her boyfriend's approval. Not for us anyway. With all of this supposition bouncing around my head, I leaned closer to Davey, attempting to insert a degree of comradeship.

'Is that why you decided to talk to us?' I breathed. Davey bit his lip and closed his eyes.

'He couldn't even *sleep*,' Hadiah insisted, just in case his silence wasn't confession enough. Perhaps hearing the accusation in her tone, she followed my lead and took his hand once more, rubbing tenderly, massaging knuckles and fingertips. Davey gratefully lapped up the attention.

'And you say this guy had a . . .' I looked at my notes, then back up at the couple. '. . . A scar on his cheek. Which one?'

'The left?'

Hadiah was frowning at her boyfriend.

'Yeah, it was the left, definitely,' he told us resolutely. 'Quite long, from jus' under his ear to one side ah his chin.'

Davey raised his head from his plate to find himself facing a warm circle of smiles. Carmen tapped my foot under the table with hers and gave me the thumbs up. I couldn't deny that it felt good.

We managed to dig a little further, even though it was easy to tell that the kids were emotionally spent. Their eyes grew heavy lidded, their speech slow, lethargic even. When they both left to use the toilets and the waitress cleared our table, I leaned closer to Carmen, grabbing her forearm and squeezing gratefully. 'Thanks, Cee. You've been something else. That's the biggest breakthrough I've had since I took this on,' I gushed.

In response, she rolled her eyes and pulled the most sarcastic grin I'd ever seen, then let her cheek muscles fall, returning to her former no-nonsense expression.

'Thanks, mate. I'd do even better wivout yuh silly little games thrown in fuh good measure.'

So she knew about my stunt in the subway. She looked far from pleased to see her suspicions confirmed. Edging away, I studied her to gauge how vex she really was.

'When did you realise?'

'As soon as yuh came back. You was so friendly an' open like usual, all the shoutin' an showin' yuhself up didn't make sense. It wasn't *professional*. The more I thought about it, the more I realised you're a guy dat does shit right, if yuh do it at all. An' dat was it.'

She was sneering in disdain at my feeble attempt to play her. I shook my head, a hand returning to her forearm while she cautiously watched my every move.

'*Woah!* I gotta be careful, you'll be runnin' my business if I don't watch out!' I half-joked. She gracefully shrugged off my hand along with my praise.

'C'mon, Vin, we was always playin' detective when we was kids; mainly 'cos you forced everyone to do it!' she teased, finally returning a grudging smile. 'I'm jus' glad yuh happy wid my work so far.'

'More than happy,' I enthused easily, equally glad that she wasn't too put out by my actions.

'So wha' d'we do?'

Carmen was right – we had to get back to business. After all, I could dwell on realisations about her when I was alone and in a relaxed enough state to think. If any of my hopes were false, I'd still found a smart and worthy friend. Warming to that idea, I followed the topic back to our homeless youths.

There was no way we could let them wander the London streets with the information they knew. Besides, the fact that they were our only key witnesses put these kids in daily mortal danger from The Foundation's thugs. Anytime the situation changed, those men could return to look for them, and I marvelled at how easily I could have been the cause of their deaths. The racists were following me, so I'd bet my cat that their eyes also remained on these kids.

'That guy,' I hissed at Carmen. 'The one that threatened them. Sounds like the same guy who roughed me up when I left Lipstick Parade.'

'You sure?' she frowned.

'Not one hundred per cent. We'll find out when we go to Eltham, won't we?'

Even with all my excitement, that thought still sent a wriggle of panic running down my spine.

'So what do we do wiv George an' Mildred?' Carmen chuckled, seemingly ignorant of my discomfort.

'Well, I can't really imagine The Foundation would dare come an' visit somewhere like Claybridge,' I mused tentatively, not sure how she'd take my plan. 'It'd be like church to a vampire or some shit like that. I reckon we take them to my mum's house, let them stay there for a bit, what d'you reckon? She uses my old room as a spare, so I know she's got space. They'll be safe, an' we'll know exactly where they are.'

Carmen's doubt echoed as loud as her laughter. I could grudgingly see her point; Tazanne was charitable enough, but dumping two adult strangers on her doorstep wasn't something she'd take to kindly. Although I agreed, I had neither the patience nor the inclination to argue. We had no choice. Carmen easily admitted that she had no other suggestions. More to the point, the youths were coming back hand-in-hand, looking as though they'd been talking just as intently.

When they reached our table, Hadiah made to sit until Davey restrained her, tugging absently at her shoulders, forcing her to straighten her legs back into a standing position. Carmen gave me an enquiring look as Davey took a deep breath and began his quick rehearsed speech.

'We've bin talkin',' he told us in an important tone. 'An' we was finkin'. Morals are all well an' good, but what's in it fuh us? We're riskin' our lives on the streets. What d'we get out of dis?'

A rush of relief flowed from me. I'd been scared they'd lied about needing to relieve themselves so they could run away; when they did turn up, I was sure it was only to inform me they'd changed their minds. Anything else the couple might want, I would find and present to them on a golden platter if I had to, they were needed that much. Luckily enough, Carmen's cheeky wink reinforced my belief that I might possess the price they were asking. Patting the seats they'd not long vacated, I offered my most pleasant expression, waving an absent hand for a nearby waiter.

18

The drive to Claybridge gave me time to reflect that I'd visited my former home more over the past couple of weeks than I had in the last 3 years. Regrettably, not that much had changed. The drunks sipping Super T and Kestrel still remained, as did groups of colourfully dressed youths lounging wherever they could find space. The pensioners, dealers and pram-wielding women were all still there. I began reluctantly picturing Dougie and Maya inserted into the tableau, doing just whatever they felt necessary in a place like this. Though it seemed strange, I'd only just realised how close their lives were to those of the people that I saw as I cruised through London's many manors. Up until recently, I'd viewed them as exceptions to the rule of the street, with little evidence to go on. I inwardly promised to try harder with them both, juggling that thought with mental preparation for the wrath of my mother.

Mum had been upset, as we'd predicted, even as she saw the serious side of our situation. I explained that while our intentions were always to offload any criminal information to the police, it was also best to check whether the evidence was true. This made for good relations, as well as keeping the nature of the work strictly professional. The last thing a PI needs is a suspect reputation. In the end, like any good Christian, she agreed to house the youths while we busied ourselves checking out their story. My relief was so acute it was physically draining.

The couple had been less than pleased with my plans for a temporary home, only perking up when I promised a thousand pounds of the money Emilia Walker had paid, as long as their evidence led to a conviction. I knew from her body language that my new partner disagreed. To me, it was clear there was little else to offer these uncaged birds in order to convince them to remain earthbound. I was yet to learn of my mistake. From that point onwards, Davey wouldn't stop talking about the things he'd buy and what he'd do with all that money. Cars, houses, private yachts, were all in easy reach if he were to be believed; indeed, he'd testify Jesus was black if it meant getting his hands on the money. Obviously, this wasn't the type of thing I wanted to hear. I wished someone else would say something to him before I had to. No such luck.

Carmen was quiet and contemplative, staring out at familiar blocks we'd called ours, an arm propping her chin, eyes shaded by dark glasses. Hadiah lay sleeping in the back seat, head thrown back and mouth wide open, looking not long dead. Mister was curled on her lap, equally motionless. Luckily, Davey ran out of steam as we approached my former home block, subdued by concrete buildings which stood like silent and foreboding gravestones.

Davey was one of those guys who play the ultimate lad until faced with a strong woman; meeting one, they behave like Mister, rolling over and exposing their soft underbelly. He was no different with my mother, oozing compliments and charm until we were laughing out loud, Mum along with the rest of us. After hugging Carmen half to death and tickling Mister the mongrel beneath his chin, Mum showed the couple to their room, where she informed us she'd spent a hurried forty-five minutes tidying the flat, thanks to me. Taking the resulting insults bravely, I held up my hands and left the youths, sitting in the kitchen with Mum and Carmen as she prepared some leftover food for her guests. As the women caught up on their respective lives, I helped myself to a bowl of rice and meat, heating it up in the microwave. When the bell rang, I headed for the table, my excitement barely in check.

'Boy, those guys dunno what they're in for. This come like the Yardie Hilton!' I joked between spoonfuls, as my mother and Carmen swapped dry looks. Mum pointed her ladle at me.

'Look, Ervine, don't tes' me bwoy. Me nuh 'ear frum you in weeks, den de nex' ting yuh know, yuh ah beg favour! Me 'ave a good mind to—'

'*Mum* . . . Mum . . .' I got up from my seat and crossed the room, reaching for a hand. She kissed her teeth and pulled away, even though I was relentless in my mission. Behind me, Carmen was laughing heartily.

'Beat 'im man,' she giggled. I felt a teacloth whip at my back.

'*Ow!* Hey, watch it . . . Mum . . .' I forced myself into my mother's sight line, letting her know by my face that I was serious. 'Mum, I need you to know that I appreciate what you've done for me. This case had me under some serious strain, but it won't happen again. I feel a lot better now I've got Carmen's help. So I'm sorry, OK? I love and appreciate you very much.'

I ended my sloppy speech with a sloppier kiss on her cheek

and a rib-cracking hug. Any normal woman would've screamed; Mum returned my gesture with all her might. Carmen applauded as if I'd performed a back flip in the confines of the kitchen.

'Apology accepted,' Mum said grudgingly. 'But yuh mus' realise yuh 'ave a family dat miss yuh, while some people 'ave none dem cyan call on. Ain' dat right, Carmen?'

Carmen gave me another whip with her dishcloth.

'Dat's right, Vinnie! Don't worry, Tazanne, I'm on his case now, he won't be able to slack no more!'

Noses high in the air, Hadiah and Davey floated into the kitchen, matching expressions of wonderment alive in their eyes. Davey's thin face was split with a lop-sided grin. Hadiah moved with her eyes half-closed and nostrils twitching like a racehorse.

'*Naah* . . . Mrs J, don't tell me dat's yuh cookin' smellin' like dat?' the white youth beamed in unbridled anticipation. My mother rounded on him. It was easy to see she was not amused.

'Now lemme tell you young people a few ting, yuh hear? Firs', call me Mrs James or call me Tazanne, nuh bodda wid no *Mrs J*. Yes? Second, yuh right, dis is my cookin'. If yuh waan food like dis yuh musse learn how to cook! So me will give yuh lesson, an if yuh nah waan learn, yuh nah eat! Unnu 'ave nuh slave in yasso!'

Davey and Hadiah stood through this onslaught, mouths wide open, noses filled with the aromatic scent of cooking meat. I knew what they were feeling. My mother used to have her children standing just like that, listening to her sermon long enough for our drool to create sticky puddles at our feet. Luckily for them, newcomers got the edited version. By the time they left this flat, they would know the true meaning of pain.

'. . . Third, yuh cyaan eat before yuh bathe. Not in dis house, not h'evah! An' me beg unnu pardon, but me believe yuh 'ave a lot ah bathin' fe do! Suh deal wid yuh business, an' when yuh done de food will be waitin' right where yuh lef' it! Gwaan nuh!'

They were both frowning at the patwa, yet had lived in London long enough to get the gist, turning meekly and leaving the kitchen in total compliance. Mum was struggling with her straight face, barely holding on long enough for their shadows to disappear from the walls.

Some time later that night, I sat on my bed with the phone by an ear and Renk purring at my feet. It'd been a long day, what with dealing with my mother, our witnesses, and the thought of what my errant siblings would say when they came back to find Hadiah and Davey treating their home like a youth hostel. Still, there was too much happening for me to worry about every move I'd made; besides, it'd already proven useless, so my new method of dealing with things was to worry about nothing.

Dialling Minister Charles Muhammad's number from his card, I waited for an answer, tickling Renk's chin as I listened. He picked up on the fourth ring. We talked for nearly fifteen minutes, catching up on the case and life in general before I asked for the favour I'd wanted, in truth, from the moment Dominique mentioned his name. Muhammad laughed, wondering what had taken me so long. He'd love to help; after all, wasn't that what the Nation was for? We arranged a time to meet before I rang off, and immediately dialled Carmen's number.

'Hello?'

In the background, Akira murdered a Destiny's Child song over the original. I spoke louder to drown her out.

'It's me, Carmen.'

'Oh hey, how'd it go?'

'It's done. I'll pick you up at half-eight.'

'No problem. See yuh den.'

'See you tomorrow.'

I put the phone down and relaxed on my bed.

We rode in a convoy of three vehicles. My Audi led, closely followed by a Space Cruiser occupied with ten suited Nation of Islam members. Behind them cruised Charles Muhammad's jet-black Granada. Jazz FM was on my radio, Abbey Lincoln playing soothingly in the background, once again matching my mood. Carmen, sitting in the passenger seat, had given me a disbelieving glance when I'd flipped the dial and music began to fill the car. By the time we got to Eltham she was laid back in her seat, eyes closed, a finger appreciatively tapping the dashboard.

The streets were silent and empty, just as they had been on my previous visit. Parking in much the same spot, I turned to Carmen and saw my own trepidation in her eyes. For a moment I thought of pretty little Akira and how wrong this could truly go. Then I was forced to bury the thought, as I'm sure she was. We smiled grimly, exiting the car. The weight of my Taurus was a firm and reassuring pressure against my lower back, giving my walk towards Muhammad's vehicle a feigned yet purposeful confidence.

'This is it?'

The minister peered up from his driver's seat, glittering eyes hidden by black sunglasses. Beside him was the bespectacled Nation member I'd swapped respectful nods with on my first visit to their offices. Two more sat in the back seat, neither less than six feet tall. They wore a firm and sullen aura, though they also managed curt, perfect manners. I nodded at the occupants, then at the minister.

'Yep, we're here. We'll handle things just as discussed, yeah?'

Muhammad was rubbing easily at his upper lip. It seemed he had none of the nerves that were making my stomach churn in slow revolutions.

'Ervine, we're here fuh you today. Whatever you want us to do, we'll do, OK?'

'OK. So we stick to our plan, yeah?'

'No problem. We'll be dere if you need us. If I sense any trouble I'm comin' in after you, y'get me?'

'Yeah. Thanks man.'

Leaving the men sitting in their cars, I headed back to mine. Carmen stood on the pavement, an expectant look on her face. We'd both agreed the perfect way to start a race war was to march up to the bookshop with a platoon of Nation members behind us. That was pointless if we wanted to achieve anything positive, so the idea was quickly discarded in favour of something a little less provocative. As they already seemed to know me, I would knock at the door again, with Carmen at my side as a non-threatening ally. The Nation would wait in their respective vehicles, a passive yet valid warning that we were not to be taken for fools. If push came to shove and we were forced into violence, I was prepared to do whatever it took to protect Carmen, myself and the men that had joined us in this task.

'Ready?' I asked as warmly as I could. She looked at her feet and kicked a tiny stone across the road, her small face pale. 'Then let's go.'

It was a long walk across that road to face the painted navy blue bookshop, which today looked very much open. The shutters were up, though blinds were pulled down behind the windows, casting the shadows of books at observers. The door wasn't open, although a sign hung on another little window proclaimed that the shop itself was, just in case any passing white supremacists might wonder. Panic was strong in my heart, thoughts of my Taurus uppermost in my mind. I looked back at the cars one last time before pushing my way into the store.

The layout wasn't far removed from the interior of an average Soho sex shop. Books and magazines lined the shelved walls, most featuring pictures of Swastikas and white fists clenched against the background of a thunderous sky. Nazi memorabilia was placed in a locked cupboard at the furthest end of the room, behind a manned counter overshadowed by a fire-blackened cross hanging on the back wall. Mannequins wore Klu Klux Klan and German Second World War outfits, price tags dangling from every item of clothing, boots to hats. Varied posters from far-right parties all over the world were pinned around the shop, their screamed propaganda as loud as the voice of any racist. As I had previously seen on their equally chilling website, The Foundation seemed to honour any organisation that believed in the Aryan way.

'Jesus wept . . .'

I was so entranced by our surroundings, I'd forgotten how they might affect my old friend. Carmen was creeping by my side, mouth unconsciously open as if unable to believe the scale of what she was seeing. In that moment, she knew why I'd been so scared. Anyone who openly praised such hateful deeds deserved cautious treatment, something I reminded myself as I approached the shop counter.

The skinny white youth I'd seen at the bus stop, then later tailing me in Shepherd's Bush, had very good reason to be upset, though I couldn't allow that to make me overconfident in here. Fear quite often made people act like trapped rats, liable to produce surprising efforts to free themselves. Somehow, I got the feeling that a wimp like this could become a very slippery customer if I let him.

'Well, well, well, if it isn't bus-stop boy,' I teased gently. 'Bet you didn't think you'd be seein' me . . .'

The youth's nerves were more than apparent as, behind me, Carmen stepped into view.

'Yuh better get out ah 'ere . . . Yuh better, or you'll be in trouble,' he panted, looking as though he was about to wet himself.

'Trouble? I don't think you've *seen* trouble yet. So you better run along an' get your friend if he's here, the one I met in the alleyway. Tell him he better be nice too. There's people outside that I'm sure he don't wanna upset, an' that's what'll happen if this lady or me get hurt.'

The kid was off and through a back doorway before my final words bounced off the walls. When I turned to Carmen she was paler than ever, her freckles as bright as a constellation glittering across her face.

'I don't like dis, Vinnie. Look ah dis stuff,' she complained, arms wrapped tight around her body. I pulled the Taurus from the small of my back, flipped the safety off and prepared for the entrance of the big guy.

'I know, but we'll be out of here soon. Don't forget to look for the scar on this guy's cheek. Left side, right? That's all we need, then we go.'

She was nodding as we heard the rumble of feet running down stairs above our heads. Before we could react, we were faced with the owner of the whispering voice in my ear, heralding violence as confidently as Santa does Christmas. He was as huge as the homeless youths had predicted. His body was round as a beer barrel and seemed to have no end. The medicine-ball head bore potato-like lumps and shaving marks, though from the angle he was standing I couldn't see any scars. Forced to ignore his features, I focused on the hands, which were wrapped around an aluminium baseball bat that he lifted as he came into the room. The skinny youth trailed behind, looking despairingly worried.

'Geddowt.'

The giant said it as one word, but the meaning was clear. His tiny black eyes refused to let mine go.

'We just want to talk—' I began in a steady voice.

'*Geddowt!*' he roared, moving our way with the bat raised.

Carmen screamed once, then I was raising the gun and stepping towards the counter, even though my body protested. The skinny kid yelled. Before the giant could do more, I was standing beside him with the Taurus pushed into his soft belly. He was now stuck that way, arms held aloft with his baseball bat, facing his worst nightmare eye to eye. It was a moment I wished I had time to savour, but we weren't out of danger. I opened my mouth and when a girl's voice came out, I found myself wondering if the fear had got me worse than I'd thought. Then I remembered.

'You. Get dat bat an' give it to me. Now!' Carmen was ordering the skinny kid as she stepped lightly behind the giant, chest rapidly rising and falling. The kid did as he was asked with as much haste as he could muster. I was sincerely grateful that he pulled no stunts. When Carmen had the bat in her hands, she called the kid forwards while moving along-side me, rolling the weapon around for heft, her face a mask of potential danger. The Foundation members stood side by side in front of us, their harsh breathing destroying the silence of the room. I backed off from the giant, keeping the gun levelled at his belly.

'I'm an Army man, so you know I learnt how to gut-shoot,' I warned seriously, venom coursing through my voice. 'Think about that. Now is anyone upstairs?'

They were shaking their heads unhappily.

'D'you wanna check, Cee?'

It was clear she didn't. Still, she pulled down her mouth and left without a word, disappearing upstairs so quietly it was hard to tell whether she was really gone. I kept my vigi-lance and gun trained on the giant, my eyes on his as we waited in silence. Carmen returned after several minutes, sweat dripping down her face in a torrent.

'All clear,' she stuttered, easing past the white men and rejoining my side.

'Thanks,' I replied, giving her a quick nod in salute of her bravery. 'OK, I just want you guys to know we haven't come here for a fight, you got that? I just wanna have a talk with you both—'

'Supposin' we don' wanna talk t'you?' the skinny kid spat, face contorting at the thought of any conversation with us.

'I think you both know the answer to that.'

Giant shot him a look. The kid ducked his head, his defiance bluffed into nothing.

'You already know who I am, so I haven't the need to introduce myself to you, though I'm eager to know *your* names. After that, you can tell me all you know about Viali Walker, starting with exactly where you were on the night of her murder.'

There was a small silence, which I didn't like one bit. By now, information should have been flowing like urine from a drunk. I could feel Carmen shooting me dubious looks, unsure of what to do.

'C'mon! I wanna hear names and where you were!'

Suddenly, the giant began to laugh uproariously. Sweat trickled from my armpits, rolling down my ribs.

'Lissen, mate, we don't 'afta do nuffin, you hear me? Yuh wanna fackin' shoot, shoot me yuh cunt, think I give a toss? I ain' tellin' yuh fack all!'

Damn. So he was gonna make this hard.

'Yeah, you're right if you're thinkin' I don't want to shoot you, 'cos I don't. But whether I *would* shoot you if I felt threatened . . . Well, d'you wanna take that risk? An' there are many, many ways I can feel threatened. You not answering my questions is a threat. So wha' you sayin', *mate*?'

Nothing. We'd reached a point of stand off, where I'd have to shoot or get the shit kicked out of me. If I fired the gun, all hell would break loose. If I didn't, I was risking death and the case would remain a mystery. The devil or the deep blue sea. As usual.

All of sudden, Carmen was piping up beside me, her mouth going a mile a minute, stunning everybody rigid.

'Look at yuh, both you fuckin' racist bastards! You lot ain' hard, yuh jus' some poor losers probably couldn't get a woman if you tried! Dat's why you fuckin' raped her you sick cunts. You wanned a black woman an' you knew you could never get one like her innit? *Innit*! Only black girls got arse like dis . . .' Here, she slapped her own as if it offended her, while my eyes bulged in horror. 'Bigger tits than anyone, an' no one ain' got skin like us, 'specially dem brownin' gyal like Viali, y'get me! But you couldn't get her so you killed her, didn't you? *You fuckin' killed her!*'

This was getting way out of control. By the end of her tirade Carmen was screaming until she was red in the face, the giant was set to explode at any second, and worst of all, I could hear Muhammad's car horn beeping impatiently from the street. Before I could say anything to halt looming calamity, the giant began to respond.

'You 'alf-breed *bitch*, yuh sound like yuh wannit. You'll get it good, don' worry about dat, luv. I ain' scared ah you cunts, I'd fuckin' kill you all if I 'ad to, but I never killed dat girl, an' neither did anyone else from 'ere! Suh stop tryin' ta stitch us up, all right! I'm warnin' you like I warned 'im before! *Stop tryin' ta stitch us up!*'

Giant was spitting all over the place. I'd let things go too far. It was only a matter of time before he went for Carmen, regardless of the gun, so I brought it down against his temple and watched him fall to one knee, wobbling, half-upright. Carmen was taking big gulps of air, while the white youth shivered with rage in one corner. He would've gone for me at that point if he'd been as brave as his larger friend.

'I didn't wanna do that, but you forced me, all right? If you won't answer our questions, we'll leave and be back with police if need be,' I warned the two men. 'So you better be more co-operative.'

'Try . . . Try an' come back,' Giant wheezed from the floor. Blood was trickling down one cheek to drip from his chin. 'We know where yuh live, remember? We'll be payin' you a little visit before you know it.'

He was grabbing for the support of the shop counter. I backed off and let him.

'I wouldn't do that, there might be a surprise waitin',' I promised, moving backwards out of the bookstore, Carmen leading me by the arm. Only when we stepped outside and onto the pavement did she finally lower the bat, her small body sagging with relief. Putting away my gun, I surveyed the road around us, sure there was no time to relax.

We'd just made it. Muhammad and the other Nation of Islam members were getting out of their cars, standing around as if wrong-footed by our appearance. The minister rushed over.

'What happened, Ervine, you were ages!'

He looked from mine to Carmen's shining faces, concern prominent. I held out my arms so he could pass no further.

'We better get out of here—' I started, trying to herd everyone away from the shop.

Then the Foundation men stepped out of the door and saw us.

Everything was silent. Even birds in the trees seemed to halt mid-song as rival factions took each other in, no boundaries of police or legalities to part them. All that was between them was Carmen and myself. It didn't take long for our unfavourable position to take root in my mind.

'Now guys, this is all over now, we're leaving—' I tried again, too late as realisation took hold.

'You fackin' *dare* to come down 'ere?' Giant roared, stepping forwards with skinny youth clutching at his arm. Muhammad and his men were quick too, their surge sparking the realisation in Giant's brain that this was not a fight he could win. He stopped dead, as did I, a hand back on my gun, ready to draw.

'You dare to bring dem down 'ere? I'll fuckin' kill you, wait an' see boy. You're gonna die,' he told me in a conversational moan.

Muhammad joined us at that point, ignoring my insistent

pleas to stay back. The sight of his attire was causing our Foundation friends no end of anxiety, and it wouldn't be long before Giant didn't give a damn how many men he was outnumbered by.

'Wha' d'you know about *killin'*?' the minister hissed out of the blue, his voice lowered. 'You think we're afraid ah you? Where I come from man was killin' on the regular, it weren't no ting. I shook a manslaughter case myself, so watch it when you talk like dat, 'cos you see man like us? Man like us don't play wid you racist white fucks, you hear? Suh start suttin' if yuh gaan start.'

With that, he backed away with his arms outstretched, the gesture an introduction to war, his message hitting home. The huge man looked from face to black face, only to be rewarded with more of the same: darkened stares, cold and lifeless as you could possibly get. I swapped a look with Carmen to see what she made of everything she'd heard and saw that she was frowning hard. For me, information had irrefutably fallen into place, leaving me breathless, winded by the force of my assumptions. Behind Giant, his skinny friend was pleading that he 'leave it alone'. He responded with a look of disgust, turning back to me.

'You keep yuh monkeys 'ere . . .' he began, until Muhammad sprang back and faced him. I barked at the minister to back off, sighing with relief when he complied. Giant continued. '. . . Stay 'ere an' I'll call some friends to even dis up. Den we'll see who's really serious. I told yuh already, we never kilt dat coloured girl. If we 'ave to hurt one ah you facks to prove it, so be it.'

Turning his back on us, Giant stomped into the bookstore with skinny kid running behind him like a puppy. The door slammed hard, sending blue paint raining to the pavement. Grabbing Carmen's hand without waiting for pleasantries, I pulled her towards my car, aiming my words at Minister Muhammad.

'C'mon, let's go,' I snapped quickly. 'You've had your say and we got what we wanted.'

'What d'you mean?' He looked around at the lonely streets, confused.

'Remember the scar I told you about? Did you see it? 'Cos I never did. Carmen?'

She was shaking her head along with Muhammad.

'Nah, he never had it, Vinnie . . . Now can you let go of my arm?'

We'd reached my car. I let go of Carmen, unlocking the doors without hesitation, breaking it down for the minister.

'See, if they were suspects we'd have every right to go bargin' through their bookshop shoutin' the odds. As we're wrong . . .'

'OK, OK, I get the picture,' he was saying in an off-hand manner. 'I'll move my guys outta here an' we'll meet back in Shepherd's Bush, yeah?'

'All right.'

We watched Muhammad stride over to his men, steering them back towards their gathered vehicles with the confident air that had driven his spirited defiance of Giant. In no time, the cars roared away. Carmen stared at me, incredulous.

'Ervine – are you thinkin' what I'm thinkin'? 'Cos it looks like you are.'

I gave a bitter smile, even though I was relieved that Carmen saw things as I had.

'Yes. I hope so anyway. But right now we gotta get outta here, so let's talk about it in the car, all right?'

'Sure.'

Climbing inside the Audi, I turned the ignition and drove, before Carmen had even closed her passenger door.

19

In the past, the aftermath of battle was something I'd relished. Coming back from the field knowing I'd survived to fight another day, all my bruises, aches and pains tell-tale signals that I was alive. Sitting down with comrades and sharing a drink in memory of those that weren't so lucky, pouring liquor onto the earth in reverence. Talking over each individual skirmish we'd seen and won, swapping stories and sharing cigarettes, celebrating as though we were going home the same day.

Along with those things came more subdued reactions, less ritualistic, but just as common and unconscious as any others. Sweaty palms, chattering teeth, a heartbeat that wouldn't stop racing. An urge to jump at the smallest of noises, no matter how far away. I came to recognise and embrace the aftershock, thinking that acceptance would help ward off nightmares. Now, after years of finding that to be untrue, I couldn't help noticing that my heart was beating rapidly and my palms were clammy once more.

Due to my fears, our drive westwards was virtually silent apart from a few muttered sentences swapped tersely, mainly to confirm our suspicions. I chastised Carmen for her actions; she had known it was coming and took my lecture bravely enough. She'd been deeply terrified by that little scene in the dusty bookshop; I only realised how much so when a stubborn tear fell from her eye, which she was quick to dispense with an angry hand. Once I knew that she was sorry for losing her temper, there was no more to be said. The jazz ran with our thoughts, filling the void.

Parking just past the London Underground elevated tracks, we got out of the car and walked the short distance to the Nation offices. Carmen looked at me, grimacing at the sorrow that coloured my face, matily rubbing my back.

'So you're gonna tell him what we think?'

'Sure. I'm pretty positive we're right. How about you?'

She puffed weightily. The answer was obvious.

'It's the only thing dat makes sense. But I dunno . . . I'm only a novice after all.'

I laughed as I pressed the buzzer, stating my name in answer to the woman's metallic voice.

'Listen to me, Cee: if there's one thing you're not, it's a novice. You'll see when we go up.'

The buzzer sounded. I kissed Carmen's forehead reassuringly, before we climbed the stairs and headed through swing doors into the Nation of Islam's second floor office.

A hum of activity was strong in the air. Nation members of both sexes were gathered, going over differing views of what occurred back in South-east London. Soft drinks and biscuits were being served. Various people clapped me on the back in congratulations, acknowledging my role as peacemaker, while eager to know if they had helped in any way. I assured everybody who would listen that they'd saved us from getting our arses well and truly kicked, while trying to scan the throng to see if I could catch sight of Muhammad.

'Over dere,' Carmen guided, taking the lead.

He was standing just outside the door to his office, as if the Nation member talking animatedly by his shoulder had way-laid him. With Carmen at my side, I wandered through the crowd and appeared just beyond the men. Muhammad saw us, nodding once in our direction, before turning back to his cohort, the bespectacled man I'd acknowledged in his car. From what I could overhear, the man wanted to know if the Nation of Islam were going to take a more active role in the Viali Walker investigation. Muhammad said something about planning to work very closely with me in the future, which was a cue to introduce myself, along with my new partner. The man responded courteously, saying his name was Richard X, then excused himself and moved to another group on the far side of the room.

'A good man, Richard, good heart,' Muhammad told us convincingly. 'So, how d'you feel, Ervine? Was it a success?'

I thought about that, glancing over at Carmen. She was attempting not to notice how tall and good-looking he was. I forgave her; she was great at the job, not infallible.

'Yeah, I'd say it was pretty successful. Actually, we wanted a word with you on that score, Charles. In private if you don't mind.'

He stared a minute longer than necessary, then smiled again, exposing those perfect white teeth.

'Of course. Come through.'

We walked inside, Muhammad first, then Carmen, me last. I shut the door and strolled further into the room. Carmen sat on the seat I'd inhabited on my last visit, staring our quarry dead in the eye with an unflinching gaze. I couldn't allow her to lead this particular interview no matter how good she was, so I grabbed a spare seat and put it next to hers. When I sat, the naked anger on her face was unmistakable. I desperately willed her not to speak prematurely.

Despite Carmen's silence, Muhammad definitely noticed something was amiss, for he faced us with his eyebrows locked together.

'What's goin' on? Is it about what I said to dat racist? 'Cos I don't take it back, I meant every word.'

I shrugged casually. Chatter and laughter from the office area could still be heard as a steady buzz, everyone secure in the midst of their negligible victory.

'Don't you want to get your tape recorder out, Charles? Just so we both agree on everything said from here on in.'

He frowned once more, confusion emanating from him. At once, I felt extremely bad for what I was about to do. I liked the man, but fact was fact. Muhammad's body language wasn't helping either. It grew hard for me to speak the words that once uttered would soon become reality.

'What d'you mean? Is this an interview?'

I answered his question with one of my own.

'Where were you on the night Robert Walker was murdered?'

He paused, took a deep breath, started to laugh.

'Is dat it?! Dat's what you're on about? I don't need a tape recorder for dat! I was right here, in my office.'

'Who saw you, Charles?'

'Sister Veronica at the reception desk,' he returned confidently.

'Until what time?'

He stopped and didn't say another word.

'Until what time, Charles?'

Carmen abruptly got to her feet. Her stony expression was still in place.

'Is Sister Veronica the dark-skinned woman on the desk as you come in?' she muttered sweetly, though I could hear the acid beneath her words. Muhammad nodded once in silence.

'I'll jus' go ask,' she finished resolutely. Needing no more prompting, Carmen left. We were alone in the room.

Muhammad watched her go, then smiled again.

'Nice sister,' he enthused warmly. 'Smart, too.'

Bridling, I became upset that his easy-going manner had worked on me the first time around.

'I only wish you were as smart, Charles. I really thought you were, but you're playin' me for an idiot, an' you can't be smart if you're gonna do that. If you had any sense, you'd know that's only gonna piss me off.'

All civility dropped from Muhammad's body language. It flowed out of his face and left it free of expression. He slumped into his seat and watched me coldly now that I had dropped any pretence of friendship.

'So what's goin' on, Ervine? We help you out an' you start t'rowin accusations my way? Start switchin' on yuh own kind because dere's no way you can solve dis ting? Typical brothaman, help him out an' he shits in yuh face! Dat's all right man. I can take it, I bin takin' it fuh years! I still love my brothers – even the Judas brothers, the ones who try talk white an' act white, don't even know they'll never *be* white. In fact, I love you guys more. Because you need it!'

Now it was my turn to laugh, but there was no joy in the sound, only disbelief and disgust. What Muhammad had to say wasn't new. I'd heard it before and it still didn't impress me. Anyway, now wasn't the time for a debate on what 'being black' really meant. It was a bullshit conversation anyway.

'C'mon, Charles, we both know that isn't true. I didn't shit on you, but you did to me, didn't you? Listen to me a minute. You've had a manslaughter case already, right? Robert an' you never got on in all the time you knew him. In fact, you hated everything he stood for, everything about him apart from his daughter. Now check this. I was at Robert's house the morning after he died, when the police were there. They had Forensics and all that shit in the place, Charles. If it *was* you

who did that murder, the only reason the police haven't questioned you is because they don't know about you yet. If that
changed – if I made that change – how long would it be before
they found evidence that you'd been there? From your files
perhaps? It's not just fingerprints these days you know,
Charles. Hair on clothes, skin beneath nails, DNA . . . It all
contributes to the evidence.'

Muhammad was breathing hard, eyes wide and darting all
over his office like pinballs. He was guilty as hell and we both
knew it. The office doorknob rattled, making us jump. Carmen
came back inside, then stopped when she saw the set of our
faces, propping the open door with a shoulder.

'What's up?' I probed cravenly.

'Sister Veronica left Charles here at around nine PM,'
Carmen informed the room, staring at Muhammad all the
while. 'He told her not to worry about lockin' up, cos he'd do
it. She wouldn't like to say where he went after dat.'

We all paused a moment to take that information in, none
of us knowing what the other would do next. Then, before I
could move a muscle, Muhammad jumped up and grabbed
his chair, throwing it over the desk and making a run for the
door. For one moment I couldn't see anything, I was so busy
defending myself from the chair's metal legs. When they hit,
the pain was intense, yet over in a flash. Next thing I knew, a
Nation member was lifting the heavy weight from my chest
and asking if I was all right. When I looked at the office door,
Carmen was gone. Pushing away the man and his concern, I
jumped up and ran out of the office, down the stairs and onto
the West London streets.

Outside, I stopped and looked around, wondering which
direction he'd taken. Footsteps on the stairs thumped behind
me. Richard, the courteous young man I'd only recently met,
burst out of the door followed by two others.

'What's goin' on?' he demanded.

'I think Charles had something to do with Robert Walker's

death. When I asked him about it, he ran,' I snapped back, my eyes on the busy streets.

I couldn't see Muhammad, but all of sudden I saw Carmen sprinting hard on the next block from us. She immediately took the right by a fried chicken shop and was gone. I launched myself into a headlong run after her, the Nation members shouting loudly in my wake. By the loud beeping of car horns that followed as I crossed the main road, I thought it would be safe to assume they were giving chase. Whether they were after Muhammad or myself was just another question I had no time to answer. If they *were* chasing me, I was determined to make it hard.

Running as fast as I could manage, I soon found a pace that seemed to work. When I took the right at the chicken shop, I saw Carmen tearing through a small estate, while Muhammad was a barely visible flapping of coat-tails yards in front. I put my head down and pumped until I was just behind her. Our prey turned right at the top of the next street, going in the direction of the Uxbridge Road. If he could last that long, he'd find it quite easy to disappear amongst the crowds of shoppers and children, providing he didn't get enough of a lead to find a garden to hide in. If that happened, I was pretty sure there was no way we'd catch him.

Checking to make sure the Nation men were still with us, I began to accelerate past Carmen, who was running fast, though not fast enough to do any serious damage to Muhammad's lead. I, on the other hand, jogged regularly; anyone doing a job like this had to be reasonably fit. This training gave me a clear advantage. By the time the running minister had gone a few hundred yards further, he was beginning to flag. His speed slowed considerably, his steps becoming erratic. The shiny black shoes began to clatter on the concrete as though he was tap dancing. When he made the fatal mistake of looking back to see where we were, what he saw made him panic even further. He attempted to sprint, and managed another twenty yards before the stitch hit him. Stumbling, he eventually fell to the ground holding his side and wheezing brutally.

It didn't take long for us to gather around him, looking down while kids watched from a safe distance on their mountain bikes and push-scooters. I shot Carmen a questioning glance to make sure she was all right. She was standing bent over with her hands on her knees, giving only a tired look of acknowledgement. Richard was puffing and sweating, but still wore an angry expression, displeasure forcing him to Muhammad's side, jabbing a finger down on him.

'Wha' you runnin' from, Charles? Tell us what's going on, or is what these people say true?'

It was hard enough for him to breathe, let alone speak, and his panic would make things worse if we weren't careful. I was both surprised and relieved when the minister held up a hand commanding that Richard wait, sucked in a deep lung's worth of air, then gave a strained reply in my direction.

'Yeah, well done, Ervine, you got me. I'm tellin' you now, though, you won't catch the man that murdered Viali, you know why? 'Cos he's dead. I killed him an' I don't give a damn. I'll go jail fuh Viali, I don't business about goin' inside, done tell yuh. Now you gonna call the police fuh me or what?'

Carmen covered her mouth with a hand, her face turning pale once more. Richard's eyes were closed and he shook his head as he tried to come to terms with what he'd heard. The other Nation members were equally stunned. Before I could stop him, one spat on Muhammad. The minister glared upwards, just in time to catch the next blast, which hit him just above his cheekbone. At that, he attempted to get to his feet. Even as I moved, Richard and the others were shrugging their jackets to the floor.

'Yeah, get up,' the first warned. 'I can't wait to say you tried to resist a citizen's arrest.'

The minister thought about that while he paused halfway up on his feet, a stubborn scowl revealing his barely reigned temper. It took a moment, but after a look at the men surrounding him, he was forced to sit back down. I thought I better get involved before things got very ugly in front of the gawping children.

'Hold on a minute, I think we better let him get up. The police station's only a short walk from here. We can escort the minister there in five minutes, make sure he doesn't get away again.'

My idea went down well enough, with Richard and his men nodding agreeably in response. When I looked at Carmen to see how she felt now, she was still out of breath, but standing upright and looking pleased. I reached for her. We hugged, then busied ourselves getting Muhammad back on his feet again.

It was inevitable that we spent many hours at the station going over question after question, most of them an attempt to see whether I was who I claimed, and whether I'd been involved in Walker's death myself. Carmen, Richard and the two Nation men were also put in cells, then interviewed many times. By the end of it all, the police could see that our stories were too close to be fabricated. After five hours, I received the cell visit I'd been waiting for – Detective Inspector Ryder. He verified my hopes that we'd all be released when the paperwork was taken care of, congratulating my hard work. Muhammad had formally admitted the murder of Robert Walker and was currently awaiting transport to HMP Wormwood Scrubs. He'd told how he had phoned Walker on the night of the murder, suggesting that he had new information about Viali. Leaving his car in Shepherd's Bush, he met Walker at a pub near his home, where Muhammad apparently charmed the MP into a relaxed frame of mind. When the call for last orders came, the minister asked for the use of Walker's home phone so he could call a cab. Robert had responded with his usual generosity. Once inside the house, Muhammad struck almost at once.

The police had questioned the minister about Viali's murder, and though Ryder warned that his alibi for the night seemed ironclad, we both agreed that there was a good chance he could be our man. However, as far as the police were concerned, her killer remained on the streets, and they were no nearer to finding him than before. After divulging this information, Ryder thanked me profusely and left. I waited. And waited some more.

Finally, I was released with an idle apology and nothing further. I left the cells to see Carmen in the main lobby area looking desolate and alone. She seemed unhurt, though a little fed up and exhausted. We embraced and headed for my Audi, parked five minutes away.

'Thanks for waitin',' I eventually acknowledged softly. The heater was on full blast, jazz drifting through the interior of the car like perfume. Carmen, who'd been half-asleep with her head back for most of the ride, opened one eye lazily.

'Ah, don't worry about it. I only waited 'cos I 'ad no taxi fare.'

She was rewarded with a sour look, before we laughed insanely at ourselves, beginning to talk over events of the day. All our nervous moments, all of the parts that we fucked up, all of the things we felt we should've said but never did because it sounded stupid . . . It felt great to go back and relive everything I'd done from someone else's point of view, to be able to see myself through outsiders' eyes. Most of the things that I'd been worried about, Carmen thought I'd handled with calm and dignity. Most of my fears were visions that had also gone through her mind.

'I'm really, truly sorry about how I acted today, Vinnie,' she told me in earnest, as we finally reached North Peckham Estate. 'I knew it was the wrong ting to say as soon as the words came out ah my mouth, but I couldn't stop 'em. He jus' made me so *mad* . . .'

I held up a hand in understanding.

'Yeah, but we can't get so mad we lose ourselves. Ever. We have to keep that shit under control, use it against them. You see how anger got Charles?'

'Yeah,' she nodded empathetically. Only time would reveal whether or not she had learned that most vital lesson. We were pre-programmed by society, all of us, pre-destined to follow rows already furrowed, even though there was always choice. Discernment came only with realisation, and was nothing if the human brain didn't truly believe.

I let Carmen out at the front of her block, then switched off the engine and began to get out. She waved a forbidding hand.

'Oh no yuh don't, home you. I can see myself upstairs.'

'But it's late an'—'

'No! Yuh fuckin' eyes are all red an' swollen an' you look half-dead. Go home will yuh!'

I kissed her cheek sleepily, submitting to her will.

'Well, I think I'll stay at my mum's actually . . . By the way, we're long overdue goin' up to Leicester. We might have to leave as soon as the end of the week. Is that OK with you?'

'Sure,' she grunted, even as I saw pain in her eyes. Feeling like a slave driver, I peeled £100 from my wallet and handed it over. Carmen grinned her appreciation, though I could tell she wasn't really seeing the money beyond the image of her bed.

'Thanks, Vinnie. You're the best boss I ever had, trus' me!'

Another kiss and she was off, running her key tag against the blank panel, waving once and disappearing inside the block. I smiled to myself, yet found depression floating back like an evil spirit. I'd found a partner I could quickly grow accustomed to. I hoped my feelings wouldn't make me vulnerable in a way never before possible, in my career, or even my life.

We took a couple of days off after the drama with Muhammad; time I used to splice together last strands of evidence. Though I looked into Muhammad's claim that Robert had murdered his daughter, it only led me into spending time talking to Birkett and Ryder, trying to match what the minister said in taped interviews with what the police knew about Viali. It was no use. There were still holes big enough to fit a bus through, most importantly the fact that Walker's alibi seemed to check out. I knew what that meant: travelling to the Midlands was vital. Somehow, from somewhere in my innermost being, I'd hoped the Foundation men would get sick of the pressure and confess. Other than that, there wasn't much else I could pin my hopes on.

From my mother's house, where I had made another makeshift bed on another sofa, I used my Pay As You Go credits to book a modest hotel in Leicester, then informed Carmen, Sadie and Emilia that we'd be leaving the next day. After that, I made the phone call I'd been putting off: the call to the Nation of Islam. Expecting at least some slight awkwardness, if not animosity, I spoke to Richard X and caught up on what had been happening since Charles's arrest. He was cordial as ever, praising my detective work, telling me that the organisation had been stunned by Charles's actions, though of course, they were eager to weed out any bad seeds and grateful for any assistance. We rang off, with Richard promising both more work and also to stay in touch. I felt infinitely better after that conversation. Part of me was still stung by Muhammad's accusation that I was a sell out, a wanna-be. All I wanted to be was good at what I did.

The day we were due to leave London, Hadiah and Davey were sitting along with Carmen and myself, all huddled around my mother's kitchen table looking nervous and excited at the same time. Mister was there too, lying beneath the table, only stirring when someone spoke or offered him a snack from above. As it was just past eleven in the morning, Mum was already at work. Maya was out, as usual. Dougie wandered through a few times, nodding at the others but virtually ignoring me. I knew my brother wasn't happy about the new living conditions. Blame was clear in his eyes, but I couldn't dwell on his anger. As soon as he'd dug what he wanted out of the fridge and left the room, I shut the kitchen door, sitting down in front of the earnest trio of faces staring back at me. It was time.

'OK, so you both know what's goin' on?' I addressed the question to the youngsters.

Davey was scratching dangerously close to the inside of his nostril. I was glad my mother wasn't there to see.

'Yuh goin' up north ta see if da bruvva can 'elp you lot owt, innit?'

Carmen was smiling balefully.

'That's about the size of it,' I agreed. 'Now how are you guys handling things here? Can you cope with my mum and brother all right?'

The couple nodded.

'Oh yeah, they've bin lovely, really nice,' Hadiah gushed, her tone unable to disguise the truth behind her words.

'Yuh mum's pukka,' Davey chimed in, with so much passion I knew he wasn't just being polite. Still, I could tell I wasn't getting everything. I cleared my throat.

'All right, no bullshit. I believe everything you're sayin', truly I do, but what are you guys missin' out? I wanna know the truth.'

They exchanged glances. Hadiah put a hand on Davey's for comfort.

'Well . . . We're used to bein' able to come an' go as we please. Your mum's got so much rules . . .'

'. . . An' we're used to havin' our own gaff . . . in a manner of speakin',' Davey finished for his girlfriend. Carmen nudged me with an elbow.

'Told yuh,' she muttered smugly. I nodded, taking no offence. She had indeed told me.

'All right then, would you guys like to come with us? It'll all be paid for, you just need to stay out of trouble while you're there. An' it's useful, 'cos it keeps you out of the way of Mystery Man an' his Foundation cronies.'

'I thought dat Foundation guy didn't have the scar?' Davey insisted, twirling around in his seat.

'Yeah. So?'

'So 'ee couldn't be Mystery Man, could 'ee?' the youth continued. 'The one dat threatened us 'ad the massive scar innit. Oi you lot, 'ave you even bin lissenin' to us?'

There was a sudden silence in which the couple watched us with avid attention, waiting to see what we'd say in return.

'Course we 'ave,' Carmen piped up before that particular conversation went any further. 'But if it weren't 'im it means he's still out dere somewhere, which means you'd be a lot better off out of his way. Besides, don't you wanna see some fields an' flowers, or you wanna stay in grotty old Claybridge an' study the concrete jungle till we get back?'

Their answer was predictable enough. We told them to get their sparse belongings together, put a lead on Mister, get their coats and be ready to leave in half an hour.

20

Our motorway journey was nowhere near the confined calamity that I might have imagined. By the time we reached Milton Keynes, Hadiah and Davey had seen enough blandness; instead of watching the scenery, they dozed with their heads together, forming a single mass of hair and winter clothing in my rearview mirror. Carmen chain-smoked beside me, surprisingly enough saying next to nothing. Any attempts at conversation were limited to idle musings over Viali's half-brother.

I'd already called Mason Booth on the number Emilia had given me, arranging a meeting for that evening, which he'd readily accepted. The voice on the phone had been deep and toneless, flat with the fatigue of grief, each word weighted by the pain of his recent losses. I expressed condolences and ended the call swiftly, something that I felt I'd become adept at of late. When I replaced the receiver Mason's desolate voice echoed within my mind, haunting as a graveside hymn.

Though no one was talking, the strident ring of my mobile occasionally broke the silence of the car. Carmen insisted on answering the calls, saying she had a young daughter to look after, so there was no way I was driving while speaking on the phone. With each call, she'd relay the information she heard in clipped sentences, paraphrasing my reply back to the caller. The first was from Sadie, checking to see if we were OK, as well as passing on messages from Emilia and DI Ryder. The second was from Ryder himself, giving the low down on Muhammad, who had made his first appearance in court earlier that morning. As we'd expected, the minister had denied murder, going for the lesser charge of manslaughter instead. The judge agreed and the case had been adjourned until the following month. Ryder seemed pleased with the result, sure that in this instance, justice would be done.

When Carmen finished, I asked her to phone Emilia and see how she was coping with the latest news. There was brief confusion while Carmen explained her new-found role to the widow. When that was clear, I learned that Robert Walker's funeral had been scheduled for the end of the following week. I expressed surprise that it would take that long. Through Carmen, Emilia explained that her husband's interment had to wait until after the autopsy, which would take place speedily now Charles Muhammad had been arrested. Emilia was in attendance for the minister's first appearance in court, making it clear she would continue in the same vein until the verdict. Promising I would be at the funeral service no matter what, Carmen rang off, shaking her head at the woman's sheer strength.

I agreed, my thoughts caught up with our approaching meeting with Mason, unable to deal with the prospect of what was happening back home. It was safe to say that the further we moved from London, the more distant I felt from everything going on back in my gloomy city. Mixed up with all that was a strong feeling of relief I couldn't quite justify. Things had been rapidly heating up. My feeling of exodus was strong, and part of my reason for heading north was the thought that I should get out while there was still time. The threats that had been made towards me in Eltham were venomous enough to be taken seriously. Though we hadn't talked about that aspect of the case, I knew Carmen felt the same, for she told me she'd left Akira with her ex-boyfriend in Croydon, instead of the usual North Peckham childminder. There was no mention of the reason because there was no need.

Just under three hours later, signs led us towards Leicester Town Centre, and I reduced my speed. Our sleeping beauties in the back seat moaned, stretched and then woke up, peering through the windows with half-open eyes, speaking in drowsy voices. At first glance Leicester seemed to be a strange mix of town and country. Some areas were nothing more than acres of fields, others were made up of council houses bearing more than a passing resemblance to those found in London. The population was curiously multicultural, a great deal more blacks and Asians walking the streets than I'd anticipated. This was heartening to us all, putting everyone in good spirits as I drove deeper, eventually stopping to ask for directions. A few queries later, we were on our way again. The street we were looking for could be found off a main road, strangely enough called London Road. Finding a place to park outside the B&B was no trouble.

We lugged our limited belongings onto the pavement, as I took a deep intake of air. The houses in the side street were tightly squeezed together, signs advertising rooms to rent in the windows of most I could see. Our temporary home was more like a hostel-style building than someone's house, with two floors and an entrance that even had a ramp for disabled visitors. It was quiet and clean-looking; the few people going in and out appeared to be businessmen, all briefcases and saloon cars.

When I'd locked up my vehicle, we entered and checked in, agreeing to meet fifteen minutes later in the main lobby area. My room was on the first floor, boasting a clean yet clinical homeliness that only held enough comfort for a few days' stay. There was a cheap TV, a single bed, a desk and phone. The curtains were an unattractive brown, the single window looking out onto the back of more plain houses and even plainer gardens. I put my sparse selection of jumpers and jeans into the fitted wardrobe, scrubbed beneath a quick shower, then returned downstairs. Hadiah and Davey were already there. We had to wait another five minutes before Carmen emerged, looking fresh and young in jeans, trainers and a thick winter jacket.

While in the shower, I'd realised there was nothing for our homeless couple to do here besides get under my feet. I didn't fancy having to spend my time looking after them, so I decided to give them some money and the freedom to roam the town, which turned out to be the best thing I could've offered after their confined few days on my mother's estate. With £100 between them, they grabbed a map of the town from the reception desk and were gone in the blink of an eye, leaving Carmen staring enviously out of the window after them.

'So what d'we do now?' she half-grumbled in my direction.

I got out my notebook, flicking through the pages until I found what I was looking for.

'OK, Mason said he'd meet us for five in the Metro, which is this wine bar place, I think. That gives us a couple of hours to kill. I was thinking we could get something to eat and head down there?'

'Sounds good,' Carmen quickly agreed. 'So what is it, Indian den?'

She was referring to the many places we'd seen on our drive into the town centre, boasting the best in Asian cuisine. I shrugged as my stomach vocalised its agreement. After some quick directions from the receptionist, who assured we'd find

an abundance of restaurants on London Road, we left the B&B
in search of food.

Though she'd been right about the amount of likely venues,
most candidates were unfortunately closed for the afternoon.
After a fair amount of walking, we decided to cut our losses
and take the car deeper into town, where we'd at least be able
to find some takeaway food. Not long afterwards, we reached
a compromise of sorts: McIndian, an Asian burger bar that
sold Halal chicken nuggets along with the usual quarter
pounders with cheese. Before long, we were gratefully wolfing
down our food while the mostly Indian clientele did the same
around us. Carmen looked reasonably sated by her meal, the
sparkle returning to her eyes and the life back into her skin.
Soon, she was talking at her old rapid-fire pace again. After
ten minutes she halted, took a last slurping drag on her milk-
shake, then gave me a nervous smile.

'All right, Vinnie, I'm gonna ask you something an' I want
you to tell me the truth, OK?

'If I can,' I answered curiously, frowning and wiping at my
mouth with a purple napkin. Carmen politely waited for me
to finish.

'Are you scared?' she asked, when she was sure I was done
with my preening.

I had to take a moment to think over her question. It wasn't
that I was worried about exposing my true feelings; I just
wasn't sure if I should burden her with the reality of our current situation, especially after all she'd witnessed in her brief
time as my partner. If I went even further and allowed the
truth, I knew my thoughts went far deeper than my worries
about the case. Could I also admit that there had been fear
before I ever heard of Viali; before I stepped on that plane that
flew me to the Falklands and into war; even before I roamed
Claybridge Estate as a bored kid with no prospects? That I'd
realised our living nightmares never disappeared, they only
grew until they were big and ugly enough to stand up and

demand to be faced? Would I tell her the things that I had hidden inside me for so long, things buried so deep the effort to unearth them could quite easily kill me?

'Yeah,' I began stiltedly, unable to look at her. 'Yeah, I'm scared, Carmen. I think I use most of my energy trying to convince myself I'm not.'

'I don't blame you,' she replied at once. 'I know how you felt when you come to my house dat night too, don't think dat I don't. Dis is *hard*, Vinnie. For the first time I can remember, I'm seriously scared for my daughter's life. I ain' used to dat, I ain' used to dat at all. Then when I think about you an' all the shit you bin through . . . I dunno how yuh coped on yuh own so long.'

Carmen took one of my hands in her own. The many contrasts – dark and light, small and large, smooth and rough – were amazing.

'We'll be all right, Carmen. You made me see that. I know we'll be all right.'

My old friend was studying me with an objectiveness I hadn't experienced for years. She blinked and shook her head.

'If yuh talkin' about the case, I'm fine about dat. I know it'll be OK. An' yes, I'm scared for Akira, but I'm equally scared about you. I never did find out what happened when you went away, Vinnie.'

I ducked my head, unable to deal with the probing in her eyes, feeling her delicate hands rub on mine, soft and warm, resonating care. I held tight, needing comfort and not her words. When I collected myself, my head rose by sheer willpower.

'We better get going or we'll be late to meet Mason.'

Carmen nodded stiffly in understanding. We collected our things and left the restaurant.

Despite my worries about being late, we ended up having to kill time walking around the many shops and malls, which only emphasised my question-dodging tactics. Thankfully, Carmen left things just as they were. By the time we reached our meeting place, it had started to rain in tiny droplets that made us grateful for the warmth of the modern public house, the Metro. A two-floor building, the Metro had a bar on the left, just beyond the main entrance. In front of the doors were wide steps that led to an expansive area with more tables, along with a small section where 'pub grub' could be bought. The ground floor was just as large and spacious as the upper section. We didn't have to go far before a tall and wiry man got to his feet, smiling shyly in greeting.

We approached his table, introducing ourselves one after another. Carmen offered to get the drinks. After ordering, Mason and I sat down, each of us nervous in the other's presence, each trying not to make it too obvious. He bore little resemblance to Robert or Viali Walker, save the dark and keen-looking eyes. His complexion was pale as buttermilk, his face thin, almost sunken into a mask of bone and sickly looking skin, and his hair was cropped very close. He was handsome, though his every feature was sharp and pointed, everything made up of the straightest of lines, the deepest of ridges. As we skirted through niceties and routine small talk, it was hard not to notice how tired he was, how many lines had been carved by his tragedy, how he struggled to keep the conversation at any normal level of interest. Mason wore an introspective air that I was wary of penetrating. As a result, we talked nonsense about his job as retail assistant in the local Wilkinson, a gardening chain store, until Carmen returned with the drinks. By the time she was seated, Mason had resorted to staring at his pint. I shot Carmen a frown, which she returned.

'So, Mason, you're sure you're OK talking about your sister, yeah? I don't want you to feel you're being bullied into doing this. You want to stop, just let me know.'

Mason shifted in his seat, removing his jacket and placing it carefully behind his chair, his manner saying he was ready and willing, even if his expression did not. He was still wearing his Wilkinson shirt and tie, a uniform that made him look all the more pitiful and powerless.

'Nah, I don't mind. It's gotta be done, an' if it helps in any way, I'm up for it . . .' he muttered stiltedly, his voice low-pitched and baritone.

'Good. Just remember we can stop when you like, and my assistant may ask some questions too. That OK?'

As he responded positively, I could feel the dirty look from Carmen's direction. The word 'assistant' had been a figure of speech and nothing more, though I was thankful she didn't try and pursue the matter.

'All right then. I was wondering if you could tell me about your relationship with your sister, and a little about her state of mind the last time you saw her.'

'Yeah, sure,' Mason whispered, almost too low for us to hear. 'Me and Viali got on real good, you know? She was easy to get on with, an' she never tried to act like she was better than me or nothin'; dad made sure we grew up too close for that.'

'How old were you both when you first met?' I heard Carmen ask, as I wrote some notes in my pad. Mason wrinkled his nose in memory.

'Can't remember, I was too young. My mum's got photos of us together when I was about six months, so I've known her all my life really. We always said we were real brother and sister, never mind the half bollocks.'

'How many years were there between you?'

'One.'

I kept my head down, hoping the action hid my obvious outrage. Emilia must've been deeply in love to put up with that kind of treatment. When I raised my head, Mason was spinning a beer mat between his fingers with the utmost concentration.

'So can you tell me a bit about how your parents met?' I asked, and was chilled when Mason nodded mutely, as if he'd known the question was coming. The story was recited in a bored tone, his sentences abbreviated, which told me he'd been goaded into telling this many times.

'Yeah. My dad had some kind of conference up here, I think they were organising a celebration to mark Leicester as the capital of England in Roman times. While he was here, he went for a drink in my mum's local. They met and liked each other . . . And here I am . . .'

He let the beer mat drop with an air of finality. He seemed nonchalant, yet infinitely saddened by the tale that led to his conception.

'What about Emilia? She must've bin put out; did she treat you badly because of that?' Carmen rushed in before I could block her with my own question. I felt my heart leap. As I might have predicted, Mason instantly looked outraged.

'Emilia's always been fine with me. When I was seven I went to London to stay with my dad for the summer holidays. She made it clear that whatever problems she had with Dad, it had nothing to do with me. She stuck to that all my life.'

'What about your mum?' I intercepted, eager to make the subject matter far less threatening. Mason pulled a defeated face. I could tell that I had barely succeeded.

'She passed away,' he sighed glumly. 'She died when I was seventeen. They put me in care for a year, then got me a council flat. I lost it though. Too young to handle money, so I had to learn the hard way. Won't happen again.'

As the young man spoke, it began to feel as though Mason Booth was one of the world's truly unlucky people. One of those revisited by despair so many times it became as much a part of his life as eating or breathing the air that surrounded him. Not only had he lived with the knowledge that his father would never be able to give him the affluent lifestyle that Viali enjoyed, he then lost his mother, his half-sister and eventually his father in the space of four years. There was no doubt that the burden was crushing him to the ground in agony; it was written on his face like a billboard. Even though he seemed to be coping, there must have been count-less sleepless nights, many times when he'd cursed his God for being so cruel.

'I'm sorry to hear that. Could you tell me about Viali, Mason,' I asked, trying to lead the conversation away from any more morbid stories. 'How often did you meet up?'

He told us how they met whenever he managed to make it to London, which became more frequent the older he got. Until he'd left school, every summer holiday was spent with his half-family. When Viali moved into her flat and Dominique's secrecy had been won, he'd stayed there on many occasions. There seemed no hint that he had known of Walker's affair with Viali's flatmate, so I decided not to men-tion it. He began looking for his own flat in the city, but rents had been too high and he'd been unable to find a job that paid enough to justify leaving Leicester. Even so, Mason got to know London reasonably well while hanging out with Viali, making friends in Ladbroke Grove bars and restaurants, sometimes even further afield, then meeting his sister at work and escorting her home when she had to stay on late. Mason confessed that he'd loved her lifestyle, her friends and the city.

Some seconds later, the penny dropped. I was so delighted by my conclusion I had to fight not to smile with joy.

'Mason, that place of work wouldn't happen to be Whispers would it? The lap dance club Viali worked in, down Soho way?'

Mason hesitated. The life left his blunt features and the breath caught in my throat as I watched the indecision on his face. Carmen was looking from the young man to myself, rev-elation afire in her eyes. It was a surreal moment. I was almost sure Mason would deny his sister had ever worked as a stripper, until he reached for the pint and washed his refutation down with cold lager.

'Yeah, that was the place,' he finally admitted reluctantly, eyes darting everywhere, his glass back on the table. 'There was always funny blokes hanging around, and I didn't really trust the manager. I'd never let her go home on her own.'

That sealed it. Mason was the guy Ivanhoe and the other showgirls had seen meeting Viali after her shift; a fact that thankfully closed another avenue. If Mason knew about her job, there was a very strong chance that his father had known as well, which made Walker even more suspicious as far as I was concerned. I quickly resolved to keep that particular information to myself. It was the longest of long shots, but when all other possibilities were removed, things were beginning to look very bad for the late MP.

Carmen shot me an encouraging look. I felt invigorated. Mason sat slumped in his seat as though he was glad that I knew the truth.

'I 'ated her doing that job, I 'ated it,' he growled all of a sudden, sounding more animated than he had during the whole of our former conversation. 'All those men throwin' money at her, the bitchy girls, Ivanhoe acting like a big-time pimp. She loved the money an' . . . You know, Viali was a bit of an exhibitionist, she would've been a singer if she weren't so smart. For her it was perfect. For me . . . For me, it was torture even thinking about it.'

'But you still walked her home, you still looked after her,' Carmen spoke up, admiration colouring her tone. Though Mason tried hard not to let on, I saw that he'd noticed how pretty she was, something I was grateful for after her terrible beginning. 'You loved her a lot, right?'

Mason smiled, turning shy again. I noticed his teeth, unlike his features, were crooked and twisted. It disrupted the ordered tidiness his face had possessed with his mouth closed.

'She was my sister weren't she?' he mumbled with no enthusiasm. 'I couldn't leave her to all those middle-aged men and back-stabbing girls. What was I supposed to do?'

Carmen beamed in approval, unconsciously helping the young man to relax, making him feel more comfortable with her questions. As she was doing well enough I let her continue, hoping the experience nurtured her confidence.

'So were you in London when Viali went to the South Bank?' she questioned, leaning forwards and ignoring her drink. Mason shook his head.

'Nah, I was here. I heard about it when me dad phoned an' told me. It—' He stopped a second, faltering, reliving the moment once again, though I didn't blame Carmen this time. We had to know what had happened that night.

'You OK?' I asked gently. Mason took a second and huge gulp of breath before answering.

'Yeah . . . It's just . . .'

'Take your time,' Carmen interrupted. I felt a rush of elation as she reached over and took Mason's hand, much as she'd taken mine not long before, a feeling that grew stronger when the young man allowed it. The woman's touch was definitely working.

'It's a big thing to talk about, especially so soon after. We can wait, can't we, Vinnie?'

'Sure we can,' I agreed, putting my notebook away in a show of good faith. I gestured at his almost finished pint. 'Like another drink?'

'Yes please,' he instructed, almost at once.

'Carmen?'

'No thanks, Vinnie, I'm all right.'

I got to my feet and told them I would be two minutes, then felt for some change and went to the bar. When I'd ordered, I took a quick peek over my shoulder. They were sitting closer, Carmen's chair next to Mason's, talking with their heads down low. She was really all right. I liked the way that she was never intimidated, never cowed by people's personalities, or even their foibles. Everything, even her own mistakes, were taken in stride, learnt from, used to her advantage. I could finally relax enough to admit it was a major relief to have her. I could also learn a hell of a lot.

The drinks arrived. When I went back to the table, Mason was speaking in the same barely audible voice, with Carmen nodding along solemnly. As I sat, I realised their shared mixed heritage might have had a lot to do with their solidarity, whether they knew it or not.

'How you feeling?' I questioned, pushing the sweating pint his way.

'OK,' the young man allowed, while Carmen rubbed his shoulder in her usual comforting way. 'It just gets to me some-times, you know . . . Sometimes it's too much . . .'

'Dat's fine,' Carmen told him sympathetically. 'Do you wanna stop?'

He shook his head while knocking back his pint, drinking a third with his first few swallows. When the glass hit the table, he roughly wiped at his mouth with the back of his hand.

'No. Let's finish this. It all helps, it's gotta help.'

With rekindled zest, aided by Carmen's input I guessed, Mason told us how he'd spoken to his father and helped make the funeral arrangements, then caught the first train to London, arriving late that same night. What followed was a traumatic experience for the whole family. Mason told how he'd been embraced by everyone he met. How he felt closer to his extended black relations than ever before. How he and his father had made promises to stick together, as each of them were all that the other had left. Maybe it was the untruth of that statement, maybe no fault of anyone's, but that final pact never became reality. Contact was maintained purely over the phone. Mason claimed that he'd seen his father only twice before his untimely death.

'And you haven't made it down to London yet?' I probed unwillingly, mostly because it sounded like an accusation. Mason shook his head, the shame apparent.

'I can't. I'll be there for the funeral, that's about it. I know Emilia needs me, but I've told her how I feel and she understands. I just can't take it this time around. I dunno why, I don't feel as strong as I did before.'

'You do what yuh have to,' Carmen encouraged in return. 'Have yuh got people lookin' after yuh here?'

'Yeah . . .' he sighed. 'Just friends I grew up with, workmates and all that. I'll be OK, I reckon. It's just weird, you know? All my main blood relatives are gone, there's only me left. Sometimes I wonder what the point is.'

Carmen was clutching Mason's hand once more. At that stage, I felt like an outsider, a gooseberry intruding on the private grief of some couple I'd come across in a darkened corner of the pub.

'So who do you think did it? Your sister I mean, who d'you think did that to her?' I quizzed, after taking a quick sip of my own drink for Dutch courage. Mason held me with his eyes. They were dark rimmed and sunken, dulled by time and sorrow into tiny flat pebbles.

'I don't think, I know,' he growled in quiet rage. 'That fuckin' Foundation lot. They did it. Everyone knows.'

I nodded, expecting nothing else. He was right, of course: everybody knew. It was now a case of proving it. And how could I possibly attempt that when I'd already put my life into their hands by visiting their bookstore? How far would I have to go and how long would it take for justice to be done?

Knowing who the murderers were didn't solve anything, all three of us had learnt that long ago. The fallibility of our so-called justice system was enough to drive anyone to ask what the point was, never mind somebody who had just lost a loved parent and sister. Briefly, we spoke about the arrest of Charles Muhammad and the possibility of him going down for a long time. Mason was obviously pleased by this, though gratification could only go so far before he remembered all that had brought him to that point, his tears welling reluctantly. This was both painful and terrible to watch. I wanted to free him from this torture, yet before I could, I had to ask one last question.

'Mason, I just wanted to know something, then you can get on with the rest of your day,' I told him keenly, unsure how he'd react.

'Fine,' he mumbled, swapping a quick glance with Carmen and returning his gaze to the pint.

'I know Viali received some e-mails the day that she died. I was wondering if you knew her QuickMail password so I could check the messages myself. I'm pretty sure a Foundation member contacted her, so there could be some evidence worth using. Do you know anything about that?'

Mason was looking vague and disappointed, as if he was let down that I'd asked a question he didn't have an answer for.

'Sorry, but I don't have a clue,' he admitted sadly, looking straight at me. 'I never used e-mail with Viali, always the phone. I wouldn't even know where to start with the Internet.'

'That's OK, don't you worry about it.'

I got to my feet with Carmen doing the same beside me, downing her drink in a manner that was definitely not befitting a lady. Mason ignored that, instead standing with us and hugging my friend, then shaking my hand in a robust way that told me we'd earned his trust and respect. Despite my failure to glean any results, I was glad of that. The upset I'd caused his father before his death was still in my mind, a tiny speck of guilt that lurked in a remote place I tried not to visit too often.

'If you need any more help, let me know. You've got my number,' he told us warmly, sitting back down to his unfinished pint. I smiled in agreement.

'We'll be here for the next few days I think, so we may just do that,' I replied, ignoring another curious look from Carmen.

We exchanged more pleasant goodbyes and polite gestures of respect, then Carmen and myself left the Metro, walking out onto the cold and damp streets. Though I tried to ignore her, the tug on my sleeve came within no time.

'Oi, Vinnie, hol' up a sec'. What d'yuh mean we're stayin' a few more days? I got a daughter to look after in case yuh forget. It ain' as if dere's a load for us to do here!'

Although I knew where she was coming from, I couldn't help my wandering mind, which was still caught up with thoughts concerning Mason Booth. Carmen would protest no doubt, but in my mind the case was more or less over. We'd burned our last bridge. Mason had sparked no revelations, no hunches, hadn't led me in any direction of interest or given me any additional clues. The only thing the young man had managed to do was lessen my belief in true justice, something my already addled brain didn't need at this precise moment in time. The craziest thing was, if my long withheld suspicions about Robert Walker were right, Minister Charles Muhammad had performed the task of judge and executioner, pitting one black community leader against another. I hoped nobody was stupid enough to read the implication in his actions and fan the flames of bad feeling between their organisations. The only confusion I was left with concerned the guest appearance of Mystery Man and his cronies. How had such men befriended Viali?

As I tried to compose a reply for Carmen, my eye was caught by something across the street, too bold for me not to notice. Outside a hut-like news-stand was a small placard-style advert for a local newspaper, the *Leicester Mercury*. The placard was tied around a lamp-post with some string. The headline was written in black ink, and a reminder of what we would be going back to face as soon as we made it into London. I pointed it out.

ASIAN FAMILY LATEST VICTIMS OF MYSTERY ARSON ATTACK. FATHER SPEAKS OUT AGAINST RACISTS FROM HOSPITAL BED.

'That's why we're staying,' I told my friend as she read the copy, her lips moving and a worried set to her face. 'To be honest with you, that kinda thing is exactly what and who we're running away from, Carmen. At least the racists up here don't have a death wish against us. And it's not just us we gotta think about either; Hadiah and Davey are in as much shit as we are. So we're staying as long as it takes for things to die down. At least Emilia Walker's paying.'

From Carmen's expression, our homeless travelling companions were the last people on her mind, as charitable as she could sometimes be.

'Well hurry up an' think what we're gonna do, Vinnie! 'Cos sooner or later our time's gonna run out an' they will come after us. I know it.'

'So do I,' I grumbled truthfully.

One look at her saddened face was enough to know that I'd made my point, perhaps more stridently than I had needed. I linked my arm through hers and walked us back in the direction of my Audi.

On the way back to the B&B we discussed how we felt about Mason, not surprisingly finding our views fairly similar. As I'd expected, Carmen thought his tale was the saddest we'd heard so far. Though I agreed, I was disappointed to find that meant that she also had no idea what we should do next. Our discussion quickly tapered off when we both realised the other had no solutions. I was beaten, unable to think past all the distraught faces that I'd seen since I began. As I drove, a last important detail came to mind. There was encouragement from that quarter, though not much.

When we returned to the B&B, Hadiah and Davey were already there. They'd spent their day enjoying a quick game of pool in a local Super Bowl, an arcade that also offered money-munching computer games and ten pin bowling. Tonight, they told us, they were heading to the nearest pub for a well-deserved drink. They wore a look of controlled glee about them, as though both had forgotten how much they enjoyed each other's company. We were invited, but I declined; the last thing I needed was another drinking binge. Carmen also turned them down, begging off by saying that she was retiring to her room to phone her daughter. Cursing us as the light-weights we were, the couple left for their night on the town, probably their first in ages.

Telling Carmen I'd knock for her if she were needed, I headed to my room, tussling with the thought of that long-forgotten item. Once inside, I locked the door and went through my bag. Viali's diary was tucked away in a secluded side pocket, seeming smaller and thinner than I'd remembered. Holding it in my hands, I flicked the pages until the light in the room began to dim. Switching on a bedside lamp, I continued searching, taking a pen and notepaper from a bedside table, copying random words. It was only a five-minute job, but when I was finished I had to laugh. I was either on to something or I was going mad, it was hard to tell which.

I tucked my piece of paper into a pocket and went back down into the reception, asking a man behind the desk where I could find the nearest Internet café. He responded by telling

me the guesthouse provided that service, directing me down
some stairs into a basement area that I hadn't even known
existed. Computers lined the walls, guarded by a stern
woman who managed the room. She led me to an unused
seat, marked the number stuck on my monitor onto a sheet
next to the time of my arrival, then left me to it. Placing the
sheet with my selection of words from Viali's diary in front of
me, I moved the mouse until I'd located the QuickMail website.

Selecting e-mail, I forced my misgivings down and tapped
Viali's address into the space provided. Next came the hard
part. Looking down at the list of words, I hoped that I could
find the one, if any, that would unlock the system. There were
three main contenders that caught my eye out of the six I'd
written down. Going on instinct, I plucked the first from the
roll, Viali's scribbled middle name, Louisa. Typing it into the
computer, I pressed OK.

Incorrect password.

No matter. I expected as much. To save myself chances, I
guided the mouse towards a facility that took me back a stage,
so I was on the opening page as if I'd never attempted a false
password. *My hunch just needed some time to pan out*, I told
myself, *that was all.* Going for my next choice, I typed the name
Dominique. From my inside coat pocket, my phone began to
ring.

Incorrect password.

Ignoring my failure and looking at the caller ID, I saw it
was DS Birkett. Getting up from the seat, I instructed the manager to 'keep the clock running', then left the room and
wandered back upstairs, where I found a better signal.

'Hello?'

'Ervine? It's Alain, mate, how you going?'

I found myself smiling at the sound of the detective's voice.
It felt like a long time since I'd heard it.

'Oh, not too bad, still at it, still at it . . . What about you? You sound a bit stressed out mate, you OK?'

He took a deep breath before he spoke.

'I'll get straight to the point, I know you'll appreciate it,' he said. 'Basically, your house has been vandalised, Ervine. We're pretty sure The Foundation did it.'

Closing my eyes, I sat on one of the easy chairs, a hand clutching my head, struggling to hold my tongue. If I spoke without thought I knew I'd only say terrible things. Until I worked out how to deal with this, that wouldn't be wise.

'What did they do?'

'Broke all yuh windows, spray-painted their shit on yuh wall, smashed some fings up inside, you know – stereo, TV, shit like that. They . . . They took a crap on yuh bed, mate . . .'

I moaned loud enough to bring the receptionist running, though when he saw my face, he disappeared in a vague gesture of privacy. I felt a building necessity to lash out at something, though I realised that would only bring him back. Part of me wanted to go upstairs and let Carmen know right away. Then fear for my possessions came fast, new worry replacing old.

'What about my cat?'

I heard a rustling of papers.

'Cat . . . Nah, sorry Ervine, nothin' 'ere about a cat. Probably ran away or somethin'. Your next-door neighbour was the one who found it all. She was meant to feed the cat weren't she?'

There was more rustling.

'Yeah, yeah she was,' I remembered. '*Fuck*! I knew this would happen!'

'I'm real sorry it had to go this way, but at least we can do something now. We'll be after the bastards, all right?'

'Sure.'

My gloomy tone couldn't be helped. I was already adding up the cost of replacing my possessions, not to mention the priceless security and comfort my home had given me. Birkett was trying his best, but I couldn't help being vex.

'Where are you?' he rasped.

'I don't think I can tell you that,' I replied, equally harsh and deciding to treat the world as my enemy. 'Let's just say I'm not in London, right?'

'Good. Wherever you are, stay there,' he ordered. 'I'll call you tomorrow an' give you an update, OK?'

'Sure,' I grumbled.

Birkett rang off. Pitifully, I put the phone into my pocket and marched back into the basement, determination charged by the idea that I might just be able to get them back. Settling back in my seat I looked at the list, finding it hard to push aside the image of my home in a state of disarray. My mind demanded that I concentrate. I stared at the computer screen until something caught my eye.

It was a line on the opening QuickMail page, a command for people who'd forgotten their password and needed a reminder. I clicked, and was rewarded with another screen. Here, a question was posed.

What's the name of my secret workplace?

I tapped *Whispers* onto the screen, selected OK and waited. The computer screen went blank, then gave me a new page.

I was in.

Grinning with achievement, I watched as various options came to light in front of me. One small step, though I couldn't rejoice just yet. Clicking Viali's Inbox, I waited a little longer before her e-mail list scrolled down the screen. There were at least fifty. I counted more than ten fresh ones, which would explain why her account hadn't been shut down. Most of the latest arrivals were newsletters from sites she'd subscribed to, along with random chain mail letters, something I'd been surprised to see make the leap from snail mail to here. Ignoring the bulk of the entries, I looked for ones dated November tenth, the date of Viali's death. She'd received one e-mail. The subject box was blank. What I saw in the name box sent cold tingles running down my spine.

Snakeskin.

Moving the mouse, I pointed the arrow at that strange word, then pressed the left button. An anonymous letter appeared on the large monitor. I read quickly, unwittingly shaking my head the closer I got to the bottom of the page.

```
V
Been trying to reach you but your phone's
been off. I know you're angry with me but I
need to see you tonite. I won't lie to you
mark made that call about the Purcell Rooms.
If you still care what happens next, you'll
come anyway.
SS
```

I selected the print option then closed my eyes, the words audible sentences echoing inside my head. I was close, though not close enough. Viali's killer had penned this message, though precisely who that was I couldn't even guess, much less prove. I opened my eyes; the message on the monitor was still goading me. Disgusted, I signed off and paid for the service, then retired to my room, defeated once more.

21

I spent that night alone, trying to take my mind off what I'd learned, thinking it would do me no good to dwell on things I couldn't change. Sleep had been far from my reach. Mostly, I'd turned over the thought that some people were strong enough to reach a certain distance, destined to go no further than luck and spirit could take them. Sometimes those things, admittedly assets, weren't enough to drive a being to excellence. It was hard not to convince myself that this was the case with everything I had been through over the last few weeks. Strong, though ultimately not strong enough. Thinking about it that way brought the gloom back to my demeanour. Grumpily, I left my bed sometime near nine, when I could no longer fight the feeling that I had to get up and do something. I went downstairs for breakfast in resigned misery, which only partially subsided at the sight of Carmen, Hadiah and Davey already eating.

'Hey,' Carmen grinned as I came into the small dining room and sat by a blue checked table. Her resigned look was gone, her smile bright and filled with hope. 'Sleep well?' she continued, scanning me with an eager eye.

'Not really,' I admitted, keen to skirt over my insomnia and what seemed like resident bad cheer. My full English breakfast was ordered from a man at the door brandishing a neatly typed menu complete with illustrations. 'How about you guys? How was your night out, Davey?'

'Ah, well good, we 'ad a right laugh innit, Hads?' Davey grinned through a mouthful of toast, with Hadiah smiling in agreement. Not knowing what I'd let myself in for by asking, I was subjected to a full and detailed account of every drunken conversation, joke or accident they'd had, in every bar. Carmen laughed along with them and ordered more coffee, proposing that today we all forgot about The Foundation and the Walkers, instead going for a lunchtime drink together. Bad as I was feeling, the thought was not inspiring, but I couldn't possibly say no. I said that I'd eat and join everybody in the lobby after I'd got myself in some order, which allowed me some time alone before we went on our little outing.

Back in my room with a full stomach, I sat on the single bed, gazing at the walls. Though I felt like I was going mad, I wasn't quite there yet. Sometime during the night I'd stuck Viali's photo up with some spare Blu Tack I'd found, next to the printed e-mail from my mystery author with the strange nickname: Snakeskin. Further along the wall were scribbled scraps of paper I'd ripped from my notebook, mostly sightings and descriptions of Viali's alleged assailants by Michael Josiah, Hadiah and Davey. Looking from one to another, I tried to force my mind to think: what was the connection? There had to be one. Pieces were still missing from the puzzle, but no matter how hard I thought this thing over, I could draw no conclusions. I was running out of time, even though my inclination was driving me almost as much as frustration. If I didn't find something quickly, pretty soon I would have to report my lack of results to Emilia.

Tearing my eyes away from those of Viali, I left and locked my room around 11.30, then met with the others, who were gathered in a pensive huddle. I must've been in my room a long time, because Carmen's worry was clouding her new-found good cheer, though she tried hard to hide her feelings. This reinforced my decision to keep the news concerning my house to myself. I also decided to keep quiet about Snakeskin, at least until I found out who he really was. Seemingly oblivious to the strained air, Hadiah informed us we were being taken to a pub they'd visited the night before. What amazed me most was that neither of the youths seemed particularly bothered by the prospect of drinking themselves stupid all over again. That unanimously decided, we left the building and climbed into my car, driving towards the centre of town.

The bar Hadiah suggested was known as the Orange Star, a small establishment with a trendier club feel than the Metro, complete with dimmed lights, exotic paintings and an affordable fluorescent cocktail menu. It looked like the kind of bar you'd find on a remote desert island, not stuck in the centre of a rainy Midlands town. The place was quiet and mostly empty, the House music pitched low, even though massive speakers were hung in every corner. As I was being such a grump, I felt obliged to get the first round in, collecting orders and going to the bar, telling myself that now was the time to relax. No more Viali Walker, no more rash decisions or depressions, at least until I got back to London. I should treat this time as a brief respite from my problems; a holiday. I would enjoy this drink for exactly what it was. With those thoughts in mind, I deposited the purchased drinks on the table in front of the others with a renewed, yet slightly forced, zest for life. I took a seat next to Carmen and raised my glass.

'To all you guys: Carmen, Hadiah and Davey. And to trust,' I toasted sincerely, as they smiled and joined the chant. We sipped, looking satisfied with ourselves. After all, we had drink and good company. Some people had far less.

'I know we aren't meant to ask but . . . How did it go yesterday?' Hadiah prompted suddenly. From the guarded way she spoke, I guessed it was a question that had been batted between herself and Davey for most of the morning. Carmen seemed on edge too, and just as eager to see what I had to say, as previous talk of Mason Booth had been quite limited. I told them a condensed version of our meeting, excluding my own view of the young man, to see how they might perceive his attitudes. They listened attentively enough. When I was finished, the two simply looked at each other as if lost.

'So, what next?' Davey drawled, confusion on his face. I swallowed hard in reply. The truth was hard to admit, especially to these kids.

'I don't know,' I breathed reluctantly. 'I'm still trying to think.'

That sobered the atmosphere by a good few degrees, though everybody was benevolent enough, allowing that my work was more difficult than anyone could've guessed. It was up to wily Carmen to change the subject yet again, turning the talk to the dreaded war. I'd been so caught up in my work I had only the vaguest knowledge of what was going on, though I tried my hardest to participate. We finished our drinks, which helped us relax with each other enough for conversation to flow with no uncomfortable gaps. Carmen got the next set of drinks in.

A lunchtime crowd began to seep into the bar, and the music level was raised to accommodate a busier atmosphere. Much to the girls' dismay, talk at our table turned to sport. Ignoring Hadiah and Carmen's disgusted faces, we discovered a mutual love of Formula One racing, at which point Hadiah threw her arms in the air and said she'd had enough. While we laughed, she demanded Davey get the next round, rolling her eyes as her boyfriend protested on the grounds of poverty. To avoid a funny scene turning serious, I laid another twenty on the table and told Davey it was his if he got the drinks in. When Carmen stared, I mouthed the word 'expenses'. Her expression remained, though she managed to direct it elsewhere as Davey took our orders and struggled to his feet.

I guessed something was wrong as soon as he raised himself, twisting around to face the bar while the girls decided they'd talk about what they liked best in his absence: TV soaps. Excluded by my lack of experience, I diverted my attention to the young man, watching him stop in his tracks, eyes turned towards the counter, frozen as if the wind had changed and he was stuck that way. I tried to grab his attention and find out what was wrong, though before I could, Davey slumped back into the seat, his face drained of life. Carmen abruptly broke off her impassioned plea for the return of Bianca to *EastEnders*, which instantly alerted his girlfriend. All eyes were on the frightened youth.

'Davey?' I spoke carefully. 'What's wrong?'

I was watching the collection of men that Davey had spotted standing in a messy huddle by the bar. Four burly white men, talking loudly, pints in hand, looming over other customers. The nearest had his back to me, though I could see enough to tell that he was huge and bald-headed, his neck a series of folds and ripples that emphasised the heavyweight he was. Premonition struck me as I watched the man's wide back, those powerful shoulders, that glistening head.

'Don't look, but see dat big guy standing by the bar,' the youth directed with a stricken whisper, keeping his head as still as he could manage. '*Don't look*! I swear dat's Mystery Man. You know, from South Bank. I don't recognise the others, but that's him, I'm sure. He's wearing the same jacket, same jeans, everything.'

Hadiah stiffened, unconsciously mimicking her boyfriend's actions, blood running from her face until it was as pale as his and they sat like matching moons. There was no disbelief on her part, no hesitation; she simply accepted her boyfriend's words, even though she hadn't looked. It was hard not to be affected by their fear, but if what Davey claimed was right, this could be either the best, or worst thing that had happened since we arrived in this town. Beside me, Carmen was staring intensely at the couple.

'Are yuh sure it's him?' she hissed. 'I don't see how you can tell from here.'

'I'm one hundred fuckin' per cent sure!' Davey snapped back in return, his alarm raising his voice to a dangerous level.

Worried, I pushed a finger to my lips; the last thing we needed was to draw the men's attention. This turn of events had been like everything else that had happened so far: too rapid for second-guessing, leaving only time for reaction. There was one way we could find out if Davey was right or wrong for sure. It was foolhardy, yet the only chance we had. I got to my feet.

'All right you guys, wait here, I'll be back in a minute,' I ordered in a low voice. 'Don't talk to me, don't even look in my direction until I talk to you, all right?'

I was faced with a round of mute nods. Leaving the table and all of my limited security, I went to the bar and stood behind the bald man, waving a twenty-pound note like a flag. A barman sauntered across and took my order, while I attempted to listen to what the men were saying, quickly finding it impossible; the music was too loud and their conversation angled the wrong way. When my lone brandy and Coke was placed in front of me, I paid and collected my change. Bracing myself, I turned and walked straight into the bald man.

Brandy spilled down my hand and onto the wooden floor, though thankfully for me there was none on our suspect. Nevertheless, he turned around to see who had bumped him, his drinking buddies falling silent and glaring threateningly.

Although he was as wide as two normal-sized men placed shoulder to shoulder, we stood at roughly the same height and so faced each other eye to eye. It was immediately apparent that he had the look of a bona fide madman. His face was a mask of decadence, the skin covered with drink-reddened blotches and broken veins, his piggy blue eyes sunk deep into his face until they were barely seen. His teeth were testimony to a diet of fast food and sugar-filled drinks. As he shifted his huge bulk to face me, it was easy to see the long and fleshy scar running along his left cheek from ear to chin.

It was him.

The man stared as if unable to believe I'd had the audacity to walk into him. For now, I wasn't pushing my luck any further.

'Sorry mate,' I muttered, fully aware of the stares from his three friends, clearly unwilling to forgive my feigned mishap. Mystery Man put a lot of space between my words and his reply, finally speaking in a rumble that resembled the passing tremor of an HGV.

'Let it happen again an' you will be, *mate*,' he told me in a strong Leicester accent, perfectly pitched for my ears alone. Much as I wanted to mouth some smart arse reply, part of me was glad of the fact that I couldn't. The aura of violence surrounding this man was similar to that of Ivanhoe – no matter how such men attempted to suppress their natural inclination, the attempt was as pointless as a bird subduing its urge to fly. They were what they were, no ifs, ands or buts. Taking this into consideration, I bowed my head, feeding his ego.

'Sorry,' I mumbled, moving my pride and drink into a corner of the bar that was thankfully very near the main entrance. Mystery Man and his friends watched me go, perhaps in need of more of a challenge than the one I'd just provided. Pretty soon, they were laughing and joking again, oblivious to my presence. I snatched a look over at Carmen, who was watching me reproachfully. I nodded once as imperceptibly as I could manage.

After that, there was nothing more I could do. The men proceeded to drink, ignoring me and chatting as raucously as they liked, every other word a profanity of some kind. They were obviously thugs, and I sat nursing my brandy knowing that sooner or later they'd remember my presence and pick a fight, just to add to my already sour luck. Contrary to my mind's paranoid wanderings, after half an hour the men picked up their car keys and wallets, drained their glasses then passed me by. As they left the bar, Mystery Man muttered something about them going to find a 'nigger-free zone'. Ignoring the bait, I let them leave. As soon as they were out of view, I jumped to my feet and ran back to the table to join the others.

'Was it dem?' Davey asked animatedly. The women stared, relief apparent in their eyes.

'Yeah, I'm pretty sure it's him, I saw the scar right where you told us it was. Now Carmen, I want you to do me a favour.'

'Whassat?'

Her frightened expression deepened.

'Don't worry, it's nothing major. I just need you to take my phone and stay here looking after these two. I'll call as soon as I know where they're headed.'

'Vinnie . . .' Carmen began, but there was no time. I held a hand in the air to silence them all.

'No arguments from anyone, please. I'll see you all when I get back.'

Satisfied I'd made myself clear, I turned and left them in their seats, then ran outside and peered in the direction the four large men had taken. Nobody was there. Swearing, I ran to the corner of the street to find them walking down a side road with lumbering steps. It was apparent even to surrounding pedestrians and shoppers that these were not men to be messed with; everybody who passed the gang gave them as wide a berth as possible. Peeking around the corner, I watched them approach a white Transit van, one of the smaller men clicking a car alarm and unleashing that familiar double-beep.

While they unlocked the doors, I climbed into my Audi and studied their movements from my rear-view mirror. When they started the van, I turned my car around and began the tail, trepidation a gnawing pain I tried to ignore.

The others had thought I was crazy, I could tell by the look in their eyes. It didn't matter; I wasn't losing the only real lead we had. Little by little, things were starting to make sense, and there was only one explanation for Mystery Man's presence in this town. My suspicions about what was really going on were so terrible, so fantastic, I didn't dare put them into words. Besides, the way things had worked out, there was no one to tell. I was alone in the car with all of my suppositions and worries.

The occupants of the van had no idea they were being followed, which made them a remarkably easy tail, despite my lack of knowledge when it came to the Leicester roads. I crept along, heading away from the town centre onto London Road, then along fields and A-roads surrounding the outskirts of the town, where there were large Victorian houses and people were scarce. At a roundabout, I took the second exit after them and dropped back even further, as the road became clearer. It grew harder to keep up. I was very aware that other drivers noticed my colour as I passed their vehicles, yet the Transit van's smooth and unhurried journey was infinitely encouraging. My pursuit continued along the straight road until we reached another roundabout, where they circled and took the fourth turn, a hard left into a tiny slip road. Slowing some more, I pushed my Audi along in their wake. When they took the next available right, I rolled towards the corner of the slip road, pulling up near enough to catch a glimpse of their progress.

The road they had taken led them into a modern council estate. Instead of long tall blocks or small squat blocks, these were identical red-brick houses with gardens, fencing and double-glazing. Children rode their bikes in trainer-wearing gangs, though it was clear to my discerning eye that there wasn't a hint of ethnicity to be found. Parents waddled past with bags of shopping, or stood by garden fences chatting the day away. Despite what I knew about these places, the area had a calm serenity that was warm and enticing enough.

I turned my attention to the Transit van, which had stopped outside a house situated halfway along the road. The four men got out and strode across the pavement until I could see them no more. I could only assume they had gone inside; not wanting to be proven wrong by losing them, I thought it best that I make sure.

As I gunned my engine in determination, an unnoticed car beeped behind me. Raising a hand in apology, I turned right, driving past the Transit van, looking at the vehicle in my rear-view mirror. There was nothing to be seen. Slowing as much as the driver behind me would allow, I noticed a beat-up Volvo parked behind the Transit, though this too was empty.

I continued until the car behind me took the first left, turning my Audi around and parking where I could, the council house and two vehicles in full view. Now all I could do was watch. I didn't dare attempt to find a phone box so I could call Carmen; there was every chance the men would leave in the time it would take to locate one, let alone make the call. I couldn't even take the risk of going into the boot of my car for my Taurus, or a book. I had no option but to sit things out.

For a long time, nothing happened. The door to the house stayed closed, the cars remained where they were parked, and the only things that moved were the children running up and down the road. I got out of the car after the first hour, climbing onto the back seat and lying down flat, closing my eyes, hoping I could ward off sleep.

I hadn't realised the smell of petrol was so strong back there. With the car running the fumes must have been stifling, and I promised myself that I would get it checked out on my return to London. When a car rolled by I'd struggle onto my belly and peer through my back window to see if the men had come out, or more had arrived, yet with each vehicle there remained no change. Eventually, I grew accustomed to the sound of a passing engine. The noises became old friends, part of the waiting game.

Relaxing where I lay and putting together what I knew, there was no doubt that I had Viali's killers cornered. My latest problem was that I hadn't a clue what to do with them. The only evidence I possessed was inside the heads of Hadiah and Davey, and as things stood, the courts would only label what they had seen as circumstantial. Yet I still harboured clear joy, the knowledge that things were going right for me in a way that I could never have imagined. My main concerns right now were the length of my wait, and the fact that these people would determine my next move, how I reacted. It was a precarious final position, my fate in the hands of men that hated me.

Dusk began taking shape. I settled into a light doze, prepared to camp out all night. There was no movement from the house, though lights had started to blaze from a downstairs window. Besides this, everything was the same. Eyes closed, I pictured Viali's face in my mind's eye. *Soon*, I spoke to her in my head. *Soon it would be done.* I was alive and aware, as though I could feel every particle of blood racing through my veins, as though I could sense every cell, every atom that made up my being. Now, only when it was fully within my grasp, I knew what I had been looking for so long: the rush of exhilaration that comes with success.

There were sudden raised voices, the sound of farewells.

For what I hoped was the last time, I rolled over onto my stomach and peeked through the back window. Fading light made the people coming out of the house and walking down the garden path hard to see, while a silhouette stood in the doorway seeing them off. The person waving seemed to be a woman from what I could make out. Her friends were all men, though none of them looked like the suspects I'd seen in the Orange Star. Curious, I raised myself a few inches higher, as one of the men seemed very familiar. As he shouted his last goodbye and turned to face the street, I got my clearest look at him yet.

Mason Booth turned and pushed the garden gate open with his backside, his hands full carrying a large cardboard box. Even though I had anticipated this from the minute I'd laid eyes on Mystery Man's scar, knowing his presence here couldn't be a coincidence, I was still shocked and angry that Mason had managed to deceive me. It seemed senseless that the young man had made these racists his friends and allies.

I carefully watched as he opened the Volvo, placed his box on the back seat, then got in and with a last farewell beep, drove back towards the slip road. Clambering into the front of my car, I turned the ignition and followed, ducking my head as I passed the men starting their own cars. When I reached the A-road, Mason was already gone. I kept faith that, as relaxed as he had looked, he wouldn't move too fast, though I increased my speed nevertheless and kept my eyes open in case I unintentionally passed him. It had happened before. Thankfully, it didn't take long before I saw the Volvo in the distance, stuck by some yellow lights on a lone junction. I slipped carefully into the traffic flow as the lights turned green.

Soon, Mason hit the same roundabout I had circled hours before, taking the first left, which I recognised as the road that led to my B&B. He passed a petrol station and a girl's high school, before he turned right onto another side road. I did my same trick, pulling up at the corner of the street, watching him drive a third of the way and eventually park on an easy bend. Mason got out of his car, went into the boot and grabbed the box, then lifted it away, somewhere out of my sight.

When he was gone, I rested my head against the steering wheel, unable to explain the feelings shooting through me. Things were almost over, and I didn't know what that left me with. This was a part of the job that I had no experience in. I didn't want to mess up by doing something irreparably stupid, so I turned the car around and headed back for the petrol station. There, I found a phone and dialled my mobile number, which I'd written down in my notepad rather than attempt to memorise. Carmen answered after two rings.

'Vinnie, is dat you?'

'Yeah.' I had to smile at the worry in her voice. 'Everything's fine and I'm OK, but you won't believe what's happened.'

I told her about my journey to the small estate, the meeting that seemed to have taken place and what I'd seen of Mason Booth. Following that, I offered Carmen two choices: she could wait a little longer or go back to the B&B; either way, I would handle this next and last part alone. Call it macho, call it stupid, but there was no way I was letting her walk into a dangerous situation like this, no matter how street smart she was. She protested, yet again, but as I wouldn't tell her where I was, there was nothing more she could do. Promising to call again in an hour, I rang off, walked to my car, then drove back to the street where I had last seen Mason Booth.

22

When I arrived, the Volvo remained parked in the same space. I looked around to see if it had been joined by other cars from that small estate. There were none to be found. Hopefully, it wasn't just a case of me not recognising the vehicles they drove. For my own well-being, I dug into my boot for my Taurus and a spare clip I'd hidden away for these moments. After some thought, I took a couple of home-made plastic slides, perfect for breaking and entering. I stuffed the latter into my pocket, the former into the small of my back, and walked to the Volvo with a slow, uneasy step.

Peering through the back window of his car, everything was verified by the lone poster that had no doubt fallen from the box he'd hefted away. The familiarity of the script sent more alarm through me, yet made me feel perverse excitement. Reading that blazing line again – BRITAIN FOR THE

BRITS – SUPPORT OUR CAUSE – I realised that Mason Booth was an extremely confused young man.

 Leaving the car, I crept along the nearest pathway, aware of the quiet and dark of the road, the thick silence. I hadn't seen a soul, which was nothing like London, no matter how similar the houses and roads seemed. An automatic light clicked into life, scaring me until I realised it worked by itself. When I reached a door at the end of the pathway, I peered at four buzzers that lined a silver intercom system, each with a name or initials beside them. Third on the list was a scrawled MB, enough of a clue to have me reaching into a pocket for my plastic slide, furtively looking around as I moved closer, hiding my actions from the road. Seconds later, there was a click and I was in. Feeling blindly along the wall until I touched a light switch, I pressed and moved upstairs.

It was a door as plain as the man that inhabited the flat: emulsion white with a silver number screwed dead centre. I stared, fully aware that if I was wrong I would be going to court for breaking and entering. Not that I cared at this stage. Producing my makeshift slide, I pushed it into the crack of the door, jiggled it about and was rewarded with another familiar click. Cautious now that there was no going back, I gingerly stepped inside noting the sound of music from a far away room.

Small and somewhat cramped, there seemed only enough space for one person in that matchbox of a home. I moved towards three doors, one on the right side of the passageway, the others located at the end. One of the far doors was closed, which tweaked at my senses; that wasn't quite right when the others were standing wide open. Drawing the Taurus from my back, I breathed through my nose, feeling my heartbeat increase, my mouth go dry, the hairs on my neck begin to rise. In seconds I was nineteen years old again, dressed in fatigues with the sound of gunfire around me. I heard the noise, smelt hot earth, felt the ground beneath me shake until I blinked my eyes and saw that shut door again. Swallowing hard, I pushed on down the corridor trying not to imagine what lay beyond.

The first open door revealed a small kitchen, the tidy space painted yellow and blue, with matching plates and cutlery. By the time I reached the end of the passageway, it was apparent the music was coming from a radio inside the last open room; this had a large TV, a video and sofa, piles of Nintendo games scattered about. Turning to the closed door, I thought awhile, laughed at my silly musings, then decided there was nothing else for me to try. Hoping that I wasn't making a big mistake, I knocked three times.

'Hello,' Mason's voice came back. 'Is that Ervine?'

Stunned, there was a moment when I didn't know whether I should answer. Mason solved my problem by adding to my bewilderment.

'Come inside, mate. Come on, it's all right!'

Gun raised, I turned the door handle awkwardly with my left hand and let myself in. It was a typical man's room: an unmade bed, computer screen, posters of supermodels all over the walls. As I looked around, I realised not all of the pictures were of models, and not every pin-up was a poster. Some were press clippings, exclaiming shocked headlines that told of house fires, beaten youths, attacks by groups of men with baseballs bats. Most showed family pictures of the victims, who were more often than not Asian, though sometimes black. Scanning further, I saw the newspaper picture of Viali placed in the centre of the others.

Sitting on his unmade bed beneath this cutting was Mason Nathaniel Booth. He was holding a gun in both hands, pointed at himself. His manner was serene, his expression unworried by his own pistol, or my Taurus. I wasn't even sure where to point my weapon, faced with the surreal scene before me.

He turned my way as I froze by his bedroom door.

'Come inside,' he ordered gently.

'Mason . . .' I began, unsure of what to say. As I spoke, his expression changed into something fierce, more animal than I could imagine. He jammed the pistol against his temple.

'*Fuckin' come inside!*'

I sighed. He was indeed as smart as his father and sister. Mason knew that I would respond correctly if he threatened to harm himself, rather than attempt to turn the gun on me. Angry, but unable to show it, I followed his instructions and moved inside until I stood at the foot of his single bed. Mason was paying me little attention, now looking straight into the sightless black eye of his automatic.

'Mason . . . Mason, we can do this another way . . .'

His dark-rimmed eyes turned to me, freezing my words into a tiny snowball inside my throat. I could see that despite his calm, Mason was crying. In the silence between us, I could hear the radio playing some mournful indie song, which wasn't exactly ideal for the current mood. He cocked an ear in appreciation.

'Radiohead,' he told me in a satisfied voice. 'Great band they are. '

I was frowning tightly.

'So you're . . .' I had to clear my throat to free the previous sentence. 'You're . . . Snakeskin?'

The gun wriggled in Mason's hands as the young man's eyes crawled all over me. It was a vile feeling, the displeasure that laced his glare adding to the growing feel of being trapped inside that room.

'You know about that?' he whispered. I was tempted to make a leap for the gun, even though I knew that any slight miscalculation could leave one of us dead. When he looked up, my rational mind was so elated, I almost missed his next sentence.

'It was all over anyway,' he continued, his words spoken not to me but to himself.

'What d'you—'

'Sit down!' he barked, nodding at a seat beneath his computer desk.

Perching on the metal chair would put me in Mason's direct line of fire. Knowing it was almost useless anyway, I put my Taurus on the floor before complying with his instruction, hoping the young man would perceive this as an act of trust. When he saw my manoeuvre, Mason laughed out loud, making me flinch.

'That's right, Ervine, I don't wanna shoot you. Don't be afraid of me. If I wanned to kill you, I would've already done it. They saw you followin' me from the house, you know. I knew you was comin'.'

My brow remained tense, knitted like steel wool. I took the seat, anger trying hard to claim me, even though the emotion couldn't help.

'This isn't the movies, Mason. Put the gun away and tell it to the police. You'd be doing me more of a favour.'

In front of me, he was still laughing, wrapping his thumb tighter around the trigger. He saw me watching his awkward clutch, and even had the nerve to wink.

'Don't say another word, Ervine. My dad told me about you. Did you know that? Told me that he thought there was an edge to you. He was right, wasn't he? Mind you, Robert was hardly ever wrong.'

I clamped my lips together. Mason chuckled in return.

'All right, Ervine James, sit back and relax, cos I'm gonna tell you a story, OK? Listen carefully, I haven't time to repeat myself.'

He giggled. I cursed myself for thinking sanity had still been within Mason's grasp. Now I could truly see him for who he was, I wished my insight had been better. *Mind you*, I thought, *at least if I die in this shitty little room, they could write on my tombstone that I solved the case. Very comforting.*

'You don't have any idea what it's like livin' in a place like this,' Mason began, and intentional or not, his voice took on a storyteller's cadence that was only slightly less unsettling than the scene before me. 'No matter how I tried to fit in, I was an outsider. Growing up, I lived with my mum on that estate you jus' come from, an' I was the only coloured kid for fuckin' miles. Mum was always on at me to be proud, but what did she know? She didn't have to go through the shit I did. No matter where I went, I was noticed. For a kid, that's the worst feelin' in the world, that isolation. You'd do anything to be part of things.

'I went through all of the usual shit, all of the insults. You must've heard 'em before, so there's no sense me going inta detail. I was bullied, teased, beaten up, until one day I found a way to stop it. "At the end of the day", I told them kids, "I'm only half-black. My mum is as white as you." But that wasn't enough for them. They wanted me to prove my white side was as important to me as they said it was. I started doing the things they told me to. There was a gang of us that used to do it, the same lot I hang with now.'

'What did you do?' I asked slowly, trying to keep the strain from my voice. Mason snatched a look, then returned his gaze to that single black eye, aiming his answer that way.

'We beat up kids around our area. You know, all the Pakis and coons that live around here, we used to chase 'em an' kick shit out of 'em, about fifteen of us. That was the time that one of our little lot, Mark, started going to these meetings with his older brother and telling us what happened. At the meetings they'd talk about how we'd get the area back, drive all the immigrants out and everything would be great again. How we'd get more jobs and better houses when they were gone. Us kids wanted to go to those meetings. Next thing I knew, Mark's older brother said, "Yeah, great, come along". I remember that day . . . All of the hardest blokes from all over Leicester was there, an' they treated us like little princes, even me. They said I couldn't help the mistake my mother made, an' at least I looked white from far enough away. From that day to this, those people in that room was like family to me.

'We started to do little things to let the immigrants know we weren't havin' it. We'd rob their shops, or beat up their kids, or threaten them for a laugh. No one would dare grass us up – when one lot tried, they soon found out how we dealt with that. One night, we went over their way and burned down their house. They moved the family out, and everyone knew not to fuck with us. Mission accomplished. Mark's older brother was well pleased, 'cos it was mostly our boys that had gone an' done the raid. His mates told us that the only language those people could understand was violence. So we went an' did it again. An' again. An' again.'

He waved a hand at the wall behind him. I could feel the horror alive on my face, unable to control it. There were at least eight different cuttings, eight separate families that had lost loved ones, or homes, or possessions. My cold glare was useless against Mason, whose eyes remained locked on his gun barrel, tears silently racing down his cheeks. The weapon trembled in his hands. I was tempted to make my move once more; he didn't notice, but tightened his grasp on the pistol all the same.

'What about Viali? Did she know what you were doing?'

I wasn't sure I should be asking questions, but I needed to know. Contrary to his growled order, Mason seemed not to mind, though he continued to speak blindly, as if he were alone.

'Viali didn't know a thing,' he whispered sombrely. 'I was such an idiot. I loved her so, so much, all the things they'd been tellin' me, the things I'd been doin' when I was here seemed . . . wrong . . . evil, you know . . . when I was with her. I could've been a different person in London. In the right places, no one took any notice of me . . . You know that in Leicester, even the kids know you're different, point you out? So what chance did I have? In London I could disappear, there were thousands of people that looked like me. I wanted to disappear with Viali. Live a life like hers, a life *with* her.'

The true horror of what Mason was saying dawned on me as I sat there listening to his painful confession. His love for his sister had been no ordinary, run of the mill, brother's love. It became sexual, and had caused Viali's death.

'How many times, Mason?' I dared, unable to hold the thought back. He cried out in anguish, the tears flowing faster, the gun trembling once more. I stared as if hypnotised, my ears only just picking up his despair-filled reply. His tears and change of vocal pitch were making the words progressively harder to hear.

'It happened once,' he choked into the silence that followed. 'Only once, but Viali was sick about it. I'd stayed in her house for the weekend. Dominique was away an' I walked her home from Whispers one night, then it happened by itself, I'm tellin' you! I never meant it! We were both to blame! She was actin' strange afterwards, so I thought I'd give her some space, you know? When I got back here she stopped callin', stopped e-mailin', broke off all fuckin' contact! I didn't know what to do. I fuckin' loved her, you understand? I always loved her, even when we was kids! Then Mark asked if I wanted to go down to London in the van an' talk her round. You know, it was funny – even after all we'd learnt in those Foundation meetings, he still fancied her like mad. They met a few times an' got on well, too, even though he looks like a right thug. So we went, an' Mark called her without me knowing, pretending to be from Dad's office, arranging to meet. When he told me I was fuckin' pissed, so I e-mailed her right away an' told her the truth. She said she'd come an' see me anyway.'

'Why Snakeskin?' I mouthed, still gazing at his pistol in concentration. Mason wiped his nose with one hand, his laughter harsh and filled with bitterness. Imperceptibly, I raised a quarter of an inch from my seat, only to sit back down when he saw and moved the weapon closer to his face.

'That's a good one, that. Viali always used to ask an' I wouldn't tell her. I wanted to see if she found out for herself, you know? She was smart as anyone, but she never did. In the end it was up to me to tell her, and she hated me for it.'

He shifted on the bed in an attempt to get more comfortable, while I perched on my chair, scared to move a muscle.

'In a way, you know, she was the one who made me go by that name. You know how Afro-centric she was, don't you? Always on about black this, black that . . . The amount of times Mark would have to bite his fuckin' tongue . . . Anyway, she was always talkin' about black people sellin' out – movie stars, singers, politicians. And all the while, whenever she started rantin' about dat shit, I'd agree. Whenever me dad started talkin' about racial equality, I'd be right there with him, givin' my own experiences; which most of the time were jus' stories where I swapped places wiv the Pakis me an' my mates had beaten up, robbed, or intimidated over the last few weeks. 'Cos when I was back here, back home, I went the opposite way an' sided wiv Mark an' the rest. England for the English an' all that lark. Pretty soon I didn't even know what I really thought or believed, whose side I was on. All I knew was I'd become the kind of person Viali hated. A sell-out, someone that would rather keep their own kind down in order to get ahead in life – and I was such a dozy bastard, I'd sold out both sides. I was nothing more than a snake amongst other snakes, not black or white, shedding my skin for each race, trying to convince them all I was like them. So I made it me nickname.'

I wasn't satisfied with Mason's flimsy excuses for his actions, but held no desire to voice my opinion, especially as I got the feeling that he had somewhat enjoyed his turncoat role. There were many pieces of this puzzle that remained separate enigmas, each one equally compelling in their own right: whether his father had known what he had done to all those families; if he'd ever loved Robert Walker, or if the MP's presence in his life only added to his self-hatred, his confusion; if Mason had gone to meet Viali with the intention of killing her, or if he'd wanted to walk off into the sunset with his sister, hand-in-lover's-hand. So many questions to be asked, even though I knew there wasn't time. I had to talk the gun from Mason's hands before he decided to take his anguish out on me, the only man within striking distance of his pain.

'Mason ... You've got to stop what you're doing, it's making things that much worse. You can't point a gun at yourself and expect everything to go away. You've got to face up to what you've done. You've started the process, so let's continue. You owe it to all of these people!'

For the first time since his confession, Mason looked back into my eyes, his own glistening.

'Nah, nah, you don't understand what happened. When I met Viali that night I told her, you know, like I jus' told you. You know what she did? She threatened to grass! Someone like me ... I can't go to jail for what I did ... They'd all hate me. I'm not one or the other ... I'd die in there ...'

Mason jammed the gun between his jaws. I wanted to jump from my seat even though I knew there was little I could do to stop him. In seconds, my forehead was red hot, sweat dripping like Mason's falling tears.

'No! C'mon Mason, don't do this, there's no need! You can be looked after, people can take care of you! *Mason!*'

Delicately, he took the barrel from his mouth and turned my way. I felt deep relief, preparing to jump no matter what.

'Viali's dress is in my wardrobe. That should be all the evidence you need. All right mate?'

He replaced the pistol and fired before I could scream his name again.

There is no greater horror than the sight of a corpse. Whether male or female, adult or child, it carries the same terrifying weight. The only thing worse was witnessing

death first-hand. No demise was more final than the one I
had just seen. Mason may have lived for a few seconds – or
was it his nerves twitching, sending messages to places that
couldn't possibly respond? I couldn't tell. All I could fathom
was that I had been faced with my worst fear, the thing that
I had never wished to see again. The vision flashed in my
memory over and over like a record stuck in the groove. It
hadn't killed me, so I hoped that the remainder of the saying
was true.

When I could stand to look down at my coat and trousers,
I saw they were covered in the young man's blood. Instead
of recoiling, as all of my urges insisted, I chose to ignore the
sight and perform one last task before I called the police. I
had to make sure that when the lawmen came, they knew I
wasn't the criminal. Strengthened by the thought, I stumbled
to Mason's wardrobe, which was thankfully close to the
door, so I wouldn't have to pass the body. Looking carefully
inside, I moved jumpers, jackets and T-shirts until I could
see something glittering behind his dull and dusty clothes.

At the sight of the tiny outfit, the torn and scuffed patterned blue dress, tears threatened to rain from my eyes. I
took deep breaths and gulps of air until the feeling passed.
When I'd collected myself, I shut the wardrobe door and
walked into the sitting room. Finding the phone, my trembling finger dialled two nines, thought about it, replaced the
receiver, then dialled again; only this time the number was
the usual seven digits. The familiar voice answered after three
rings, just like I'd taught her.

'Good afternoon, James' Private Investigations, how may I
help?'

'Sadie?'

'Ervine? What's goin' on? I had a call from Carmen, she's
practically frantic! What's goin'—'

'Everything's fine, Sadie, I'm OK. It's over. I know who did
it, but I'm calling because I want you to do something for me.

I need you to call Emilia Walker an' tell her that Mason Booth confessed to Viali's murder, then took his own life. I want you to say it to her just like I said it to you. Can you do that? Do you *mind* doing that?'

'Well . . . I don't . . .' She caught herself, breath trembling a moment before she continued. 'Nah babes, course I don't mind . . .' She sighed. 'But are you all right? You don't sound too clever, luv . . .'

'I'm fine, Sade, just a bit shaken up, you know? I'll be OK. I just need you to phone Emilia right away and let her know.'

'". . . Mason Booth confessed to Viali's murder, then took his own life . . ." Is there anything else?'

'Only that I'll call her when the police have finished with me. Thanks, Sadie.'

'No trouble babes, I'll get on with it right away. Now you hurry up an' get down here.'

'Yeah, I will. I gotta go, but thanks again.'

'No problem, luv.'

'Oh, an' Sade?'

A pause.

'Yeah, go on, I'm here.'

'I think' – I took a huge gulp – 'I think we're about to be in business. Seriously.'

'That's good, darlin'. That's all we can ask innit?'

'Innit,' I agreed.

'See you when you get back.'

''Bye, Sadie.'

I cut her off with a finger and held the receiver in my free hand, then sat motionless for a long time, thinking about everything I'd just said. All of my fighting, all of my anguish and sweat, yet the reward still didn't seem nearly as valuable as the life in the next room. Maybe time would make me happy about the prize I'd won. Lifting my finger again, I pushed three nines, waiting for the ring tone to purr in my ear once more.

THE SCHOLAR

Courttia Newland

Cory and Sean Bradley are cousins, but grow up
as brothers on the Greenside Estate in West London.
Young, black, good-looking and smart enough to want
to leave the poverty trap of the estate, their escape routes
are as different as their personalities.

Sean, 'the scholar', sensible, serious and anti-drugs,
studies hard to get a university place. Cory, streetwise
and impulsive, has discovered the more instant rewards
of crime and the pleasures of weed, E and whiz.
Each cousin seems to have made his choice;
but plans have a habit of going awry . . .

As the violence escalates and options dwindle,
Sean and Cory face the impossible task of trying to do
the right thing in the wrong place at the wrong time.

'Real tension and suspense . . . an absorbing debut from
a writer who clearly has something to say'
Observer

'Vividly rendered, powerful'
Nicholas Royle, *Time Out*

'Feisty and real'
Mail on Sunday

SOCIETY WITHIN

Courttia Newland

Set on the Greenside Estate, West London,
Society Within starts with the arrival of newcomer Elisha:
sweet, bright, sassy and just eighteen. As Elisha negotiates
a territory with more than its fair share of dark corners, we
take in the vividly interlocking lives of the other Greensiders:
cool, ambitious Valerie, with some bad secrets to deal with;
Little Stacey, looking for his first girl; Orin, dealing, stealing
and trying to stay away from anything too lethal; Nathan
and his plans for pirate radio station Midnight FM,
the music which provides an irresistible soundtrack
to this extraordinary novel.

'The rising star of Brit-lit and chronicler of inner-city life . . .
the comparison with [Irvine] Welsh . . . is apt for two
reasons. First there is a clear parallel in creating a new
literary language and second, with luck, Newland will also
open up the world of fiction to a whole new audience'
Guardian

'This is a real life story that comes with pain and dreams,
friends and lovers, trust and betrayal and despair and hope'
Untold

'A truly gifted storyteller'
Time Out

Now you can order superb titles directly from Abacus

☐ The Scholar   Courttia Newland   £6.99
☐ Society Within   Courttia Newland   £6.99

The prices shown above are correct at time of going to press. However, the publishers reserve the right to increase prices on covers from those previously advertised, without further notice.

──────────────── ⟨ABACUS⟩ ────────────────

Please allow for postage and packing: **Free UK delivery.**
Europe: add 25% of retail price; Rest of World: 45% of retail price.

To order any of the above or any other Abacus titles, please call our credit card orderline or fill in this coupon and send/fax it to:

Abacus, PO Box 121, Kettering, Northants NN14 4ZQ
Fax: 01832 733076   Tel: 01832 737527
Email: aspenhouse@FSBDial.co.uk

☐ I enclose a UK bank cheque made payable to Abacus for £ . . . .
☐ Please charge £ . . . . . . to my Visa/Access/Mastercard/Eurocard

Expiry Date ☐☐☐☐   Switch Issue No.   ☐☐

NAME (BLOCK LETTERS please) . . . .

ADDRESS . . . .

. . . .

. . . .

Postcode . . . . Telephone . . . .

Signature . . . .

Please allow 28 days for delivery within the UK. Offer subject to price and availability.

Please do not send any further mailings from companies carefully selected by Abacus ☐